ASK MY

Mood
Ring

HOW I FEEL

ASK MY Mood Ring HOW I FEEL

BY DIANA LÓPEZ

SCHOLASTIC INC.

ISBN 978-0-545-68809-3

Copyright © 2013 by Diana López. All rights reserved. Published by Scholastic Inc., 557 Broadway, New York, NY 10012, by arrangement with Little, Brown and Company, a division of Hachette Book Group, Inc. SCHOLASTIC and associated logos are trademarks and/or registered trademarks of Scholastic Inc.

12 11 10 9 8 7 6 5 4 3 2 1   14 15 16 17 18 19/0

Printed in the U.S.A.   40

First Scholastic printing, January 2014

To Amabel, Marina, and Soli

9 BIKINIS

I spent the entire month of May waiting for summer—for waking up when I felt like it and not when the alarm told me to, for wearing cool skirts and no shoes, for spending time with my friends at the park and pool, and for our family vacation—this year a trip to Carlsbad Caverns, a giant cave system in New Mexico—and on to Roswell, where aliens once crash-landed. Of course, I knew aliens were a hoax, but I looked forward to Roswell anyway, if only to see how many people could be fooled by such a silly story. So when Mom said she was going to shop for bathing suits, I didn't think twice. Sure, New Mexico was a desert, but every vacation spot had pools—not to mention the Texas coast, which we visited two or three times a year. And when she brought home nine bikinis, I thought it was odd, but only for a second, because Mom did funny things sometimes, like making potato chip pancakes or talking in a computer voice inspired by *Star Trek* shows.

"Come look, Chia," Mom said, waving me into her room. "You too, Carmen."

I stepped in, my nerdy little sister following.

"What do you think?" Mom asked, arranging the bikinis on the bed with the care of someone setting the table for Thanksgiving dinner. Their colors were bright like piñatas. One bikini top was striped, another polka-dotted, a third checkered. One had tropical flowers, and another, little palm trees.

"They're very pretty," I answered.

"Yeah. Real pretty," Carmen said. "Are these for vacation?"

Mom shrugged. "You could say that. I bought one for each day of the week."

Carmen's finger pointed at each as she counted. Her math brain always counted things. "But there are nine bikinis here," she said. "Does that mean we're having a nine-day vacation?"

Once again, Mom said, "You could say that."

Mom took the bikini bottoms and threw them into the small wicker basket she used as a trash can, then folded the tops and stacked them neatly in her lower dresser drawer.

"What are you doing?" I asked. I could totally understand potato chip pancakes, a computer voice, and buying nine bikinis, but throwing away something new was beyond me.

Before she could answer, my two-year-old brother walked in. "Gimme, gimme, gimme," he said, grabbing a bikini top. When I tried to take it away, we got into a tug-of-war match.

"Let go, Jimmy!" I cried.

"It's okay," Mom said. "Let him have it. He'll give it back after he's had a good look." She ran her fingers through his hair, but he was too interested in the bikini top to notice. Then she lifted him, hugged him tight, and said, "My baby, my beautiful baby," even though he wasn't a baby anymore. When Jimmy wriggled free, Mom grabbed Carmen and me for a group hug, and she said it again, "My babies, my beautiful babies."

"Is everything okay?" Carmen asked.

"Of course. I'm just showing a little affection."

"But you're acting weird. Right, Chia?"

"Maybe," I said.

"What do you mean by 'maybe'? She *is* acting weird."

Truth was, I *did* think Mom seemed a bit…off…but there were a lot of things I'd rather do than take Carmen's side—like sleep on a block of ice or drink tomato sauce with crushed Oreos.

3

"It's not weird," I said. "Mom doesn't need a special occasion to hug us or call us her babies."

Mom said, "You're so sweet," and kissed the top of my head.

Carmen hated to be wrong, but more than that, she hated for me to be right. She glared at me. If her eyes were claws, I'd have a dozen scratch marks on my face.

"Okay, girls," Mom said. "Why don't you go to the other room? It's time for Jimmy's nap."

"Gimme nap. Gimme nap," Jimmy said, climbing onto the bed and grabbing a pillow. Carmen and I left him there and made our way to the kitchen.

A long time ago, Mom and Dad had bought us matching desks and placed them side by side in the den, but we preferred to hang out in the kitchen because it was huge and had a table as big as a stage. Besides, it usually smelled good in there—sometimes like Mom's *charro* beans or beef stew, other times like biscuits or coffee—and when we were lucky like chocolate cake. Today, though, it didn't smell like anything, but it would as soon as Mom started dinner.

Carmen and I sat on opposite ends, the rest of the table like a long hallway between us. Carmen made a skyscraper of library books about dream interpretation, Egyptology, and renewable energy. I had to roll my eyes. I mean, she wasn't in college—*yet*. Besides, it was summer. Who spent the summer studying? Only *my* sister begged for a trip to the library each week. No thank you. I'd rather hang out with my friends or watch TV than read boring books.

Speaking of friends, I flipped open the laptop and spotted an e-mail from Iliana, with "Park?" in the subject line. "Hey, guys," she wrote to me and a few other friends, "want to meet at the park tomorrow?" We all lived in the same neighborhood, and the park was a short walk from our homes. It had lots of shade, skateboarding ramps, swing sets, and a pool.

"Mom!" I called out. "Can I go to the park tomorrow?"

"Sure," she called from the bedroom.

I hit the "reply" button and wrote, "I'll be there."

After checking the rest of my messages, I glanced at the shipping information for the Endless Band Mood Ring, the one Dad ordered for me after I said "please" a dozen times. Mom mentioned having one when she was a teen, and when I learned that mood rings change colors according to your emotions, I had to get one, too. My friends always wanted to know how I felt, and pointing to a mood ring seemed a lot easier than having a whole conversation about my feelings. It was scheduled to arrive tomorrow. Good. I needed to make sure I was here because the last thing I wanted was Carmen stealing my übercool ring, and she'd do it. No doubt in my mind she would.

"Did you know," Carmen began, "that when Egyptians were turning dead bodies into mummies, they sucked the brains out through the nose?"

"I wonder if they used a sippy straw?" I said.

"And then they took out the intestines and put them in jars."

"Imagine seeing that in a pantry—not strawberry preserves but gut jam."

She ignored me. "They put *all* the organs in jars. Except for the heart. Do you know what those jars were called?"

I took a second too long for a comeback.

"They're called *canopic* jars," Carmen said, all proud of herself.

"I knew that," I lied. "I was just testing you. Now, quit being a show-off." I crumpled a napkin and threw it at her, but it missed.

Her way of knowing a bunch of useless details really bugged me, especially after I learned that she'd be joining me in middle school next year. She was supposed to be in the fifth grade but she got bumped up to sixth. So when she started acting like the narrator of a Discovery Channel show, I did my best to make jokes or ignore her. I didn't want Carmen to know how dumb she made me feel. She'd never stop teasing me if she did.

Forget her, I told myself. I had my own intellectual pursuits. Carmen liked ancient civilizations and math equations, but I liked to mind-travel—that's what I called it when I let my imagination take me somewhere else, somewhere far from my pesky sister. I loved to visit Google Images. Today, Mom's bikinis made me think of the ocean, so I typed "seaside" in the search box. So many pictures came up—peaceful coastlines with water as blue and clear as marbles, busy boardwalks with roller coasters right over the ocean, resort towns with rows of condominiums, and places where waves splashed against giant rocks. I finally settled on a crowded beach. Every inch seemed full of people in lawn chairs or on blankets, their coolers beside them, their umbrellas providing shade. The sand was dotted with footprints. I mind-traveled and felt the wind, the sun, and the gritty sand. I heard gulls, waves, laughter, and flapping towels. I tasted the salty air and an ice-cold—

"Gimme Chia. Gimme Chia," Jimmy said, interrupting my "vacation." He had walked in, dragging a pillow and bikini top across the floor. He dropped them and pointed at the baker's rack. "Gimme Chia. Gimme Chia," he said, reaching for our SpongeBob Chia Pet. Chia Pets are clay figurines with little holes, usually where hair or fur belongs. When you water them, grass grows through the holes. So instead of pies and cookies on the baker's rack, we had green-haired characters. On the top shelf were actual Chia

Pets—a cat, a puppy, a lamb. Then we had the patriotic shelf with George Washington, Abe Lincoln, and Barack Obama. Below that, we had SpongeBob SquarePants, Scooby-Doo, Homer Simpson, and Dora the Explorer, all with green hair. In the middle of our collection was a picture of me when I was one. I had thick curly hair back then, so for my first Halloween, Mom and Dad painted it green, put me in a Onesie the color of terra-cotta, and told everyone I was a real live Chia Pet. That's why they call me Chia now. It isn't my actual name. My actual name is Erica. Erica Montenegro. By the time I was three, I had long straight hair, but the family called me Chia anyway. In fact, I didn't know I was Erica till I started school.

I never asked for a Chia Pet, *ever*, but after Mom and Dad framed that Halloween picture, my aunts and grand-parents, and later my friends, bought them for me as Christmas or birthday gifts. So the surprise wasn't what I was getting, since I knew a Chia Pet was in the box, but which one. When I complained that I was getting too old for Scooby-Doo and Dora the Explorer, they started to buy me historical figures, even though I really meant "no more Chia Pets." Then I said, "I'm not really into politics," so they started buying animals. I didn't bother to complain because I knew they'd just discover another Chia Pet cate-gory. In fact, I absolutely loved my collection. In a way, the

Chia Pets were like a timeline of my life, a happy timeline since they mostly came gift wrapped at a party.

"Gimme Chia!" Jimmy said again. He looked so cute with his wide, innocent eyes. I almost forgot how destructive he could be until I noticed a blank spot on the shelf.

"Gimme!" he insisted.

I tried to break the news gently. "I can't. You'll break it. Remember what you did to Garfield last week?"

"But I wan' it! I wan' it!" He started to cry. Jimmy didn't know about sniffles or sobs. When he was upset, he went straight to bawling.

"Sorry," I said. "I don't want you to get in trouble."

This time, he added stomping to the tantrum.

Carmen whined. "I can't concentrate with all this noise. Where's Mom? She's the only one who can handle Jimmy."

"I can take care of him, too," I said, heading to the pantry because a snack was a great way to calm him down. I offered him a cookie. He slapped it away from my hand.

"No cookie!" he yelled.

"Will you be quiet?" Carmen said, scolding him. "Where's Mom? Can't she hear him?"

I wondered too, especially since pep rallies were quieter than this.

"Maybe she's sleeping," I guessed.

Just then, Dad got home from work.

"What's going on?" he said as he stepped into the kitchen. "I can hear Jimmy from outside."

"He wants to play with SpongeBob," I explained.

Dad stooped down to Jimmy's level. "Is that right, little buddy?"

Jimmy nodded and stomped again. "Gimme Chia!"

"Okay, okay," Dad promised.

"Dad, don't!" I warned. "He'll break it."

"We're just going to touch it, right, Jimmy? We're not going to play with it because it's not a toy."

Jimmy nodded again. Then Dad picked him up and let him pat SpongeBob's hair. After a minute, Jimmy said, "Down now." He was perfectly quiet again. He picked up the bikini top and the pillow and headed to the hallway. I made a mental note: when cookies don't work, just give Jimmy what he wants.

"Where's your mother?" Dad asked.

"Asleep," we said.

He looked toward their bedroom. "Okay. We'll let her rest awhile longer."

He took off his coat, tie, and buttoned-up shirt. His undershirt looked funny with his pressed slacks and shiny black shoes, but we were used to seeing him like this. He worked at USAA, a giant insurance company and one of the biggest companies in San Antonio, so he had to wear a suit every day, what he called his straitjacket. He couldn't wait to take it off when he got home, especially in the summer when it was so hot.

After he got comfortable, he opened the fridge and took out ground beef, lettuce, tomatoes, and cheese. Then he opened the pantry and took out a package of corn tortillas. After that, he pushed aside all the cans and boxes and reached *way* back into the pantry. He scratched his head a minute, then opened all the cabinet doors, even beneath the sink where we kept cleaning supplies. Then he peeked on top of the fridge, behind the microwave, and under the toaster.

"What are you looking for?" I asked. "You look like a kid on an Easter egg hunt."

"I'm looking for that packet of spices for the tacos," he said. "I want to start dinner."

"We ate tacos last week," Carmen answered. "Mom hasn't been to the store since then."

His shoulders slumped. "I guess we'll eat *migas* instead."

Migas was our favorite Tex-Mex dish—a mix of corn tortillas, eggs, tomatoes, onions, and cheese. We loved the recipe. Thing was, *migas* were for breakfast, not dinner.

In a way, it made sense for Dad to make them because he always cooked breakfast. After all, my parents believed in "division of labor." Dad made breakfast, Mom made dinner, and Carmen and I cleaned the kitchen at the end of the day. We used to wash dishes together, but since we kept fighting over who washed and who dried, who cleared the table and who swept the floor, Mom and Dad came up with a new "division of labor" plan. Carmen would clean on the odd-numbered days, while I cleaned on the even-numbered. Sounded great to me. Of course, Carmen quickly pointed out how unfair it was since months like January had thirty-one days, which meant she'd have to clean two days in a row because the next day was always the first. So to make things *exactly* equal, Mom or Dad cleaned when the last day of the month ended with an odd number.

"We can't eat *migas*," Carmen complained. "That's for breakfast."

Dad took out the cutting board and started to chop an onion. "The only dinner recipes I know are tacos and barbecue. Anyway, who says breakfast is just for the morning? We might have to get used to eating breakfast at night now."

"Why?" Carmen asked. "Is Mom going on strike or something?"

Dad stopped a moment, closing his eyes tight. I thought he was going to cry, but that was silly. Dads didn't cry. Must have been the onions he was chopping.

"Well?" Carmen said.

Dad didn't answer. Instead he said, "Jimmy's too quiet. Go check on him."

When Carmen didn't move, I said to her, "He means you."

"No, he doesn't," she sassed back. "It's your job to baby-sit. You're the oldest. Whoever heard of the *second* oldest taking care of little kids?"

"Girls," Dad said. "Not now. Why don't *both* of you check on Jimmy?"

We still didn't move.

"One, two," he began.

"Okay, okay," we said. The last thing we wanted was Dad to hit three. Once he hit three, we hit some kind of punishment. Usually he took away our iPods or computer privileges for a day. But we never knew. Punishment could mean pulling weeds or dusting baseboards. It could mean writing a five-paragraph essay about the possible conse-quences of our bad behavior. Like, what if we *didn't* check on Jimmy? What's the worst kind of trouble he could get into? I'd heard stories about little kids sticking their fingers in sockets and getting electrocuted or swallowing small toys and choking. That was the last thing I wanted for my brother, even if he was a pest sometimes.

I bolted from my chair and sprinted past Carmen, who hadn't budged an inch. Once again, I had to look after Jimmy, while Carmen got to stay with her precious books.

I searched all over the place, even called his name. He never answered back. I finally discovered him in the coat closet where we kept our tennis shoes and hiking and work boots. He'd taken out all the shoelaces, so now they were in a giant tangle. How could he make such a mess in fifteen minutes?

I picked up a shoelace, and it was wet with saliva. "Gross!" I said to Jimmy. "Did you put all these in your mouth?"

He laughed. Then he said, "Gimme!" as he opened and closed his hand.

I didn't hand it to him. Instead, I ran the shoelace over his face, tickling him.

"Let's clean this up," I said.

He shook his head to say no, and then he ran back to the kitchen. That brat!

I grabbed my cell phone from my pocket and wrote to Iliana. "Can we trade bros?" A few seconds later, she replied, "Let's." If only it were that simple. Iliana had twin brothers in high school. They were super cute and athletic. They were smart too, and polite. And they were exactly identical. Sometimes I wished I were their girlfriend because if the first one couldn't take me to the homecoming dance, I could ask the second one. It'd be like having two iPods with the same playlists. That way, when the battery ran out on one, I could switch over to the other. My dad always said it was good to have a backup plan. Twin boyfriends and twin iPods sounded like good backup plans to me.

I shook the wishful thinking from my mind as I untangled the shoelaces and threaded them through the tennis shoes and boots. Then I returned to the kitchen and found Jimmy tearing paper towels into tiny pieces, while Dad spooned *migas* onto our plates and Carmen set the table.

"Thanks for helping," she told me, all sarcastic.

"No, thank *you* for helping *me*." I could be sarcastic, too.

"You're the one who snuck off to text Iliana so you wouldn't have to work in the kitchen."

"Well, *I'm* the one who had to clean up Jimmy's mess after Dad asked *you* to check on him."

"He didn't ask me. You're the oldest, remember?"

"*¡Por favor!*" Dad said. He still had the spoon in his hand and was clenching it so tight. I could see the muscles and veins in his forearm. "I just want to have a nice dinner for Mom. A nice, peaceful dinner. She had a really hard day, understand?"

Carmen and I glanced at each other. Why did Mom have a hard day? As far as we could tell, she went shopping and got a good deal on bathing suits. Something was up, and we both knew it. We'd never admit that our brains were hooked on the same idea, but they were.

"Take your seats," Dad ordered. He picked up Jimmy and placed him on his booster chair. "All of you stay put. And don't say a word till I get back."

We obeyed, but it was tough. Staying quiet was impossible for my little brother and sister. Jimmy kept blowing bubbles through the straw of his sippy cup and Carmen kept tapping her fork against her glass. I could see her lips moving, which meant she was counting. Later she'd tell me exactly how many times she tapped her fork, plus whatever else she'd counted. She couldn't help herself, and Jimmy couldn't help making a mess, even with his spill-proof sippy cup. I loved them, but I couldn't stand it sometimes, couldn't stand *them*.

Finally, Mom and Dad stepped in. As soon as she saw the table, Mom said, "What's this?"

"I made dinner," Dad announced.

"And I set the table," Carmen added.

"But I could have made dinner," Mom said. "I was planning to. I *always* make it, don't I?"

"Just wanted you to have a day off," Dad said, all cheery.

He pulled out her chair. He could be a real gentleman, but since he pulled out Mom's chair only at fancy dinners or weddings, this was weird. Mom must have thought so too, because she hesitated before sitting down. Then Dad went to his seat and told us to dig in. We did. Quietly. For once, Carmen wasn't acting like a know-it-all and Jimmy wasn't begging for something to hold. It was a perfectly quiet dinner like Dad had wanted, but it sure wasn't peaceful.

Finally, Jimmy broke the silence. "Gimme juice!" he said, holding out his sippy cup.

Mom scooted back her chair, but Dad said, "I got it."

"That's not..." she tried.

"It's my pleasure," Dad said. "You get Jimmy's juice every night."

She crossed her arms. "That's right. I do."

"So let the rest of us help," Dad said. "There's no need for you to do everything."

"And there's no need for me to do *nothing* at all."

I felt totally confused. Dad was acting super nice, but Mom was acting mad. "What's going on?" I had to ask.

"Your father's treating me like an invalid," Mom said.

Carmen jumped in. "Chia doesn't know what that is. You have to define it for her."

"I know what 'invalid' means," I protested.

"What does it mean then?"

"An invalid is what you're going to be after I break your legs because you're such a brat all the time."

"Quit fighting, girls," Dad scolded. "You're upsetting your mother."

"They're not upsetting me. I'd rather see them fight than see you cater to me. Their fighting is normal. It's...it's *energetic*."

That was a strange thing to say. My dad thought so too,

because he stared at my mom for a long time—she stared back—whole paragraphs passing between them. The entire time, Jimmy kept saying, "Gimme juice. Gimme juice." But Mom and Dad were motionless. Finally, Mom stood up, and then—she pulled off her shirt! She was wearing a hot-pink bikini top, and she straightened her shoulders to show it off.

"You can't walk around like that," Dad said.

"You're *not* going to make me cover up."

"But we're not at the beach!"

Mom laughed. "Well, I can pretend. I've got nine days to pretend."

"Mom? Dad?" Carmen's voice cracked a little, and then Jimmy started to cry. Maybe he was tired of waiting for juice, or maybe he was scared like Carmen.

"Is this how you want to tell the children?" Dad said. "While they're all upset?"

"Tell us what?" Now *my* voice cracked. Once again, my parents stared at each other. This time, whole chapters passed between them, while a dozen scenarios ran through my mind. Were they getting divorced? Were they going bankrupt? What secret were they keeping from us?

"Your mother is sick," Dad said calmly.

"What kind of sick?" I had to ask because I knew this was bigger than a stomachache or the flu.

Mom took Jimmy's cup and refilled it. I could tell she was stalling. When she handed it to him, she kissed the top of his head. Then she returned to her seat, grabbed her fork, and pushed the remaining *migas* around her plate. And finally, without looking at us, she said, "I have breast cancer. I'm going to have a mastectomy in nine days."

5 ROBINS

The next day, Iliana stopped by my house so we could walk to the park together. Like me, she was skinny and had brown eyes, but Iliana wore gobs of mascara, so sometimes her eyelashes looked like spider legs. Our hairstyles were different, too. I had long brown hair, usually in a ponytail, while Iliana had short hair with lots of curls.

"OMG," she said (she loved to speak text sometimes), "my brothers' friends are so cute."

"Your *brothers* are cute," I said.

"To *you*, maybe. To me, they're a pain. They are so protective. I have to tell them everywhere I'm going to be and when I'll be back and they'll probably still check up on me. They're stricter than my parents. And they *torture* me!"

"How?" As far as I could tell, they were the nicest brothers in the world. At least she didn't have to live with a walking encyclopedia.

"First, they invite their friends over to play video games. Did I mention how cute their friends are?" She didn't let me answer. She just kept going. "Then, they shut me out. Literally. They close the door to their bedroom and tell me to stay out. So there I am standing with my ear to the door, just listening to all the video game sounds and to these really cute guys cheer after shooting some monster or who knows what, and then..."

I didn't mean to tune out. Normally, I loved hearing about Iliana's brothers, but how could I get excited about video games and cute boys when Mom was scheduled for surgery next week?

Suddenly, Iliana yanked me off the sidewalk, seconds before a skateboarder whizzed by.

"What planet are you on?" she said. "Didn't you hear the skateboard? Didn't you hear Chad call 'Sidewalk!' right before he almost bumped into you?" She held up two fingers to show me how close he'd been. "You have to pay attention because knocking a cute guy off his skateboard is not the best way to make a first impression, even if it is a close encounter of the fourth kind."

"Close encounter" is how we describe our relationships with boys. We got the idea after Iliana did a report on space aliens and learned that scientists call UFO sightings "close encounters." They even have different categories depending on whether you saw a vague shape in the sky or an actual life-form. Since boys seem as strange as aliens, Iliana and I decided to invent our own categories:

- Close encounter of the first kind—boy knows you exist.
- Close encounter of the second kind—boy talks to you, but only at school and only about boring school stuff like "Can I borrow a pencil?"
- Close encounter of the third kind—boy talks to you *and* sends you text messages about interesting stuff like favorite video games or funny YouTube videos.
- Close encounter of the fourth kind—actual physical contact!

I still hadn't experienced a close encounter of the first kind with Chad, which was disappointing because, with his blond hair and perfect tan, he topped my Boyfriend Wish List, along with Forest Montoya, Alejandro Guzmán, Lou Hikaru, Jamal Grey, Derek Smith, and Joe Leal.

I shrugged. "Chad's never going to notice me," I said. "I'm like that crack in the sidewalk that he jumps to avoid. I'll have to become a skateboard ramp or a pair of Vans before he notices me."

Iliana punched my shoulder. "Stop it, will you? Of course he's going to notice you. You've got nice, silky hair and a cute figure."

I had to disagree. "A lamppost has more curves," I said, pointing to one.

She laughed. "Only because of the way you're dressed. What's with the baggy, uninspired outfit? Even your T-shirt seems depressed."

I glanced at it, a faded brown V-neck. Usually, I wore T-shirts with punch lines or funny cartoons, but I couldn't laugh when Mom was sick. I shouldn't be going to the park, either. I should have stayed home and helped her. I offered, but she got mad just like the night before. She said, "Don't start acting like your dad by treating me like an invalid," and she ran me out of the house, even gave me extra money.

"You're not listening to a word I say," Iliana complained. And she was right. I had no idea she'd been talking.

"I got some really bad news," I explained, immediately regretting it. Sometimes, I didn't want friend-to-friend counseling sessions. They made me feel…weak. I could take care of myself, thank you.

"What happened?" Iliana wanted to know.

I shrugged. "Nothing. It's no big deal. I shouldn't have said anything."

We turned a corner and the park came into view. I sped up, nearly jogging.

"Wait!" Iliana reached for my arm but missed. "Don't you want to talk?"

"Sure," I called back. "Let's talk about boys."

"That's not what I meant," she said.

I pretended not to hear. "Hey, look. There's Patty waving us over."

We headed toward a picnic table with the Robins, our special group of friends. We have five members: me, Iliana, Patty, Shawntae, and GumWad, whose real name is Roberto. He had a purple tongue today because of his grape bubblegum. He really grossed me out sometimes. And to think that without the gum, he could be a decent-looking guy. He wasn't athletic and he didn't wear anything more interesting than T-shirts with sports logos and jeans. But he had a cuddly type of body like a teddy bear and dimples when he smiled. Too bad the dimples were on either side of a rainbow-colored mouth.

The Robins were my best friends, though we didn't choose one another—not at first. Our second-grade teacher put us together. Her classroom had four big tables, and in the center of each was a nest with a stuffed bird—one with a cardinal, another with a mockingbird, and another with a blue jay. Our table had a robin. When you squeezed its belly, it sang—*cheerily cheer-up cheer-up*. We'd have contests. Whoever finished an assignment first or made the highest grade got to squeeze the bird's belly. It seems silly now, but in second grade, squeezing the bird was a big deal.

As we approached the table, Iliana and I gave our friends a big Texas "Hi, y'all."

"Hey," they replied, hardly missing a beat in their conversation about some movie. This time, I tried my best to pay attention, especially since Iliana had already forgotten about my bad news. After a while, though, I started to feel really hot. In San Antonio, the temperature regularly hits the nineties, and the humidity made it feel like a hundred degrees. I grabbed a rubber band from my pocket and gathered my hair for a ponytail.

"You look hot," GumWad announced.

"Ooh, Erica," Shawntae teased. "Roberto thinks you're hot." She made a sizzling sound.

"That's not what I meant," GumWad said. "She's not sexy or anything…just hot, like overheated, like there's sweat running down the back of her neck."

"Gee, thanks," I said. "You sure know how to flatter a girl."

"I was just noticing you were hot. I wasn't trying to flatter you."

"Obviously," I said.

Shawntae punched me. "Leave the poor guy alone."

"You started it, Shawntae, with all those sizzling sounds you made."

"Yeah," GumWad said, taking my side. "You started it. Erica's not the only one who's sweaty. We all are. Look." He lifted his arms to show us round, damp splotches on the underarm parts of his T-shirt.

Patty pinched her nose. "Quit giving the skunks competition."

"Do I smell that bad?" GumWad said, full of dismay.

Patty, Shawntae, and I nodded, but Iliana said, "Don't listen to them. They're picking on you because they don't have anything better to do."

"I can think of something better," Patty said. "Let's go see who's skateboarding."

Her suggestion reminded Iliana about our close encounter with Chad earlier, and as we walked toward the ramps, she told the group about it. We reached the skateboarding park and sat on some bleachers just as she finished her story. Then we scanned the cement hills before us. "There's Alejandro," Iliana said, pointing.

In fact, several cute guys from school were showing off

grinds, kickflips, and ollies. We had fun watching them, giggling when they stumbled or fell and sighing when they took off their shirts. At one point, Forest stopped by. He said, "Hey, girls," and we said "Hey" back. Then he turned to GumWad. "Where's your board?"

"Left it at home."

"You should bring it next time."

"Sure thing."

When Forest skated off, Patty hit GumWad's shoulder and said, "You don't have a skateboard."

He shrugged.

"So why'd you lie?"

He shrugged again and glanced at me. He seemed embarrassed to be caught in a lie, but I could totally understand.

"I know why," I said. "It's a lot of trouble saying 'I don't have a skateboard' to a guy who thinks skateboarding is life. Then you have to explain *why* when there isn't a reason. You have nothing against skateboards. They just don't interest you. But try telling *them* that. They'll think you're weird, which can cause all kinds of awkwardness. So it's best to pretend, get them off your case."

"Yeah," GumWad said as grateful as someone who had just been rescued from an overturned ship.

Just then, we heard bells from the *paleta* man, a guy

who hauled an ice chest between the back wheels of a three-wheel bike. He stored *paletas* in there, frozen fruit bars. They cost one dollar each.

"You want one?" GumWad asked me, but before I could answer, the other Robins were handing him money.

"Thanks for offering," Iliana said. "You are so sweet," she cooed.

Shawntae jumped in. "Yeah, you're as sweet as...as sweet as..." She snapped her fingers, my cue to finish the sentence.

"As sweet as a cookie dough pizza topped with chocolate chips, marshmallows, and caramel."

Everyone smacked their lips as they imagined it, except Patty. She rolled her eyes and said, "You'd have to run ten marathons to work off all those calories."

Patty looked like the sweetest girl on the planet with her freckles and blue eyes, but if she won a million dollars, she'd focus on the extra taxes instead of the extra fun she could have.

"Well, I guess I could get some for all of us," GumWad said, taking the not-so-subtle hint. We told him which flavors to buy, and he took off. The skateboarders and kids from the playground and pool had already formed a long line in front of the bicycle. That *paleta* man knew exactly when to show up.

While GumWad waited in the line, Shawntae, Iliana, and Patty went on and on about boys, which was usually my favorite topic, but I couldn't stop thinking about Mom. How could she be sick? She seemed perfectly normal, full of energy. I couldn't imagine cancer eating away part of her body, especially when she hadn't complained about pain. Maybe it didn't hurt till it was too late. Maybe cancer was like a termite, silent and invisible until you noticed the walls falling down.

"Erica!" Iliana said. "This is the second time you totally ignored me."

"I ignored you?"

Patty explained, "You didn't answer when Iliana asked who was cuter, Alejandro or Chad. You were looking right at them, but your mind was somewhere else."

Just then, GumWad returned and passed out the *paletas*. I had ordered banana, but the other girls got strawberry, while GumWad got mango.

"Fess up," Iliana said. "Time to tell us about your bad news."

"What bad news?" Shawntae wanted to know.

"It's private," I said.

The Robins stared at me, silently eating their fruit bars and waiting. If I didn't tell, they'd spend the whole day pestering me.

"Okay," I said. "If you really have to know." I paused, secretly hoping they'd let it go but knowing they wouldn't. Taking a deep breath, I said, "My mom has breast cancer."

If I was scared about cancer before, I was more scared now, because all of them stopped eating, stopped *breathing*, it seemed. They were as frozen as the *paletas* we held in our hands, but like the *paletas*, their initial shock was quickly melting away. "When did you find out?" they asked, and "How serious is it?" and "Is she in the hospital?" and "Is she…is she…is she going to die?"

"I don't know!" I said, throwing my *paleta* to the ground. "This is why I didn't want to tell you guys. I knew you'd have a million questions that I can't answer." I got a lump in my throat, the one that meant tears were on their way, so I swallowed hard and breathed deeply. I was *not* going to cry. Sure, these were my friends, but that didn't mean I should act like a baby around them. "All I know for sure," I said, more calmly, "is that my mom's going to have a mastectomy."

"What's that?" GumWad asked.

"It's an operation," Patty said. "They cut off your breast."

Iliana, Shawntae, and I winced and crossed our arms over our chests as we imagined the pain. GumWad winced and crossed his arms, too.

Then he said, "My uncle had an operation last year. He had a stone in his gallbladder."

"How did he get a stone in there?" Shawntae asked.

"I don't know. He didn't swallow it, if that's what you're thinking. It's something his body made." He blew and popped a bubble before going on. I couldn't believe he was chewing gum while eating a *paleta*. "They took out his gallbladder," he went on, "and then they put the stone in a little jar with some formaldehyde and gave it to him—like a souvenir. He keeps it by his computer and he named it Bob."

"That is so weird," Shawntae said.

"No, it's not," I said. "It's like having a pet rock."

"Yeah!" GumWad smacked a little more quickly. "You're the first person to get it!"

Maybe I understood pet rocks because of the Chia Pet zoo in my kitchen.

"Is your uncle okay now?" Iliana asked.

GumWad nodded.

"See?" she said to me, putting her hand on my shoulder. "Lots of people have surgery, and they come out okay. I'm sure that's how it'll be for your mom."

"But it makes you wonder," Patty said. "What do they do with the breast after the operation?"

"Patty!" Shawntae punched her. "That's so rude!"

I shivered, suddenly feeling cold even though it was

ninety-plus degrees. The image of Mom's breast displayed in a jar on someone's desk was freaking me out. But Patty had asked a good question: When ladies had mastectomies or when soldiers had arms or legs cut off, where did the body parts go? Were they sent to some crazy scientist's lab? Or were they thrown away, like garbage? And was that what we became when a part of us died or when our whole body died? I looked at the fruit bar I had thrown on the ground, how quickly it was melting, how the banana had been plucked from its tree.

We sat silently for a while. The Robins knew my mom and were probably feeling worried like me. Soon the skateboarders returned, and I focused on the sounds of their wheels, how they rolled and thudded after jumps.

Finally, Shawntae leaned forward and said, "You're not going to believe this, but..."

"Not another dream!" I moaned, because this was the one thing that bugged me about Shawntae.

"I can't help it," she said. "I have psychic powers. You guys are just jealous because you can't predict the future like me."

"It's not a prediction," Iliana explained, "when you tell us your dreams after the fact."

"This isn't after the fact. I had the dream last week."

We knew she'd tell us about it, so we slumped in our seats and sighed. Only GumWad seemed interested.

"So what did you dream?" he wanted to know.

Shawntae straightened her shirt and smoothed back her hair like an anchorwoman with a news flash. "I saw Erica's mom wearing a bikini, but she had a thermometer in her mouth. Who wears a bikini and sticks a thermometer in her mouth? So I thought she was at the beach and the thermometer was a symbol of how hot it was. But now I get it. The thermometer meant she was sick. Like when the nurse takes your temperature."

"You didn't have that dream," I said. "You're just repeating stuff from our conversation. That's what you do. You take a few clues, and you make something up."

"I *did* have that dream. Last week."

"Why didn't you tell me then? This is serious, Shawntae. My mom has cancer. What's the point of seeing the future if you can't warn your friends?"

"That's not how psychic powers work."

I stood up. "How many times do we have to tell you? You do *not* have psychic powers!"

I stomped away, heading to my house, but Iliana caught up to me. "Don't be mad," she said. "We're just trying to help."

"Then tell me why my mom's sick." When she didn't answer, I repeated myself. "Why is she sick, Iliana?"

"I don't know."

"That's right. Nobody does," I said, realizing that I wasn't angry about Shawntae's dream. I wasn't angry with my friends at all. What bugged me, what *really* bugged me, was that no one knew the answer to the most important question: Why did cancer choose my mom? After all, cancer had always been the big, scary end to bad habits. If you smoked, you got lung cancer and a hole in your throat. If you drank beer, you got liver cancer and yellow eyes. If you went to the pool without sunscreen, you got skin cancer and a dark mole creeping over your body. But what bad habit made breast cancer?

As far as I knew, Mom lived right. Several times a week, she pushed aside furniture and did a step aerobics tape. She drank eight glasses of water each day, and when she felt like coffee, she drank the decaffeinated kind. She didn't eat doughnuts or chocolate bars or syrupy pancakes. She never sped past the yellow lights or told lies or cheated or cursed or stole.

And every night—every single night—after saying "sweet dreams" to Carmen and me and singing lullabies to Jimmy, she made the sign of the cross, clasped her hands, and prayed.

30,000 PEOPLE

Most people slept late on Saturdays, but I had a brother who thought he was the six o'clock alarm. Jimmy Gimme's room was next to the one Carmen and I shared, so I piled pillows over my ears, hoping to drown out his cries. No use. Even if Jimmy were miles away, I'd still hear him scream.

"What's the matter, *mijo*?" we heard Mom say. "You've got no reason to cry. Everybody loves you, don't they?"

She must have lifted Jimmy from his bed because he calmed down. I rolled over and found a comfortable spot, hoping to get back to my dream about the guys on my Boyfriend Wish List. But six o'clock was my normal wake-up time, so I was awake, wide awake. That was okay. Daydreams were just as good; even better, since I could put myself into a pretend situation—like imagining Alejandro

Guzmán on crutches after breaking his leg while skate-boarding and me pushing his wheelchair to the park, then him realizing how sweet and dependable I could be, unlike the girl who dumped him as soon as he wasn't a cool skate-boarder anymore. I was just about to imagine the good part, when Alejandro looked in my eyes, whispered sweet nothings, and leaned in close, then closer, and then...

"Wake up, sleepyheads!" Dad called, stepping into the room and tugging at our feet.

"But it's Saturday," I said.

"Yeah." Carmen yawned. "And we're still tired."

I tried to hide beneath the blankets, hoping Dad would feel sorry for me. No such luck. He started to sing. *"Hi ho, hi ho."* He marched like one of Snow White's dwarfs, the whole time singing and stomping.

"Stop it!" I cried, covering my ears for the second time this morning.

"Hi ho. Hi ho," he kept singing.

"He won't stop till we get out of bed," Carmen said. She was right. This wasn't the first time Dad had tried to annoy us with cheesy Disney songs.

"Okay, okay." I threw back the covers and sat up. "We're awake now."

"Bueno," Dad said. He stooped over to kiss Carmen's

forehead, and then he kissed mine. "After you get dressed," he told us, "I want you to pick something special for Mom."

As soon as he mentioned something special, I thought about my Chia Pets. Then I thought about the brand-new mood ring that had arrived in the mail yesterday.

"Why do we have to pick something special?" Carmen asked.

"Because of her operation," I said, glad to know an answer before she did.

Dad nodded. "That's right. We've got big plans today. We're going to the valley."

The valley was at the southernmost tip of Texas. Carmen and I glanced at each other, both of us wondering why we were driving more than two hundred miles to go there.

"We leave in forty-five," Dad said. Then he stepped out, and a few minutes later, I heard him tickling Jimmy.

I sat on the edge of my bed for a minute. Carmen and I shared a big room, split in half by an imaginary line that was as real to us as that bold yellow line down the middle of a street. To the left was my side, and to the right was Carmen's. We had our own furniture and our own style. Above her bed, Carmen had tacked a poster of the human body labeled with interesting facts like how many miles of blood vessels we had and how many times we blinked each day.

Above my bed, I tacked posters of my favorite movies. I updated them periodically, but right now, I had posters from *Twilight*—one with the guy who played a vampire and another with the guy who turned into a wolf every time the girl of his dreams was in trouble. Carmen didn't like them since they weren't educational. But she left them alone because of our invisible line. It was our lifesaver, and we respected it. The only time Carmen crossed to my side was to get to the closet, and the only time I crossed to hers was to get to the door or to wake her up, something I had to do nearly every morning.

I fixed my bed and washed up. Carmen still hadn't moved. I nudged her. She groaned. I nudged her again. And one more time. If it weren't for me, Carmen would lie in bed till noon.

"Hurry up!" I told her.

She mumbled, but she managed to sit up. After stretching a bit, she made her way to the closet, while I picked out my own outfit. Today, I selected a T-shirt that pictured a chicken and an egg with legs racing through victory tape, a photo finish, with the caption, "Which came first?" I modeled it for Carmen, but she wasn't impressed. Why did I even try?

Carmen put on jeans, but instead of blue, they were

pink—only Carmen said they were fuchsia. And she wore a T-shirt like me, but she wore it inside out. On purpose!

"What's wrong with you?" I asked.

"I'm a nonconformist," she announced. "And in case you're wondering, it means I don't follow rules."

"I *wasn't* wondering," I said, even though I was. "And besides, you follow rules. I can think of a trillion rules you follow."

"Really? A trillion? Do you even know how many zeroes that has?"

I pulled my hair. I actually pulled my hair! It was too early for this. "Stop it, already! Don't you get it? I'm exaggerating."

"Where I come from, we call that 'hyperbole.'"

"And where do you come from? Please tell me. Because last time I looked, you and I came from the same place."

"That depends on how you define 'place.' It doesn't have to be a physical location. It can be—"

"Mom!" I yelled. "Dad!"

"What is it?" they called from the other room.

"Carmen's getting on my nerves!"

"Just ignore her."

Easier said than done. Even though I could never have the last word with Carmen, I could have the longest, most intense stare. So that's what I did. I stared at her, and she stared back. We were two growling dogs waiting to see who'd back down first. Carmen might have a dictionary, a calculator, and the entire Wikipedia in her head, but she was still my little sister. No way could she outlast my stare-down. Finally, after the longest two minutes of my life, she looked away. Gotcha!

Okay, quit wasting time, I told myself. Find something special. It's for Mom.

"I guess I'll pick one of my awards," Carmen said, studying a bookshelf where she kept trophies, ribbons, and binders with every assignment from every teacher she'd ever had in her entire life. "This one's special, don't you think?"

She held out her spelling bee trophy. Last year, Carmen was the best speller in the district. Our whole family followed her to Austin for the state competition. She made it all the way to finals before the word "eidetic" tripped her up. It sounded a lot easier to spell than "confabulation," which she got right, no problem, so I was surprised she missed it. Then I learned that "eidetic" meant having a super-duper memory, which cracked me up. Imagine a girl with an almost perfect memory missing the word "eidetic" at the spelling bee. I made a joke about it, and she cried. I felt horrible. Sure, my sister really got on my nerves, but when she cried, I went into big-sister guard-dog mode. Same with Jimmy.

"You should pick an award, too," Carmen said. "Oh, I forgot. You don't have one."

I was about to point out the bike rodeo ribbon I won in third grade, but she beat me to it.

"That one doesn't count," she said, "since it's for participation. They give those so people like you won't feel bad. It's to help your self-esteem."

"At least I signed up," I said, remembering how I knocked down every cone on the obstacle course. "At least I tried."

"That's about *all* you did."

I threw a pillow at her. She caught it and tossed it back. I threw it again, this time harder and with a secret wish that instead of a pillow, I'd thrown an ink balloon. That's right. A balloon filled with ink instead of water.

"Don't get mad at me," Carmen said. "It's not *my* fault you don't have something special." For a second, I thought about asking her to spell "eidetic"—just a friendly reminder to put her in her place—but if I knew Carmen, she had memorized the spelling by now.

She walked out cradling her trophy. That brat. Maybe I didn't have any awards, but I did have something special. I had a whole baker's rack of Chia Pets. But with so many to choose from and so little time, I knew I had to pick something else. I had my new mood ring, but I hated to give it up, especially because I still had to learn what the different colors meant. I searched through my jewelry box, not the top shelf, where I kept my earrings and bracelets, but the secret compartment beneath. This was where I kept the spearmint gum wrapper from a piece that David Bara once offered me. I had a crush on him last year. I also kept a pencil with Alex Herrera's tooth marks. I'd saved it after he left it on his desk one day. I'd had a crush on him, too. And I'd had a crush on Allen Gibbs, so I stole one of his homework assignments when the teacher accidentally gave it to me. It was stuck behind my paper. I noticed it right away, but I didn't say anything when Allen said, "Hey, where's *my* assignment?"

I looked lovingly at each of these "souvenirs," but I wasn't planning to give Mom a gum wrapper, a chewed pencil, or a strange boy's homework. I had something else in mind, so I picked up an envelope that Iliana had given me last spring.

"This made me think of you," she'd said. "We're supposed to pass it along."

Inside the envelope was a pink note card that said, "Friends are forever." The envelope also contained a black pebble, a small crystal, and a "kindness" coin with a happy face that said, "You made me smile! Pass this smile along!"

I don't know why I kept it instead of following the directions. Then again, I liked remembering that Iliana chose me over all the other people in the world, over all the Robins too, and it made me feel special. Special like Mom.

I put the envelope in my pocket and went to the living room, where I found Carmen pulling crayons from Jimmy's hands while Dad complained about Mom's rainbow-striped bikini top.

"You're not wearing that today," he told her.

"Yes, I am. I explained already. I bought one for each day before my surgery."

"But, Lisa, we're going to a church."

"I know. I'll put a shirt over it when we get there."

Carmen finally freed the last crayon from Jimmy. "Why are we going to a church all the way in the valley?" she asked.

"We're going to a shrine to say special prayers," Mom said.

"Can't we say special prayers here?"

"Yes, but this is different."

"Why?"

"Quit being a pest," I told her.

Dad sighed. I thought he was going to scold me, but instead he answered Carmen's question. "Because a miracle happened at that church. There used to be another church there, but it was destroyed when a man crashed his plane into it. Over a hundred people were at mass when the church burned to the ground, but no one, except for the pilot, got hurt."

"There's another part," Mom went on. "The statue of La Virgen de San Juan was also spared. La Virgen has healing powers. She's helped many people in my family over the years."

Even though I thought the story was amazing, I wasn't convinced it was a miracle, but since it meant so much to Mom, I didn't say anything.

"Now let's get going," Dad said. "You girls take Jimmy to the car while your mother changes into something more appropriate."

"I *am* wearing something appropriate!" I heard Mom say as Carmen and I chased Jimmy, who had run out of the house screaming, "Gimme bye-bye! Gimme bye-bye!" as soon as he'd heard "car."

Jimmy liked going bye-bye, but he hated the car seat. In order for us to strap him in, Carmen had to hold down his arms while I buckled the straps.

Finally, Mom and Dad came out. Mom must have

won the argument because she was still wearing her bikini top. She looked beautiful, in my opinion, with her long flowing hair, curvy jeans, high-heeled shoes, flat stomach, firm shoulders, and breasts as full as the ones on Victoria's Secret models. I wanted to look like her someday. I wanted her hair, face, legs, and stomach. But did I want her breasts? I would have said yes a week ago, but now I wasn't sure.

The drive between San Antonio and the valley was nothing but flat land and cows. We finally reached the shrine around noon. For some reason, I thought it would look like the Alamo, but it was much bigger and more modern. The first thing I noticed was a giant mural facing the highway. It pictured Jesus in a blue robe, standing over the Virgin Mary. Her robe was also blue and was spread out like a triangular tent. She wore a crown and stood on a gold crescent moon.

"That's her. That's La Virgen de San Juan del Valle," Mom said when she caught Carmen and me stretching our necks to get a better look.

Dad found a parking spot and told us to grab our special items. Then we jumped out of the car and found ourselves near a fountain between the church and a group of buildings that included a school, a convent, and a gift shop. Many flowers surrounded the walkway. We pointed so Mom and Dad could tell us the names—blue plumbago, pink bougainvillea, and yellow esperanza. Carmen repeated the names as if prepping for a quiz. I'd probably forget which plant was which by tomorrow, but Carmen would still remember in twenty years. Mom put a shirt over her bikini top and told us to wait while she went to the gift shop. As soon as she left, Jimmy ran to the fountain. "Gimme money!" he said when he saw the coins there.

"You can look but you can't touch," Dad told him as they leaned over the pool. "See how shiny the money is?" Jimmy opened and closed his hand, so Dad reached in his pocket and gave him a penny. Jimmy looked at it, then threw it into the water.

"Hey, you're supposed to make a wish," Carmen said, holding out her own hand. Dad gave her a penny. She closed her eyes, took a deep breath, and tossed it in. Then Dad handed me a penny, keeping one for himself. We closed our eyes, made our wishes, and tossed the coins. All of us kept our wishes secret, but I felt certain that we had asked for the same thing.

Mom returned a few minutes later. She had bought a stuffed puppy for Jimmy. He was so delighted. For the rest of us, she bought candles. They featured La Virgen on one side and a prayer with *"ayúdame"* on the other. I couldn't speak much Spanish, but I knew that *ayúdame* meant "help me."

"When we get there," Dad said, pointing to the church before us, "we're going to pray."

"Then we're going to make *promesas*," Mom added.

"What's a *promesa*?" I asked.

"A promise, just like it sounds," Mom said. "Only this is a different kind of promise. A 'thank you' promise."

"What are we being thankful for?" I said.

"We're going to ask God and La Virgen to help your mother," Dad explained, "and in return, each of us is going to do something special."

"Like what?" Carmen asked.

"That's up to you," Mom said. "Some people promise to say extra prayers every day. Others promise to work for charities or do something for the church."

"I heard of a man," Dad added, "who promised to run a thousand miles."

"All at once?" Carmen sounded totally amazed.

"No. But every day he ran and recorded how far he went till he got to a thousand."

"And I had an uncle," Mom said, "who promised not to cut his hair for two years. This was in the 1950s, when men weren't supposed to have long hair."

"So it's like a bribe," I concluded. "We're bribing God to help us."

"No," Dad said. "We're *thanking* Him."

"But He hasn't helped us yet."

"But He will."

"Because of our prayers and *promesas*?"

They nodded, all of them, even Carmen. Apparently, I was the only one who thought this was a bribe. It just didn't make sense. Weren't you supposed to say "thank you" *after* someone helped you?

We entered the church and stepped into a giant, fan-shaped room with a floor that sloped down like in a theater. High above the altar stood the legendary statue of La Virgen de San Juan, an exact copy of the mural outside. I was expecting a giant statue, life-size, but this was a small doll with a dark brown face. She stood in a nook surrounded by a huge wooden frame that reminded me of an Aztec sundial with its ring of hieroglyphics and shapes that looked like snakes and leaves.

Mom and Dad led us to a chamber behind the altar, where hundreds of candles flickered and dozens of people knelt to utter prayers. As I overheard their different accents, I realized that they had come from all over the United States and Mexico to visit this shrine.

"Here's where you light the candle," Dad said. "Say a prayer and make your *promesa*, okay?"

Carmen and I nodded. Then the whole family filed into an empty section of the kneeling pad. I placed my candle in a slot, lit it, and said the Our Father and Hail Mary. I didn't know what else to say, so I added the Act of Contrition and asked to be forgiven for all the times I fought with Carmen. Then I was done feeling guilty, but when I glanced at my family, they were still praying, so I pretended to keep praying too, though I was actually thinking about Mom's surgery, like how she would sleep on a cold, metal table surrounded by strangers wearing masks and gloves. I thought about the medical dramas on TV, how they always showed clamps on the patient's chest while doctors gave one-word orders like "scalpel" or "suction," and how something bad always happened. The doctors would snip an artery or inject the wrong drug, which made the patient have a heart attack. Then the doctors would call, "Code blue!" as they charged paddles to jolt the patient back. Sometimes the heart monitor would bleep again, but other times, it stayed flat till someone said, "Call it," and a frustrated doctor announced the time of death. I trembled as I pictured the scene, though I knew TV wasn't real life. Sometimes, though, the fake world of TV actually *did* happen, and that's why I got so stressed, and the only way to deal with stress was to…well…to think about the boys on my Wish List. I knew it was totally wrong to think about boys in church, but I couldn't help it. My mind just went there.

Enough of that, I told myself. Think of a *promesa*. I silently brainstormed, but I had absolutely no inspiration, so I felt even *more* stressed. I considered Mom and Dad's examples, but I couldn't concentrate enough to say extra prayers, and I couldn't grow long hair because my hair was already long, and I couldn't run a thousand miles—at least, not in one lifetime.

"What are you going to do?" Carmen asked.

I shrugged. "What about you?"

"I'm going to clean the bathrooms till Mom gets better."

I had to admit, Carmen had a great idea—practical but also a real sacrifice since cleaning toilets was so gross.

"Look it! Look it!" Jimmy said, showing me his fingers, black from squeezing the tips of burned-out matches.

"Mom," Carmen tattled, "Jimmy got ashes on his fingers. It's all Chia's fault."

I elbowed her. "No, it isn't."

Mom glanced at me and jerked her head, a signal that meant "get him out of here." I couldn't believe it. I got in trouble even when I was praying.

"Come on, Jimmy," I said, happy to get away. I led him to a doorway, where I found a basin with water. I lifted him. "Wash all that black stuff off your hands."

He splashed his hands, getting himself and me all wet.

"Hey," a lady hissed. "That's holy water."

I set Jimmy down. "I didn't realize," I said, but she just glared at me. She must have thought I was the most sarcastic teenager. After all, I was in a church. Of course it was holy water. How dumb could I be? Maybe I shouldn't go to church at all. I seemed to get in more trouble here than in the Land of Temptation outside.

I grabbed Jimmy's wet hand and took him through a hallway, hoping to find a way out before I'd have to say more Acts of Contrition, but instead, I discovered the most amazing room. It wasn't very big, but it was filled, ceiling to floor, with flowers, wedding veils, communion dresses, locks of hair, jewelry, car keys, cards, toys, empty prescription bottles, letters, rosaries, shoes, braces, crutches, postcards, newspaper clippings, dog tags, expired licenses, eyeglasses, helmets, and pictures. Lots of pictures. Not an inch of the room was bare.

Jimmy's mouth opened as if he wanted to swallow the whole scene. I'd never seen him look so astonished. His eyes widened as they glanced across the room. "Gimme?" he said, for the first time not knowing what to ask for.

I picked him up so we could look at some of the letters on the wall. Most were in Spanish, but I did find a few English ones. One read:

Dear Virgen de San Juan del Valle,
Thank you for your intercessions. When my husband fell off a ladder last summer, he suffered a serious head injury. The doctors said he would never talk again, or if he did, he wouldn't make sense. But thanks to you, he's talking now. And he makes sense. Escúchame, Madre. Your generous heart has made this possible. For this, and for all the kindnesses you have shown to my family and to all those throughout Earth and time, I thank you. Please accept my humble offerings. I have planted roses in your honor and will make rosaries from its petals for patients at the hospital where my husband stayed. In that way may I share your message of love and hope.

All the letters were about the sick, injured, or those at war. They gave thanks for people who survived or requested blessings for people who had died.

"They're testimonials," I heard Dad say. He took Jimmy from me, and immediately my brother put his head on Dad's shoulder, since this was when he usually took a nap. "This is *el cuarto de milagros*, the miracle room," Dad continued, "where people share stories and make offerings." He nodded toward Mom. She had removed one of her bikini tops from her purse and was placing it on a table. Then she took out a notepad and started to write a letter. Carmen was with her. She seemed reluctant, but after a few seconds, she decided to leave behind her trophy.

"Do you have your special item?" Dad asked.

I reached into my pocket, pulled out the envelope, and showed him the pebble, crystal, and coin. Then he reached into his pocket and pulled out two movie tickets for *Back to the Future*.

"From my first date with your mom," he explained. "I kept them all these years. Isn't that silly?"

"Not at all," I said, remembering the "romantic" mementos in my jewelry box.

We placed our special items beside one another, right next to a newspaper article from the *San Antonio Express-News* with a picture showing a giant mass of people by the Alamodome, almost all of them in pink shirts, and a caption that read "Over 30,000 Race for the Cure." I read the first paragraphs of the article and learned that they were participating in a fund-raiser for breast cancer research. Wow! I thought to myself, wondering what it was like to be with thirty thousand people, all walking in the same direction and wearing the same colored shirt. I couldn't help it. I mind-traveled. I put myself right in the middle of the crowd, imagining people lightly bumping into me as we walked, and everyone chanting the names of their loved ones with cancer. I imagined myself peeking over shoulders and looking for breaks in the crowd so I could make my way through, stopping at the water stations for a drink, and waving to the people on the sidelines. But mostly I imagined the energy, the positive energy, and the joy. If I actually *did* the race, then I wouldn't have to mind-travel about it. Maybe the race could be my *promesa*. Then again, it was only five kilometers. It didn't come close to being a thousand miles, and if it wasn't a thousand miles, would it be good enough to cure Mom?

45 BILLION BEES

The next Wednesday, Mom went in for surgery. When my parents were gone for an hour or two, they let me babysit my brother and sister, but since Dad would be at the hospital the whole day and Mom even longer, Grandma came over to be with us.

As soon as she arrived, Carmen said, "Did you hear about the honeybees?"

"No, sweetie. What happened to the honeybees?"

"They have a disease called colony collapse disorder. I read about it in that magazine you ordered for me."

Last Christmas, Grandma had given Carmen subscriptions to *Discover Magazine* and *National Geographic*; she gave me barrettes.

"That sounds awful," Grandma said.

"It *is*," Carmen agreed, "and it killed around forty-five billion bees last year."

I knew bees lived in hives the way people lived in cities, so when I heard that number, I pictured downtown San Antonio totally abandoned. I saw the city going dark because no one was around to fix the electricity. I saw the boats slapping against the edges of our famous River Walk. I saw parking lots like empty seas. Then I pictured other big cities, like New York, Chicago, and Houston, all of them completely silent with no people around.

"Imagine forty-five billion *people* dying," I said.

"That's ridiculous," Carmen told me.

"It could happen," I insisted.

"No, it couldn't." She snapped. "Not when there aren't forty-five billion people on the planet."

Grandma patted Carmen's head the way a trainer pets a dog that jumps through a hoop and fetches a stick. Why did I even try to join the conversation?

In order to distract us, Grandma kept us busy. First we baked cookies. Then we played Monopoly. Carmen won— but only because I had to keep Jimmy from grabbing the pieces. For lunch, Grandma took us to Alamo Cafe, one of our favorite restaurants, and after, to a shopping center that had a bookstore for Carmen, a toy store for Jimmy, and a T-shirt shop for me. I bought a shirt with a teddy bear wearing a feathered hat and reading from a scroll. According to the caption, his name was Shakesbear. I thought it was totally cute, but I couldn't get excited. I didn't even feel like sending a picture of it to Iliana. Grandma meant well, but her plans to distract me weren't working. In fact, I felt worse. I couldn't stop moping or thinking of some doctor putting Mom "under the knife." And why did we use that word, "under," when we talked about surgery? It made me think of "*under*ground," as in graveyards. I knew I shouldn't think the worst, but my mind kept going there.

Soon after we got home, GumWad called. "Hey," he said. "How's it going? Is your mom still in the hospital? Today's the day she's having that operation, right?"

"Yeah," I said. "But you don't have to sound all cheery about it."

"I'm not cheery. That's just how my voice is." He paused a moment. I could hear him smacking on the other end and wondered what color his gum was today. "How are you holding up?" he asked, using a totally fake low voice.

I couldn't help laughing.

"What's so funny?" GumWad wanted to know.

"Your voice," I explained. "When you make it deep, you sound like a frog with a serious sore throat."

He sighed. "I guess I can't win. I'm either too cheery or I sound like a sick frog."

"That's okay," I said. "I shouldn't have snapped at you. But all this waiting while my mom's in surgery is driving me nuts." I glanced at my new mood ring. The stone was black, which, according to the mood ring color chart, meant I was severely anxious.

"You have to think positive thoughts," GumWad said.

"That's tough for a girl who's wearing a T-shirt that says, 'I used to be a pessimist, but now I just think the worst.'"

He laughed. "I love your 'I used to' series."

"My what?"

"You have a lot of shirts that start with 'I used to.'"

"I do?"

"Yeah," he said. "Like 'I used to be doubtful, but now I'm not so sure' and 'I used to be infallible, but now I'm perfect.'"

"'I used to be a loner,'" I added, "'but now I hang out with myself.'"

"And 'I used to be apathetic, but now I just don't care.'" He laughed again, still managing to smack his gum.

When he settled down, he said, "I stopped by your house but no one was there."

"We went to Alamo Cafe. Why did you come by?"

"To drop something off. It's in your mailbox, okay?

There's no stamp on it or an address because I put it there myself. I mean, it's no big deal. Just a little something. But don't read it when people are around, okay?"

"Are you nervous?" I asked.

"No. Why?"

"Because you're saying 'okay' a lot. You always do that when you're nervous."

"Ha-ha." He laughed, smacking extra loud now. "Okay, gotta go." He hung up before I could say good-bye.

I went out the front door, reached into the mailbox, and pulled out an envelope. It had my name on it and a blue smudge, probably from GumWad's gum. I was about to open it, but I heard a loud crash, followed by Jimmy's screams, so I stuffed the envelope in my pocket and rushed back inside.

I found everyone in the kitchen.

"Jimmy was climbing the counter, trying to get at the cookies," Carmen explained. "He dropped the plate, and it broke. Now all the cookies are on the floor. They're all dirty and mixed up with the broken plate, so we can't eat them after all." She started to tear up. "And I really wanted one!"

This only made Jimmy scream. Grandma was holding him and saying, "Now, now," as she kept him from grabbing the cookies on the floor.

"This wouldn't have happened if Mom were here!" Carmen whined. She was really crying now, which upset Jimmy even more.

Grandma looked at me and said, "I'm getting too old for this."

Poor lady. I could tell Jimmy was wearing her out. He really wanted the cookies, but how could he eat them without swallowing a piece of glass?

First things first, I told myself. Remove the temptation. I grabbed a broom and started to sweep. Step two, find another temptation. "Hey, Jimmy, isn't it time for your favorite cartoon show?" I winked at Grandma. "Don't you want to see it? If not, let me know because I've got a lot of shows I want to watch."

"No!" Jimmy said. "*My* TV!"

"I don't know," I went on. "As soon as I finish cleaning up, I'm going to watch the afternoon news. Whoever gets there first gets to choose."

"Gimme TV," Jimmy said, pointing to the living room. "Gimme cartoon!"

"Are you finished crying?" Grandma asked.

He nodded, so Grandma took him out. A few minutes later, I heard cartoon music in the other room. Meanwhile, Carmen hadn't moved. She kept sniffling, while I swept the mess into a little pile. As I cleaned, I got more and more frustrated. The least she could do was help. But no. She just stood there, watching, not lifting a finger.

"Why don't you go read a book or memorize some vocabulary words if you're not going to help? They're just cookies, anyway. They probably tasted gross."

"I'm not Jimmy," she said. "You can't lie to me and act like today's a normal day, because it isn't."

With that, she kicked the pile of broken cookies and glass, respreading them across the floor. "Hey!" I shouted. I wanted to pinch her, but she ran to the backyard, slamming the door behind her. Fine, I thought. Let her melt outside. It had to be over ninety degrees today.

I was prepared to let her stay outside all afternoon, but the last thing I needed was for Dad to discover a badly sunburned child. He had enough on his mind with Mom's surgery. Since she'd probably ignore me, I asked Grandma to call her in, and we all sat in front of the TV. For the next hour, I put on a happy face as I watched cartoons with Jimmy, but every few minutes, I glanced at my watch. All this waiting was torture.

At last, the phone rang. Grandma rushed to answer it. She kept saying, "I see" and "okay" and "uh-huh." Finally, she hung up and said, "Your mom's out of surgery. She's doing okay."

The knot in my stomach relaxed a bit. I could finally

ignore my watch. And maybe, just maybe, the stone on my mood ring would change to a color that was happier than black.

An hour later, Dad picked me up. "Tomorrow, we'll all see Mom," he said to Carmen and Jimmy. "But she's really tired today, so I'm only taking Chia."

Carmen pouted. "I'm the one who should go. Chia needs to take care of Jimmy."

"Grandma can take care of him just fine," Dad said.

I knew he was right, but I also knew that Jimmy would cry as soon as Dad and I stepped out the door. So I asked Grandma to take him to the backyard. That way, we could sneak out while he was on the swings. When we heard Jimmy laughing outside, Dad and I quietly left the house.

Once we rolled out of the driveway and turned the corner, I spotted a group of kids from school, including Lou Hikaru. What a heartthrob! Iliana and I had been trying to engineer a close encounter with him, but no luck so far. Wait a minute. Why was Lou walking so close to Paula Wilson? Were they an item? Oh, no! They *were* an item. He'd just grabbed her hand. This was not good. Lou was a top pick on my Boyfriend Wish List. We hadn't moved beyond nodding hello and good-bye, but that didn't keep me from hoping. After all, he was the star of our baseball team. Then again, Paula was a pep squad captain, so they made total sense as a couple. I shook my head. I'd have to text Iliana to tell her that Lou was on the Currently Unavailable List.

Luckily, Forest Montoya was with the group, too. With him, I actually had a chance because last year, we paired up for a science project, and in front of the whole class, we demonstrated how potatoes conduct electricity. When the teacher gave us an A, Forest gave me a high five. I secretly cheered. Physical contact, at last! Okay, so it wasn't exactly *romantic* contact, but I still put it in the close encounter of the fourth kind category. And he did say hello when he spotted me at the skateboarding park last week.

"You like him?" Dad asked, nodding toward Forest.

I covered my face, all embarrassed. I couldn't believe Dad had caught me staring at a boy.

"No," I said. "Well . . . yes . . . maybe a little."

"So what's his name? What's he like?"

I squirmed. "I don't know."

"So you like a total stranger?" he teased.

"He's not a total stranger. I mean, we had a class together last year, so we kinda know each other, a little bit."

"Oh, yeah? Which class were you in? Did he get good grades?"

"Stop with the twenty questions," I pleaded. "I can't discuss boys with you."

"Why not?"

"Because you're my dad. It's…it's…" I glanced at my mood ring, the stone a yellowy orange, which meant my emotions were…"unsettling. It makes me feel unsettled."

Dad glanced at me. "Unsettled" wasn't one of my usual vocabulary words.

Dad finally drove out of the neighborhood and onto the major road. He didn't ask any more questions about boys. Instead, he turned up the volume for his favorite radio talk show, *All Things Considered*, and we listened to people from NASA discuss the space program. Dad usually shared his opinions about the stories, but today he was quiet. I couldn't tell if he was *really* listening. With Mom in the hospital, he was probably too preoccupied to pay attention.

We finally reached the Medical Center, a section of San Antonio crammed with hospitals, clinics, and the University of Texas Health Science Center, where people learned to be doctors, dentists, physical therapists, and researchers. Mom was at Methodist Hospital, but instead of going there, Dad parked at Baskin-Robbins.

"What are we doing *here*?" I asked.

"Getting ice cream, what else?"

Even on the worst days, I wasn't the type to turn down ice cream, especially when I had a chance to enjoy it without Carmen and Jimmy around. Come to think of it…I hardly *ever* had one-on-one time with Dad. I liked pretending that I was the only child sometimes, a totally spoiled only child who could order whatever she wanted.

"Can I get whatever I want?" I asked.

"Of course," Dad said.

I got two scoops, Rocky Road and Chocolate Chip Cookie Dough, in a chocolate-dipped waffle cone. Dad ordered two scoops too, Chocolate and Vanilla, but he asked for his ice cream in a cup. I shook my head. Sometimes, adults have no imagination.

I was halfway through my dessert when Dad said, "I wanted some alone time with you before going to the hospital. We need to discuss a few things."

"Like what?"

He took a spoonful of ice cream and stared at it. "We need to discuss your mom," he said. "Today's surgery is a very important part of Mom's treatment, but the doctors need to make sure they get rid of all the cancer cells. They're worried the cancer might have metastasized."

"What does that mean?" I asked, glad Carmen wasn't around to supply the definition.

"It's a fancy word for 'spreading.'"

"You mean the cancer traveled outside the breast?"

"Maybe, but to make sure it doesn't grow into tumors, your mom is going to have radiation therapy."

"That's good, right?"

"Yes, but the treatment has a lot of side effects, so your mom's going to be under the weather for a while."

I moaned.

"What is it?" he asked.

"I hate the word 'under,'" I explained.

"Why?"

"Because it's so negative. I was thinking about it this morning—how we call anesthesia 'putting the patient under' and surgery 'going under the knife'—and now you're telling me Mom's going to be 'under the weather.' What does that mean, anyway? If the weather is something that happens in the sky, then aren't we *always* under it? If being 'under the weather' means we're sick, then being above the weather should mean we're feeling healthy, right? But think about it. No one ever says 'above the weather.' They might say they're on 'cloud nine,' but that's not the same thing. And why cloud nine, anyway? Why not say you're on cloud five or cloud sixteen? Who came up with the number nine? Did someone look at the sky one day and count?" I didn't mean to go on and on about weather and clouds, but when I feel nervous, I tend to ramble. Okay, I ramble a lot, but usually I don't ramble out loud.

Dad took my hand and squeezed it. I guess I had an "off" switch on my palm because I immediately hushed. Usually when Dad silenced me this way, he let go of my hand right away, but this time, he kept holding it. He bit his lower lip, and I knew that if he had a mood ring like mine, it would be black, too.

"I just don't know why your mom got sick," he said. "It's not fair."

"Lots of things aren't fair," I said, thinking about how Carmen was so smart without even trying, while I broke a sweat every time I opened a textbook.

Dad smiled and released my hand. "You're right, Chia. We can fill a whole book with things that aren't fair. Lots of people, for example, don't have a nice house like we do. They don't get new clothes every season. They don't go to places like Baskin-Robbins for ice cream. Lots of them are alone in this world." He paused a moment because his voice was starting to tremble.

"It's okay, Dad."

"Nobody asks to be sick," he went on. "It just happens and all we can do is deal with it."

I nodded, wishing I had the perfect words to comfort him. But all I could say was "it's okay" again.

I looked into my ice-cream cone. The last bites had melted, making the cone all soggy. Why did all the good stuff melt?

Soon, we left the ice-cream shop and headed to the hospital. The lobby had an information desk and signs to the cafeteria, the gift shop, and a chapel, but Dad walked straight to the elevators and pushed the "up" arrow. First, the elevator beeped, and when we got to Mom's floor, beeps from call buttons echoed through the hall. The doctors' and nurses' pagers beeped too, and so did heart and blood pressure monitors and the intercom before every announcement. All that beeping reminded me of items being scanned at the grocery store. Who knew hospitals were so loud? And how could anyone rest with all that noise?

"She's in here," Dad said, leading me to a door.

When I thought about Mom in the hospital, I pictured a dozen machines attached to her body and a tube stuck down her throat and a bloody bandage wrapped around her head. Of course, this was ridiculous. Mom's head was fine. I must have watched too many hospital scenes on TV. Luckily, she looked okay. She was asleep, her hair spread upon the pillow. Her lips were pale but only because she wasn't wearing lipstick. She had an IV and a splint on her finger with a red light to monitor her blood pressure. With the sheets tucked in at her armpits, I couldn't see her chest, but I could tell it was bandaged.

Dad took the chair beside her bed, reclined it, and stared at the newscast on TV. The sound was muted, so we had to read the headlines: "Burglar Caught on Tape," "Car Accident on Loop 1604," and "Local Unemployment on the Rise." How depressing, I thought. No wonder I hated to watch the news. I walked to the window ledge to examine a vase of roses. I smelled them and touched their velvety petals. The card said, *"Abrazos y besos"*—hugs and kisses— followed by all our names. I recognized the handwriting— Dad's. He'd also brought a present from Mother's Day, a photo of Carmen, Jimmy, and me in a frame that said, "World's Best Mom."

I turned to him. "You're really sweet, Dad. These are the perfect things to cheer Mom up."

He nodded. "Maybe we can buy her a big balloon tomorrow. Jimmy would love to pick it out, don't you think?"

"He'll want to keep it for himself," I said, and Dad had to agree.

Then he pointed to an empty chair. "Why don't you sit down?" he suggested.

I nodded an okay, and when I sat down, I thought about my *promesa* again. Would a 5K be enough? Maybe I could promise to do it two times in a row?

Dad had closed his eyes for a nap, so the room was quiet. How could he relax when I was feeling—I checked my ring—still unsettled? Then I remembered the blue-smudged envelope that GumWad had left in our mailbox. I pulled it from my pocket and opened it. Inside was a card with a kitten clasping a branch, its legs hanging free. The front cover said, "Whatever you fear, you can overcome," and inside, it said, "because you are not alone." The inside picture showed the same cat, but this time a pair of hands reached to catch it. There was a personal note, too. "Just wanted you to know," GumWad wrote, "if you need help with anything, you can count on me. Your friend, Roberto."

Leave it to GumWad to mess up. *I* wasn't the one who needed a "get well" card. He meant this for my mom. She's the one who called him "Roberto," anyway. I shook my head as I stood the card beside the roses.

That's when I heard someone whisper my name.

I turned. Mom's eyes had opened. Her fingers weakly waved me over.

"Hi, Mom," I said, taking her hand and kissing her forehead. Some hair had fallen near her eyes, so I brushed it aside. "How're you feeling?"

"Woozy."

"Want some water?"

She nodded. I filled a glass, lifted it to her lips. When she finished drinking, she turned her head aside, and then she clenched her lips and blinked as if fighting back tears. That's when I saw the ninth bikini top. She must have worn it to the hospital.

"Chia," Dad said, his voice startling me because I thought he was asleep. He nodded toward the dresser. "Can you put that away?"

I picked up the bikini top. "I'll take good care of it," I told Mom. "I'll hold it for you, okay? Just for a little while."

She smiled. "You can have it, *mija*. You can have all of my bikini tops. Take them from my room when you get home, okay?"

"Okay...but...they don't fit."

She laughed a little. "They will, Chia. Someday soon, they will."

50 PAIRS OF SHOES

The next day, Dad promised to pick us up around dinner-time so we could see Mom. In the meantime, Grandma was spending another day with us. She took Jimmy outside before it got too hot, while Carmen and I sat at the kitchen table, me with the Sunday tabloid and Carmen with the laptop. I loved glancing at pics of movie stars with and without their makeup, especially when they were doing normal things like buying groceries or pumping gas.

"Did you know," Carmen began, "that there are different kinds of surgeries for breast cancer?"

I shrugged. I was not in the mood for one of Carmen's lectures.

"A mastectomy and a lumpectomy," she explained. "Do you know the difference?"

I lifted the tabloid to block my view of her.

"I figured you didn't," Carmen said. "And you probably don't know what 'sentinel lymph nodes' or 'immunotherapy' are or what the word 'metastasize' means."

"It means 'spreading,'" I said, remembering the conversation with Dad yesterday.

"And the others?"

I put down the paper. "I don't care, Carmen. You're not my teacher. You're my little sister, which means you're supposed to do what I say. And I say quit being a pest right now."

"You're not my boss," she snapped back.

"Am too."

"Are not."

We locked eyes for a stare-down. I was not going to blink first. Who cared about the strand of hair tickling my temple or the ceiling fan drying out my eyes? Carmen might be smarter than me, but she wasn't tougher.

After a few intense moments, my phone pinged. Carmen blinked.

"Gotcha!" I cheered.

She just shook her head and went back to her computer screen.

I glanced at my text message. It was from Shawntae to all the Robins. "I'm totally bored," she wrote. "Anyone free? If so, come over. Save me, plz!"

I peeked into the backyard to ask my grandmother if I could visit my friend for a while. "I'll put Jimmy down for a nap first," I said, so she wouldn't have to worry about him crying.

"Sounds like a deal," she answered.

So I texted back to Shawntae. "CU in an hour." Then, I went back to the tabloid. I was just starting to read about the strange names stars gave their kids when Carmen interrupted.

"Did you know that the mastectomy rate in the United States is fifty-six percent?"

"I'm not a doctor," I replied. "Why would I know something like that?"

She ignored me. "The rate in Central and Eastern Europe is seventy-seven percent," she went on. "And in Australia and New Zealand, it's thirty-four percent."

I had to admit, I was a little interested. After all, this related to Mom. But what did it matter? All those percentages were meaningless to me. What did Carmen expect me to do with those numbers? When I thought about breast cancer, I didn't see an equation. I saw a picture—Mom in a light blue gown, her hair spread upon the pillow, and a quiet tear when she realized that she wouldn't wear bikinis anymore.

I folded up the paper and scooted back my chair.

"Where are you going?" Carmen asked.

"I'm going to get Jimmy. It's almost time for his nap."

"But don't you want to learn more about breast cancer?"

"When you can tell me why *our* mom got sick," I said, "I'll listen." With that, I headed out the door.

An hour later, I was at Shawntae's. She lives on the next street over. Her bedroom is an explosion of color—bright yellow walls, a rainbow-striped bedspread, and a tall bookshelf for her pumps. She has *so* many pumps. She organizes them by color. Lots of people wear black, red, or gray pumps, but Shawntae has orange, green, and pink, too. She has pumps with animal prints and some with bows or buttons. She must have more than fifty pairs! I imagined she slept with them because the only time I saw her bare feet was at the pool.

When I stepped in, she said, "Thank goodness you're here. I'm *dying* of boredom. Feel this."

She held out her wrist, so I touched it.

"I don't feel anything," I said.

"You see? No pulse! Like I said, I'm *dying*."

"Sorry to burst your bubble, but I heard heaven's boring, too. You don't get to chase boys, and heels are useless when you're walking on clouds. Plus, the only instruments they have up there are flutes and harps."

"That does sound worse than being cooped up in my room all day," Shawntae admitted. "At least I have a computer."

I put my hands on my hips and cleared my throat.

"And cool friends like you," she added.

"Thank you," I said. "It's nice to be remembered. So who else is coming over?"

"Iliana and Roberto are busy," Shawntae said, "and Patty…" Her phone rang. "Patty's calling right now."

She turned to answer it, so I decided to mess around with my own phone while she talked. I went to a screen saver site. I found one called "ribbons," bands of color running across the screen like shooting stars or glow-in-the-dark eels. Another screen saver had glowing light like the aurora borealis, and another had fireworks. I finally settled on a screen saver with bubbles. They changed colors—pink, blue, and yellow. They floated and bounced against one another. I picked one and followed its trail across the screen.

"I don't believe this!" Shawntae said, looking over my shoulder. "I *dreamed* about this."

"You dreamed about the screen saver?"

"No. Yes. Kind of." She took a minute to compose her

thoughts or, rather, to make up one of her silly after-the-fact predictions. "In my dream, you were in a giant bouncy ball. It was see-through, like a bubble. You were screaming because you wanted to get out, but you couldn't. There wasn't a door, only air holes. And you were bouncing down the street. Sometimes you hit the side of a building and sometimes you bounced right on top of a car. When I woke up, I thought you were going to join the basketball team, but now I see that my dream was actually predicting that you would stare at the screen saver."

I didn't feel like arguing, so I said, "Hmm...very interesting." Then I went back to looking at the bubbles.

"Wake up!" Shawntae said, snapping her fingers in my ear. "Why are you acting like a zombie?"

I sighed. "I can't help it."

"Because of your mom?"

I nodded. "She's still in the hospital. She was so weak yesterday. She could barely open her eyes. It was like her eyelids were bricks or dumbbells or boulders. That's how heavy they were."

Shawntae put her hand on my shoulder. "I know it's tough, but you can't mope around all day. She'd feel awful if she knew you were moping around."

"And the other thing that's stressing me out," I went on, "is my *promesa*."

"What's that?" Shawntae asked.

"It means 'promise.' I'm supposed to do something or make a sacrifice in honor of my mother. That way, all the angels will know she needs help. It's like giving thanks. My sister's cleaning the bathrooms, and I decided to walk a 5K, which is a bit lame, but what else can I do?"

"Maybe you can plant a garden," Shawntae suggested.

"Maybe. But if the plants die, I'll think it's a sign."

"Then write a poem every day."

"I would if I could, but I'm not smart enough to write poems."

Shawntae thought for a minute. "That's it!" she blurted.

"You have a good *promesa* for me?"

"No, but I totally understand my dream now. It wasn't about you staring at a screen saver. It was about you feeling trapped and hopeless. It's like you're bumping into things, with no control over where you're going."

"Gee, thanks," I groaned. "I feel a whole lot better now."

"Don't blame me," Shawntae said. "It's not my fault you're stuck in a bouncy ball. I gave you some good suggestions."

"Suggestions for what?" Patty asked as she stepped into the room. She slurped through the straw of a giant Slush from Sonic, took a big swallow, and said, "Major brain freeze." Then she kicked off her flip-flops and plopped on the bed. "Well?" she said, all impatient.

"Erica has to walk five whole kilometers for her mom," Shawntae explained. "It's so the angels will hear her."

"It's called a *promesa*, which means 'promise.'" I glanced at my feet, imagining them in tennis shoes. "I wish I were more inspired."

"I told her to think of another promise," Shawntae said.

"It has to be some kind of sacrifice," I explained.

"A *painful* sacrifice, huh?" Patty said, thinking about it. I nodded, even though I hadn't mentioned pain. "Why don't you promise to walk over broken glass or hot coals? I saw some guys do that on TV once. They didn't even get hurt. You just have to put *mind over matter.*"

I shook my head, remembering how walking barefoot on the hot cement made my feet blister.

"How about fasting?" Patty said. "Or you could ask your dad to drop you off in the middle of the desert and then you can find your way back. That's what the Indians did, and they always returned with the answers to the universe."

"I don't want the answers to the universe," I said. "I want my mom to get better."

"She had the operation yesterday," Shawntae explained. "And Erica's all stressed."

Patty slurped from the giant cup again, and then said, "So have you seen your mom's chest? Did it creep you out?"

"Don't ask that!" Shawntae scolded.

Patty just shrugged. "Feeling creeped out is a normal reaction to something like this, right, Erica?"

I nodded. "Just thinking about it creeps me out."

"So have you seen it yet?" she asked again.

"No. I visited my mom, but she was all covered up."

"It's not like she's going to ask her mom to take off her shirt," Shawntae said. "Things like that are private."

I shivered as I imagined women without breasts. I didn't want to think about it, but I also had this weird desire to know what it looked like.

Patty took another long slurp. Then she turned to me. "Your mom has joined a warrior tribe of women," she announced.

"Because she's fighting breast cancer?"

"Yes. I mean, that, too. But I also mean a *real* warrior tribe of women. Have you heard of the Amazons?"

"You mean the rain forest?"

"No, I mean Amazon women. Back in ancient times, they decided to live without men."

"No guys?" I felt scandalized. How could you have a Boyfriend Wish List when there weren't any guys around?

"Sounds like a good idea to me," Shawntae said. "I like guys, but sometimes they're overrated. This world would be a better place with more women as mayors and presidents."

"That's what the Amazons thought," Patty said. "But the men kept trying to take over. So they had to learn to defend themselves, and their favorite weapon was the bow and arrow."

"That's cool," I said, imagining arrows arcing across the sky.

"But there was a problem," Patty added. "The Amazons had big breasts that got in the way."

Shawntae stood up, pretended to pull back on a bow. "I guess it'd be hard if you had giant boobs."

"You want to know how they solved the problem?" Patty asked.

Shawntae and I nodded.

"They cut off the breast. Can you imagine a whole group of women walking around like that? But it worked. They were the best archers around."

"They weren't sick?" I asked.

"No, they weren't sick at all. They volunteered to do this, and it made them stronger."

I imagined a tribe of women warriors in the forest. They had long hair, muscular arms and legs, and white tunics, one side flat. But they were wrestling, swimming, and running through obstacle courses. And Mom was with them, doing all of those things—not sick but strong.

180 TILES

A few days later, Mom returned from the hospital.

"Be careful," Dad said as he helped her sit at the kitchen table. "You're still recovering."

As soon as she sat down, Carmen and I gave her hugs and took the seats beside her. Dad poured her a cup of coffee and then went to the sink to rinse dishes, while Jimmy rolled a ball across the floor.

"How are you feeling?" I asked Mom.

"I'm tired, but I'm glad to be home."

She wore a shirt that buttoned down the front. I couldn't help glancing at her chest and noticing that the right side was flat now, just like an Amazon. Mom must have caught me looking because she said, "I'm going to get a special bra. A prosthetic."

"What's that?" I asked.

Carmen turned into Little Miss Factoid again. "It's a replacement part, like a fake leg or a fake arm."

"That's right," Mom said. "I'm going to have a fake boob." She was silent a moment, and then she laughed. She winced as if the laughter hurt a bit, but the chuckles kept coming. Soon, Carmen and I were laughing, too. Even Jimmy joined in.

"Okay," Dad said, his voice stern. "Quit laughing at your mother."

"Oh, lighten up," Mom told him. "They're not laughing at me. We're just having some fun. You have to admit that a bra with a fake boob is funny."

"No, it's not." Dad turned from the sink to face us. "There's nothing funny about cancer, about having to get…"—he glanced at Carmen—"replacement parts."

Mom frowned. "I'm the one who's sick," she said, "so *I* get to decide what is and isn't funny about *my* body. Isn't that right, girls?"

Carmen and I didn't want to take sides, so we kept our mouths shut.

"I'm just saying…" Dad began.

Mom held out her hand to hush him. He stared at it for a second before turning back to the sink. When I looked across the table at Carmen, I caught her biting her lower lip. I almost bit my lip, too. That's how tense the room was. I wanted to lighten the mood, change the subject, talk about something fun and easy, like boys or Jimmy's cartoons. I wanted to suggest we eat ice cream, fly a kite, or go to the movies. But when you're sitting beneath the gloom of cancer, everything that's *not* cancer seems silly. You wonder why boys or ice cream or kites ever mattered in the first place.

Dad finished the dishes and left the room. A few minutes later, I heard him vacuuming the den.

"Can you refill this?" Mom asked me, tapping her coffee cup.

I brought the pot over, poured the coffee. Mom lifted it, a bit awkwardly. She spilled some on her shirt. "I don't believe this," she said, all frustrated.

"Why are you using your left hand?" Carmen asked—a good question because Mom was right-handed.

Before she could answer, Jimmy walked to her and climbed onto her lap. He hugged her tight, making Mom grimace.

"Careful, Jimmy," I said. "Mom's sore, remember?"

She hugged him back but with her left arm only, and since Jimmy wiggled a lot, he slid off. He tried climbing onto her lap again, but she waved him off.

"Up, up," he told her.

"I can't, *mijo*. At least, not right now."

"Up!" he cried.

Mom looked at Carmen and me. "My right side's weak," she explained. "When they took my breast, they took some muscle tissue too, so I won't be using my right side for a while."

Mom looked like an Amazon, but she didn't feel like one. Not yet. I still hoped, though, that soon she'd feel stronger.

Jimmy reached for her again. She leaned over and kissed him. "I can't carry you, but you can sit right next to me."

"Gimme Mommy," Jimmy said as he started to bawl.

Now it looked like Mom wanted to bawl, too. "Chia," she said, her voice a little choked, "will you take him? I'm going to the bedroom to rest."

As she walked out, Jimmy kicked her chair. "Mommy's mad!"

I picked him up. "No, she isn't," I said. "She really wants to carry you, but she can't right now. She's sick, remember?" His whole chest shook with sobs. "She'll get better," I went on, "and then she'll hug you and carry you and never let you go. I promise."

At that, Carmen said, "I'm going to clean the bathroom," and she hurried off. Carmen never volunteered to clean, so I thought an alien had taken over her body. Then I remembered her *promesa*. She was going to clean bathrooms till Mom got better. My sister could be a real brat sometimes, but once in a while, she did something nice.

I decided to follow her example and work on my *promesa*, too. I told Dad I was going to start training, and since he was so busy cleaning, I offered to take Jimmy. He loved being pushed in his stroller, even though he was getting too big for it.

"Come on, Jimmy," I said, and he happily joined me.

We walked down the block, and by the time I reached the next street, sweat was dripping into my eyes and stinging them. My hands were swollen, too. I could tell by how tight my mood ring felt. And my T-shirt, this one with beetles and ants over a caption that said "You're bugging me," was getting damp. Was I crazy? No one exercised when it was near one hundred degrees. Then again, the *promesa* was supposed to be a challenge, so I walked on, refusing to turn back until I reached the major street at the end of our neighborhood.

When I got home, I took a shower in the sparkling clean bathroom. Carmen probably spent a whole hour polishing the counters and floors. I couldn't blame her. Even though I felt tired, I went to the laundry room, sorted the darks and lights, put in a load, and dusted furniture while I waited for the wash cycle to end. In a strange way, cleaning made me feel like I was accomplishing something. Carmen and Dad probably felt the same way because they were doing extra chores, too.

Later that night, I heard Carmen turning pages in a book. The lights were out, and since she didn't have her book lamp on, I knew she wasn't reading.

"What are you doing?" I asked.

"Counting the pages."

"What for?"

"I like counting things," she said. "Did you know," she went on, "that there are one hundred eighty tiles around our bathtub?"

"I can't believe you stood there and counted tiles."

"At first, I multiplied the number of tiles in a row by the number of tiles in a column. Then, I double-checked my calculation by counting each and every tile. And then, I triple-checked. If you don't believe me, you can count them yourself. You'll see. There are one hundred eighty tiles."

"That's amazing," I said, my sarcasm as thick as the cheese on the pizza we ate for dinner. "I always wondered how many tiles there were. How can I ever thank you for enlightening me?"

She didn't reply, but a few seconds later, I heard the rustling pages again. How annoying!

"Will you stop that?" I said.

"I'll stop when I get to the end of the book."

"Why on earth are you counting pages when they're already numbered?"

"I told you," she said. "I like counting."

"But it's ridiculous. No one who's sane counts pages in a book."

"Then I guess I'm not sane," she said, getting out of bed and heading to the door. "Don't worry. I won't be bothering you anymore. I'm going to the living room to count in peace."

She stepped out, and I almost said "good riddance" because without the sound of rustling pages and mumbled numbers, I could finally fall asleep. At least, that was the theory. For some reason, though, I couldn't relax. Sure, Carmen got on my nerves with all her counting, but at least she had cleaned the bathroom. I spent a while resisting the urge to call her back, but eventually, my guilty conscience got to me.

I found her in the living room. The porch light's yellow

glow came through the window. Carmen was asleep with the book open on her chest. I shook her.

"Hey, Carmen," I whispered. "Come back to the room."

She opened her eyes partway, reaching for the book and mumbling, "Not finished yet."

"You can finish tomorrow," I said. "If you start early enough, you can count all the pages before you fall asleep."

She nodded, and without saying another word, she followed me to our room.

1 BELLY FLOP

Because of Mom's weak arm, I had to put away the heavy pots and pans, carry the baskets of laundry, and vacuum. She didn't ask me to do these things, but when I caught her wincing at the chores or giving up, I decided to do them myself, but secretly. That way, she wouldn't feel like an invalid. And when things were settled at home, I'd go walking. After a while, I could walk around the whole neighborhood without feeling tired, even though I still had to deal with sweat and swollen hands. I kept thinking a 5K wasn't enough, but since I had no other ideas, it would have to do.

I kept in touch with my friends, though I wasn't seeing them very much. They invited me to all their outings, but I felt too guilty to go when I had so much to do at home. So when Iliana called to invite me to the pool, I said, "I wish I could go, but I hate to leave my mom. She's still not one hundred percent."

"Go where?" I heard. I turned around and spotted Mom at my bedroom door, eavesdropping on my conversation. She held out her hand. "Give me the phone." When I handed it to her, she said, "Who's this?" and then, "Oh, hi, sweetie." She quietly listened for a while. "Of course, I'm fine. Getting stronger every day. You know Erica. She tends to worry over nothing." She listened some more. "Of course she can go. She can't spend the whole summer moping around here. It's not healthy. She'll be ready in thirty minutes. I promise." She hung up, handed me the phone, and said, "Time to put on your bathing suit."

I should have felt excited about seeing my friends, but I felt angry instead. "Why did you tell Iliana that I'm all stressed out and worried? That I'm moping?"

"Because you are."

I glanced at my mood ring, wondering if Mom knew how to interpret the colors. "No, I'm not," I lied. "But even if I *was* stressed out, it's none of Iliana's business."

"She's your friend, so it *is* her business."

"But that's the problem," I complained. "She's going to tell *everybody* and they're going to feel sorry for me, and instead of having fun, they're going to give me useless advice, like the kind you find on a cheesy card, because even if they *really* try to understand me, they don't. Then I'm going to get mad. But if they think everything's fine, I *won't* get mad because instead of talking about me, we'll talk about other things."

"So tell her I was exaggerating," Mom suggested. "That way, you can have some fun." She pointed to my dresser. "Now get ready."

"But I'll have to—" I stopped myself.

"You'll have to what?" Mom asked.

I hesitated, not sure I wanted to finish my sentence. "I'll have to wear a bathing suit."

Mom crossed her arms. "Is that the *real* reason you don't want to go?"

I shrugged.

"So how many times have you turned down a trip to the pool?"

I shrugged again, not wanting to admit that my friends had invited me three times already. "I don't want to hurt your feelings," I said instead. "If you see me in a bathing suit, you'll think about having cancer."

She sighed. "*Mija*, I think about it anyway. I feel worse knowing you're avoiding fun because of me. Now get ready. That's an order."

She left me alone in my room, shutting the door behind

her, so I hunted in my drawer for a bathing suit, finding one of Mom's bikini tops instead. I decided to put it on. It sagged because I wasn't developed enough. I made fists and put them inside the cups, so I could see what I'd look like as a *real* woman and picture my body as beautiful as Mom's...as Mom's *used* to be. I took my hands out of the bikini top. I made a fist again, placed the other hand over it, trying to form the shape and size of Mom's breast and then imagining that part of her body being cut away. How could she stand it? Didn't it hurt? Didn't she hate looking at herself in the mirror now that she wasn't whole? If she did, she never mentioned it. But that was Mom, strong and brave. She didn't feel sorry for herself. Or maybe she did. Maybe she kept her true feelings inside, wearing a brave face for the rest of us, because that's how mature people acted. They *handled* things.

So in the spirit of handling things, I went to the pool. It was at the neighborhood park, on the opposite side of the skateboard area. The pool was fenced in, and you had to sign a guest list before going in. Behind the entrance was a covered patio with picnic tables. Mostly parents sat there, reading magazines or visiting as their children played in the water. The pool itself was a giant rectangle, three to ten feet deep, with black swim lanes painted on the floor. Lifeguards sat upon high perches beneath colorful umbrellas, and high school girls tanned on the chaise lounges.

"Over here, Erica!" I heard the Robins call. I spotted them, waving to me from the five-foot section of the pool. I went over and jumped in. The water felt cold. I shivered, but it felt so refreshing, a perfect cure for the heat.

"Iliana says you're all depressed," Patty told me. "That you aren't sleeping because you're worried about your mom."

"You do have bags under your eyes," GumWad said, his mouth full of red gum today. When I touched the area beneath my eyes, he said, "I didn't mean that in a bad way. Baggy eyes are pretty."

"She does not have baggy eyes," Shawntae said. "You're imagining things. But"—she turned to me—"you do look skinny. Have you been eating? I heard depressed people lose their appetites."

"It's true," Iliana said. "They don't feel like doing anything like going to the pool. I just hate the thought of you feeling too sad to come to the pool. You have to get out and *do* something."

I thought about how busy I'd been—helping with the chores and walking around the neighborhood to train for my *promesa*, things you can't do while sleeping—so if I looked a bit skinnier, it was because I'd been working, not because I'd been skipping meals. I probably had bags under my eyes because Jimmy woke up at six o'clock every morning. Mom slept right through his cries for attention, and even though Dad was awake, he was too busy getting ready for work. So I had to help Jimmy instead. And although Carmen cleaned the bathroom, that's *all* she did. My friends didn't have younger brothers or lazy sisters. How could they possibly understand?

They circled, waiting for me to share a true-confessions moment. When I didn't say anything, Iliana put her hand on my shoulder to encourage me to talk. This is exactly what I tried to tell my mom. I had the nosiest friends on the planet.

"I am not depressed!" I yelled, and I went under the water, making my body heavy so I could sink. My friends' voices were muted, and their legs wavered in the flickering sunlight. What a wonderful way to disappear. If only I could sink into a quiet place whenever people got on my nerves. After a moment, GumWad came underwater too and did all kinds of hand signals. Who knew what he was trying to say? The way his hair floated like a wild mane and his cheeks puffed out as he held his breath made me want to laugh, so I had to go up for air.

"What were you trying to say down there?" I asked GumWad when he surfaced a few seconds later.

He said, "I was trying to let you know that I'm going to Disney World next week."

"You go to Disney World every summer," I told him.

"No, I don't." He glanced at the other Robins, but they could only agree with me.

"*Every* summer," Iliana repeated. Then she turned to me. I knew she was about to question me again, but before she could, a bunch of boys from our Boyfriend Wish List walked in.

"It doesn't get better than this," Shawntae said, nodding toward the guys as they got ready for the water.

Iliana turned to us. "Quick. Do a face check. Do I look okay?" After we gave her a thumbs-up, she gasped. "They're taking off their shoes and their shirts!"

"Big surprise," Patty said, unimpressed. "We're at the pool, remember?"

"Yeah, that's why *my* shirt's off, too," GumWad said, sticking out his chest. He probably meant to look muscular, but he looked like a puffed-up rooster instead.

I turned away. After all, GumWad was like a cousin. I'd been meeting him at this pool for as long as I could remember. He has a dime-size birthmark behind his left shoulder and a scar on his belly from the time he ran into a barbed-wire fence at his uncle's ranch. So, of course, the other guys were more interesting. I wondered if they had scars or birthmarks. I scanned their bodies, but instead of scars or birthmarks, I saw nice tans and athletic arms and legs. I hadn't worn my mood ring because I didn't want to lose it in the pool, but if I *had* been wearing it, it'd be all sorts of colors because I had emotions that weren't even described on the mood ring chart.

"Snapshot," Iliana said, pretending to take a picture of the boys.

"Tattoo that image on my heart," I added.

"I *dreamed* about this," Shawntae said. "I dreamed we'd see cute guys at the pool. That's why I wanted to come today."

Our eyes followed the boys wherever they went. And, of course, they went to the diving board. Cool guys didn't bother with the pool. They weren't going to bob around like the rest of us. They were fearless. They were going to climb up the high board and jump.

Chad went first. When he got to the top, he stood at the edge, his toes curling over. Then he lifted his hands over his head and dived, doing a beautiful somersault before hitting the water. Derek Smith went next. He did *two* somersaults. Alejandro did a twist in the air, and Forest, a graceful swan dive. Each time they jumped, they got back in line to wait their turn again. And we just watched, speechless.

"Hey, girls," GumWad said, tapping our shoulders to get our attention, "check this out." He plunged and did an underwater flip, and when he came back up, his red gum was floating in the pool. How gross! GumWad coughed and snorted. "Water up my nose," he explained.

"Don't be disgusting," Patty scolded, pointing to the red blob.

GumWad obeyed. He picked up the gum and headed to the ladder so he could throw it away.

Meanwhile, we turned to the diving board. It was Chad's turn again. This time he hugged his knees and curled himself into a human bomb. The other guys copied him, bragging that they could make bigger splashes.

"I just love how they shake the water from their hair as they climb out of the pool." Iliana sighed.

"Yeah," Patty said, "like wet dogs shaking out their fur."

While we watched the guys, I decided to multitask by holding the edge of the pool and kicking my legs. That way, they could get ready for my *promesa*. Little by little, my legs felt heavier, which meant they were getting stronger, too. Soon I was on autopilot, hardly noticing that I was exercising while watching the diving board and visiting with my friends. Ten minutes must have passed when Patty said, "Is that Roberto in line?"

It *was*! We had forgotten all about him after he left the pool to throw out his gum. Patty did the Robins' *cheerily cheer-up cheer-up* whistle to get his attention, and when he glanced our way, we waved. He waved back and pointed to the high dive.

"I thought he was scared of heights," Shawntae said.

"Maybe he's conquering his fears," I suggested.

Sure enough, when GumWad reached the ladder, he paused a long time before grabbing hold. The person behind him had to nudge him. Finally, he climbed a couple of steps, stopped, climbed a few more, glanced down, and climbed a few more. At one point, he put his arms around the ladder and hugged it. Some nearby kids started to laugh. "Check out that scaredy-cat," they said. Even though I knew it was true, I didn't like other people making fun of my friend.

"Hey, GumWad!" I called out. "You can do it!"

He nodded, then made his way to the top. When he got there, he stood at the back of the board for a while, shaking out his hands. Someone said, "Quit holding up the line!" And that's when GumWad jogged forward, the board bouncing beneath him. He didn't pause at all. He simply ran off, and while he was falling, his arms and legs went in crazy directions. He looked like a rag doll, and he was screaming like someone on a roller coaster. Then he hit the water, one giant belly flop, with a splash more forceful than the stream that comes out of a fire hydrant. Everybody laughed, including me, because it was the most awkward dive I had ever seen. Poor guy. He must have felt embarrassed as he swam to the edge, where he gripped the side of the pool and coughed like someone who had swallowed the wrong way. Luckily, a lifeguard helped him out of the pool and sat beside him, patting GumWad's back till he caught his breath again.

When he returned to us, he said, "Did you see my dive?"

"Sure," Patty said, "you were as graceful as a...as a..." She snapped her fingers in front of my face.

"As a duck in ballet slippers," I said.

We all laughed.

"I wasn't trying to be graceful," GumWad explained, a bit defensively. "I was *trying* to be funny."

"If that's the case, then you scored a perfect ten," Shawntae said.

We laughed again, but then Iliana got serious. "You scared me. I thought you almost drowned when I saw you with that lifeguard."

"You were supposed to close your mouth before hitting

the water," Patty told him. "But you were too busy scream-ing." She couldn't contain her chuckles.

"It was all part of the act," GumWad insisted. "I *wanted* the lifeguard to help me. Not the guy lifeguard, but the one who's a pretty girl."

We glanced around. Sure enough, a pretty girl studied the pool from her perch.

"You're always staring at the guys," he went on, "but I *can't* because I'm a guy, too. I can't be talking about them. Sure, Chad has nice hair and Derek looks like he lifts weights, but I can't *say* that."

"You just did," I pointed out.

GumWad pretended not to hear. "So I search for the pretty girls instead, and there's a whole lot of them." He looked at me directly. "They're all around me."

"Then why are you hanging out with us?" Shawntae asked, her voice all offended.

GumWad thought about it, then said, "That's what *I'm* wondering." I could tell he was mad. He probably tried his best to do a fancy dive, and here we were, making fun of him. "See you later," he said. He climbed out of the pool and found a chaise lounge right between two high school girls. They were a lot more developed than us, and I had to admit, they looked great in their bikinis. One of them yawned as she adjusted her sunglasses. The other grabbed a water bottle, took a sip, and poured a bit onto her head. They didn't have a care in the world as they sat under the sun—the *cancerous* sun. Didn't they know that ultraviolet rays could cause cancer? I looked at their chests. I couldn't help it, couldn't help comparing them to Mom, couldn't help wondering if someday they'd have to get mastectomies.

"Are you looking at those girls' boobs?" Patty asked me.

"No."

"Yes, you are. You are *totally* checking out their boobs." She laughed at me.

I decided to challenge her. "So what if I am?"

My harsh tone surprised her. She backed off, got quiet.

I glanced at Shawntae and Iliana. They wouldn't look at me. They probably guessed that I was thinking about my mom. So I took a deep breath, made my body a rock, and sank. I'd stay under as long as possible, as long as it took for my friends to find another topic to discuss. Anything was better than facing my problems when they were around.

O TEARDROPS

A few days later, Mom left Carmen and Jimmy with Grandma, so "You and I can go pick out my new boob," she told me, laughing because it sounded like a funny way to spend an afternoon. Up till now, she'd been wearing what she called her "boob pillow." It *did* look like a pillow, a round pad with the kind of stuffing that you find in teddy bears. But now that her wound had healed, she needed to get a silicone breast form that matched the size and weight of her remaining breast. "If I don't," Mom explained, "I'll start having back problems because I'm not balanced." I nodded, remembering how I ached when I wore my backpack over one shoulder, instead of two.

We went to a medical supply store that specializes in prosthetics. There were models of artificial hands and legs, some very lifelike. There were also different kinds of shoes, some attached to braces and others with very tall soles, like the platform shoes rock stars wore. When the assistant caught me staring, she said they were for people with one leg that was shorter than the other. I thought about those who were born this way and those born with a short arm or an extra toe and those born blind or deaf. Then I thought about people born with problems on the insides of their bodies—like lungs that couldn't breathe normally or hearts that had trouble pumping blood. Our bodies could fail in so many ways. Even if we were born normal, something, like cancer, could happen to us later. No wonder my parents told me to be grateful for my health.

"Follow me," the assistant said, leading Mom and me to the back of the store and into a private room with posters about "how to fit a bra" and "types of breast forms." When the assistant said, "Let's take some measurements first," Mom started to remove her blouse.

"Mom!" I didn't mean to shriek, but I couldn't believe she was undressing in front of a stranger.

"Quit acting so scandalized. We all have the same things." She sounded just like Mrs. Garcia, our coach, after we complained about having to change clothes for PE the first year of middle school.

"Shouldn't I wait outside?" I asked, not wanting to see my mom's bare chest.

"Absolutely not. I need your help. This is a big decision for me, so I need another woman's opinion." This was the first time she had called me a woman. I felt proud but also undeserving. After all, a true woman was a lot more mature. She had a job, a marriage, children, and a developed body. I was still in middle school! I was still waiting to have my first boyfriend.

Mom removed her shirt and the bra with the pillow boob. She turned toward a mirror, and I looked at her reflection, how one side was completely normal while the other had the line of her scar. Her mastectomy side wasn't completely flat like I'd imagined but a bit caved in. I must have frowned because Mom said, "Don't be scared."

"I'm not," I replied, glancing at my mood ring, which was between colors, black and brown—nervous but with a sense of anticipation, too. Did this mean I was between emotions? That I really *was* scared, but also fascinated?

"Time to measure," the assistant said, measuring tape in hand.

She told Mom to lift her arms. Mom winced, explaining that she was still struggling since the surgery and would be starting physical therapy the following week. The assistant wrapped the tape around Mom's torso beneath her breast, then measured her cup size, and finally the length for the shoulder straps. As she wrote everything down, Mom put her shirt back on. Then the assistant took out a catalog of breast forms, along with some samples. She handed them to us. They felt like water balloons, only firmer. Some were smooth, while others had nipples. They came in different colors, too, one for every skin tone.

"Where's the Mexican one?" Mom asked, because the one she held was too peachy for her skin. When the assistant handed it to her, Mom laughed.

"What's so funny?" I wanted to know.

"Look at us," she said, "touching all these fake breasts. Imagine telling your friends that you and your mom went shopping for boobs."

"And talking about whether or not we should order one with a nipple." I giggled.

"And asking for the Mexican color even though no one's going to see it because it's going to be under my clothes."

"And discussing whether you should get the teardrop or the triangle shape," I added.

"Oh, you're definitely a triangle," the assistant told my mom, all serious.

"Did you hear that?" Mom asked me, laughing harder now. "I'm a triangle—like something you study in geometry."

We had the kind of giggles that wouldn't stop, that made our bellies ache, but eventually, we settled down and made our selections. Who knew buying a fake boob was so complicated? Not only did Mom have to choose a skin tone, but she had to decide whether to buy the adhesive kind or the kind you slipped into a pocket in the bra. When it came to the choice between the triangle or teardrop model, I said, "Yep. You're a triangle. The teardrop doesn't fit you at all."

Mom took my hand, squeezed it, and said, "That's right. No teardrops here."

The next week, Mom started going to physical therapy, so she left me in charge of Carmen and Jimmy for a few hours every afternoon. The first time, I was nervous. I kept thinking something bad would happen. When Jimmy crawled under the table, I worried that it would collapse and crush him. When Carmen went to the garage to get a hammer and nails for something called "string art," I worried that she'd lose a hand at the table saw even though she wasn't going anywhere near it. And when she started hammering the nails, I knew she was going to break a finger, so I told her she couldn't work on her project till Mom or Dad came home.

And who knew there were so many breakable things in our house? Glasses, plates, windows, vases, Chia Pets. Who knew there were so many poisons? Bleach, Windex, hydrogen peroxide, every medicine in the cabinet. I didn't want Jimmy or Carmen to leave my sight. If something bad happened to them, I'd never forgive myself.

Once, I spent the whole afternoon in a near panic. When Mom returned, I gave her a giant hug and said, "I'm so glad you're here! Taking care of kids is hard work. Do you know how many things can go wrong?"

She just laughed and said, "Well, I'm glad everyone's still in one piece."

By the second week, babysitting my brother and sister felt a little more routine, but that didn't stop me from imagining all sorts of horrible accidents.

In the meantime, Carmen kept the bathrooms clean, and I took long walks to get ready for the 5K in October. I felt stronger every week and could walk the whole distance—twice! I was still a little suspicious about the power of *promesas*, but I was beginning to believe that they worked because Mom was getting better. So maybe a 5K was enough after all.

"We do stretches in therapy," she explained at dinner

one evening. "That way, my tissues will stay flexible. Otherwise, they'll get rigid and tight, making it hard for me to move my shoulder around." She cautiously rolled her shoulder.

"Soon you'll be able to carry Jimmy again," I said.

"And do your step aerobics tapes," Carmen added.

"Are you kidding? I'll be strong enough to go to the gym and lift weights with all those musclemen."

"Let's not get carried away," Dad said. "We can't have some muscleman falling in love with you."

"One already has," Mom replied, winking at him. And then she said something in Spanish, something romantic because Dad blushed.

3 GRADES

Soon it was time to return to school. Normally, I loved school—not the classes, but the chance to be with my friends and to see cute guys. Plus, I was going to be in eighth grade, the oldest group on campus, which meant extra privileges, like first choice in the computer lab, a junior high homecoming and prom, and end-of-year field trips. But instead of being excited, I felt bummed. After all, this year my sister was going to junior high too, not because she was old enough but because she was skipping a grade, and, to make matters worse, she was skipping *three* grades in math. That meant she was taking eighth grade math like me, only she got to take the advanced class.

Carmen bragged about it nonstop as we got dressed

for our first day. "When I met my teachers at registration," she said, "they didn't remember you."

"Gee," I replied, all sarcastic. "I wonder why. Wait. Maybe it's because I wasn't in their class."

"That's what I figured, since you take the classes for *normal* people."

"You're the only one who thinks 'normal' is an insult."

"Oh, there's nothing wrong with it," she said, "but there's nothing *memorable* about it, either."

"You mean as memorable as your outfit?" I pointed at her clothes. While I, and everybody else, wore regular T-shirts and jeans to school, Carmen was wearing a pleated skirt, a starched blouse, knee-high socks, and a blazer. The blazer had brass buttons and a patch with a fake coat of arms. She wanted to look like a student at a fancy boarding school, the kind with redbrick and ivy, because she thought she was better than the rest of us.

"No," she answered, "I mean memorable like someone with a high IQ, someone like me. But what am I saying? You probably don't know what 'IQ' stands for."

I knew it meant "intelligence quotient," but I said, "It means 'idiot quotient,' and you're right. It's a perfect description of you."

She stuck out her tongue and marched out. Good. Mission accomplished. Privacy at last. Still, I kept thinking about the teachers who did not remember me, how I failed to make an impression. Well, how about *this* for an impression? For the first day of school, I put on a T-shirt that said, "I'm right 97% of the time. Who cares about the other 4%?"

Thirty minutes later, Dad dropped us off, and I walked Carmen to her first-period class.

"You're on your own from here," I said. "I'm sure you'll find your way around since you have such a high IQ."

"No problem," she replied, though she didn't sound as confident as she usually did.

I left her at the classroom door and made my way through the noisy hall of North Canyon Junior High. My campus was one of the newest on the north side of San Antonio, and like all the new buildings on this side of town, it was built in a hurry to make room for the growing population here. This meant no time for an architect to design interesting archways, windows, or courtyards. Everybody said we went to North Canyon Savings & Loan because our school, a three-story rectangle of bricks between two strip malls, looked like a bank.

"Hi, Erica."

I turned to find Derek beside me. I had seen him at the pool a few weeks ago, but he seemed taller and more muscular now. I glanced at my mood ring. It was purple, the color for love.

"Where are you headed?" he asked.

I glanced at my schedule. "Math. Room 215. With Mr. Leyva."

"Hey, that's where I'm going, too." He seemed so happy to have a class with me. Was this the beginning of a serious romance? He'd never noticed me before, so I couldn't believe he was walking beside me. "Are you going to try out for the talent show this year?"

"I really want to," I answered, "but I sing worse than a cow with a sore throat."

He laughed. He said, "You crack me up!" and laughed some more. That *had* to be a good sign, right? Didn't guys think girls should have a sense of humor?

The warning bell rang just as we stepped into class. I scanned the room for Robins. No Patty, Shawntae, Gum-Wad, or Iliana. Bummer.

"Let's sit over here," Derek said, choosing a desk in the middle row.

Did I hear right? Derek wanted me to sit next to him? So far, this was a terrific first day of school.

All the students settled into their desks as Mr. Leyva started the class. He had a reputation for being a no-nonsense teacher, but everyone said he was nice as long as you behaved and tried your best. He took roll, and when he got to my name, he said, "Montenegro. Are you related to *Carmen* Montenegro?"

"She's my sister," I grudgingly admitted.

"Well, it's nice to meet you. I'm sure you're going to breeze through this class."

I shrugged as if I didn't care, but I *did* care. Was I going to be compared to Carmen in every class? She just started coming to this school. How did he know her already? Was he her math teacher, too? I wanted to change my last name, so my teachers wouldn't make the connection. After all, having a smart sister didn't mean I was smart, too. Just ask my T-shirt.

My second class was social studies with Mrs. Gardner. I sighed with relief because everyone knew how nice she was. On my way to her room, I bumped into GumWad.

"Hi, Erica," he said, his mouth all blue from his gum. He studied my T-shirt. "Ha-ha." He laughed. "That's funny. You're really good at being sarcastic. You're the most sarcastic girl I know."

"Gee, thanks," I said. "I'll put 'sarcastic' on my résumé when I apply for a scholarship."

"Ha-ha." He laughed again. "You're such a natural."

Leave it to GumWad to think sarcasm was an admirable quality. I had to change the subject before he started pointing out other "admirable" qualities, like the big zit on my forehead.

"Do you have Mrs. Gardner for social studies, too?" I asked.

He showed me his schedule. Yep, we had the same class. And so did Patty. "Hi, guys," she said. She walked right between us and took a seat near the back of the room. GumWad and I followed, choosing the desks beside her.

Luckily, social studies is my favorite subject. I love learning about societies and cultures. Last year, for example, my teacher assigned each of us a country and asked us to create a menu featuring that country's food. I got Kenya, where they drink cow blood mixed with milk. The class was grossed out when I told them, but my teacher said that every culture has weird food, even ours. Like *menudo*. San Antonio people think it's delicious, but people from other parts of the country think it's gross because the main ingredient of *menudo* is the stomach lining from a cow.

"Let's spend today introducing ourselves," Mrs. Gardner suggested. "Tell us something interesting about your summer."

One by one, my classmates shared stories, mostly about

places they went for vacation. One girl went to Canada, a city called Banff "where the clouds are *below* you." Another girl went to a dude ranch in the Texas Hill Country. "I can ride a horse now," she exclaimed, "and start a fire with flint." One guy played on a summer baseball league and made the all-star team. GumWad, of course, went to Disney World. No surprise there, though everyone else seemed interested in his adventures.

What was *I* going to say when it was my turn? My family didn't see the Carlsbad Caverns after all, and for the first time since I could remember, we skipped going to the coast, to Malaquite Beach, our favorite spot. We didn't even have a Fourth of July picnic.

"And how about you?" Mrs. Gardner asked Patty. "Did anything interesting happen to you?"

"Oh, yeah," Patty said. "Lots of stuff." She looked at the ceiling as if to read her past there. "I startled a skunk. That was lots of fun. Then I got a bad sunburn and spent a whole week peeling off dead skin. And then"—she tapped her chin—"I threw up after getting eighth place in a hot dog eating contest."

"How many people were competing?" a guy asked.

"Including me?"

He nodded.

"Eight."

The whole class laughed—Mrs. Gardner too, even though I could tell she was trying to hold it in. Then she said, "And how about you, Erica?"

Suddenly all eyes were upon me. "I didn't go anywhere exciting," I said.

Patty punched me. "Yes, you did. Tell them about that miracle place where you saw those human scalps."

"They weren't scalps. They were braids of hair."

"And teeth and bones and little baby feet," Patty added.

Everyone leaned forward to hear more. "You're exaggerating," I said. "There was a jar with teeth but there weren't any bones. And the baby feet were made of this metal called pewter." I went on, sharing the story about the suicide pilot and how the church had burned except for the statue. I described the little doll in the Aztec sundial above hundreds of candles. "And after praying," I explained, "people leave gifts at El Cuarto de Milagros, the Miracle Room."

"Why did you go?" a girl asked.

I shrugged.

"Don't people go there when someone's sick?"

I looked down, not wanting to answer.

"Sometimes people go because it's an interesting place," GumWad said. "No one *has* to be sick. Anyone can go."

"I'm just asking," the girl said, all offended.

When the teacher turned her attention to someone else, Patty whispered to GumWad, "Good save."

"Yeah, thanks," I said, giving him a grateful smile. Once in a while, between the silly things he did or said, GumWad acted like the coolest friend.

6 QUIET RULES

After school, Carmen and I found Mom leaning back on the recliner with her legs outstretched on the footrest. This had been a first day for her, too. Her surgery had been about seven weeks ago, and now that she had healed, it was time to start radiation therapy. So I wasn't surprised to find her resting, a pillow on her lap and a glass of water on the side table. Meanwhile, Jimmy, who had spent the day with Grandma, was on the floor breaking up his train track.

"I feel sapped," Mom said.

Carmen and I kissed her. Then I sat on the floor with Jimmy while Carmen grabbed the laptop and surfed the Internet.

"According to this website," she explained, "fatigue is the most common side effect of radiation therapy."

"I believe it," Mom said sleepily.

Carmen surfed the Net a little longer. Then she asked, "So what's it like at the cancer center? How do they 'nuke' your cells?"

I wasn't sure Mom wanted to discuss this, so I said, "You don't have to tell us if you don't want."

"It's okay," Mom said. "I don't mind talking about it." She pointed at the afghan on the couch. I gave it to her, and she spread it over her lap. "The therapists take me to a room with a machine called a linear accelerator. They put me on a bed, only it's not soft and comfy like a *real* bed. It's more like a table. They position me, just so, making me lift my arm over my head, and they move the gantry, the part of the machine where the radiation beam comes out. They point it right where my breast used to be."

"Can you see the beam?" Carmen asked.

"No, it's invisible."

"But doesn't it scare you to know that something invisible is hitting your body?"

I wanted to tell Carmen to quit being nosy, but I was curious, too. I'd probably ask the same questions if my sister weren't around.

"Yes," Mom answered. "I was a bit scared because after they prepped me for treatment, they said, 'Don't move.' And then they walked out. They can't turn on the machine until they're in another room behind a thick wall that protects them from radiation. There isn't even a window. They've got cameras to see me, but I can't see them. I just hear their voices when they tell me they're turning on the beam now." She paused a minute, and I mind-traveled to a spaceship filled with mad scientists doing experiments on people because that's how I imagined the room Mom described. "When I sat up after my treatment," Mom continued, "I noticed all the 'caution' signs with the symbol for radiation. One even said, 'Danger! Radiation Treatment Area.' The therapists wear these things called dosimeter badges that change color if they're exposed. So I knew we were working with some very dangerous stuff, and I kept wondering if I was crazy for doing this. You may not realize, but I grew up during the Cold War."

"We had a cold war?" I asked, imagining battlefields in Alaska with weapons that hurled sharp, lethal icicles.

"We called it the Cold War," Mom explained, "because we fought with threats instead of weapons. The United States and the Soviet Union had made enough nuclear bombs to destroy the entire world, so we lived in fear of bombs falling from the sky, especially here in San Antonio, with all its military bases. We constantly heard about radiation sickness, how it made you burn from the inside out."

Carmen and I squirmed. "That's awful," I said.

"You know what the funny thing is?" Mom said. "I grew up thinking that radiation *caused* cancer, not *cured* it. I mean, it does cause cancer, doesn't it? Isn't that why the therapists have to leave the room? I'm sure there's a joke here somewhere." She laughed to herself.

"So does it hurt?" Carmen wanted to know.

"A little," Mom said. "Let me show you." She lifted her shirt and her arm, showing us the side of her body. The skin there was red, like a bad sunburn.

"It itches," Mom said. "But don't worry. They tell me it's perfectly normal to get a rash like this."

She covered up again and placed the pillow behind her head.

Meanwhile Carmen returned to the laptop, probably looking for information about burned skin as a side effect. "It says you might get nausea, too," she said. "You might lose weight or damage healthy tissue."

Mom nodded, her eyes droopy now. "The doctors mentioned that." She lifted the afghan to her chin and closed her eyes. I could tell Carmen wanted to say something else, so I lifted a finger to my lips and said, "Shhh." Jimmy mimicked me, putting *his* finger to *his* lips and saying, "shhh," too.

"It's only five o'clock," Carmen whispered, worriedly. "Are you sure Mom should sleep? She hasn't eaten dinner."

"It's okay," I assured her. "She might feel nauseated, remember?"

Carmen glanced at the computer again, clicked a few more times, then said, "Maybe I should go clean the bathroom."

She was still cleaning for her *promesa*, and each time she cleaned, she also counted something. So far, she had counted the tiles around the bathtub, the stripes on all our towels, and the number of ingredients in toothpaste, deodorant, hairspray, mouthwash, and soap. She even took a roll of toilet paper one day and counted out each square. She was acting weird. She *always* acted weird, but all this counting was even weirder.

I shouldn't complain, though. At least Carmen was doing her *promesa*. At least it was challenging, because no bathroom stayed clean forever. I was working on mine too, but it wasn't as challenging as Carmen's.

Soon, Jimmy wanted cartoons, so I switched the TV to Nickelodeon, and he and I danced when some funny-looking aliens started to sing. That's when Dad came home. As soon as he saw Mom sleeping on the recliner while Jimmy and I jumped around, he grabbed the remote and turned off the TV. Immediately, Jimmy said, "Gimme cartoon! Gimme cartoon!"

Dad shook his head, so Jimmy started to cry.

"Take him to your room," Dad told me.

I wanted to say that we were having fun, that Jimmy was being good, but Dad didn't give me a chance.

"Take him before he wakes up Mom."

I obeyed and picked up Jimmy. He didn't want to go to my room, so he started to bawl.

"Gimme cartoon!" he cried.

"Be quiet!" I said as I shut the bedroom door.

Poor Jimmy. As soon as the door closed, he gave up bawling and started to sob, his cheeks all wet with tears. He looked like one of those sad-eyed puppies on the Adopt-a-Pet commercial.

"Want to pillow fight?" I asked, hoping to cheer him up.

He stomped. "No!"

"Want to jump on the bed?"

"No!"

"Want to color? Want to take pictures with my iPhone? Want to play hide-and-seek?"

"No, no, no!"

I made one last effort. "Want to try on my shoes?"

He hushed, glanced at the closet door, then at me, and then at the closet again.

"Gimme shoes!" he announced as if it were his idea in the first place.

"Sure thing," I said. "You can try on *all* my shoes if you want."

We went to the closet. First he put on my tennis shoes, then my sandals, then the dress shoes I wore for special occasions, and after that, my boots. Of course, all of my shoes were too big, but he didn't care. And when he tripped over himself, he laughed. After he got bored with matching pairs, he tried different combinations—one tennis shoe with a boot, one sandal with a dress shoe. He thought the oddball pairs were the funniest things he'd ever seen.

A while later, Carmen peeked in and said, "Dad wants to have a family meeting."

I told Jimmy to pick his favorite pair, but he shook off the shoes and decided to go barefoot for a while.

We found Dad at the kitchen table. "Have a seat," he said. "We need to talk."

He sounded as serious as a strict principal. I just knew we were in trouble. I scanned my brain, trying to figure out what we had done wrong. Had I gotten in trouble at school already? Had Jimmy broken another Chia Pet? Had Carmen used Dad's PayPal account for something as useless as the motorized solar system model she bought last year without his permission? Wait a minute! Maybe one of the guys from my Boyfriend Wish List had called. Maybe Derek had called! After all, he did talk to me today. He even asked me to sit by him. Dad probably wanted to set some ground rules now that he knew I was interested in boys. He probably wanted Carmen and Jimmy to spy on me. I was about to protest when Carmen spoke up.

"Where's Mom?" she asked. "I thought this was a family meeting?"

"She's resting," Dad said. "And we *are* having a family meeting...but it's about Mom. So let's keep this between us, okay?"

Carmen and I nodded, but we glanced at each other, too. She looked as nervous as I felt. I wondered if something had gone wrong with the operation or with the radiation treatment.

"Is Mom okay?" I asked. "She seemed fine this afternoon. She was tired, but she was fine other than that."

"She's okay," Dad said. "But like you mentioned, she's tired. She needs to rest. And we need to let her rest."

I didn't know what he was talking about. Mom looked

very comfortable on the recliner earlier. She had her feet up. She had a pillow and a blanket. Sure, Jimmy and I were jumping around, but it didn't seem to bother her.

"I've come up with a few quiet rules," Dad said. "We need to make sure we follow them." He turned to Jimmy. "That means you too, little buddy."

"What do you mean by quiet rules?" Carmen asked. "You want us to whisper from now on?" She wasn't being sarcastic, only curious.

"That would help," Dad said. And then he stated the rules, counting them off with his fingers:

1. Do not turn the TV volume above level 10.
2. Use your earbuds, not the speakers, when listening to your iPods.
3. Put your cell phones on vibrate.
4. Do not vacuum or run the dishwasher or the washing machine while Mom is asleep.
5. When Jimmy cries, take him to your room and close the door till he settles down.
6. Take off your shoes when you come into the house and tiptoe when you walk around.

He paused, thought a minute, then said, "That should do for now, but if I think of any more, I'll let you know."

He pushed his chair away from the table so he could stand. It made a scraping sound against the floor. Dad thought a minute and said, "Instead of scooting your chair, lift it, so it doesn't make any noise."

Before leaving the room, he lifted the chair to set it back under the table. He was right. It didn't make a sound.

If only cooking were as quiet. Dad tried to make dinner without a sound, but he couldn't hush the vent over the stove or ask the meat to stop sizzling in the pan.

"Who knew tacos were so noisy?" he said. And when Mom woke up, he apologized over and over again.

"It's okay," she said. "I can't be sleeping all the time."

She didn't have a big appetite, so she heated up a can of soup instead. All in all, it was a normal dinner. Carmen bragged about how many times she knew the answers in class and how the teachers were excited to work with such a smart girl this year. Jimmy kept asking for things like my taco and Carmen's glass of water even though he had his own. Dad shared a story he'd heard on *All Things Considered*. And Mom didn't seem sick at all. She asked questions about our first day at school and laughed at the funny things we said. Maybe she was lucky. Maybe Mom's surgery was the worst part of her treatment. And it was over. She'd felt sick for a while, but besides being tired, she was okay. At least, that's what I thought, until Mom grabbed her stomach and raced to the restroom. She stood up so fast, knocking over her chair. It startled Jimmy, so he began to cry. It startled Dad too, and he hurried after her.

"What happened?" Carmen asked, all scared.

"I don't know," I said. "Watch Jimmy. I'll be right back."

I found Mom in the bathroom, vomiting into the toilet. Dad stood beside her. He was gathering her long hair, holding it away from her face. He kept saying, "It's okay. It's okay," but it wasn't. Mom made awful heaving sounds, and she kept throwing up, even though all she'd eaten was a tiny bowl of soup.

I *knew* walking a 5K was too easy. After all, one guy ran a thousand miles. A 5K was only three miles. Should I be doing two 5Ks in a row? Three? How much is enough? How much to keep Mom from feeling sick?

I ran to my room, ignoring Carmen and Jimmy, who were still in the kitchen, both crying now. I shut the door, grabbed a notebook, and started to brainstorm. There must be something extra I could do. I jotted down ideas, my pen hard against the paper. "Extra prayers," I wrote, "running a thousand miles, giving up chocolate, being nice to my sister." These seemed impossible.

I wrote:

Dear Virgen de San Juan,

Ayúdame por favor. My mother has breast cancer and she is very ill. She already had surgery, but the doctors say she needs radiation therapy, too. The next couple of months will be very difficult, and she will need all the help she can get. I have been training for a 5K, but it's not enough. What else can I do? If only I had a sign.

4½ PROJECT IDEAS

The following week, Mr. Leyva gave us a math quiz. We had spent the first week reviewing last year's math, so he wanted to see how much we remembered.

The quiz wasn't too hard. It had addition, subtraction, multiplication, division, and some easy algebra like "$2x + 9 = 45$." I breezed through until I reached the word problems, which I absolutely hated, especially when it had "please show your work" in the instructions.

"A blue car and a red car are at location A," the first problem read. "They both want to go to location B, which is sixty miles away. The blue car leaves at 1:00 PM and drives 20 miles per hour, while the red car leaves at 3:00 PM and drives 30 miles per hour. Which car will arrive first? Please show your work." Of course, the blue car would get there first because it had a two-hour head start. I didn't need an equation for that. It wasn't as if the test were asking about that fable with the turtle and the rabbit racing each other. If *that* were the problem, I'd have to figure out how much time the rabbit wasted as it took naps, ate snacks, and played Wii. But this was about two cars with full gas tanks driving along the same road. I could solve it with common sense. The bad news was that Mr. Leyva didn't give credit for common sense. He gave credit for showing work. What work? I just couldn't see it. This was a classic example of somebody making something harder than it really was. Besides, who cared what time the blue car got to "location B"? I mean, whose car was it anyway? And where was location B? *What* was it? A store, a park, a friend's house?

I felt so confused. Thank goodness, the bell rang. If I had to spend one more minute thinking about word problems, I'd lose all my hair.

"See you later," Derek said as he rushed out. He'd been talking to me every day and was now numero uno on my Boyfriend Wish List.

I grabbed my things and headed to the door, where Mr. Leyva stood to collect our papers. When he saw mine, he said, "You didn't finish."

"I got stuck on the word problems," I explained.

He seemed surprised. "But your sister . . ." he began.

"What about her?" I interrupted, not meaning to be rude but unable to stop myself. "I'm the dumb one, okay? She's the one who was born with all the brains."

"That's not what I meant," he started to say, but I didn't wait around. I left as fast as I could and hurried to the restroom so I could calm down. The entire first week of school, teachers oohed and aahed about my sister. It made me so angry to hear about her in every class. I literally had to cool down, so I splashed some water on my face. As I dried off, I caught my reflection. Today, I wore my "Siamese Twins" T-shirt with two Siamese cats, instead of two people joined at the hip. Is that what people thought about Carmen and me, that we were twins—exactly the same like the cats or joined at the hip like best friends? And all because we shared a last name?

Luckily, Mrs. Gardner never compared me to my sister, which was another reason to enjoy her class. I stepped in and took my seat beside Patty. She said hello and so did GumWad. Today, his mouth was blue. I always checked the color of his gum just like I checked the color of my mood ring. I couldn't help myself.

After taking roll, Mrs. Gardner said, "Every year, my students do a service learning project."

"What's that?" GumWad asked. "Is it a paper or a speech? Are we working in groups or alone? When's it due?"

Mrs. Gardner raised her hand to silence him. "A service learning project," she explained, "is one that helps the community. Activities like cleaning up a park, reading to preschool kids, volunteering, or organizing a fund-raiser."

"Great," Patty whispered to me. "More chores, only no allowance."

"At least you'll get to help people," I offered.

"Why would I want to help strangers? I barely want to help my friends."

I turned my attention back to Mrs. Gardner.

"Anybody have ideas?" she asked.

"Can we look for dogs?" GumWad said. "That would be helping the community, right? Finding lost dogs so little kids won't cry."

"That's a good idea," Mrs. Gardner said. She wrote it on the board. Then she asked us if we had other suggestions. Lots of hands went up. Someone wanted to start a community garden. Someone else wanted to teach people about recycling. Another wanted to paint over graffiti.

While the class brainstormed, I wrote "service learning project" on a piece of paper. Normally, I got excited about projects like this, but I also had "study math," "read three poems for English," "fix the toy train Jimmy broke," and "remind Dad that we're almost out of toilet paper" on the list.

"Erica?" I heard.

I looked up. Mrs. Gardner was staring at me. I'd been too busy with my list to notice that she had called on me.

"Yes, ma'am?" I said.

"Do you have any ideas?" she asked.

I looked at my classmates' suggestions, but none of them interested me. Then I thought about my *promesa*, how perfectly it fit.

"Does walking a 5K for cancer research count?"

Mrs. Gardner nodded, but then she said, "Maybe you can do more than walk. Maybe you can get people to sponsor you. That way, you can raise more money and increase awareness."

I glanced at my mood ring. Bright blue for happy. Of course I was happy! Here was the answer I'd been looking for. I was going to ask for sponsors—lots of sponsors! It was the perfect service learning project and the perfect *promesa* for Mom.

Later, I met the Robins in the cafeteria for lunch. Only the second week of school, and we had already staked a claim on our table. As soon as GumWad joined us, Shawntae saw his tray and said, "You do *not* have blue Jell-O. Can you believe I had a dream about that last night? Seriously. I dreamed that you got blue Jell-O, and I remember thinking, 'GumWad doesn't like that flavor.'"

"You're right. I don't," he said. "But it was the only color left." He stuck his fingers in his mouth and pulled out his gum. "Guess it matches this," he said, showing us the slobbery mass before sticking it beside his milk carton.

Patty was mashing her peas, but when she saw his gum, she said, "Really? You're going to make us stare at that while we eat?"

"You don't have to look at it," GumWad said.

"I look at everything that's gross. I can't help it. I see someone with a giant, oozing zit, and guess what—I *stare*. It's human nature."

"Hey, this isn't a zit," GumWad said, all offended.

"Maybe not," Iliana interjected, "but it *is* kinda gross."

"Amen to that," Shawntae added.

"Fine, then," GumWad said. He wrapped it in a paper towel and left to throw it away. "All better?" he asked when he returned, and the rest of us nodded.

"Guess what!" Iliana said, all excited. "I had a close encounter of the third kind with Alejandro. He asked me if I've seen any movies lately. Do you think he's trying to ask me out? I mean, why else would he mention the movies?" She reached in her purse, took out a compact, and checked her mascara. "Do you think he likes my thick lashes or should I put on more mascara?"

"No!" Patty, Shawntae, and I said in unison, because Iliana had gobs of black around her eyes.

"Are you girls going to talk about boys again?" Gum-Wad asked. "That's all you ever talk about sometimes."

"If you don't like it," Shawntae said, "sit somewhere else. But before you do, consider this. If you pay attention, you'll get special insights about girls. You'll be the only guy in school with insider knowledge about the mysterious workings of a woman's mind."

GumWad thought a minute. "You make a good point."

"Of course I make a good point. I'm going to be captain of the debate team this year. It's my job to make a good point." She then turned to Iliana. "So what else did Alejandro say?"

We spent a while hearing about Iliana's close encounter, and then we moved on to other topics. That's when I said, "I figured out my service learning project *and* a new and improved *promesa*."

My friends leaned forward to hear more.

"I decided to get a lot of people to sponsor me for the 5K. All they have to do is sign their names and make a donation."

"That's a great idea," Iliana said. "I'll be your first sponsor."

"I'll sponsor you, too," Shawntae said, and GumWad also agreed.

"That makes three sponsors so far," I said. "I'm off to a good start."

We all stared at Patty, expecting her to donate too, but all she said was, "How many people is a lot?"

"I don't know," I admitted. "I guess I should be specific."

I glanced around the table. Five Robins, five hundred names.

"I hereby promise to get five hundred sponsors for the 5K."

"Five hundred people?" Patty said. "Are you crazy? It's easier to get five hundred people to pull off their toenails than to do something nice like help a real cause."

Iliana sighed. "Don't you believe in *anyone*?"

"Absolutely not," Patty answered, mashing a few more peas.

"If you ask me," Shawntae said, "getting sponsors is a great idea, and five hundred is even better." She took a sip of water. "So you want to know what *I'm* doing?" She and Iliana had Mrs. Gardner, too. "I'm going to educate everyone about the upcoming election. I plan to design brochures listing this year's hot topics and what each candidate believes. Then, I want to do a YouTube video of random people to get their opinions. Finally, I'm going to collect links to articles and post them on my Facebook page, so everyone can keep up-to-date."

"Sounds like an awful lot of work," Patty said.

"Sounds like fun to me," Iliana countered.

"Especially the random people part," GumWad said. "I like helping random people. That's why I'm going to look for lost dogs."

Patty poured milk into her mashed peas. It looked totally gross. Then she turned to GumWad and said, "You're not looking for dogs because you want to help people. You want the reward money. Why don't you admit it?"

"I'm not doing it for reward money."

"Sure, you are."

GumWad plopped a fresh gumball in his mouth even though he hadn't finished his lunch. "I know what it's like to lose a pet," he said. "How you're always wondering what happened. Did he run away? Did he get hit by a car? Did someone steal him? And I see these poor dogs running around, probably trying to get back home. So I don't care about the reward money at all."

He seemed a little mad, so I said, "I wouldn't blame you

if you took it. After spending all day in the heat, you deserve a little reward."

"But that's not why I'm doing it," he insisted.

"I know," I said. "You're doing it because you're nice."

He smiled, and his dimples looked really cute, but then he blew a big orange bubble, and when it popped, gum got on his upper lip. He licked it off, which was really gross, in my opinion, especially since we were at the lunch table.

"Well, I came up with an idea, too," Iliana said. "I'm going to volunteer at the hospital by playing with the little kids. Some of them have to stay for a very long time, and they get bored. Besides, I want to marry a doctor someday, so this will be good experience."

"But these kids are in the hospital," Patty said, "which means they're sick. They have diseases, and diseases are contagious. Do you really want to get some awful disease? You might get sores on your body, or your arms and legs might swell up. You might have to eat through a tube for the rest of your life. The only doctor you'll have a relationship with is the one who's treating you."

"Quit being so negative," Shawntae scolded. "You're really getting on our nerves."

"Yeah," I said. "You have a criticism about everything.

So tell us about your great idea. It's obviously better than what we're doing."

"I don't have any ideas," Patty confessed.

We spent a moment thinking in silence.

"What about picking up garbage?" I suggested.

She shook her head. "I'm supposed to do a narrative. How can I write a narrative about throwing away trash?"

"Don't throw it away," I said.

"You want me to *keep* it? I thought *I* was the one with the dark sense of humor."

"I'm serious," I went on. "Use the trash for something else."

"That's a great idea," Iliana jumped in. "You take art every semester. Maybe you can do something artistic."

"Hmmm..." Patty tapped the table a few times. "I'll think about it," she said.

We eventually moved on to other topics, mostly glancing around to see who had changed the most. Some guys, for example, were cuter this year, or they walked around with more confidence. A few boyfriend-girlfriend couples had broken up over the summer, while others had gotten together. With so many changes, we definitely had to revise our Boyfriend Wish List.

A large group from a nearby table stood to return their trays. That's when Shawntae spotted my sister. Every table in the cafeteria was rectangular except for the circular one Carmen picked. She *would* sit at the only oddball table in the room. After all, she was wearing that silly school uniform again and had already earned the nickname Miss Prep, as in "prep school."

"Your sister's so cute," Shawntae told me, "with that fancy uniform and her suitcase."

"But it's got to be hot under that jacket," Patty said. "She probably has big underarm stains from sweating a lot. And that suitcase must weigh a ton."

"It *is* hot in that blazer," I said. "I keep telling Carmen to wear normal clothes, but she won't listen. And that suitcase is full of books, too many books for a normal backpack. She likes to pretend she's in private school instead of with the rest of us dummies."

"I'm sure she doesn't think we're dumb," Iliana said.

I shook my head. "She doesn't think we're smart, that's for sure."

"She looks so focused," Shawntae noticed. "It's like she's working out problems while she eats."

"She's counting," I explained.

"Counting?"

"Yes. She counts how many times she chews. She won't swallow till she reaches a certain number."

"What a chore," Patty said.

"She can't help it. Ever since my mom's operation, she's been counting. It drives me *insane*." I knew I shouldn't tell everyone about Carmen's quirks, but I couldn't stop myself. "We can't take her to the grocery store anymore. Too much stuff to count. Once, she wouldn't leave till she counted all the bananas, the ones in the fruit section *and* the ones by the cereal."

"Maybe counting makes her feel better," Iliana said. "Instead of stressing out about your mom, she counts. It takes her mind off things."

I shrugged. "I guess."

"It must be tough," Iliana continued, "to be so smart."

"What's tough is being the *sister* of someone smart," I said.

Iliana ignored me. She started to wave Carmen over, but I grabbed her arm before Carmen noticed.

"What are you doing?" I asked.

"Trying to get her attention. She looks so lonely all by herself."

"Well, that's her fault," I said. "She can get her own friends. If she's smart enough to do advanced math, then she's smart enough to meet people on her own."

I must have sounded angry because all the Robins, even Patty, looked at their plates and stayed silent. They were not about to disagree with me.

5 CUL-DE-SACS

The next Saturday, Carmen had a practice meet for the University Interscholastic League A+ academic competition. She was competing in calculator applications, science, and number sense. "I could enter all the contests if I wanted," she bragged, "but there isn't enough time in one day."

I could only roll my eyes and be grateful she was limited to twenty-four hours. Our room already looked like a pirate's chest with all the fake gold of her trophies.

Dad planned to drop her off and take Jimmy to the zoo while she competed. Meanwhile, Mom's sisters were coming for a visit. That meant I finally had a free day. No Carmen, no Jimmy, no chores. So I went to Iliana's house to work on my social studies project. My mom had experienced the worst week, throwing up several more times. I needed to fulfill my *promesa* as fast as possible. I had to show La Virgen how much Mom needed her help.

"Do you think Chad knows I exist?" Iliana asked, and "Have you noticed that Alejandro talked to me every day this week?"

Instead of answering, I grabbed my spiral notebook. "Mrs. Gardner wants us to write out the steps for our projects."

"I can't believe it!" she cried. "You really want to do homework. No wonder my parents like you so much."

"Don't get mad because I'm being responsible," I said as I wrote a title on the first blank page.

"Fine," Iliana said. "But if you get bored, my brothers are around."

I looked up. "Really?"

"And they've been exercising a lot because of football season, so they're all muscular right now."

"I can't imagine your brothers being *more* muscular."

"You should say hi to them. They're always asking about you."

"They *are*?"

She nodded, and I glanced at her bedroom door, imagining her brothers somewhere on the other side, the garage probably, since that's where they kept all their weights. Normally, I'd pretend to get thirsty and, on my way to the kitchen, peek into the garage and catch them working out. I'd stay there for a while offering to get them water and answering their questions because they always asked me about school and family. It sure was tempting.

"Well?" Iliana said. "You want to spy on my brothers?"

My mood ring was yellow, the color for feeling creative but also for feeling distracted.

"I can't," I decided. "This isn't just for school, remember? It's for my mom."

She sighed. "Suit yourself."

I returned to my notebook. "Steps for completing my service learning project," I wrote. "Visit 'Race for the Cure' website and learn how to become an official participant. Print a sponsor form. Go to people's houses and ask for donations." I thought a moment. What happens after I get donations? "Continue training to get in shape for the event." I looked at the ceiling and scratched my head. Hmmm… this sounded like a complete plan to me. "All done," I said.

Iliana glanced up. "No way! You finished in two minutes?"

I shrugged. "It's not that complicated."

"Lucky for you," she said. "It's going to take me all day

to work out a plan. I don't know the first thing about play-ing with little kids or working at a hospital."

"Doesn't Santa Rosa have a volunteer department?" I asked. "All you have to do is make an appointment, right? And then you show up and play with the kids. What's so hard about that?"

"I wish it were that easy, but in my house, *I'm* the little kid, so I never have to babysit."

I nodded, thinking about Jimmy Gimme. "Yeah, it's tough. I babysit a lot, and my little brother can be a giant headache sometimes."

"But he's so cute."

"You're right," I admitted. "He's a really cute, giant headache."

She laughed and threw a pillow at me, and I remem-bered how Jimmy liked to throw things too, especially after he begged to hold them, and of all the things in the world, his favorite objects to hold were...

"Chia Pets!" I blurted.

"What about them?" Iliana asked.

"Jimmy loves to hold our Chia Pets, just like you would a real puppy or kitten. He likes other stuff too—crawling inside the closet, jumping on the bed, and climbing on the table—but the hospital kids are probably too sick for activities like that. Still, they're kids. And all kids are the same in certain ways. So I thought, what does Jimmy like to do? We call him Jimmy Gimme for a reason. Every minute of every day, he's grabbing something, and one of his favorite things to grab is a Chia Pet. Something about them calms him down, but they make him laugh, too. He thinks green hair is hilarious. I'm sure the hospital kids would think so, too. You should find a way to get people to donate Chia Pets. Then the kids could keep them in their rooms, make sure they're watered, watch them grow. They could name them. They could have Chia Pet parties. They could—"

"Slow down!" Iliana said. "I can't write fast enough."

"They could set up a pretend farm or zoo in the play area and even sponsor Chia Pet adoption days if they want to trade or if someone new gets admitted."

Iliana scribbled frantically. "Pet parties," she mumbled, "farm or zoo." She wrote a few more lines, put down the pen, and shook the stiffness from her hand. "Wow," she said. "You really know how to brainstorm."

"If only brainstorming were useful for math." I sighed. "I'm so nervous about the test next week. I just know I'm going to fail. I already failed a practice quiz."

"But you do great in your other classes, so you can't be *that* bad in math."

"Yes, I can."

Iliana smiled at me, but instead of being happy, her smile seemed to say, "I'm sorry," even though it wasn't her fault I couldn't solve word problems.

Maybe I couldn't pass Mr. Leyva's class, but I *could* pass social studies. I took Iliana's laptop and began the first step for my project, "Visit the Race for the Cure website." On the home page was a slideshow from past races. Most of them featured groups behind company banners or runners crossing the finish line. Beneath the slideshow, a box offered fund-raising tips like "most people donate simply because they were asked" and "make the first donation and watch your family and friends follow." Another box listed the top fund-raisers. One lady raised more than $67,000. That was probably more than I could ever get, but lots of people had raised $5,000 or $6,000. Maybe I could, too. After all, how hard could it be? All that money must mean people really wanted to help.

Eager to get started, I clicked on "Register as an individual." The form asked for information, like my name, address, phone number, and T-shirt size. I cheered because I love cool T-shirts. After my contact information, the registration form had a questionnaire. "Please tell us the primary reason you are participating," it said, followed by a drop-down menu. My choices included "I care about finding a cure for breast cancer," "I enjoy walking or running," and

"My workplace organized a team." Nowhere did it say, "School project" or "*Promesa*" or "My mom's sick," so I selected the first option. After all, I *did* care about finding a cure even though it wasn't my *primary* reason for doing this. The next question asked, "How did you hear about this event?" and luckily "Newspaper article" appeared in the drop-down menu. Finally, I had to pay a fee. I didn't have $35, so I called Dad's cell and asked to use his PayPal account. He said, "Sure thing, *mija*. You have a great idea, so just let me know about whatever you need for your *promesa*." Now as an official participant, I printed a donation form that had the Race for the Cure logo on the top, a "please sponsor me" paragraph, and a grid where people wrote their names, addresses, and donation amounts.

The entire time I worked, Iliana talked to people at the hospital and set up an appointment. She hit her "End" button at the same moment I shut the laptop.

"Ready for the next step," I announced.

"Me too," Iliana said. "But I can't do anything until next weekend. I have to go to volunteer training before I can work with the kids."

"What a bummer."

"Actually, I'm glad. I *need* that training. I'll probably feel more confident after I go. And maybe I'll meet a cute guy there, too."

I laughed. Iliana could turn any event into a setting for romance.

"I guess I'm ready to bug people for donations," I told her. "I'm going to do it the old-fashioned way, by going door to door."

"Sounds like fun," she said. "Want to start right now?"

"Sure, but you don't have to go with me." I didn't mean to leave her out, but part of me wondered if a *promesa* counted when you didn't do it by yourself.

"I want to," she insisted. "It'll be fun."

"Well, okay," I said, not wanting to be rude.

I pinned the fund-raising forms to a clipboard, grabbed a pen and a manila envelope for the money, and we headed out the door.

Our neighborhood has several winding streets with cul-de-sacs. When I was in elementary school, I called the cul-de-sacs "mushrooms" because that's what they reminded me of, and now my family and friends called them mush-rooms, too. We live in a suburb, so the houses are still new. My dad said this area had nothing but rocks, shrubs, and creek beds when he was growing up, but I can't imagine it without houses, especially because we moved here when I was two. He must be telling the truth, though, because the trees don't tower over the houses on my street like they do in the neighborhoods closer to downtown.

"Let's do your mushroom first," I told Iliana.

"Sure thing. We can start with my neighbor."

We knocked on the door, and an old woman answered. Her face was as wrinkled as a wadded burger wrapper, and she moved as if every muscle ached.

"Hello, Señora Alderete," Iliana said. "Is Carolina here?"

"*No, no está aquí.*"

Iliana turned to me. "Señora Alderete is my neighbor's mom. She doesn't speak English, but she can understand everything we say."

I glanced at Mrs. Alderete, and she nodded.

"Is it okay if my friend asks you something?" Iliana said.

"*Por supuesto,*" Mrs. Alderete answered.

"That means 'of course,'" Iliana explained.

"I know," I said. "I speak Spanish, remember?"

"Since when?"

"Since right now." I was totally lying. I wasn't bilingual. Not really. My last name is Montenegro, but that didn't matter when everyone spoke English at home. I could count to one hundred in Spanish and order at a restaurant, but beyond that, I got confused. Still, I hated to admit that I wasn't bilingual because it made me feel dumb. I was already weak in math, and I didn't want to be weak in Spanish, too. So I turned to Mrs. Alderete and said, *"Buenos días."*

"Buenos días," she answered.

"Mi mamá está … está …" What was the word for "sick"? I looked up, trying to remember.

"Enferma," Iliana whispered. "And remember, she understands English."

I nodded. *"Mi mamá está enferma."*

Mrs. Alderete sighed. *"La pobrecita,"* she said. *"¿De qué está enferma?"*

I stared at her, trying to find the words, but I didn't know how to say "because she has cancer" in Spanish. So how could I explain my mom's situation to Mrs. Alderete? How could I say, "My mom had an operation to remove her breast and two weeks ago she started radiation treatments so the doctors could 'nuke' the extra cancer cells and it is making her feel worse on top of how frustrated she feels about not being able to wear bikinis anymore." How could I say something so complicated in Spanish? Sure, Mrs. Alderete understood English, but even so, how could I answer in English? In *any* language? It was too personal.

"Her mom has cancer," I heard Iliana say. "And my friend's raising money to help find a cure. There's a race coming up, so she's asking people to sponsor her by making a donation."

Mrs. Alderete nodded the whole time Iliana spoke. After a moment, she said, "*Lo siento, pero no tengo mucho dinero.*" She held out empty hands. Then she reached in the pocket of her housedress. "*Solamente tengo diez dólares.*" She handed us a ten. "*¿Está bien?*"

"Oh, yes, Mrs. Alderete," I said. "*Es muy bien.*" I took the bill and put it in the envelope. "*Muchas gracias.*" I bowed as if Mrs. Alderete were the queen of the cul-de-sac.

"*Vaya con Dios,*" she said, about to close the door.

"Just another minute," I pleaded. "Can you fill this out?" I handed her the sponsor form. She wrote her name, address, and donation amount, and we thanked her about twenty more times before we left.

"She's so nice," I said to Iliana as we walked along the sidewalk. "With people like her, I'll reach my goal in a couple of weeks."

"If not sooner," Iliana predicted.

We went to the next house and rang the doorbell. No one. Same for the second and third houses.

"That's strange," Iliana said. "Their cars are in the driveways."

When we rang the fourth doorbell, a lady peeked through a curtain, but she didn't answer. I knocked and heard movement inside. I knocked again. Nothing. "We know you're in there," I called. "We just want to ask a question." But the lady didn't respond. I turned to Iliana. "She's ignoring us."

"That's so rude," Iliana said.

A few people answered their doors, but they weren't very nice. "Can't help you," they kept saying.

Now and then, we met someone who had an experience with illness. One person, for example, had a cousin with cerebral palsy, and another, a grandmother with leukemia. They were more than happy to donate. We went through several mushrooms, and after an hour, we had four yeses, eight nos, and countless unanswered doors.

Getting five hundred people to sponsor me was not going to be easy.

30 QUARTERS

We never missed church on Sundays. During mass, we made petitions, which meant thanking God or asking Him to help us. Last year, I mostly asked God to help me with my Boyfriend Wish List—no miracles like the cutest guy in school becoming my boyfriend, but small things like moving from a close encounter of the first kind to a close encounter of the second kind. This year, asking for help with boyfriends seemed so immature. Sure, I was still boy crazy. How could I *not* be? There were so many cute guys in the world. And Derek had been talking to me every day. We were definitely having close encounters of the third kind. But I couldn't waste my petitions on boyfriends anymore. Last night, Mom ate applesauce and toast with strawberry jelly. She didn't throw up, and we all cheered like during a Super Bowl. But by seven thirty, she was completely exhausted. She tried to stay awake and watch videos with us, but she fell asleep sitting on the couch. Dad told us to turn down the volume, and then he helped her to the bedroom. We finished the movie, but then Jimmy still needed a bath. I couldn't let him go to sleep all dirty, so I got the tub ready for him. The whole time he fought me and cried, "Gimme Mommy! Gimme Mommy!" And when I tried to read him a bedtime story, he grabbed the book, threw it to the floor, and cried for her again. That's when Dad came in and told me to settle Jimmy down.

"I *am* settling him down," I said, all frustrated, "but he's not listening."

Eventually, Jimmy wore himself out. He wore me out too, but my night wasn't over. When I walked into the bedroom, Carmen had toppled over a big jar where we dumped spare coins. She was sorting them. "And then I'm going to count them," she explained.

"Tonight?"

She nodded. I didn't want the light on, and I didn't want to hear her mumbling numbers. But I was so tired, and since it took too much energy to fight, I just put on my earphones and listened to my iPod. Normally, good music calmed me down, but my mood ring was the amber color that meant I felt unsettled, probably because I couldn't help thinking that even though only Mom had cancer, my entire family seemed sick.

On Sunday, I was still thinking this at church, so during petition time, I closed my eyes and asked—no, *begged*—for help. "And for my part," I prayed, "I'm going to work on my *promesa*."

Keeping my promise, I changed into some comfortable clothes as soon as I got home. I wore a T-shirt that had a picture of the Abominable Snowman with a caption that read, "Yeti or not, here I come." I grabbed my clipboard and headed out, approaching the cul-de-sac with more determination than Jimmy when he wanted an ice-cream cone. Most of these neighbors didn't answer yesterday. Maybe they weren't home at the time. Maybe I'd have better luck now, especially since it was Sunday. Weren't people nicer on Sundays after they came back from church?

I knocked on the first door. Nothing. I knocked on the second. Nothing again. The third person answered but quickly said, "I already give to charities," and the fourth one said, "I have diabetes. Are you going to raise money for my diabetes, too?"

What was wrong with these people? Any amount was acceptable. I'd take one dollar if that's all they could afford.

I looked at their houses. They had two-car garages, chimneys, and automated sprinkler systems. Many had signs that let everyone know about their security alarms. Security alarms meant expensive stuff inside. If they could buy expensive stuff, then surely they could donate five bucks to a good cause. So why were they being so selfish?

I was getting angry. I wanted to stand in the middle of the street and scream, "I hate this neighborhood!" But I didn't. Instead, I dragged my feet, dreading the next doorbell. At one point, a little dog joined me. He had white fur that was all muddy. He stayed with me for a whole cul-de-sac, and then he disappeared.

I decided to try one more set of houses. I walked up to the first door, pushed the button, and heard the ding-dong and then some footsteps. I knew someone was spying on me from the other side of the peephole, so I rang the doorbell again. A few seconds passed, and then a man answered.

"Weren't you here yesterday?" he asked. "You and another girl?"

"Yes," I said. "But you didn't answer."

"Because I don't like to be bothered."

How rude, I thought, wanting to walk away but remembered my mom and stood firm.

"I'm sorry. I didn't mean to bother you," I said.

"Then why did you? And why are you here today? You're not selling Girl Scout cookies, are you? Those things are overpriced, if you ask me."

"No, sir. I'm not a Girl Scout."

"Then why are you carrying that order form? You want money, don't you?"

I nodded.

"You kids," he said as if being a kid were the worst thing in the world. "I can't go one week without some kid bugging me for money. First, it's the school band. Then it's the church choir. And always those Girl Scouts. Haven't you kids heard of working for things?"

"I *am* working for it," I blurted. "If you'll only let me explain. I plan to walk in this year's Race for the Cure. It's for breast cancer, and the reason it matters so much is because my mom's sick. She had an operation this past summer, and now she's getting radiation treatments. They're making her sick, but it's all the doctors know how to do. So I'm out here, ringing doorbells, *working*, to raise some money. But if that isn't enough for you, I'll wash your car or mow your lawn or bathe your dog if you have one. I'm not asking for a lot. Just whatever you can spare." I had to catch my breath after all that.

He stared at me a moment. I thought for sure he'd slam the door in my face, but he didn't.

"I'm sorry to hear about your mom," he finally said. Then he pulled out his wallet and handed me a twenty-dollar bill. "You don't have to wash my car or anything."

"Thanks," I said, handing him the clipboard.

He signed my sponsor form, and as he returned it, he said, "You keep bothering people, okay?"

"I will," I said.

He smiled, and then he shut the door. This was going to be tough, but maybe it wouldn't be impossible.

I spent another hour bugging people. A few more offered to help, but most ignored me or gave an excuse. Maybe going door-to-door wasn't the best strategy, but I didn't know how else to reach people.

I was about to head home when I heard a familiar voice calling, "Rover! Hey, boy! Where are you?" Sure enough, GumWad turned the corner. He carried a stack of papers in one hand and a dog leash in the other. From a distance, he looked like a normal guy, even a little cute, though his arms and belly were a bit soft.

"Hey, GumWad!" I called. "Over here."

He spotted me and jogged over. "Didn't think I'd see you today. What are you doing out here?" He smacked a yellow piece of gum.

"I'm working on my social studies project," I explained.

"Me too." He blew a bubble, popped it, and licked the gum off his upper lip. "Look here," he said, handing me the stack of papers. They were "lost dog" signs. One had a caption that read, "Have you seen me?" over a picture of a sad-eyed dog that reminded me of Jimmy when he didn't get what he begged for. The others were like police descriptions with the color, size, and breed of dog. All of them had reward amounts.

"Are you sure you aren't going to keep the rewards?" I asked.

"No. I really want to find these dogs. I don't care about the money at all."

He seemed a little mad as if I'd accused him of something awful. Maybe I should have apologized, but I didn't do anything wrong. Honestly, if I found a lost dog, I'd keep the reward, and no one would think I was a bad person. We stood there without saying a word, the only sound his constant smacking. Being alone with GumWad was... awkward. Usually the other Robins were around so I hardly noticed him, but out here, away from school and alone, I *had* to notice him. But I didn't want to look at his face, so I looked at the dog posters instead. That's when I saw a picture of the muddy white dog.

"I just saw him!" I exclaimed.

"Really?" GumWad beamed. "Where?"

"Follow me. I'll show you."

I hurried to the last place I saw him. Now that I knew his name, I could call out. "Max! Come here, Max!" Gum-Wad called for him, too. It took a while, but eventually, the muddy white dog appeared. He ran to me, all happy. While I petted him, GumWad checked his dog tag. Sure enough, he was the one on the poster. We managed to get the leash on him, and then we walked him home.

"Did you see how happy those people were?" GumWad said after we returned Max.

"Max seemed happy, too. I bet he hadn't eaten in days."

"And he was probably drinking water from a ditch," GumWad added. Then, "Speaking of thirsty dogs, do you want to get a Slush from Sonic?"

"Are you calling me a dog?"

"No," he said. "I just thought you'd want a drink since you've been working so hard to get names for your mom."

Great. I didn't look like a dog; instead, I looked like someone who was about to pass out after working so hard.

I didn't *really* want to spend more time with GumWad, but how could I turn down an opportunity to go to Sonic, especially when the cute high school boys liked to go there, too? Besides, it was close by, right at the end of the major street that branched into the cul-de-sacs.

"Sure," I said, "I'll go, but I don't have any money." I glanced at the manila envelope. "This is for my project," I explained.

"Don't worry. I got cash." He reached into his pocket and pulled out a handful of quarters. I'd never seen so many quarters in my life. He must have had thirty. "See?" he said. "I got enough here for a hamburger too, if you want."

"Okay, okay." I laughed. "Let's go, then."

I sent a text to my dad, telling him where I was going and when to pick me up. Then GumWad and I headed to Sonic. As we walked, he told me about his gumball machine, how his parents bought it one Christmas and how they gave him enough quarters to buy the gum. When he ran out, his mom bought a fresh supply. Then he took the quarters from the machine and started over. The same quarters have been going into that machine since he was eight.

We both ordered lime Slushes at Sonic, and GumWad surprised me by throwing out his gum instead of sticking it to the side of his cup. While we enjoyed our cool drinks, he told me about the dog he lost when he was in kindergarten, how he never got over it.

"That's the real-life story of why I'm looking for lost dogs," he explained.

"You're too sentimental."

He said, "Just because I care doesn't mean I'm sentimental." He was so serious when he said this, but then he started to laugh. "You can put that on one of your 'used-to' T-shirts." My face must have looked confused because he added, "I used to be sentimental but now I care too much. Get it?"

After a moment, I got the joke and laughed. "You're right," I said. "That's a perfect line for a T-shirt. I'm going to write that down." And I did, right on my manila envelope.

GumWad talked on about the cool rides at Disney World, where his family had spent vacation, but I hardly paid attention because I had already heard his Disney World story. Besides, a sporty black Volkswagen had parked at the ordering console right in front of me. When the tinted window rolled down and the driver leaned out to push the call button, I saw a god. Honestly, a god. Not like *the* God at church, but like the gods in mythology, the ones with long hair and bulging muscles, the ones who rescued helpless mortals like me from evil stepmothers or seven-headed monsters. I couldn't stop looking at him. He was a shiny new toy, and my eyes were Jimmy begging, "Gimme, gimme." And then he caught me staring. He rubbed his eyes. To get a better look? Then he winked. I couldn't believe it. He winked!

"What are you looking at?" GumWad said, turning around and seeing the VW guy I was secretly calling Thor. "Are you staring at *him*?"

I could only sigh.

"Why are you staring at him?"

"Because he's super handsome and because he's winking at me. Can you believe a cute guy like that is flirting with me?"

"He's not winking," GumWad said. "He's got something in his eye. Either that or his contacts are bothering him."

I studied the guy's frantic winking. Okay, maybe Thor's contacts were bothering him. That's probably why he kept rubbing his eyes. But it didn't matter because he was handsome even with all those tears and blinks.

"When guys are flirting," GumWad went on, "they wink in a different way."

"Like how?"

He ran his hand across his face as if erasing a chalkboard. Then, he opened his eyes, looked at me, and winked, putting his whole cheek and forehead into it. Seriously, he squeezed half his face.

"That's not flirtatious at all," I said. "You look like Popeye."

"Let me try again," he insisted. "I got all nervous."

"Why would you be nervous? It's just me."

He didn't answer. He just looked away for a minute.

After a while, he said, "That guy's old enough to be in high school. He's probably old enough to be in college."

"Maybe," I said.

"You should be interested in guys your own age, not guys like him. He's too old for you."

"Says who?" I asked. "At most, he's six years older than me. I've got an aunt and uncle who are eight years apart, and they get along just fine. Besides, I'll be in high school next year." I glanced at my mood ring. "Look, it's purple!" I lifted my hand to GumWad's confused face. "The stone is purple!"

"So?"

"So that's the color of smoldering passion."

"How can you feel passion for someone you don't even know?"

"It's called 'love at first sight.' People have been writing poems about it since forever."

GumWad frowned. He probably hadn't discovered love poems yet.

Just then, Dad pulled into the parking lot and waved me over.

"Gotta go," I said. "Thanks for the Slush."

"Sure. You're welcome. Anytime. We should—"

I hopped into the car, and as Dad drove away, I glanced back to get another glimpse of Thor, but GumWad was blocking my view.

1 SILLY DREAM

On Monday, Mr. Leyva announced that we would have a math test later in the week. This wasn't a pretest. This would be a recorded grade. I panicked just thinking about it. Luckily, I was doing well in my other classes, especially social studies. Mrs. Gardner asked us to discuss our projects. Some of the students hadn't started yet, but I was right on schedule. I talked about asking for sponsors, and Gum-Wad talked about searching for dogs, running into me, and having Slushes at Sonic.

After everyone gave an update, Mrs. Gardner said, "Since a few of you are behind, let's take fifteen minutes to catch up. Write out a plan for accomplishing your goal, and for those who have already tried the first steps, write a narrative about your experience so far."

"How do I write out a plan for picking up trash?" Patty whispered. She was definitely resisting this assignment, but she opened her notebook anyway.

I took out my own paper and wrote, "My friend Patty said people would tear off their own toenails before helping me raise money for cancer research. I didn't believe her, but now I know she's right." I went on, describing in detail all the variations of "can't help" I'd heard as I knocked on door after door. Then, because I hated to be so negative, I described the people who *did* help, like Mrs. Alderete and the man who thought I was a Girl Scout.

"Finish your thoughts," Mrs. Gardner said when the class was about to end. I completed my sentence and then glanced at Patty's page. She had drawn a tattered cardboard box, a crushed soda can, and a banana peel.

"Trash," she said. Then she tore out the page and wadded it. "*Real* trash."

I had to take my science book to the cafeteria. I hadn't read the assigned chapter because I was so busy with my *promesa* over the weekend. I was frantically skimming the pages when Patty arrived.

"Why are you studying during lunch?" she asked.

"Because I have a quiz this afternoon, and I didn't have a chance to study." I quickly glanced over the bold print words in the chapter and tried to memorize the definitions, but concentrating was difficult when my friends were nearby.

As soon as Shawntae took her seat at the lunch table, she said, "GumWad and Iliana told me about your weekend."

I glanced at them, and they nodded.

I couldn't believe my friends were talking about me again. When were they going to stop sharing my business with the whole world? Even if they weren't saying anything negative, it still bothered me. Shawntae must have noticed because she said, "I'm your friend, remember? I need to know these things. Besides, I *knew* you wouldn't get a lot of names. I *dreamed* it. You should have talked to me. I could have saved you some time."

"And when *exactly* did you have this dream?" I asked, feeling myself getting impatient. Honestly, I had a lot on my mind. The last thing I needed was to hear another one of Shawntae's fake predictions.

"Friday night, before you went looking for sponsors."

"And I'm supposed to believe you?"

Shawntae crossed her arms. "Yes, you're supposed to believe me. Just ask Patty. She knows all about my dream."

Patty was tearing her napkin in half, but she stopped in

the middle of the rip, looked at Shawntae, and said, "You told me you dreamed that Erica and GumWad were looking for candy in a dark, scary forest and that it must mean they were going to dress up as Hansel and Gretel for Halloween."

"That's so cute," Iliana said. "You think Alejandro and I could dress up as a fairy-tale couple, too? We could be Snow White and Prince Charming. That is, if he really likes me. I can't tell. What do you guys think?"

No one had a chance to answer because GumWad turned to me and said, "I don't mind being Hansel if you want to be Gretel. We can give gum to the little kids." He reached in his pocket and pulled out a handful of gumballs. I saw lint on one and wanted to gag.

"I don't believe in trick-or-treating anymore," I said. "No one in my neighborhood gives out candy. I live next to the most selfish people on the planet."

"Hello!" Shawntae interrupted. "Can we get back to the *real* subject? We're supposed to be talking about my dream."

"What else is there to say?" I asked. "You had some silly cartoon dream that, in my opinion, has nothing to do with what happened this weekend."

"You can't take dreams so literally, Erica. They're not

facts; they're symbols. Just think about it. The candy symbolizes the money you were trying to earn. The dark, scary forest symbolizes the rude people you met."

Patty was tearing her napkin into smaller and smaller pieces. "I liked it better when Erica and GumWad were going to dress up as Hansel and Gretel," she admitted. "It's such a cool story, especially the part when the witch throws the kids in a giant pot of boiling water."

"I don't know about symbols," Iliana said, "but I do see similarities between Shawntae's dream and what really happened."

"Thank you," Shawntae said.

"That's the problem with dreams," I explained. "People can interpret them however they want. They aren't predictions about anything. And even if they were, what's the point if they're always so symbolic, if you have to decode them all the time, and if they don't make sense until it's too late? For once and for all: No…more…predictions!"

"I'm going to make a believer out of you," Shawntae decided.

"It'll never happen."

She ignored me. "I'm going to tell you my dreams," she went on. "I'm going to tell you as soon as they occur. Then we can see what happens next. That way, we can test my abilities."

"That's a great idea," GumWad said. "Can you call when you have a dream about me? I'd love to get a preview of my life, especially if it involves something like me getting hit by lightning or chased by a tornado."

"Sure thing," Shawntae said, and she and GumWad shook on it.

"And can you let me know which guys like me in a romantic way and which ones only as a friend?" Iliana added.

"If I dream about it, I'll let you know."

"Are you serious?" I asked Shawntae. "You're going to call me every morning and report your dreams?"

"Well, not *every* morning, since I don't remember my dreams sometimes, and not *every* dream, since you're not the only person in my subconscious mind, but if I do dream about you, I'm going to call. You can count on it."

"She doesn't mind calling *me* every morning," Patty said, her napkin pieces as small as confetti now.

Shawntae lightly punched her. "That's because you need a wake-up call or both of us will be late for school." They often carpooled together, and at least once a week, they had to run to class so they wouldn't be late.

Iliana jumped in with her opinion. "I think you should try it, Erica. What can it hurt? We'll finally know whether or not Shawntae's a psychic."

I took a minute to consider the plan. Maybe Iliana was right. Maybe this *was* a good idea. Shawntae wanted to teach me a lesson, but *she* was the one who had a lesson to learn. When her predictions did not come true, I'd get to say "I told you so." And then I'd be free of Shawntae's dreams forever because she could *never* predict the future, just like I could never make a perfect score in math.

"It's a deal," I decided. I held out my hand, and Shawntae shook it, the whole time with one of her big, flashy smiles.

2 SPARE INVITATIONS

Dad took Thursday off so he could go with Mom to her radiation therapy appointment. He said he'd pick me and Carmen up after school, but he was running late because he had to get Jimmy from Grandma's house first. Carmen waited in the sixth grade area, while I waited in the eighth. Nobody had assigned waiting spots for different grades, and there weren't any signs. But somehow everyone knew that the sixth graders were supposed to wait on the hot cement around the flagpole, while the eighth graders waited beneath the shady trees. The seventh graders had their own spot, too. Luckily, Shawntae and Patty's ride hadn't arrived yet, so I waited with them. We barely had time to discuss the afternoon when Derek showed up.

"Hi," he said to me. "I wanted to talk to you after class, but you were still working on the test."

"Yeah," I admitted. "Math isn't my best subject. And the test really takes a long time when you have to show all your work."

"Tell me about it. I barely had time to finish."

"At least you worked through all the problems. I still had five to go."

Patty stomped on a line of ants crawling along the curb. "That means you failed it," she said.

My shoulders drooped. I felt as crushed as the ants beneath her shoe.

"I'm sure you passed," Derek said. "You probably got all the other questions right since you were taking your time."

"Yeah, probably," I said, though I wasn't convinced.

"So why did you want to talk to Erica?" Shawntae asked, all nosy.

Derek reached into his backpack, took out a stack of postcards, and handed me one. It was red with black letters that said, "Let's party!" In the middle was a black-and-white photo of Derek and on the back were the details.

"I'm having a birthday bash," he explained. "My cousin's a DJ, so there's going to be music, dancing, and food." He handed postcards to Patty and Shawntae, too. "You should *all* come. Your *presence* is the only *present* I need. Get it?"

"You are so corny!" Shawntae said, slapping his arm with the postcard.

"Maybe so, but I made you smile, right?"

Patty said, "She smiles for everything. She'd smile at a funeral." She glanced down at the dead ants and smiled at *their* funeral, looking away only when Shawntae elbowed her.

"Thanks for the invitation," I said to Derek. "It sounds like fun."

"Good," Derek said. "Then I'll see you there. And you girls, too," he added, pointing to Patty and Shawntae before walking off to join a group at the basketball court.

"Can you believe that?" Shawntae said to me. "He is totally into you."

I shook my head. "No, he isn't."

"Oh, yes, he is." She mimicked Derek's voice. "Here's an invitation for *you*, Erica. I was waiting for you after class, but since you took so long with the test, I had to hunt you down after school, so I could personally hand you this invitation because the only present I need is your presence. Oh, and by the way, I guess I can spare two invitations for your friends."

"It wasn't like that," I said, secretly believing it was. "He meant to invite all of us from the beginning."

"No," Patty said, "you were the main objective. We were total afterthoughts."

"Are you serious?"

They nodded.

My fingers and toes got all wiggly. Who knew fingers and toes could feel excitement? Finally! I was making "close encounter" progress with a guy from my Boyfriend Wish List. I fumbled in my backpack for my phone and texted Iliana. "OMG. On solid level 3 w/Derek. Details later." After a few seconds, she replied with the happy face icon.

Just then, I spotted Dad's car.

"See y'all tomorrow," I said to my friends.

"Your presence is the only present we need," they teased as my dad pulled up.

I jumped in the backseat with Jimmy because Carmen had grabbed the front since Dad reached the flagpole first. As soon as Jimmy saw the postcard in my hand, he wanted it. "Gimme paper. Gimme paper."

"No, Jimmy. It's important."

"What is it?" Dad asked.

"An invitation to a party."

"Let me see," Carmen said.

"No, it's not for you. It's for me."

Just then, Jimmy grabbed the postcard, and when I tried to snatch it back, it tore right across the picture of Derek's cute face.

"Ha-ha," Carmen said. "That's what you get for being selfish."

"Girls," Dad said with a tone that meant "you better behave."

We didn't want to upset him, so we stayed quiet and listened to *All Things Considered*, this time with a story about elephants and how they communicate across long distances using something called infrasonic rumbles.

"Isn't that amazing?" Dad said. "I wonder what they're saying to each other."

Secretly, I wondered, too. I'm sure the elephants gave boring announcements like "cool watering hole one mile to the east" or "three zebras grazing on our turf," but maybe they sent love letters, too. Maybe they had parties and used their infrasonic rumbles to invite their friends. Maybe they told stories about warrior elephants that trampled dangerous beasts of the night or brainy elephants that devised plans to outsmart poachers. If only I could be an elephant interpreter. Wouldn't that be a cool job?

"I wish humans could talk across the miles, too," I said.

"We *can*." Carmen held up her cell phone and pointed to it. "It's called using a phone." She exaggerated each word as if talking to an infant or a monkey. I hated the way she always made me feel like a dummy.

"Gimme phone. Gimme phone," Jimmy cried, reaching for Carmen's.

She pretended to hand it over, then snatched it away at the last minute. Poor Jimmy bawled.

"Look what you started," I complained. "He was fine a few minutes ago."

He cried even louder. "I wanna phone! I wanna phone!"

"Here," I said, taking mine out. I let him touch a few buttons, and he immediately settled down. Then I showed him pictures of my friends.

"Who that?" he asked, pointing at each one. When we got to a picture of GumWad sticking out a purple tongue, Jimmy laughed.

"He looks funny, right?" I said.

Jimmy laughed even louder. Then he got bored. He was always begging for things and getting bored two minutes later. I handed him his toy puppy, the one Mom bought in the valley. We kept it in the car so Jimmy could have something to play with. Jimmy and I growled like angry dogs and barked like happy ones. He was a pest most of the time, but sometimes I really liked playing with him.

When Jimmy settled down, I held up the torn postcard and said, "Can I go to the party? Lots of my friends will be there."

"Including boys?" Dad asked.

"Yes," I said, blushing because I hated discussing boys with him.

"Chia's totally boy crazy," Carmen squealed. "That's why she can't concentrate in school. If you let her go, you'll be feeding her boy-mania."

"You're just jealous," I said, "because the boys at school don't know you exist."

"They *do*."

"Oh, really? Then why do you sit by yourself during lunch? Why do you walk by yourself to class?"

"Is this true?" Dad asked Carmen. "Are you always by yourself at school?"

"Yes, but not because I'm pathetic or something. I *like* being by myself. The kids at school are total morons. They don't even care about calculating their carbon footprint."

I rolled my eyes. "That's because they wear regular tennis shoes, not carbons."

"Your carbon footprint has nothing to do with shoes," Carmen said. "It's about creating carbon dioxide and destroying the environment, but how would you know? You're a moron just like the boys at school."

"*Por favor,*" Dad said. I was about to complain because she did it again, made me feel like a dummy, but Dad added, "Not another word from either of you."

We reached the stop sign a few blocks from our street.

Dad braked and let the car idle. "Let me see that invitation." I gave it to him, and he held the two parts together. "It says, 'Feel free to bring guests.'"

I nodded. "That's why I want Iliana to come. You see? It's not like I'm going to be alone with boys. A lot of girls are going to be there, too."

Dad returned the invitation and edged the car forward. "That's right," he said. "A lot of girls, including your sister."

"Really?" Carmen nearly hopped out of her seat. She hadn't been this excited since the Discovery Channel promised to air a new documentary about black holes.

"I thought we were morons," I told her.

"I was just kidding," Carmen said. "Besides, I'm sure I was going to be invited anyway."

Just then, Jimmy threw his toy puppy on the floor. "Gimme dog. Gimme dog," he said.

"She can't go," I insisted as I handed Jimmy the toy, which he immediately threw down again.

"Gimme! Gimme!" he cried.

My mood ring was brown, which meant I felt feisty, troubled, and mad.

"No!" I snapped, and I meant it. No to Jimmy and no to Carmen.

Dad pulled into our driveway and turned off the car. While we unbuckled our seat belts, he said, "Carmen, help

Jimmy out. Take him inside. I need to talk to Chia for a minute."

"You are in so much trouble," she gleefully whispered as she lifted Jimmy from his seat.

As soon as they entered the house, Dad said, "Listen, I want you to take Carmen to the party. It's not because I don't trust you, but because she never gets invited places. I don't like how she's by herself all the time."

"She's by herself because she's a brat."

"She's not a brat. She's"—he thought for a minute—"different. That's all. And sometimes people who are different have trouble fitting in."

"She doesn't *want* to fit in. You heard her. She thinks everyone is a moron."

Dad sighed. "Just take her to the party. Do it for me, okay? Do it for Mom."

I could not believe he would manipulate me this way, but I knew what would happen if I refused—an ultimatum: either take Carmen or don't go at all.

"Fine," I said, exiting the car and stomping toward the house.

20 MESSAGES

Saturday began with a phone call from Shawntae. At seven o'clock in the morning!

"Not another dream!" I complained. So far, she had called to tell me about dreams with sports cars, hot air balloons, and talking lockers. I was a character in each, but honestly, the only thing remotely connected to my real life was my school locker, and it had *never* uttered a word. Why couldn't Shawntae dream about me with a guy from my Boyfriend Wish List or about me getting a good grade in math or about my mom feeling better?

"In this one," she began, "you're roller-skating on a beach."

"You mean on a sidewalk or pier?"

"No, on the sand."

I wanted to pull out my hair. "Are you serious? Have you tried roller-skating on sand? It's next to impossible."

"But that's the point," Shawntae insisted. "In the dream, it *wasn't* impossible. Not only were you skating, but you were gliding. People were pointing at you and talking about how easy you made it seem. You should really buy a new pair of skates."

"But we don't have a beach in San Antonio," I reminded her.

"I had another dream, too."

I sighed. "And what was this one about?"

"You were with Iliana's brothers."

"Really?" Now this sounded like a dream I could relate to. "What were we doing?"

"Talking."

"That's it?" I couldn't help being disappointed. I was hoping for a close encounter of the fourth kind.

"Yes," Shawntae said. "And their words were very clear. They said, 'You can be two places at once if you ask your twin for help.' "

"What's *that* supposed to mean?"

"My subconscious is showing you how to cover more ground when you look for sponsors."

"But I don't have a twin," I said, all frustrated. Shawn-tae didn't seem to notice.

"Buy those skates," she commanded, "and ask your parents if you have a secret twin somewhere."

I sighed. So far, Shawntae wasn't scoring well on this test of her psychic abilities. The only thing she truly accomplished was waking me up with her phone calls.

"I wish I did have skates," I admitted. "I have to walk around the neighborhood again for my *promesa*."

"That's great. I'll go with you."

At first this seemed like a good idea, but last week, Iliana had joined me. I liked her company, but all she did was talk about boys. Shawntae didn't discuss boys so much, but she loved to give me advice and share her strategies for becoming the first black woman mayor of San Antonio. Plus, she'd probably make up more dreams. No, this was something I had to do by myself.

"That's okay," I said. "I better go alone."

"Are you sure? I have terrific persuasive skills. I'm on the debate team, remember? That means I know how to talk people into things."

"I know. You *are* great. But this is something I have to do on my own."

"Suit yourself," she said. And with that, she hung up.

After breakfast, I headed out, deciding to start on the other side of the neighborhood. The weather had cooled, so lots of people were out mowing grass and washing cars.

"Hello, sir!" I called to a man edging his lawn. He didn't hear me. "Hello!" I shouted.

He looked up and turned off the edger when he saw me. "Can I help you with something?"

As I told him about needing sponsors, a woman came from the side of the house. She had gardening gloves on and her clothes were full of dirt and leaves. "What do we have here?" she asked.

"This girl," the man explained, "is asking for donations." He turned to me. "Sorry, but we can't help today. Maybe another time."

"Now wait a minute," the woman said, pushing him aside. She took off her gloves, stuck them in her pocket, and held out her hand so I could shake it. "My name's Ann. What's yours?"

"Erica."

"Well, Erica, what are you raising money for?"

"Breast cancer research. It's for a service learning project I'm doing at school, but mostly it's for my mom."

"She has cancer?"

I nodded.

"You poor thing," she said. Then she looked at her husband. "Don't just stand there. Go inside and get some money." I wanted to laugh at the way she ordered him around, but I didn't want to ruin this chance at a sponsor. "How old's your mom?" the woman asked as we waited.

"Forty."

"That's young, which means she's strong. I bet she's going to be just fine."

"I hope so," I said.

Her husband returned and handed me thirty dollars. I gave him the clipboard, and he filled out the sponsor information.

"Can I get back to the yard?" he asked his wife, the way kids ask parents for permission to play.

She nodded, so he turned on the edger. As soon as he got back to work, Ann put on her gardening gloves and headed to the side of the house again. I tried to say goodbye, but I don't think they could hear me over the loud machine, so I moved on to the next house.

I really wanted to get more sponsors, but almost everyone waved me away. A lot of them said "not now" or "come another time." I knew they never wanted to see me again, that they were trying to get rid of me, but I wrote their addresses on a list called "Come Back Later," vowing that I would return in a few days. After all, the 5K was one month away! So I kept walking, the day getting hotter and hotter, my nose feeling sunburned, sweat trickling into my eyes, and blisters forming on my feet. Once in a while, someone donated, but at this rate, it would take a year to get five hundred names. I didn't have a year! *Mom* didn't have a year! I glanced at my mood ring—amber again, a deeper shade, which meant I had moved from feeling unsettled to feeling despair. No wonder my shoulders drooped.

I noticed that I was near Patty's house, so I decided to stop for a break. She wasn't the best cure for despair, but maybe she could help me take my mind off my own problems for a while.

When I knocked on her door, her grandfather answered. He had moved into her house after his wife died two years ago. Patty was real close to her grandparents, so when her grandmother died, she felt awful. We Robins bought and signed a card for her, and then we got together and baked cookies. We must have given Patty four dozen. Normally, she loved cookies, so we thought they'd cheer her up, but when she bit into the first one, she didn't smile. She didn't frown, either. She had no expression at all. And when I watched her eat that cookie, I imagined it was as bland as pasta with no sauce or spices. We wanted to help Patty, but when you're sad, nothing, not even cookies, can make you feel better.

Is that how I would feel if Mom died? I hated to think about it, but I had to be prepared. What if radiation therapy didn't work? What if Mom got sicker and sicker till she couldn't take it anymore? Would I ever get over the sadness? A few weeks after her grandmother died, Patty returned to her old self, but I don't think I could ever get back to normal if something awful happened to Mom. My mood ring would probably stay black for months, maybe even years.

"Are you okay?" Patty's grandpa asked. "You look like you've seen a big, hairy watermelon."

I looked up at him. "I've never seen a *hairy* watermelon before." Then I tried to imagine a watermelon with hair. What a ridiculous image! I couldn't help laughing, and it was such a relief to smile after spending the whole morning with a frown.

"Grandpa!" I heard Patty's voice behind him. "Quit teasing her." He moved aside and Patty waved me in. "I'm so glad you're here," she said, leading me to the kitchen, where a bunch of papers had taken over the table. "Can you believe my English teacher called and told my parents I hadn't done a single thing this week?"

"You haven't," I said, remembering how Patty had complained about her homework.

"Sure, but did she have to call?"

"It's her job."

"So now I have a whole bunch of homework," Patty went on, "and if I don't finish, I'm going to be grounded."

"I'm going to be in trouble, too. I can barely keep up. Who knew eighth grade was going to be so hard?"

She nodded.

"How long will you be grounded if you don't catch up?" I asked, hoping she wouldn't be grounded during Derek's party.

"For forever," her grandpa said from the other room.

Patty just rolled her eyes. In a quieter voice, she said, "I have a serious case of writer's block. You have to help me. You *never* have writer's block."

"I don't?"

"No. Everybody knows you're the one to turn to when we can't think of ideas."

"Really?"

"Yes, really. So will you help?"

"Of course," I said, pointing at my T-shirt. It had two stick figures. One had a circle for a head, but no body. The other stick figure was complete. It held a straight line in one hand, and its speech bubble said, "I've got your back."

Patty studied it a minute. Then she laughed. "Oh, I get it. This one guy's holding the line that would make up the other guy's back."

I shrugged and nodded at the same time. Except for GumWad, my friends always took a while before getting my T-shirt jokes.

"So what's your homework?" I asked.

"I have to write similes, and I can't think of a single one."

I thought a moment. "How about as droopy as a thirsty sunflower or as panicked as a cat-chased mouse."

She wrote them down, and together we thought of a few others. Then she had to pick a popular story and write it from a different point of view.

"I don't even know what that means," Patty complained.

"It means to forget the main character and pretend the story belongs to someone else."

"So instead of Cinderella," she said, "pretend the story is about the fairy godmother?"

"Sure. You could do that, but how about pretending the story is about the glass slipper?"

"But that's an object, which means it doesn't have a brain. How can something without a brain tell a story?"

"That's the fun part," I said. "What's the slipper thinking as it dances around the ballroom? As it gets left behind when Cinderella runs off? And as the stepsisters stick their fat, smelly feet in it?"

She thought about it. "I guess I could write a story about

that." She sounded doubtful, but an intense brainstorming session convinced her that she could write the story.

Just then, her grandfather walked in. "All done?"

"Almost," Patty said. "At least I know what to do now, thanks to Erica."

"Sounds like you owe her one," her grandfather said.

"That's okay," I said. "I had fun helping with the homework." I stood, ready to leave.

"And where are you going?" Patty's grandfather asked.

"I need to walk around the neighborhood. I'm raising money for cancer research." I grabbed my clipboard. "Would you like to donate?"

Patty's grandpa reached into his pocket and pulled out a five. "I guess I should," he said, "since you helped my Patty with her homework."

"Thank you so much," I said, taking the money and handing him the form.

As he filled it out, he said to Patty, "You should return the favor and go with Erica."

"You want me to knock on a bunch of weird people's doors? Can't I pay her back by buying her lunch or something?"

"I don't need help," I said. "I can do this on my own."

Her grandfather thought a minute. "Make sure you knock on that red door two houses over."

"I already did."

"So Mrs. Cavazos signed your form?"

"No. She didn't even answer the door."

Patty's grandpa put his hands on his hips. "Well, I'll be." Then he said, "Just a minute." He took out his cell phone and dialed a number. "Hello?" I heard him say. "How are you doing, Mrs. Cavazos?" A woman spoke on the other end of the line but I couldn't understand her. "And how's that pipe I fixed last month?" He listened a bit. "I'm so glad to hear it isn't giving you any more trouble and that I was able to save you from hiring an expensive plumber." While he listened, he winked at me. "Actually, I do need a favor," he said to the phone. "I'm sending Patty over with a friend. She's raising money for a fund-raising event, and she's been going around the neighborhood looking for sponsors. I told her how nice you are and that you'd really like to donate." I don't know what the woman said, but when Patty's grandpa got off the phone, he said, "Mrs. Cavazos is going to help, so you two go over right now before she changes her mind. And, Patty, go to Johnny's, too. Tell him he can borrow my lawn mower any time, and tell Sally that I'll feed her dog when she goes out of town next week." He paused, looking up at the ceiling. "Oh, yeah, tell Jamal he can donate the ten dollars he owes me. Got all that?"

"Johnny, Sally, Jamal," Patty repeated, counting them off on her fingers. "Got it."

I didn't really want her help, didn't want her to see me get doors slammed in my face. That was the *last* thing I wanted my friends to talk about. They had already gossiped about my troubles last week when I wasn't *supposed* to have any trouble. And I worried that my *promesa* counted only if I did it on my own. But Patty's grandpa was forcing her to help me.

"Let's kill two birds with one stone," I suggested to Patty. "Grab a trash bag and we'll pick up garbage along the way."

"What a sensible girl," her grandpa said, all impressed. Patty just rolled her eyes, but she grabbed the trash bag anyway.

As we walked to the house with the red door, Patty said, "Before my grandpa moved in, I didn't know any of these people. But he went and made friends with everyone, which means they're always in our business. It's such a pain." The red door was open, so instead of knocking or ringing the doorbell, Patty called through the screen. "Mrs. Cavazos? Are you in there?"

A middle-aged woman approached. She said, "Patty, it's nice to see you."

"Nice to see you, too," Patty replied. "My grandpa's glad

to hear the plumbing's okay. Those leaky pipes can sure mess up your floor." Patty paused a minute before remembering why we were really here. "This is my friend Erica."

"*Mucho gusto,*" Mrs. Cavazos said.

"*Mucho gusto,*" I replied.

"Her mom has cancer," Patty said, "so she needs money for a cancer race next month. My grandpa said you'd help."

I couldn't believe how blunt Patty was, but Mrs. Cavazos didn't seem to mind. She said, "*La pobrecita.* What kind of cancer does your mother have?"

"Breast cancer," I said, and since she had a small statue of La Virgen de Guadalupe on her porch, I added, "I made a *promesa* at that shrine in the valley, so I have to get five hundred names."

Mrs. Cavazos nodded. I could tell she knew exactly what a *promesa* was. She had probably made one herself. She told us to wait a minute, and then she returned with a check for twenty-five dollars. As she filled out the sponsor form, she said, "Mrs. Martínez's car broke down last week. When you get to her house, tell her to call if she needs a ride to the grocery store. I'm going in a couple of hours."

Patty nodded, and when we got back to the street, she said, "See what I mean? Everybody knows what's going on with everybody else. No privacy at all."

How awful, I thought. After all, I hated my friends

talking about me even when they were just reporting what happened over the weekend. Iliana wasted no time telling the Robins about my mom's cancer or about my first attempt to get sponsors, and GumWad told our whole class about Sonic. Never mind Shawntae, who blabbed about every dream with me in the starring role.

As we walked, Patty found some bottle caps at the curb and a crushed aluminum can. When I pointed at a burned-out match, she shook her head.

"Are you being selective about the trash you collect?" I asked.

"Yep."

Who knew what that girl was up to?

We soon reached Mrs. Martínez's house and mentioned the grocery store. *"Gracias, gracias,"* she said, all grateful. For a minute, I thought *we* were giving her a ride. When Mrs. Martínez saw that her friend had already given money, she matched the donation.

When we got to Johnny's house, Patty said, "Your yard looks great. My grandpa said you could borrow his mower whenever you want."

When we got to Sally's house, she said, "So are you looking forward to your trip next week? My grandpa said not to worry about the dog. It's no trouble for him to come fill his bowl."

And when we got to Jamal's, she said, "My grandpa's in no hurry to get back his ten dollars, but if you have it on you, he said you could give it to my friend. She's raising money for cancer research." As we walked away, she said, "I'm really getting the hang of this." She sounded excited.

I didn't like the way she blabbed my whole story to everyone, but how could I complain when her blunt attitude resulted in sponsors and when Patty was having fun? It seemed as if everyone donated, and like Mrs. Cavazos, they gave us messages, too. We must have passed along twenty.

"Call us the pony express," Patty joked.

"Or the ponyless express," I said.

She giggled at that. "Ponyless but not penniless," she added, glancing at my manila envelope. Seeing Patty in a good mood was putting *me* in a good mood, too. Even my mood ring sensed it and turned to a sapphire blue.

One message led to another. A guy named Luke said he had extra tomatoes from his garden. Mrs. Johnson said she would donate them to the soup kitchen. Hector said he could drop them off when he picked up his daughter, who volunteered there and who agreed to babysit for a lady named Lindsay, who in turn said she had coupons for free car washes at the gas station and was giving them away on a "first come, first served" basis.

"Isn't it crazy?" Patty said about all the messages. "My grandpa doesn't mind, but it drives me nuts."

"Maybe," I said. "But look at us. You found some cool trash, and I got twenty-five new sponsors. This has been my most productive day yet!"

3 SIDE EFFECTS

After spending time with Patty, I made my way home. I felt exhausted but excited, too. Finally, I was having success with my *promesa*.

As I turned onto my street, I heard the familiar roar of a lawn mower. Mr. Landon, our neighbor, was working on his yard. I could tell he had just started because most of the grass was still long. When I got to my front yard, I waved at him, and then Dad stepped out.

"Hi, Dad," I said, eager to show him the names I had collected.

"In a minute," he answered. He seemed angry, and I wondered if Jimmy was acting up. Maybe I should have stayed home. With Mom ill, Jimmy was hard to control, and Carmen liked to pick on him, making things worse.

But Dad wasn't angry at the family. He was angry with Mr. Landon because he went straight to him and said, "Can you mow another time? My wife can't rest with all that noise."

Mr. Landon shrugged. "Sorry. Got to do it now."

"But she needs her sleep," Dad said.

"If it's too loud, tell her to wear earplugs. Why's she turning in so early anyhow? It's only four o'clock. Who goes to bed at four o'clock?"

"Do you want to know who goes to bed at four o'clock?" Dad said, his voice getting loud. "You really want to know? People who are sick, you hear? People who have cancer."

I could tell Mr. Landon felt bad because he got apologetic. "I'm sorry to hear that Lisa's sick. Really, I am. She's always been a kind lady."

Dad stood there a minute, took a deep breath. "Thanks," he said, calmer. "Thanks for understanding and for agreeing to do your yard another day."

"Now wait a minute," Mr. Landon quickly said. "I said I'm sorry, and I meant it, but I have to mow today. I work all week, so it's the only time I have. I'll do it quick, though, I promise."

For a minute, Dad looked like someone who had just lost a championship game. Then he looked like someone who felt cheated by the referee. "How's this for a promise?" he said. "Next time you need something, don't bother to ask because I *promise* not to help."

"Oh, come on now, don't be that way," Mr. Landon said. "Don't be making a mountain out of a molehill."

Dad ignored him and stomped toward the house. He didn't even remember that I was standing right there. Somehow the anger had blinded him.

But Mr. Landon saw me and said, "Tell your folks I'll just be an hour, if that. Sorry about the noise, but I have to do my yard. Hope you understand."

"It's okay," I said, feeling embarrassed because Dad wanted quiet rules for the whole neighborhood now.

I went inside and found Jimmy on the floor with his toy cars, while Mom lay on her recliner all bundled up. Her lips looked chapped and her skin paler than usual because she hadn't been enjoying the sun. She was watching TV, but her eyes were nearly closed. When her head fell forward, she jolted, surprised. I could tell she was fighting to stay awake awhile longer.

"I got some more names for the cancer race." I held up the clipboard and my manila envelope.

"That's wonderful," Mom said.

I sat on the couch, got comfortable. "Are you doing okay?" What was I thinking? I just asked the dumbest question in the world. Of course Mom wasn't doing okay. She was sick.

She answered anyway. "I'm fine."

Dad must have heard because he stepped in. I could tell he was still mad. "You are *not* fine."

"Maybe not," Mom said, "but why worry if I don't have to?"

"What do you mean?" I asked, sensing that something had happened.

Mom sighed. "Last night," she began, "my arm started to feel funny. It didn't hurt, but it felt tight, like something inside was pushing against my skin. And when I woke up this morning, it looked like this."

She pulled down the blanket and showed me.

"Fat arm! Fat arm!" Jimmy laughed as he pointed at Mom. Her right arm was totally bloated. I could see her skin stretched tight like a spandex gym suit. She had no wrist, so her arm looked like a preschool drawing, a puffy rectangle with five sticks for the fingers. "Fat arm! Fat arm!" Jimmy laughed again.

"One more time," Dad said through clenched teeth, "and I'll spank you."

He gave Jimmy the harshest stare-down, and Jimmy's eyes started to water. I couldn't blame him for wanting to cry. Dad *never* got this angry.

"What's the matter with you?" Mom said to him. "Jimmy's just making an observation."

"He's making *fun* of you."

"But he's only two," Mom said. "He doesn't know what he's saying."

Jimmy started to sob. I picked him up, and he wrapped his arms around me, putting all his strength into the hug.

"You're upsetting him," I scolded. Now *I* was angry, and I sounded like the parent instead of the kid.

"We're sorry, *mijo*," Mom said to Jimmy. He hid his face in my shoulder, but little by little, he calmed down. "Besides," Mom added, "I *do* have a fat arm." She lifted it and studied it as if it were a separate part of her body. "It looks like an elephant leg. And it's got these hard cable things under the skin. Come touch it."

"Lisa," Dad warned.

"It's *my* arm," she snapped back. "I can't hide it or pretend it's normal. Maybe I'm crazy, but I think the way the body reacts is fascinating, too."

Dad stared at her. Then he stared at her arm. He looked...afraid.

"Don't fight," I pleaded.

"We're not fighting," Mom assured me. "Sometimes your dad takes things too seriously."

"And sometimes your mother doesn't take things seriously enough," Dad answered. "Like the neighbor. If he weren't mowing the lawn, you'd be able to rest, and your arm would feel better. I'm sure of it."

"He has every right to mow his lawn," Mom said. "I told you to leave him alone, but you talked to him anyway. Now you're all short-tempered."

Dad shook his head, too tired to argue. After a few seconds, he stepped out. When he left, Mom seemed sad. I could tell she wanted to fight the sadness just like she had tried to fight sleep a minute ago.

"Don't worry," she said. "These are tough times, and we're all a little anxious."

That part was definitely true. Lately, my mood ring's favorite color had been black, for "100 percent stressed out."

"Come touch my arm," Mom suggested again.

Jimmy and I poked it. There *were* hard cables under the skin but the areas between were squishy.

"Does this mean the cancer spread to your arm?" I asked, trying not to sound afraid but unable to keep my voice from trembling.

"No," Carmen said, walking in with the laptop. She must have been in the other room doing research. She set the computer on the coffee table and studied the screen. "This is a side effect from the treatment. It's called lymphedema. It happened because Mom's lymph nodes were damaged, and one of the things they do is drain tissue fluid. It's like she has a clog in her armpit, so the fluid is all backed up."

"That's what it feels like," Mom said. "It's very uncomfortable. I already called the doctor, and he wants to see me tomorrow. He said I'll have to go to physical therapy again."

"They're going to massage you and put wraps on you," Carmen said. "Look." She showed us pictures of swollen arms and legs being wrapped. Most of them were a lot bigger than Mom's. "That's how they get the fluid to move along. But it'll take several days for the swelling to go down. If you don't do anything, your arm will just get fatter and fatter."

"I sure hope this is the last side effect," Mom said. "I'm already dealing with nausea and fatigue. The arm isn't so bad as long as something else doesn't happen. I want to do things again. I feel like I can't do *anything* anymore."

So why *was* she having these side effects? It made no sense, especially after I'd been working so hard on my *promesa*. Was it because I wasn't working fast enough? But what else could I do? I had gone to lots of doors, many of them twice. I had asked all my friends and called my aunts and uncles. Why did I promise five hundred names when I didn't even know five hundred people?

"Since I can't lift my arm," Mom continued, "I won't be able to go to radiation treatment for a while."

"Does that mean the cancer's going to spread?" I sounded more panicky than before.

"I don't think so," Mom said, though I could tell she wasn't exactly sure.

Carmen scrolled down the website and started to read. "It says that lymphedema can happen after surgery and that it occurs on the same side as the mastectomy. That's exactly what's happening to you." Mom nodded. "You'll have to wear compression bandages to 'assist with lymphatic flow.' How cool is that?" She was getting more and more excited, while I was getting more and more butterflies in my stomach. "Can I go to therapy with you?" Carmen asked. "Maybe they'll let me help. Maybe they'll teach me how to bandage the arm. That way, I can take care of you at home."

Mom nodded. "You should be a doctor," she told Carmen, and my sister smiled as if she had just received the biggest compliment. That's when I stopped listening to all her medical facts. After all, no one ever told *me* I could be a doctor. But why would they? You had to be smart for something like that, and I couldn't even come up with a *promesa* that was good enough to help Mom.

2,051 PAGES

Monday morning, my hair flipped up in every direction. That's what I got for going to bed right after taking a shower. I didn't want to go to school looking so awful, so I tried leave-in conditioner, the straightening iron, and even wetting my hair and blow-drying it, section by section, just like a professional stylist. But my hair was as uncooperative as Jimmy when he needed to go in his car seat. So I grabbed a rubber band, made a ponytail, and slipped on a T-shirt that said "Bad hare day" over a picture of bunnies in striped prison uniforms.

Then I went to school, excited about seeing Derek in math. He was still at the top of my Boyfriend Wish List, but before I had a chance to talk to him, Mr. Leyva called me to his desk. School hadn't officially started, so the room was mostly empty. He said, "I'm glad you came early, so we could talk about your test."

My whole body slumped. "I failed, didn't I?"

"Now, now," he said, as if calming a baby. "If you knew you were struggling, why didn't you ask your sister for help? Sometimes students learn better from their peers, and you've got the best math student right there in your house. I'm sure she'd be happy to tutor you."

I looked up at him, wishing my stare could zap him like a stun gun.

He must have seen how angry I was because he said, "It's just an idea."

"A bad idea," I grumbled.

Mr. Leyva studied me a moment, to figure me out, I guess. After a while, he said, "Well, you didn't complete the test, so at this point, you haven't technically failed."

He showed me my paper. Some of the answers were wrong, but others were correct. Mr. Leyva explained how I was "on the bubble," and how, if I got the remaining questions right, I could pass. "Go to the library," he said, "and complete the test. Take the entire hour if necessary and remember to show all your work."

I felt so grateful for the chance to complete the missing questions. Maybe a bad hair day didn't have to mean a bad math day, too. I wanted to salute Mr. Leyva and say, "Sir, yes, sir." After all, I felt like a soldier going to war against math. Maybe this time, I'd be victorious.

I gladly took the test and headed to the library, getting there just as the tardy bell rang. Since classes were scheduled for visits, the librarian let me use her office. "Make yourself comfortable," she said.

So I did. I pushed aside her papers to clear a spot. Then I readjusted the height and the armrests of her chair, took a pencil from a cup on her desk, and turned up her radio. To loosen up, I popped my knuckles and did a few neck stretches. Time for battle, I told myself. Math is your foe, but it can be conquered.

The first problem went like this: Mary went to the store to buy a dress. The price of the dress is $40, but a sign announces that the store is offering a 20 percent discount. How much will Mary pay?

How was I supposed to know the answer? This was the most ridiculous problem on the planet. First, what store was this? Because stores like Macy's had sales all the time with big red signs that said "20% off." But it was never that simple since the small print always began with "discount does not apply to..." How could I know if the discount applied to Mary's dress when the problem didn't list the exceptions? Second, *when* was Mary buying the dress and what kind of dress was it? What if the sale was happening right now, in the fall? What if the dress was a sundress? Would Mary really buy something she couldn't wear for the next six months? Next, what condition was the dress in? Sometimes the clothes on sale were stained or missing a button, which meant Mary could argue for a bigger discount. That's what Mom did. She *always* got a few dollars taken off. Finally, how much money did Mary have? Did her parents expect her to pay for the whole thing or did they plan to pitch in? Did Mary even have parents, or was she an adult with a job?

I couldn't stop fretting over the question. How could the word problem ignore such important details? This *had* to be a trick. I tapped the pencil on the desk, wondering what to do. "Need more information," I wrote beside the word problem. Then I saw in bold print, "Show all your work." Suddenly, I understood. Mr. Leyva wanted me to explain what kind of information I needed. I grabbed a sheet of notebook paper since there wasn't enough room to explain on the test. I wrote down everything that might affect the price of the dress—the store, the small print on the ad, the style, the condition, the season, and even Mary's personal situation.

The remaining questions were similar, so I wrote "Need more information" again and again, explaining why each time. My hand got so stiff from all that writing, but passing the test was worth the pain. After forty minutes, I was done.

I put the librarian's supplies back in order and headed to the circulation desk to say thanks, but then I spotted Carmen. I didn't want her to know about my math test, and I didn't want to talk to her, especially in front of a cute guy like Joe Leal, who was checking out the display of graphic novels. Sure, everyone knew Carmen and I were sisters, that she was a genius while I was *not* a genius. But if they didn't see us together, maybe they'd forget. So I hid behind the office door, and while I waited for a moment to escape, I spied.

As usual, Carmen had on her prep school uniform with its plaid skirt, knee-high socks, and blazer, and, as usual, she carried a stack of books that was as tall as Jimmy. The books were about to topple over, so as she walked, she swayed like a circus clown on a tightrope. Carmen approached a table, but the students there laughed and waved her away. She approached another table, but one of the girls threw a purse on the last empty chair and said, "We're saving this." When she approached a third table, a guy shook his head as if to say, "Don't even try it." So Carmen lugged her books to the counter. She wasn't far from me, but luckily, she faced the other way. I should have said hello because part of me felt sorry for her, but another part felt like telling her, "That's what you get for being Little Miss Factoid all the time and making me feel like a dummy." Okay, so maybe I *was* a dummy because I needed extra time on my math test, but at least I had friends.

Carmen went directly to the last page of each book and wrote something on a piece of paper. She had just finished going through the stack when her teacher approached.

"What you got there?" she asked Carmen, who answered by reading out titles: *When a Parent Has Cancer*; *Is Pollution Making Us Sick?*; *Breast Cancer: What Every Teen Girl Should Know*; *The Disease Sourcebook*; *Cancer Treatments and Their Side Effects*; and *The Complete Medical Guide for Teens*.

"That's a lot of reading," the teacher said.

Carmen shrugged it off. Then she read out the numbers she'd written down. "It's 54 plus 212 plus 340 plus 298 plus 424 plus 723 for a total of 2,051 pages. If I get to keep these books for two weeks, that's 146.5 pages a day minus the pictures and glossaries and tables of contents and indexes." She glanced at the book spines again. "These books are okay," she said, "but they're written for teens. This"—she held up the thinnest book—"has pictures. Not photographs of tumors or blood cells, but illustrations like the kind in a kid book. What do the doctors read? That's what I want to know because I want to be a doctor when I grow up."

"You'll have to visit a university or hospital library for doctor books," the teacher said. "They're very technical."

"I know, but I don't mind reading technical stuff if it gives me the real answers."

"I don't think anyone has the real answer for cancer. But I'm sure the medical books are more detailed than these."

"That's what I want," Carmen said, "details."

The teacher patted her shoulder. "Why don't you start simple, okay, sweetie?"

Carmen nodded, then took the books to the checkout line. While she was busy with the librarian, I slipped out without letting her know I'd been there.

Later at home, Mom showed us her compression dressings. She was wrapped from armpit to hand. Carmen, Jimmy, and I couldn't help touching the bandages.

"You look like a mummy," I said.

She laughed. "Mummy, Mommy, not much difference."

"You should have taken me with you," Carmen said. "I really wanted to learn."

"You learn more in school, *mija*."

"No, I don't. I have to draw pictures." She reached in her backpack and pulled out pages of lines looping over themselves, forming odd shapes that she had colored in. "I finish my work before everyone else, so this is what I do. I try reading, but…"

"But what?" Mom wanted to know.

Carmen glanced at me. She probably didn't want to admit how nerdy she was. "Nothing," she said.

"She doesn't read because she's too embarrassed," I guessed aloud. "She doesn't have any friends."

"I have friends," Carmen said, all offended.

"Name one."

She crossed her arms. "No, because you don't know them."

"I don't know them because they don't exist."

She stared at me. If her eyes were boxing gloves, I'd be knocked out by now. That's how angry she looked.

"That's enough," Mom said. "Carmen, go outside and water the plants for me. I'm not supposed to get my wraps wet. And Chia, get the towels from the dryer and fold them."

"You're giving us chores?" Carmen whined.

"About time you helped out," I said as I headed to the laundry room.

After I folded towels, I noticed that the furniture in the living room needed dusting, and the Chia Pets needed watering, and Jimmy's toys needed to be put away. When Dad came home, I helped him with dinner, *migas* again, even though it was my night to clean the kitchen. Then I bathed Jimmy and read him a bedtime story so he could go to sleep. Finally, at about eight thirty, I had time for homework. By then, my feet throbbed and my back ached as if I'd been standing all day. I had trouble concentrating, not because I felt distracted but because I had a headache, probably from stress. I shouldn't be doing homework this late. I should be watching TV or chatting with my friends on Skype. I should be sleeping!

My cell phone rang. Shawntae. When I answered, she was all panicky.

"Erica, you have to help me. I'm in so much trouble."

My mind raced. Were her parents in an accident? Did her house burn down? Did she humiliate herself in front of one of the guys on our Boyfriend Wish List?

"What happened?" I asked, fearing the worst.

"I ran out of ink!" she cried.

I sighed, and even though she couldn't see me, I rolled my eyes. That girl had more drama than a reality show.

"Can you help me, *pleeeaase*?"

"Sure," I said. "What do you need?"

"I'm forwarding a file for my social studies class. Can you make fifty copies? It's an invitation to a presentation about the election. I'll buy you a new ink cartridge if you do this giant favor."

"Of course, I'll do it. No problem."

"I *knew* I could count on you," she said.

A few minutes later, she e-mailed the file. I made sure my printer had enough paper and asked it to print. Maybe now I could do my own homework and finally get some sleep. But when I pulled Shawntae's invitations from the printer, I noticed that they weren't flyers, but cards, which meant they had to be folded. More work! But what could I do? I already told Shawntae I'd take them to school tomorrow.

So I started folding, trying my best to get the lines straight because if Shawntae were doing this, *she'd* get them straight. She was a perfectionist. Never a hair out of place or a shoe that didn't exactly match her outfit.

When I was about halfway through, Carmen walked in. "Still doing homework?" she said as if I were too dumb to get it done in time. I ignored her, kept on folding, and realized that I was getting tired. There was no way I'd be able to concentrate on my own assignments.

Carmen got into bed. After a minute, she sat up. "Do you think Mom's going to be okay?" she asked.

I shrugged. "I don't know."

"But do you think—"

"I don't know," I said, impatient. I had so much on my mind and didn't want to deal with Carmen right now.

"But can't you guess?"

"No, because I can't see the future. Do you want me to lie? Do you want me to pretend everything's going to be fine?"

"Never mind," she said, turning away and hiding under the covers. A moment later, I heard, "One...two...three..."

"What are you counting now?" I wanted to know.

"The fan's on," she said. I glanced at our little fan, the one that turned back and forth. Every time it pivoted, it made a little sound. It made that sound twenty-three times before I finished folding cards. My homework would have to wait. If I woke up extra early, maybe I'd have time to do it then.

532 DOLLARS

The next morning, Mr. Leyva returned my test. I failed even after the second chance. I just wanted to hide. From everyone. I let my hair fall over my face as I stooped over my backpack to put away my test. I didn't notice Derek until he knocked on my desk and said, "That's funny."

How could he joke about my low grade?

"Your T-shirt," he explained, probably noticing that I had no idea what he was talking about.

I glanced at it. Today I wore a shirt with a dog dressed as a cowboy walking into a saloon and saying, "Who shot my paw?" His arm was bandaged. I guess it reminded me of my mom's lymphedema, but I couldn't explain that to Derek. He'd think I was weird for having a mother with a bloated arm.

"Was that your test?" he asked, staring at my backpack.

"Yeah," I sighed. "My grade's lower than the aquifer level."

He frowned. Each night the weatherman told us about the aquifer, our underground water supply. San Antonio was in the middle of a drought, so we had water restrictions.

"Cheer up," Derek said. "It's just one test. Everybody has a bad day. I bet you'll ace the next one."

Easy for him to say. He didn't live with a genius sister. But I acted as if it didn't bother me because I liked Derek and no guy wants to be with a girl who feels sorry for herself.

Who was I kidding? I *did* feel sorry for myself. At least I had social studies next, my favorite class. On my way there, I ran into Shawntae.

"Do you have the invitations?" she asked, her hands ready to take them.

"Sure," I said, reaching into my backpack. I pulled them out and gave them to her.

"I can't believe you folded them," she said, surprised but happy, too. "That was so nice of you. You saved me a lot of time."

"You didn't want me to fold them?" I asked.

"You didn't *have* to, but I'm glad you did. Now I don't have to skip lunch. Thanks a million!" With that, she took off, her zebra-striped pumps clacking on the floor.

I replayed our conversation last night. She *didn't* ask me to fold. I did all that work for nothing!

When I stepped into my social studies class, I mumbled hello as I took a seat by my friends. Patty didn't seem to notice my gloomy mood, but GumWad sent a note. "Are you okay?" it said.

I wrote, "I guess."

He looked at it and frowned. "Are you okay?" he wrote again. "Circle yes or no."

I circled no.

"What's wrong?" he wrote back.

"I don't want to talk about it."

He glanced at my note, and then he took out a clean sheet of paper and started to draw. After a while, he sent me a picture of a cat hanging from a limb, two hands reaching up to save it, and he wrote, "Remember the card I gave you when your mom had her operation?"

So that's why it looked familiar. But why was he sending me a picture of a card he gave to my mom? My life was hard enough without GumWad confusing me with mysterious riddles. Luckily, Patty got tired of passing the notes between us. She said, "Will you two stop writing notes to each other and just talk when class ends?"

And then, an eternity later, class ended.

"See you guys during lunch," Patty said as she grabbed her things to leave.

"Wait for me," I said, but GumWad interrupted.

"Hold on a second," he told me.

Soon everyone was gone, including Mrs. Gardner, who had stepped into her storage closet while the class emptied out, and since she had a conference period next, the classroom stayed empty.

"Are you okay?" GumWad asked. "You were all fidgety during class. Do you have to go to the restroom? Why didn't you ask Mrs. Gardner? She's real nice about the hall pass."

"No," I said. "I don't have to go to the restroom. I'm stressed!" I held out my mood ring to prove it.

"Why?"

"You really want to know?"

He nodded.

So I told him, my words as fast as a caged hamster sprinting in its little wheel. In two or three minutes, I blabbed the whole story about math, my mom's fatigue and fat arm, my dad's quiet rules, my sister's nonstop counting and medical facts and how everyone bragged about her extremely intelligent brain, and my little brother, who was starting to think that *I* was his parent. I told him about the chores I had to do and how I was such a long way from getting five hundred names. "It's too much," I said, "and there's no one I can talk to at home. And all Iliana talks about are boys and Shawntae about running for mayor. And Patty's an awful listener because she always complains."

"You can talk to me," GumWad offered.

He was the *last* person I wanted to speak to, especially with all that gum-smacking. But how could I say that without hurting his feelings? Plus, I didn't want him to feel sorry for me. I hated when people felt sorry for me. So I said, "Maybe, but it's easier to talk to girls."

GumWad sat there and thought quietly for a few minutes. He didn't even chew the gum that was in his mouth. Finally, he said, "Don't worry. I'll figure something out. I promise."

Just then, Mrs. Gardner came out from her storage closet. "What are you still doing here? You better hurry to your next class."

So we left, GumWad running through the hall so he wouldn't be late and me dragging my feet. I walked in a daze, as unaware of my surroundings as Jimmy when he got a new toy.

During third period, Iliana sent a text, "Where were

U?" because I didn't stop by her locker as usual. Between classes, I bumped into a guy, not realizing it was Chad until five seconds too late, but then not caring about the brief close encounter. And when I heard Shawntae's pumps clicking behind me, I didn't turn till she tapped my shoulder. She said, "Remind me to tell you about last night's dream," before rushing to her next class. Usually, I had some sassy comment about her silly dreams, but I couldn't think of one sassy thing to say.

I felt totally lost. I couldn't stop worrying about math. I really thought I did well on the test. I had put so much effort into those questions. I showed all my work, every detail. So where did I go wrong? How could I have failed? It just didn't make sense. Unless, of course, I was dumb. That *had* to be it. Whatever math intelligence was supposed to go into my brain went into Carmen's instead. That's why she was the genius, while I was the moron.

Honestly, I was too confused to tell the difference between a letter of the alphabet and a number. I took my science book to English, forgot my locker combination, and walked into the bathroom instead of my fourth-period class. The only thing I knew for sure was that I had issues. Lots of issues. No wonder my mood ring kept changing! It went from black for tense to pink for uncertain to white for frustrated. I kept waiting to see blue, the color for calmness and peace, but no such luck. With all the craziness in my life, I couldn't see blue if I looked at the sky.

When lunchtime arrived, Iliana said, "Where have you been?" as soon as I got to the table.

"Nowhere. Hiding. Bad day."

"Why?"

"I don't want to talk about it."

Her face was full of worry, but she didn't press the issue. Patty said, "What day *isn't* bad?" and Shawntae said, "Here's something to cheer you up."

"Another dream?" I guessed.

"This one's about your mom," she said.

I leaned forward. "Good news?"

"Yes."

"Will she be cured?" Iliana asked.

"I don't know, but she *is* going to win the lottery. Pretty cool, right?"

Iliana and Patty cheered, but I felt a little disappointed. Winning money *was* cool but only if it could buy a cure for Mom.

"In my dream," Shawntae went on, "your mom's at a convenience store, all decorated with pink streamers, like when my aunt had a shower for her baby girl."

"That's weird," I commented.

"I know, right?" She paused before returning to the dream. "So your mom gives the cashier a Snickers bar."

"Wait a minute," I said. "She never eats chocolate."

"Well, she should. Apparently, chocolate brings her good luck because when the cashier scanned it, confetti fell from the sky and a big band started playing."

"At the convenience store?" Patty asked, all skeptical.

"Of course. That's where the dream took place."

"Since when do convenience stores have live music?"

"Since *I* started having my dreams," Shawntae said. "Can I continue now?"

Patty nodded.

"Next thing you know, the cash register drawer shot out and a number flashed on its screen. The anchorman from Channel Five said, 'Congratulations, Mrs. Montenegro! You are the winner of five hundred thirty-two dollars!' He handed her a check while a dozen photographers took her picture."

"Wait a minute," Patty said again. "When did the news guy and photographers come in?"

"Who knows?" Shawntae answered, getting impatient. "It's a dream. They just appeared. Let me finish, okay?"

Iliana laughed. "You mean there's more?"

Shawntae ignored her and turned back to me. "Meanwhile, your mom kept saying 'I can't take this check. You have the wrong Mrs. Montenegro. I never bought a lottery ticket, so how could I win?' But no one listened. They just wanted to party. Suddenly all the shelves of chips and candy bars disappeared and the store became a dance hall."

"Are you sure you weren't dreaming about Derek's party instead?" I asked.

"I wondered that, too. The streamers, confetti, and dance floor don't really fit. But the clearest image was the five hundred thirty-two dollars that flashed on the cash register, so this dream was definitely about your mom. My subconscious mind is probably merging two realities, your Mom's big win and Derek's party."

"I guess," I said, doubtfully.

"So you know what she needs to do, right?" Before I could say anything, Shawntae answered her own question. "She needs to go to the convenience store *today*. Tickets are only a dollar, and the jackpot is up to twelve million."

"I thought you said she was going to win five hundred thirty-two dollars," Patty said.

"I did, but my predictions aren't completely accurate, remember? There's always one detail that's off. That's why we have to interpret them."

"Are you sure it's the prize amount that's off?"

"No, Patty, I am *not* sure," Shawntae said, punching out her words because she was getting impatient again. "Why do you think I've been telling you my predictions after the fact? My dream interpretation skills are still in the development stages."

"Okay," Patty said. "I didn't mean to get you mad."

"Well, stop being such a critic."

The conversation moved toward things we could do with twelve million dollars. Iliana wanted to get a makeover so she could attract the cutest guys, Shawntae wanted to finance her political campaign, and Patty wanted to buy her own island so no one would get on her nerves. Nobody asked what I would do, probably because they knew I'd donate it to cancer research.

All of a sudden, GumWad arrived. "Hi, y'all," he said.

"Why are you late?" Patty asked.

"I went to the library."

"Since when do you skip lunch to go to the library?"

He shrugged.

"So where are your books?" Shawntae said, all suspicious.

"I didn't get any. I was looking for quotes—the kind that cheer people up." He reached into his backpack and pulled out a spiral notebook. It was almost new, although I could tell a few pages had been torn out. He handed it to me. "Here you go," he said.

"What's this?"

"A journal. So you can write down your feelings."

I opened it. The first page had a collage of phrases like "U is for unique," "the inner me," "one of a kind"—and sayings like "Dare to be remarkable" by Jane Gentry, "For a long time she flew, only when she thought no one else was watching" by Brian Andreas, and "It is not given us to live lives of undisrupted calm, boredom, and mediocrity. It is given us to be edge-dwellers" by Jay Deacon.

"This way," GumWad said, "you can have someone to talk to. Well, it isn't technically a person since it's just a bunch of paper, and it isn't technically talking since you'll be writing instead. But you know what I mean. The next time you get mad, you can write down your thoughts."

"Thanks," I said.

"So where's *my* special journal?" Shawntae asked, all jealous. "I want a spiral notebook with motivational quotes, too."

"And I want one with beauty tips," Iliana said.

GumWad reached in his backpack. "Well...um...I only had one extra, but I'll go to the store after school if you want."

"Will you? That's so sweet," Iliana said.

"Really? You guys think I'm sweet?"

"Sure," I said. "And thanks again for the notebook. It's exactly what I needed."

He smiled, and for the first time, he didn't have any gum in his mouth.

9 CHIA PETS

Another Saturday rolled around. I had promised to help
Iliana with her service learning project. She rang the doorbell at exactly nine o'clock, but I wasn't quite ready.

"Give me a minute to grab my stuff," I told her.

I ran to my room, slipped on some shoes, and put the
manila envelope and the clipboard with the sponsor forms
in my backpack. Then I put my Chia Pets in a laundry basket, leaving SpongeBob for Jimmy since that was his favorite. When I returned to the living room, Mom was talking
to Iliana. I felt a little embarrassed because Mom was in her
robe and her hair was all messy.

"Have fun today," she told me.

I noticed how she leaned against the doorway as if to
hold herself up.

"Should I stay?" I asked. "I don't have to go. I can lend Iliana my Chia Pets."

"That's right," Iliana said. "If you need Erica to stay..."

"Don't be ridiculous," Mom interrupted. "Go have some fun."

I nodded, even though part of me felt guilty for thinking about fun when she was still sick.

"Miguel!" Mom called out. "Chia's leaving. Come say good-bye."

Dad rushed over, but instead of saying bye to me, he took one look at Mom and said, "What are you doing out of bed? I thought you were sleeping."

"I was," she answered. "But I heard the doorbell and wanted to say hello."

"The doorbell woke you up?" He sounded upset, and I couldn't help thinking that if the doorbell were a kid, it would be grounded.

For her service learning project, Iliana was going to play with the children at Santa Rosa Hospital, which is across from a popular tourist spot called El Mercado, where visitors could eat Mexican food, watch ballet folklórico dances, and buy souvenirs. Her father drove us, and the hospital soon came into view. Its most impressive feature was an eight-story mural on its outer wall, a mosaic of tiles featuring a guardian angel in shades of purple and blue. She hovered over a Mexican boy with a dove in his hand. When I saw it, I glanced over my shoulder. I couldn't help wondering if I had a protective spirit, too. After all, I almost got hurt so many times—like when I ran into the street and a car screeched to a stop right before hitting me, and when I slipped and nearly fell off a cliff at Lost Maples State Park, and when a library bookcase tipped over as I climbed it, spilling its books but failing to crush me because a column kept it from crashing to the floor. Surely, I had a guardian angel, and if I had one, then my friends had one too, and my mom. But what about the times we *did* get hurt...or sick? Where were the angels then? Weren't they watching all the time? I was beginning to doubt because I'd been working so hard on my *promesa*, yet Mom was still sick...sicker, in fact, with her swollen arm and with dark circles under her eyes. I knew I shouldn't think this, but sometimes those angels did a terrible job.

Iliana's father dropped us off, and we carried the basket of Chia Pets to the children's ward. Every time we saw a cute guy in scrubs or a lab coat, Iliana said, "Do you think he's a doctor?" And every time we passed a glass door, she checked her makeup and said, "Do I have enough mascara?" or "Is my lip gloss shiny enough?"

"Are you here to help kids or find a boyfriend?" I finally asked.

She shrugged, but I knew what the answer was.

"Don't you think doctors are too old for you?" I said, remembering how GumWad had said the same thing to me at Sonic.

"It doesn't hurt to *imagine*. I *might* marry a doctor someday. You never know."

I could only shake my head.

We made our way to the nurse's station on the pediatric ward. I got a visitor pass, while Iliana got a special "I'm a volunteer" button. The nurse said, "They're waiting for you," as she led us to the patients.

"That's great," I said, and I asked how old the children were and what they normally did when volunteers came. Meanwhile, Iliana didn't say a word. She kept slowing down, and because we both carried the basket, I had to slow down, too.

Finally, we reached the play area. It had a giant floor mat with brightly colored squares, each featuring a letter of the alphabet or a number. Against the wall, goldfish swam in a tank with multicolored gravel, fake plants, a scuba diver bobbing up and down as he released bubbles, and a sunken ship with windows big enough for the fish to swim through. Buckets of crayons and colored pencils were on the tables, and toy boxes filled with stuffed animals, puzzles, and board games lined the walls. A few parents stood around, too.

"Have fun," the nurse said before returning to her station.

"What do I do now?" Iliana whispered. She sounded panicky.

"Talk to the kids," I suggested.

But she didn't say anything. She just stared at them. A few kids were in wheelchairs. Others had IVs or oxygen masks. One boy didn't have a leg, and one girl was bald with a long scar on her head. There were also kids who didn't seem sick at first. Except for the hospital gowns and ID bracelets, they looked like students on a field trip. But then, you noticed that they were tired or pale or extra thin. You noticed something else, too. All of them had added a personal touch to their hospital clothes—slippers shaped like fire trucks or teddy bears, crazy socks with stripes or polka dots, robes with cartoon characters, or baseball caps with the logos of their favorite teams. Sure, the children weren't feeling 100 percent, but that didn't stop them from having a sense of humor and a sense of style. They had a special kind of bravery, the kind I saw in my mom whenever she laughed at her own situation. She wasn't in denial, like my dad thought. She was trying to make the best of things.

I nudged Iliana. She didn't move. The kids stared at us, full of expectation, so I nudged Iliana again. Nothing. This was going to be a disaster if I didn't act fast.

"Good morning, everyone," I said.

They stayed silent.

"Good *morning*," I said again, this time with a big smile and my arms moving like a drum major's urging the band to play.

This time they said, "Good morning."

I glanced at Iliana. She was looking at me. Very quietly, she said, "Go on."

So I said, "My name's Erica, and this is my friend Iliana. You can call me Erica the elephant, and you can call her Iliana the iguana."

The children laughed at that.

"So who are you?" I asked, pointing to a girl who wore a jangly bracelet.

"Susan the swan."

"Hello, Susan. You have beautiful feathers."

She brushed her arm as if smoothing a wing.

"And you?" I pointed to a boy.

"I'm Hugo the..."—he looked up—"Hugo the hyena."

"And I'm Clarisa the camel," another girl said.

After that, everyone jumped in, all of them giving us

their names and laughing at the animals they chose. Soon, Iliana the iguana was laughing, too.

"Why don't we make name tags?" she said, finally warming up to her job.

She pulled some blank stickers from her purse, and the children wrote their names and drew their animals. Then they pressed the stickers onto their gowns. Now everyone knew everyone else.

"What's in the basket?" a boy named Juan asked.

"More animals for our zoo," I announced. I reached in and pulled out Mickey Mouse, his big ears peeking through the green hair.

The kids giggled.

Juan laughed, "Mickey doesn't have hair!"

"Well, this isn't Mickey," I explained. "This is Mitch, his green-haired cousin."

The giggles turned to laughter. The children wanted to see the other Chia Pets, so Iliana and I took them out, telling a story for each one. Then we handed them to the children.

Some were too weak to hold the Chia Pets, so we put them on their laps or nearby tables. They smiled and petted the funny green hair. Soon, Iliana and I heard animal noises even from Chia Pets based on historical figures. Abe Lincoln barked, and Einstein mooed. One girl had a kitten, but instead of meowing, it quacked. Why not? If a kitten could have green fur, then it could quack, too. We were acting so silly, all of us, and I caught myself laughing till my belly hurt. When I glanced at my mood ring, it was red, which meant I was feeling energized and adventurous.

Now that Iliana knew what to do, I decided to work on my own project. Since I was at a hospital, I figured lots of people would know how I felt about my mom. After all, if they were here, then they knew someone who was sick. Surely they wanted to cure diseases, so I went to the lobby to ask for sponsors.

"Hello, can I speak to you?" I said to the first group who walked in. When they saw my clipboard, they hurried away. I asked the next group. They shook their heads and said, "Not now." This was turning into a repeat of going door to door. But eventually, people stopped to listen, and they were very understanding. Some even admitted knowing someone with cancer, too. So I was able to collect more sponsors. After a while, I was on a roll. Maybe this had been the answer all along. Instead of ringing doorbells, I should go to hospital lobbies. San Antonio had lots of hospitals. Maybe I could visit them all. What a great strategy! I finally had a genius idea. At least, that's what I thought until a security guard approached and said, "I'm sorry, miss, but you are not allowed to solicit here."

"I'm not soliciting," I explained. "I'm just trying to get donations."

He put his hands on his hips as if to scold me. "That's what 'soliciting' means," he said.

I felt so stupid. If I were Carmen, I would have known the definition and wouldn't have made a fool of myself. But I *wasn't* Carmen. I wasn't a child genius. I was Erica, dumb Erica, a failure at math, at vocabulary, and at finding five hundred names.

"I'm afraid I have to ask you to stop," the security guard said.

So I left, returning to the pediatric ward, all down in the dumps. When I got there, most of the kids were gone, and those who remained had moved to other activities, which meant my Chia Pets were scattered about, completely ignored. One was on the floor, not broken but on its side, the leaves getting squished. And over by the giant window, Iliana was giggling with some guy. Okay, he was amazingly cute, but he wasn't wearing a hospital gown, so he wasn't a patient, which meant she had no business talking to him. She was here to work with the kids.

"What are you doing?" I said to her.

She didn't catch my anger at all. "Oh, Erica. Back already?" She glanced at her watch. "I guess time flies when you're having fun," she said, smiling at the boy, who smiled back. He was even cuter when he smiled, which just made me angrier.

"Aren't you supposed to be playing with the kids?" I said.

"I was. We had a great time, but then I met Alan, Clarisa's older brother. You remember Clarisa, right? Clarisa the camel?" She told Alan about the name game we played, taking all the credit. He said she was clever, and she giggled again.

Normally, Iliana's flirting wouldn't bother me. In fact, I'd be flirting, too. But not today, when we were supposed to be working on our projects! How could she play around like this in a hospital where people were sick or dying— even little children, the very children she came to meet? There I was, in the lobby, begging for sponsors and then being humiliated by the security guard, while she was up here playing around. This was a game to her, but for me it was life and death, my *mom's* life and death.

I knew I was about to cry. That's how angry I felt. So I decided to calm myself by collecting my Chia Pets. That's when I noticed some were missing. I counted. Yes, nine Chia Pets were gone!

"Where's Tweety?" I asked Iliana. "Where's the president?" I held out the basket to show her how empty it was.

She shrugged. "A couple of kids asked if they could have them, and I said yes. I guess the other kids thought they could take them, too."

"You gave away my Chia Pets?" I couldn't help it. I shouted.

That's when Iliana finally realized I was angry. She got apologetic. "I'm sorry, Erica. I thought you *wanted* to give them away. I thought that's why you brought them."

"I've been collecting them since I was a baby, so why would I give them away?"

"I don't know," she admitted. "I thought you were tired of them."

"But I *love* my Chia Pets. They make me laugh. They're like my friends! And my whole family calls me Chia. It's like my identity. What are they going to call me if I don't have the pets anymore?"

I wasn't making any sense. Even as I spoke, I could tell how ridiculous I sounded.

"My mom's the one who started the tradition," I said.

Iliana's eyes got watery. "I'm sorry."

I wasn't in the mood to forgive, but I didn't want her to cry, either. I glanced at my mood ring to figure out how I felt. It was orange, a firebrick shade, which meant I was feeling vexed. Breathe in, breathe out, I told myself. I did this three times, trying my best to change the color of my mood ring.

"My sister took one," Alan confessed. "I'll go get it for you."

He turned toward the rooms and was almost out of the play area when I called him back. "Wait!" He stopped and looked at me. "She can have it," I said.

"Are you sure?" he asked.

I nodded. After all, how could I take a Chia Pet away from a sick child, especially one as cute as Clarisa the camel? If she was anything like Jimmy, she'd start to cry. All the kids would cry. I didn't want to cause so much sadness, especially when I came here to make them laugh.

"Are you sure?" Iliana repeated, and I nodded again. Sometimes, it was too late to get things back even if they were still close by.

I made another pass through the play area in case I had overlooked a Chia Pet, but, no, they were definitely gone. Meanwhile, Iliana and Alan exchanged cell phone numbers and said good-bye. Then Iliana asked a nurse to sign her timesheet, and we headed to the elevators. When we got there, I spotted a directory of the hospital departments. I pointed at the word "oncology" and said, "That's where the cancer patients go."

And that's when the tears finally came. I couldn't push them down anymore.

"Oh, Erica," Iliana said. She hugged me. She probably knew I wasn't crying about Chia Pets, but about my mom.

A moment later, the elevator doors opened. Some people came out. They saw my tears, but they didn't say anything. Why would they? We were in a hospital, where tears were more normal than smiles.

28 CARS PASSING BY

Because of the lymphedema, Grandma had been driving for Mom, and while I was in school, she watched Jimmy. But by the end of the day, she was ready to go home. "Your grandpa gets cranky," she explained, though I knew she got cranky, too.

When she dropped us off on Thursday, Carmen and I found Mom at the kitchen table, sound asleep, her cheek on top of a place mat. The swelling in her arm had finally gone down, so she had returned to radiation therapy. The treatment knocked her out, but Jimmy thought she was playing night-night, a bedtime game.

When he tugged at Mom's robe, Carmen pulled him away. "Mom's not playing," she said, but he didn't believe her. He curled up on the floor, closed his eyes, and said, "I go night-night, too."

She was about to stand him up, but I stopped her. "Let him pretend," I said. Then I gently shook Mom. She lifted her head, confusion all over her face. "Come on," I said, helping her stand and letting her lean on me as I walked her to the bedroom. Once we got there, I pushed aside the blanket, and when she crawled into bed, I tucked her in and kissed her cheek.

She smiled. "Who would have thought?" she said sleepily. "You acting like the parent and me acting like the child?"

"You're still my mom."

"And you're still my baby."

She patted the bed like she used to when I was Jimmy's age. I shook off my shoes and curled up beside her. I knew I was leaning near her sore side, but she didn't complain. I was almost as tall as she, and I'd been washing clothes, vacuuming, and giving Jimmy a bath every night. I'd been trying my best to keep peace with Carmen even though she got on my nerves. But right now, I wanted to be a child again, Jimmy's age because he was too young to understand what was happening.

Mom stroked my hair and hummed my favorite lullaby

about little chicks who cried when they were hungry and cold. *"Los pollitos dicen, pío, pío, pío, cuando tienen hambre, cuando tienen frio."*

That's how I felt, like a *pollito* crying—not like Jimmy, whose shoulders shook, but like Dad, who got still as a wall.

As I lay there, I thought about the Race for the Cure and my project, both only a week away. Little by little, I'd been gathering names, but I still didn't have five hundred. Last Sunday, I had asked Dad to take me to the Medical Center area because lots of hospitals were on the same street. I went to the lobbies, asking for sponsors, and leaving only when the security guards explained the "no soliciting" rule. I knew it was lying to pretend I didn't know the rule, but each time, I managed to get several sponsors before getting caught. And I never really got in trouble. I just apologized and went to the next hospital. What else could I do? I had already knocked on every door in my neighborhood and called all my relatives. I had even bugged people after church. But it still wasn't enough, and I was starting to panic because it seemed impossible to get five hundred names in time for the walk—in time for Mom.

After a while, Mom's voice faded out, and her hand slipped away. She was asleep again. I wanted to stay and dream that things were back to normal, back to the time before Mom brought those nine bikinis home, but something fell in the kitchen and the loud crash made Jimmy cry. So I crawled out of bed, took a deep breath, and went to investigate.

When I got to the kitchen, I discovered the trash flipped on its side. Last night's chicken bones were scattered on the floor, along with dirty paper towels and broken eggshells.

Jimmy was holding up a jar and saying, "Throw away!" It was a half-empty peanut butter jar. We'd made a few sandwiches from it, but the rest of the peanut butter was on his face, shirt, and hands. He even had peanut butter in his hair.

"How did you get this in your hair?" I asked.

He just held up the jar and said, "No more!" even though there was enough for several sandwiches.

"Why weren't you watching him?" I complained to Carmen.

She didn't answer because she was counting, her eyes staring at some invisible point. She said, "Twenty-three," and a few seconds later, "twenty-four," and a whole minute later, after I had time to dampen a towel and wipe Jimmy's face, she said, "twenty-five." That's when I realized she was listening for cars passing by. We didn't live on a busy street, and you could barely hear the cars from within the house, so counting them took a lot of concentration, something

249

Carmen had gobs of right now. She looked obsessed, in my opinion.

"If you're counting cars, you'll never get to the end," I said. "There will *always* be cars driving down the street."

She just said, "Twenty-six, twenty-seven"—long pause—"twenty-eight."

I could only shake my head. My sister was going nuts.

I looked at Jimmy again. If I wanted to wash off the peanut butter, I'd have to give him a bath. Lots of kids probably cried about taking a bath but not Jimmy. He loved it. I filled the tub with bubbles and threw a bunch of toys in there. I helped him into the water, and then I sat on a stool beside the tub to make sure he didn't drown. While he invented adventures with his pirate ships and toy shark, I invented a story in the journal GumWad had given me. I'd been writing in it every day. And GumWad was right. Having a place to express myself helped. Maybe it didn't solve my problems, but it made me feel calmer. Often, I didn't even mention my worries. I wanted to forget them, so I wrote whatever came to mind—stories, lists, conversations I'd overheard, or letters to famous people.

Today, I wrote a story about a girl who liked to count. First, she counted the cans of soup in the cupboard. "It took her twenty-two seconds," I wrote. Then, she counted the lightbulbs in the house, which took five minutes and forty seconds. She went outside and counted the trees on her street. Since the street was long, it took over an hour. She then made her way to the grocery store to count the cars in the parking lot. Cars weren't like trees. They kept leaving and arriving. The girl had to start over numerous times. Finally, around midnight, when the last person left, she finished counting. One car. "The girl wondered who it belonged to," I wrote, "since all the customers and employees had gone home. Finally, she looked at the sky and started to count the stars. She's still counting because you could never figure out how many stars there are. It would take a lot more than one lifetime to get that number."

All my stories were short and simple. When I had time, I went back and drew pictures. Sometimes, I read my stories to Jimmy, very quietly—not because of Dad's rules but because I didn't want Carmen to overhear.

I was just about to read him this one when Dad walked in. He sat on the edge of the tub, scooped up some bubbles, and threw them at Jimmy, who was too preoccupied with his toys to notice.

Then Dad said, "The counselor from your school called today."

"Is Carmen getting another award?" I asked, already dreading the news.

"No," Dad said. "She called about you."

"Me?"

I thought for a moment. The counselor called only when it concerned Carmen, usually to invite my parents to some type of recognition ceremony. No way was I getting an award. I hadn't done anything special. That could mean only one thing. The counselor called because I was in trouble. Of course I was in trouble. I'd been falling behind. My grades were okay, but I'd missed some assignments and my quiz scores were low Cs.

"She wanted to schedule a conference with some of your teachers next Monday," Dad said. "She mentioned Mr. Leyva. Isn't that your math teacher?"

Of course, I thought, dropping my head. "Yes," I said, my voice small because I felt like such a loser.

When the school called about Carmen, it was because she'd done something spectacular, like gotten a perfect score on a national test that's for seniors in high school. But when the school called about me, it was because I was... well... I was *not* spectacular. And because I was not spectacular, I was failing math. Sure, I could count, just like everybody else, but the most interesting thing I did with numbers was remember my locker combination.

"Any idea why he'd want a conference?" Dad asked.

"I think I'm failing his class," I admitted.

"Really? What's your average?"

"If I were good with numbers, I'd tell you." I couldn't help being sassy. After all, who cared about my average? I was failing, plain and simple. It didn't matter if my average was a sixty-two or a twelve because it was still an F in the grade book.

"I don't understand," Dad said. "Your sister…"

I stood up. "Don't even go there," I warned. "I'm so sick and tired of hearing how smart Carmen is and how dumb I am."

"I didn't say you were dumb."

"You were going to tell me to ask Carmen for help. To ask her for *tutoring*. That's what *everybody* tells me. They think Carmen has all the answers, and guess what…*she* thinks she has all the answers. And I'm the one who has to hear it all the time, who gets *corrected*. So excuse me if the last thing I want is to give her another reason to wave her superior intelligence in my face!"

With that, I stomped out. I knew Jimmy was still in the tub, but I thought to myself, *Let Dad deal with it!*

43 PHONE CALLS

About an hour later, Dad told us to start dinner without him. He wasn't hungry yet, so he was going to take a shower and watch the news first. I served our food on paper plates and handed out plastic forks so the clinking of *real* forks and plates wouldn't wake Mom. But she woke up anyway, and when she saw us at the table, she said, "There you are. I thought I was all by myself. I thought you guys went for pizza and left me behind."

Carmen and I glanced at each other. Somehow, this felt like getting busted for doing something wrong.

"Well?" Mom said. "Where's the cat?"

"What cat?" Carmen asked.

"The one that bit your tongues," Mom joked. When we

didn't say anything, she got suspicious. "Why are you being so quiet?"

That's when Jimmy blurted, "Rules!"

"What's that, Jimmy?"

This time he whispered, "Quiet rules."

"What's he talking about?" Mom asked Carmen and me.

"Just something Dad made up," I said. "It's not important."

"Yeah," Carmen added. "Just a few quiet rules."

Mom raised her eyebrows, curious. "And what are these rules exactly?"

We knew we had to tell her, so we described putting a towel against the crack beneath her bedroom door to drown out noise, and lifting the dining room chairs instead of scooting them, and not blow-drying our hair or hooking up our iPods to the speakers.

"And last weekend, Dad disconnected the doorbell," Carmen said, "because Erica's friends were waking you up."

"They're not the only ones who ring the doorbell," I snapped, because she was trying to make things my fault again. "Anyway," I continued, "Dad went a little overboard with that rule."

"With *all* of them." Carmen laughed.

I laughed, too. Dad's rules seemed ridiculous when you really thought about them.

Somehow, I expected Mom to join the laughter. After all, she made fun of her lymphedema and her replacement breast. She joked that she glowed in the dark after so much radiation. But when she heard about the quiet rules, she slumped in a chair, her shoulders drooping. Then, when Dad came into the room, she stood up, mad.

"No more quiet rules, understand?" she said.

Dad took a step back. "What? Who? What…do you mean?"

"The girls told me all about it."

I didn't want Dad to get in trouble, so I said, "Mom, we *like* being quiet. Right, Carmen?"

Before she could answer, Mom made the "stop" gesture with her hand, so we didn't say another word.

"I want to hear my children," she told Dad. "I want to hear their voices and footsteps. I want to hear toilets flushing and vacuums running. I want to hear Jimmy crying and laughing, and the girls fighting. And I want to hear you, too—tapping on the computer, shaving, brushing your teeth. Why aren't you brushing your teeth anymore?"

"I am," Dad admitted. "But I'm using the kids' bathroom now."

"Why?"

"So I won't bother you. So you can rest."

"But I can rest just fine with noise!"

She startled me because she rarely raised her voice. She startled Jimmy, too. He didn't cry, but he ran to me and lifted his arms so I could carry him.

Mom came toward us. She kissed the top of Jimmy's head, patted my back, and tousled Carmen's hair. "I'm sorry, kids," she said. And then her voice got shaky. "I feel tired all the time. That part's true. The radiation just zaps me, but I'm still alive." She turned to Dad. "Can't you see I'm still alive? Don't make this place like a tomb. I don't need to feel buried already. You understand? Noise is life, that's what I'm saying. Noise is life."

Dad approached her, hugged her, and said, "I thought I was helping you. I didn't mean to…"

I don't know what he said next because I carried Jimmy out and Carmen followed. We could be the nosiest kids on the planet, but we knew when it was best to leave our parents alone. But we were worried. As soon as we got to our room, Carmen said, "Mom and Dad never fight."

"You're right," I said. "I guess it's the cancer."

We just stared at each other for a minute, the way hikers in a blizzard might stare at each other, not because they're angry but because they're scared that if they look away, they'll be lost and all alone.

"I'm going to clean the bathroom," Carmen said, and she stepped out. A few minutes later, I could hear water running in the tub.

I grabbed a few toys from Jimmy's room. "You play with these, okay?" I said. He grabbed them, and soon was making crashing sounds as he rolled toy cars into the wall.

While he played, I made a list of everyone in Mrs. Gardner's class. They had to do a service learning project too, so maybe they'd help. Then I listed students from my other classes. After brainstorming two whole pages of names, I took out my school directory and made phone calls. I called forty-three students. Of course, some people didn't answer the phone, and other calls went to voice mail. But I did reach a lot of people. A good number were more than happy to sponsor me, so when my classmates said, "I'll think about it" or "I don't have any money" or "Let me talk to my parents first," I didn't feel so bad. I was still a long way from my goal, but every bit helped.

144 OUTFITS

My phone rang at six o'clock in the morning on the day of Derek's party—when I couldn't afford to lose a single minute of beauty sleep!

"Not another dream," I answered, because only Shawntae called so early.

"I'm calling about your mom's lottery ticket. I had that dream a week ago, and you still haven't told her."

"Because it's not going to happen."

"I haven't had any more dreams about you," she said. "You know what that means, right?"

I shrugged, but then remembered she couldn't see me because we were on the phone. "No, I don't know what that means."

"It means that the last dream is the *real* one. Your mom's going to win the lottery. I can feel it in my bones."

I sighed, unconvinced. "And we'll all live happily ever after. We'll have lots of money, and you'll put 'psychic' on your campaign posters when you run for mayor."

"Don't be sassy with me," she scolded.

"I'm sorry," I said. "It just sounds a little far-fetched."

She was quiet for a moment, but then she said, "Just make sure she goes to the store, okay? It only costs a dollar to buy a ticket, so even if my psychic abilities aren't one hundred percent accurate, she won't lose much."

"Okay," I promised. "Can I go back to sleep now?"

She said yes, but we talked a bit longer about Derek's party before hanging up. I couldn't fall asleep after the conversation, so I hid under the blankets and made my own prediction. Tonight, I was going to have a close encounter of the fourth kind—physical contact—maybe even a kiss! I just *knew* it, and I didn't need to dream about it first.

Iliana and GumWad planned to carpool with Carmen and me. After leaving us at Derek's house, my parents were going to take Jimmy to Chuck E. Cheese. He *loved* that restaurant. Three or four times a week, he said, "Gimme pizza. Gimme pizza," while pointing to a flyer with the

Chuck E. Cheese mouse on it. As for me, I hated the place. All those bells, whistles, and kiddie songs gave me a headache, but if Mom needed noise to feel alive, Chuck E. Cheese was the best noise factory in the city. She admitted, though, that she had no appetite for pizza and that she'd probably just sit at the table while Dad and Jimmy played games. Still, she was going out, which was a good sign, in my opinion.

Iliana arrived an hour and a half before the party. She brought a suitcase of clothes and a gym bag of shoes so I could help her find the perfect outfit. I'd been trying on clothes since midafternoon, so when she came, she stepped into a room with skirts covering the beds, blouses spilling out of drawers, and shoes littering the floor.

"What a mess!" she exclaimed.

She pushed some clothes aside to make room for her suitcase, and as she matched up different combinations, I finally settled on a black, ruffled miniskirt with an under layer of tulle peeking out below the hem. I also wore a pair of strappy, silver sandals, and a silver ankle bracelet with cute charms—an "E" for "Erica," the Pisces zodiac sign, a puffy heart, an angel, a tiny T-shirt, a laptop computer, a cell phone, and my newest charm, the pink ribbon for breast cancer awareness.

"What do you think?" I asked as I slowly turned to model.

"Thumbs-up for the skirt and shoes, but that T-shirt has to go."

I was wearing my faded brown T-shirt, a total yawn on the fashion meter. "I'm still trying to pick a top," I explained.

Just then, Carmen burst in. She had dressed in the laundry room because she wanted to iron her clothes first.

"I'm ready!" she announced. "At least, I think I'm ready." She had on black Mary Jane pumps, a black skirt, and a white, long-sleeved blouse buttoned all the way up.

"You look like a nun," I said.

Carmen glanced at Iliana to see if this was true. Iliana hates to hurt people's feelings, but she had to agree.

"I'll never figure out what to wear!" Carmen moaned as she threw herself on the bed. "Not counting my school uniforms, because you can't wear them to a party, I have five skirts, three pairs of jeans, four other types of pants, and twelve blouses. That's 144 potential outfits. I can't possibly try on *all* of them."

"I guess you can't go then," I teased.

Iliana threw a blouse at me. "Be nice," she warned. Then, turning to Carmen, she said, "I'll help you out. Besides, I've always wanted a little sister to play dress-up with."

"You can have my sister for free," I said. "In fact, I'll *pay* you to take her."

They just ignored me.

While they picked through clothes, I asked Iliana for her opinions. First, about a T-shirt featuring a gigantic ring with a glittery diamond and the words "You rock my world!"

"You'll scare the guys with that one," she said. "They'll think you want them to propose."

"What about this one?" I asked, pointing at a shirt with a picture of bowling pins and the caption "You're out of my league."

"Too intimidating," she said.

When I held up a shirt that said "Luv my badittude," she said, "Too sassy." For the one with butterflies, "Too cutesy." And for a shirt that said "Sacred Heart Church. Come in for a faith lift," Iliana could only roll her eyes.

Finally, I discovered the perfect T-shirt—a hot pink V-neck that said "dress shirt" over outlines of a wedding dress, a flapper dress, a ball gown, a sundress, and a muumuu.

"I'm ready!" I said, turning around to discover that Carmen was ready, too. As much as I hated to compliment my sister, I had to admit she looked great. The white blouse was now a loose jacket over a turquoise camisole, and a scarf with swirls of turquoise and gold acted like a belt for her jeans.

"That looks a lot better than the nun outfit you had on earlier," I said.

"Really?" Carmen ran to the mirror to see for herself. She flipped back her hair and put her hands on her hips. I think she meant to pose like a runway model, but she looked like Supergirl instead. And that's when I noticed...

"You have nubs," I said.

"What?"

I pointed at her chest. "You have nubs."

Iliana leaned forward for a closer look. "That's right," she said to Carmen. "You're developing."

I thought my sister would be excited, but instead she covered up and said, "Quit looking at me! It's embarrassing."

Iliana put an arm around her. "No, it's not. It's just nature. You should feel excited."

"Well, I'm *not*. How can I go to the party with nubs?"

"It's no big deal," I said. "Just put on a bra."

"I can't. I don't have one."

"Why not? All you have to do is ask Mom. You should have seen how happy she got when it was time to buy *me* a bra."

"I don't want to ask because... because..."

For once, I knew what my sister was thinking. "Because of the surgery?"

She nodded.

Poor Carmen. She didn't want to remind Mom about losing a breast, so she'd kept quiet about needing a bra. Luckily, she had me for an older sister. I reached into my underwear drawer and searched for my training bras, finding three in the back corner beneath the bikini tops Mom had given me. The bras seemed tiny—just a bit of padding and some straps. I couldn't believe they fit me two years ago. I tossed them to Carmen and said, "They're yours." She thanked me as she turned away to try one on. The straps were too big so she asked Iliana for help, and while they made adjustments, I glanced at the C cups of my mom's bikinis. I took one and put it against my chest, but I was a long way from fitting into it. I could *never* fill that bikini, I decided. Funny, how I could seem so big next to Carmen yet so small next to Mom.

Just then, my cell phone beeped with a text from Gum-Wad: "Want something from the store?"

I remembered Shawntae's dream. Before winning the lottery, my mom was buying candy at the convenience store. I decided to give Shawntae's prediction a try, so I wrote, "Snickers. Thx."

"OK. BRT," which means, "Be right there."

"GumWad's on his way," I announced. "We've got to hurry!"

Because she'd spent so much time helping Carmen and

me, Iliana had to rush her own outfit, but she didn't complain. She picked a short denim skirt with rhinestone-studded flip-flops and a shimmery white blouse. Simple but classy. We applied lip gloss and combed our hair once more. We were finally ready for the party, and just in time, because we heard knocking at the front door.

When we answered, GumWad said, "I think your doorbell's broken. I've been standing here for five minutes."

"My dad broke it on purpose," Carmen tattled.

"It's a long story," I said, not wanting to explain.

After a few awkward moments, he handed me the Snickers bar. "I got you a king-size."

"Thanks," I said. "Double chocolate, double luck."

Everyone looked at me. I could tell they were wondering if I'd lost my mind.

Just then, my parents and Jimmy showed up.

"Everyone ready?" Dad asked.

We all nodded.

"But first," I said, handing Mom the chocolate. "You have to eat this."

"But..." GumWad tried. Before he could finish his thought, Jimmy started crying. "Gimme candy. Gimme candy."

"Also," I explained to Mom, "you have to go to the convenience store, preferably one decorated with pink streamers and a mirror ball, and you have to buy a lottery ticket because tonight's the big night. You are going to win the jackpot."

"Oh, please," Carmen said. "Statistically speaking, a lottery with six numbers from one to fifty gives you only…"—she stared at the sky where, I imagined, a gigantic calculator flashed the answer—"only a one-in-thirteen million chance of winning."

If Iliana and GumWad weren't around, I would have stuck out my tongue and said something really immature like "nanny-nanny boo-boo." As it was, I could only stare at her and wish that I were Medusa so I could turn her to stone because, as far as I knew, stones were awful at math and they never, ever acted like Little Miss Factoid.

"Gimme!" Jimmy begged as he reached for the candy.

Mom peeled back the wrapper and handed him a piece. "What makes you think I'm going to win?" she asked.

"Shawntae."

"Really?" GumWad said, all excited. "Did she have another dream?"

I nodded. "You were in the library when she told us about it last week, and ever since, she's been bugging me." I turned to Mom. "She wants you to buy a ticket *tonight*."

"You really should," GumWad said to my parents. "Shawntae has psychic abilities. Last week, she told me I was going to eat enchiladas on Wednesday, and I did. Then she told me I was going to find a dog for my social studies project, and I did. I actually found four. Then she told me a pink gumball was going to come out of my gumball machine, and it did, right after the yellow and blue gumballs came out. And she also told me I was going to have a test in one of my classes, and I *did*. I had a test in science. So you see? She's been predicting all kinds of stuff for me, and they've been happening right before my very eyes."

"Well," Iliana said, "those predictions are kind of… well…those predictions are *predictable*. I mean, you always eat enchiladas on Wednesday, and you've been searching for dogs so it was likely you'd find one, and there's always a test in some class."

GumWad stared at her. He opened his mouth. I think he wanted to blow a bubble, but he hadn't chewed gum in over a week. After a minute, he spoke again. "I believe, Iliana. That's all I'm saying." Then he turned to Mom. "And if I were you, Mrs. Montenegro, I would buy that ticket."

Mom tore off another piece for Jimmy. "What could it hurt?" she decided. She glanced at Dad to see if he agreed.

He nodded. "I have to stop at the gas station anyway," he said. "We can buy the ticket while we're there."

I still doubted, but it was fun to hope. Winning would be great, but if none of her numbers matched, at least I'd get to say "I told you so" to Shawntae and finally put an end to her silly predictions and early-morning phone calls.

2 INTERRUPTED SLOW DANCES

When we got to Derek's house, he was out front, ready to greet his guests.

"Make yourself at home," he said, pointing toward the backyard. "There's lots to do and plenty of food."

A few more kids showed up, so he said, "Catch you later," before running off to greet them.

He had a great setup. As we entered the backyard, we walked beneath a giant banner that said, "Happy Birthday, Derek!" The detached garage meant a long driveway for the dance floor, and the DJ's huge speakers meant we could hear the music over the talking and laughing. A soft glow came from tiki torches and strings of white Christmas lights on the trees, garage, and patio. Also on the patio was a Ping-Pong table, so a bunch of kids stood around waiting their turn to play. A glass sliding door led to the dining room with a table full of chips, dips, a veggie plate, a fruit bowl, hot dogs with all the fixings, and a giant chocolate birthday cake. In the next room was a TV with a Wii console.

A few adults stood around here and there, but they mostly left us alone. They were probably Derek's relatives, making sure we didn't break or steal anything.

As soon as we finished our "tour" of the party, Gum-Wad headed to the Ping-Pong table, while Iliana searched the crowd for Patty and Shawntae.

Before joining her, I told Carmen, "I hope you don't plan on being a tagalong. I'm not here to babysit, you know."

"I don't need a babysitter."

"Finally, we agree on something. The last thing I want is to hang out with you all night."

"Don't worry," she snapped back. "I've got my own friends to hang out with."

"Good. I'm glad to hear it," I said as I left to join Iliana.

I found her at a picnic table with Shawntae and Patty. We talked for a while, then Shawntae pointed at me and said, "Come on. Let's go liven up this party."

I followed as she clopped away in tiger-striped pumps.

"Nice shoes," I said.

"Tonight, I'm a wildcat," she explained. Then she held up her hand, made a claw, and growled.

I couldn't help laughing. "You're crazy, that's what you are."

"Boy crazy," she admitted.

She grabbed my elbow and walked me toward a group of kids.

"How come y'all aren't dancing?" she asked, all accusing. No one answered. "We've got good music and plenty of space, so quit standing here doing nothing like…like…" She glanced at me.

"Like lint on a sweater?" I offered.

"Like lint on a sweater," she said. Then she snapped her fingers and pointed to the dance floor. And the group went there and started to move, just a little at first, until a girl decided to go wild. That's all it took. Once she let go, everyone started laughing, clapping, and hopping around.

"How'd you do that?" I asked Shawntae. "How'd you get them out there?"

"I'm a natural-born leader," she explained. "Now, come on, let's dance, too. After all, your mom's going to win the jackpot tonight, so you have a lot to celebrate."

We joined the crowd. Shawntae found the beat in no time, but I felt so awkward. Except for the square dances we did in elementary school and a couple of dances with my dad at somebody's wedding, I had no experience. So I just snapped my fingers, tapped my feet a bit, and hoped I wasn't embarrassing myself—especially in front of the guys from my Boyfriend Wish List, because all of them were here. In fact, at one point, Forest appeared, gave me a high five, and moved on before I could say anything to him. At another point, Iliana was in front of me. She said, "This is so much fun!" And later Patty tapped my shoulder. She danced too, if swinging your head without moving your feet counts as a dance. That's how it was. No one danced with a partner, but no one danced alone either. Soon I warmed up and let myself move a bit more, especially after seeing how silly some of my friends looked, how they didn't care if they were as stiff as zombies or as clumsy as clowns. There was no right or wrong way to dance, I decided. You just let your body find the rhythm, and if it *never* found the rhythm, that was okay, too.

After several fast songs, the DJ played a slow one. Most of the kids left the floor, but a few paired up, including Lou with his girlfriend, Paula; Forest with Shawntae; and Alejandro with Iliana. I stood on the sidelines feeling a bit lonely until Derek grabbed my hand and walked me to the floor. Next thing I knew, I was in the official dance position, holding one of his hands while my other hand rested on his shoulder. Was this really happening? Was I really in the middle of the closest encounter of the fourth kind I had ever experienced? No wonder my palms felt sweaty and the beat of my heart was stronger than the beat of the music.

"Are you having fun?" Derek asked.

I couldn't speak, so I just nodded.

After a few seconds, he said, "Did you get something to eat?"

I nodded again even though it wasn't true.

"You're being really quiet tonight," he said.

This time, I *did* speak. A whole two words! "I know."

He squeezed my hand. He *actually* squeezed my hand, like some private code letting me know it was okay to be quiet. I could enjoy this moment without having to say interesting stuff. I could just be me, Erica, the girl who wears funny T-shirts and hates math.

This was the first slow song of the evening, and Derek was dancing with me. That meant he liked me. He *had* to. After all, lots of girls were here, and since he was the birth-day boy, he could probably dance with anyone he wanted. Yet he picked me. I suddenly remembered the afternoon he gave me the invitation, when he told me, "Your presence is the only present I need," and when Patty said that I was definitely the main idea of that conversation while every-one else was the afterthought. Is that why he had this party? For me? So he and I could spend time together, dancing like this? He probably wanted to ask me out a long time ago, but didn't know how I'd react. Then he had the perfect excuse—his birthday. He could invite me *and* everyone else, so it wouldn't seem as if he liked me, at least not until he knew exactly how I felt. And that's why I had to tell him. I had to admit my true feelings.

"Derek?" I began, but before I could say another word, someone tapped my shoulder.

"Hi, Auntie," Derek said to the woman standing beside us. I guess he was embarrassed because he let me go.

"I don't mean to interrupt," she apologized, "but are you Erica Montenegro?"

"Yes. Why?"

"Well, it seems your sister has locked herself in the bathroom."

I couldn't believe it. Of all the moments for my sister to be a brat!

"People are waiting," Derek's aunt continued, "but she won't come out. Do you think you could talk to her?"

Just then, the slow song ended, the couples split apart, and the dance floor filled up with a clapping, hopping crowd again.

"Sounds like your sister really needs you," Derek said. "You should go talk to her. I'll catch you later, okay?"

"Okay," I said as his aunt led me to the bathroom. I couldn't help feeling disappointed. I wanted to spend time with Derek, not with my sister. I *knew* she should have stayed home.

We reached the hallway, and outside the bathroom door was a line of edgy girls. I wondered how long they'd been waiting.

"Your freak sister is having a meltdown," one said.

And another said, "Who invited her, anyway?"

Okay, I often called Carmen a freak and said mean things about her, but that's because I was her sister, which meant I had *permission* to pick on her. After all, we shared a room, so I had personal experience with her weirdness. It interfered with my peace of mind sometimes, my very sanity. But sharing a room also meant that no matter how mad Carmen and I got, we had to apologize and forgive because we couldn't avoid each other, at least not for longer than a few hours. So, yes, I could be mean to my sister, but I did *not* appreciate when other people acted mean.

"I invited her," I said. "And she isn't a freak, understand? She's a genius."

Usually, these girls liked to have the last word, but they didn't argue because they really needed to pee. Each one of them was about to have an emergency right there in the hallway. I could tell by the way they stood with their legs crossed tight.

"Carmen?" I called through the door. "You have to

come out now, okay? You can't hog up the bathroom when there's a long line waiting."

She opened the door, just a crack. I could smell Pine-Sol and bleach. My crazy sister had been cleaning again.

"Move," the first girl in line said as she pushed through.

Carmen stumbled out and the girl slammed the door behind her.

"Would you like a place to talk?" Derek's aunt asked us. We nodded.

She led us to the living room. It was dark, so she turned on a lamp. She said we could stay as long as we liked.

When she left, I said to Carmen, "Your eyes look red. Were you crying?"

Instead of answering, she said, "They have eighteen towels in the linen closet. Eight bath towels, four hand towels, and six washcloths. There are two hand towels on a rack by the sink, so actually they have *twenty* towels in there."

"Will you stop?" I asked.

"There's an arrangement on the counter with five flowers and a jar with thirty-six cotton balls."

"Carmen!" I said, shaking her a bit. "Stop counting. What's wrong with you? Why are you locking yourself in the bathroom?"

She sniffled. "Because no one likes me."

"That's not true," I said, at the same time remembering how her classmates had acted in the library earlier in the week.

"Yes, it is. Every time I open my mouth, people roll their eyes and turn away. They ignore me. Sometimes, they actually walk away. It's like I have a disease, and maybe I do. Maybe I *do* have a disease."

"That's ridiculous," I said. "You don't have a disease."

"Then why do people run away from me?"

I thought a minute. "When you talk to them, what do you say?"

"All kinds of interesting stuff," she answered. "Like those things I told Grandma the other day about the bees, and how the United States has more tornadoes than any other country in the world. And when this girl complained about the heat and how she was sweating, I told her that she should be grateful because that's how humans cool themselves. Sweat is a great evolutionary advantage. I mean, dogs and deer don't sweat. That's why they get heat strokes a lot faster than we do. And on top of that, our sweat glands carry pheromones."

"What's a pheromone?"

"That's what *they* wanted to know," she said, pointing in the general direction of the party. "So I explained how pheromones emit this smell that helps attract mates. And they started laughing at me, *everyone*, just like you are right now. Stop laughing, Chia!"

"I'm sorry," I said. "I can't believe you were lecturing about sweat. So what happened next?"

"That girl, the one who was sweating and who started the whole thing, said, 'Hey, everybody, Carmen thinks BO is like perfume.' A couple of kids said I was totally gross. And they laughed at me. Then everyone walked off. They just left me there. It was the third time a group left me standing all alone. And I don't even know what BO is!"

"It stands for body odor," I explained, surprised to be the one giving her a definition.

She sniffled again. Luckily, a box of Kleenex was beside the lamp, so I handed her a tissue.

"Look," I said. "You can't go around talking about people's sweat."

"But I wanted to join the conversation. She *did* say she felt hot."

"I know, but instead of a lecture, just fan yourself and say something like, 'You're right. It sure is hot in here.'"

"But where do you go from there?" Carmen asked. "What do you talk about next?"

"Nothing. You let the other person talk. That's what a conversation is. You're supposed to go back and forth. Sometimes, most of the time, when *you* talk, you start to act like a professor. You make us feel like we're in school, like we're going to have a test on all the information you tell us. That's why people walk away. No one wants to talk to a textbook."

She dabbed her eyes with the Kleenex. After a minute, she said, "You always look like you're having fun when you're with your friends, like it's easy to be with them."

"It is."

"But—and don't be offended, okay?—but if you don't know any interesting facts, then what on earth do you talk about?"

I thought a minute. "We mostly tell stories about stuff that happened to us or about things that we saw."

She sat silently as she considered what I'd said. "Are you going to tell *this* story?" she asked. "About me locking myself in the bathroom?"

I laughed a bit. "Probably."

And instead of getting mad and begging me not to say anything, Carmen laughed, too. "I guess it *is* funny, even if it's really embarrassing."

"People *love* embarrassing stories," I said, "especially when they're about someone *else* being embarrassed." After a minute, I added, "You don't have to be perfect, sis. It's okay to laugh at yourself."

She nodded as she crumpled the tissue in her hand.

"Forget about those other girls," I suggested. "Come hang out with the Robins. Iliana wants to adopt you as her little sister, so she'll be thrilled."

"But I thought you didn't want me to tag along."

"I didn't," I said. "But we can make a deal. You can hang out with my friends as long as you don't act like a professor. Every time I catch you starting a lecture, I'm going to tap your leg so you can stop, okay?"

She considered it. "Okay," she agreed. "I'll try my best."

So Carmen followed me to the picnic table where the Robins were stuffing their faces with hot dogs. When she started to list the ingredients of "processed meat products," including "preservatives like sodium nitrite," I tapped her leg, and when she mentioned that Patty's freckles came from something called melanin, I tapped her leg again. But when we heard an owl and Carmen explained how one of its ears was slightly lower to help it pinpoint sounds, I didn't tap her leg. Some of her facts were actually interesting, especially when she wasn't trying to show off. After a while, Carmen started to understand the give-and-take rules of conversation, and she started to enjoy herself. Maybe my sister wasn't so weird after all.

For the most part, I was having fun, but one thing bothered me—Derek. He came by a few times to check on us, but every time the DJ played something slow, Derek asked a different girl to dance, including Shawntae and Iliana, who were nice enough to make an excuse because they knew I liked him so much. So what was going on? Was Derek trying to make me jealous? If so, his plan was working because every time I saw him with another girl, my mood ring turned amber, which meant I felt insecure. Then again, how could Derek know I liked him? I hadn't told him yet. I was about to confess my true feelings when we got interrupted. So maybe he thought I just cared for him as a friend. But didn't he notice that I wasn't dancing with anyone else? Every time another guy asked, I said, "Thanks, but not right now." This whole situation was more confusing than a word problem in math.

"I need your honest opinion," I said to the Robins. "Does Derek like me or not?"

They glanced at one another, afraid to answer. Finally, Iliana said, "I don't think he likes *anybody*, at least not for a steady girlfriend."

"That's not it at all," Shawntae said. "Derek is a player. He wants to be the center of every girl's universe. I've been watching him flirt with *all* the girls tonight. Including each one of us."

"Yeah," Patty said. "Even me."

"No way!" We gasped because no one flirted with Patty.

I'm sure a lot of guys thought she was cute, but she could be intimidating, too.

"He tried to be poetic," Patty went on. "Instead of the roses-are-red poem, he said, 'Your freckles are red, your eyes are blue, that's why there's no one as special as you.'"

"Gag me!" Shawntae screeched, sticking a finger in her mouth.

"Yeah, gag me, too." Carmen laughed.

"So how did you respond?" Iliana wanted to know.

"I answered with my own poem," Patty said. "I told him, 'Your pimples are red, your teeth are yellow, that's why you're such a lonely fellow.'"

"You did not!" Iliana said.

"Did too. And to think, I've been struggling in English. Apparently, the only time I can come up with poems is when I'm insulting someone."

We cracked up. Only Patty could invent an on-the-spot comeback like that.

After our laughter died down, I said, "That settles it. I'm not ruining my chance for love because Derek wants to flirt around. I'm saying yes to the next guy who asks me to dance."

"Looks like I have perfect timing, then." I turned to see GumWad standing behind me. He'd been at the Ping-Pong table all night. I actually forgot he was at this party. The DJ had just put on a slow song, so GumWad bowed and said, "May I have this dance?"

I didn't answer right away because GumWad, in my opinion, didn't count as a guy, at least not one worthy of the Boyfriend Wish List. He was one of us, a Robin. This wasn't the type of close encounter I was looking for, but since no one else was asking me, I said, "Sure. Whatever. Okay."

So I found myself in the official slow dance position again, only this time I made sure there was at least a foot between GumWad and me. We danced for a little bit. Then GumWad said I looked pretty tonight, so I said thanks. And when he said I had a great sense of humor because no one in the whole school wore T-shirts as witty as mine, I said thanks again. And I said thanks when he told me that I was a real special person to keep asking for sponsors after so many people refused, and an even *more* special person to look out for my brother and sister and help my folks around the house. Then he said my mood ring was purple, and I just nodded because I wasn't paying attention to him. I was in auto-response mode, like when a friend is talking about something boring and you say "really" or "uh-huh" or "wow" but you don't mean it. You're just pretending. That's what I was doing. I was *pretending* to listen to GumWad, but

I was *really* watching the couples around me. Derek, of course, was dancing with yet another girl. Alejandro and Iliana were dancing for the third time tonight. But the couple who really had my attention was Lou and Paula. They were so in love. I couldn't help staring because that's what I wanted—a boyfriend, a *real* boyfriend, one who was as athletic, handsome, and popular as Lou.

"So which one would you like better?" GumWad asked.

For a second, I thought he was asking me which *guy* I liked better, but that made no sense. So I said, "What are you talking about?"

"Which charm? I noticed you wear that bracelet—"

"Anklet," I corrected.

"Oh, yeah, I get it. Because it goes around your ankle. Well, I noticed you wear it sometimes, and the other day, I saw some charms in this James Avery catalog my mom gets. Would you like the little angel with your birthstone or the little bird?"

"Why are you asking me about charms?"

"So I can buy one for you," he said.

"Why do you want to buy me one?"

GumWad looked at the space between our feet and blushed, all embarrassed or ashamed, I couldn't tell, but since he was avoiding eye contact, he had to be feeling something awful. And then, all these details flooded in—the card he sent on the day my mom had surgery, the Slush, the journal, the way he defended me on the first day in social studies class.

"The presents," I said, "the compliments, the way you've been super nice. It's all because of pity, isn't it?"

"What do you mean?"

"You feel sorry for me. Admit it. My mom is seriously sick, and here you are rubbing it in my face by treating me like a person who's about to fall apart."

"I don't think you're about—"

I wouldn't let him finish. "I'm not some orphan girl," I said, "so don't give me any handouts."

"I don't think you're an orphan girl," he rushed to say, and he stepped forward like he wanted to hug me the way I hug Jimmy when he's acting like a baby.

I waved him off. "I'm not helpless. Don't you get it?"

And I marched to the picnic table, leaving GumWad alone on the dance floor. When I got there, I crossed my arms, refusing to talk. All night, the Robins asked what was wrong, but I said, "Nothing." When they kept pestering me, I said, "I don't want to talk about it."

GumWad had returned to the Ping-Pong table. Every time I glanced over, he was looking at me like I was the saddest *pobrecita* in the world.

When my parents finally picked us up, GumWad sat at one end of the SUV, while I sat at the other. My parents asked about the party. Carmen and Iliana filled them in, but GumWad and I stayed silent.

Finally, we dropped off my friends and made our way home. As soon as we walked in, we turned on the laptop to check the lottery numbers, but Mom didn't win the jackpot, or even $532. I didn't expect her to, but I still felt disappointed, so I sent Shawntae a text. "No jackpot for us," I wrote. "Once and for all, you do not have psychic powers!"

4 TEACHERS, 2 PARENTS, 1 COUNSELOR

Monday, my parents took us to school thirty minutes early. Carmen made her way to the library, while my parents and I headed to the office for the teacher conference.

"Don't worry," Mom said. "I'll tell them how hard you've been working on your service learning project." I dropped my head. She meant well, but that didn't stop me from feeling humiliated. How I hated being the dumb kid. For the past month, I had tried my hardest to juggle school with my new responsibilities. I was doing my best, yet here we were, walking through the counselor's door.

I thought wearing my TGIF T-shirt would make me feel better. It didn't stand for "Thank God it's Friday" like most people thought. Instead, TGIF stood for "Thank God I'm fabulous." At least, that's what the back of my T-shirt said. But I didn't feel fabulous. Once again, my mood ring was black for stressed.

We entered the office, the counselor's desk buried beneath folders, papers, and writing supplies. Luckily, she had a large, round table in the middle of the room. Mr. Leyva waited there, as well as Mrs. Gardner; Mr. Watson, who taught science; and Mrs. Silva, who taught English.

The counselor introduced everyone as we took our seats at the table. Then she began. "We don't want to alarm you unnecessarily, but since it's still early in the year, we wanted to touch base before Erica's situation gets too serious."

"And what is her situation exactly?" Dad asked.

That's when my teachers chimed in. Mr. Leyva said I was failing. Mrs. Gardner said I was doing okay in her class but that I was often distracted. Sometimes, she had to call my name twice before she got my attention. And Mr. Watson and Mrs. Silva said that even though I wasn't failing their classes yet, I was about to because I hadn't turned in all of my homework assignments.

"Is this true?" Dad asked. "You haven't done your homework?"

I felt too ashamed to look at him, so I kept my head down and nodded.

"Why aren't you doing your homework?" he asked.

"I don't have time," I said, my voice small.

"What do you mean you don't have time? As soon as you come home, you should sit at the table and do your work. That's what Carmen does."

I looked at him. I could feel the anger like hot laser beams shooting out of my eyes. I could not believe Dad compared me to Carmen in front of all my teachers when every day I worked so hard to escape her shadow. Why was she the perfect one? Why did she get all the credit? At first, I was asking myself these questions, but then I started to ask them aloud.

"Do you really want to know why I'm not like Carmen? Do you really want to know why I can't find time to do my homework? Do you think it's because I'm lazy or something?"

"Erica, settle down," Dad warned, but I couldn't. I wasn't about to listen to these people talk about how dumb I was.

"When am I supposed to do my homework? That's all I'm asking. After I clean up the mess Jimmy makes? After I give him a bath or make him a snack? After I wash the clothes? After I go through the medicine cabinet and pantry and fridge to make a list of things we need from the grocery store? After I put away all those groceries? Or spend all my energy working on my *promesa* and trying to keep Carmen and Jimmy quiet so they won't break your precious rules?"

Dad just sighed, but Mom blurted, "This is all my fault!" Her eyes were teary, and I felt horrible because the last thing I wanted was to make her cry.

The counselor and teachers stared at us. They probably thought we were the most messed-up family in the world.

"I have cancer," Mom admitted, but she couldn't go on because she was crying. And now, I was crying, my shoulders trembling, too. That's how upset I felt. Mrs. Silva placed a box of Kleenex before us, so Mom and I could grab tissues.

"Why didn't you tell us?" Mr. Leyva asked once we settled down, and I shrugged because I truly didn't know. Maybe I thought Mom's illness didn't matter to my teachers. Maybe I thought I was strong enough to handle it on my own.

"Erica's very independent," Dad said. "She's like an adult in a kid's body."

"And sometimes," Mom said, "we forget she's still a teen. She's so *responsible* at home."

"We don't have to ask her to do anything," Dad added.

Mom put her arm around me. "We're sorry, *mija*. We had no idea you were dealing with so much."

"We don't want you to fail school because of us," Dad said.

"That's why we're here," the counselor explained. "Now that we know what's going on, we'll be able to help."

"I can see how pressure at home is affecting your work," Mr. Leyva said, "but in math, at least, another factor is interfering with your success."

"What factor?" I asked, already thinking of "factor" as a math term.

"I've discussed your work with your other teachers," Mr. Leyva went on, "and we all agree that you're a divergent thinker."

"Oh, no," I moaned. I didn't know what "divergent thinking" meant, but it had to be some kind of learning problem. The last thing I wanted was for Carmen to find out I had a problem with learning.

"It's not bad," Mr. Watson said. "In fact, being a divergent thinker is a benefit in many classes."

He went on, and I listened patiently as my teachers explained how I saw lots of possibilities when faced with a problem or task. Mr. Leyva discussed how I wrote six pages to explain elements that might affect the solution to a word problem, and Mrs. Gardner and Mrs. Silva shared how my in-class writing assignments often went beyond the prompts, sometimes going in "new and startling directions." They said that divergent thinkers didn't do well on tests that had one answer, "like IQ tests," the counselor explained. "And multiple choice tests in science," Mr. Watson added. Divergent thinkers were far more comfortable with essay tests that asked open-ended questions, which, I learned, was a question with no right answer. That part was true. I hated multiple choice tests. I could figure out a way to make every choice correct, so I never finished on time.

"Divergent thinkers have lots of imagination," Mrs. Silva said.

"The problem with math," Mr. Leyva explained, "is that it makes more sense to people who are sequential thinkers." He turned to me. "But that doesn't mean you can't do well. You just have to recognize what is and isn't important when you work through the problems. I know you don't want to hear this, but working with a good tutor will really help."

"I don't mind working with a tutor," I said, "as long as it's not Carmen. I am the older sister, and I wouldn't want to upset the natural order of things." Everyone laughed at that. Maybe they were starting to understand how hard it was to live with a genius sister.

Together, we made an intervention plan. Mr. Watson and Mrs. Silva were going to let me complete the missing homework assignments. Mrs. Gardner wanted me to move to the front of the class, so I could pay more attention to her lectures. Mr. Leyva was going to tutor me himself, Mondays and Wednesdays, before school started. And my parents were going to make sure I didn't work too hard at home.

We had just finished our discussion when the nurse peeked in. "I'm sorry to interrupt," she said, "but Carmen told me you were here. She isn't feeling well and would like to go home."

"What's the matter?" Mom asked. "Does she have a fever?"

"No, but she says her body aches."

Dad said, "She was fine this morning."

"Maybe it's just nerves," the nurse said. "In any case, she's insisting that she's too sick for school."

I shook my head. Carmen wasn't sick. She probably wanted to skip school because she was embarrassed about the party. Someone probably teased her this morning. They must have said something really mean because Carmen *never* missed school. One year, my parents made her stay home because she had the flu. Instead of being grateful for having people who cared for her, she blamed them for ruining her perfect attendance record. Another time, we got a "bad weather" day due to an ice storm. This meant we got to stay home. All the students celebrated the extra day off. Meanwhile, Carmen wrote a letter to the school super-intendent *and* to the editor of the *Express-News*. She used a lot of big words, but her message was very simple—bad weather days are a dumb idea. "If you can get the TV stations to announce the day off," she wrote, "then you can get them to present our lessons. That way, we won't have time away from school." If you asked me, Carmen wasn't sick at all. She probably just wanted attention.

Even though the intervention plan sounded like a good idea, I still felt bummed. How was I going to finish my *promesa* when I had to catch up on my classes? Even if I didn't do any chores, I would still need every night this week to catch up.

I was going to try my best to focus on class, so as soon as I stepped into Mrs. Gardner's room, I took a seat at the front, telling Patty that I needed to concentrate when she asked why I was moving. GumWad came in late, so I didn't have a chance to explain. Then again, I didn't want to talk to him because I was still mad about the way he felt sorry for me.

Today, some students were scheduled to show their projects. Luckily, I had an extension till next week because the race was on Saturday. A few of my classmates had poster boards with pictures showing what they did, and others, like GumWad, went high-tech with PowerPoints.

He had a few slides about animal shelters, including one with a graph showing how many pets were euthanized each year. Then he had pics of the dogs he found and the happy reunions with their families.

Finally, it was Patty's turn. She walked up to the front of the class.

"I picked up trash," she said. "Trust me, it's not hard to find garbage. It's everywhere."

She stared at us as if waiting for us to ask a few questions, but no one's hand went up. Was that it? Her whole presentation? This was the worst presentation so far. I thought for sure Patty would fail, but then she turned to Mrs. Gardner, who nodded and went into the storage closet. When she came back out, she handed Patty some mobiles.

"So this is what I did with the trash," she explained. "I used wire hangers to hang stuff from them."

One had origami birds made from scraps of newspaper and magazines. "It's called *Birds*," Patty said. Another had strings of bottle caps. She held it up. "This one's *Bottle Caps*." A third had aluminum cans that were squished flat. Patty said, "*Cans*," as she shook it, making them clink against one another like chimes. The last had three clear plastic bottles. Inside one were small blue things she found—buttons, string, a plastic petal, but mostly candy wrappers. In the other two were red and yellow things. I expected her to say "Plastic bottles," but instead she said, "I call this *Primary Colors*." Then she said, "The whole point is that trash doesn't have to be ugly. You can find a way to make it nice." She paused a moment, stared at us again. "And I guess there's a recycling message here, too."

This was definitely a new side to Patty. I was so impressed that I beamed, making my mood ring blue for joyful. But the blue didn't last long because when I went to my next class, I remembered how far behind I was and how I had only a few days before the race. Sure, Mrs. Gardner would be pleased by how many sponsors I'd found, but my personal goal was five hundred. I *had* to reach it.

So I felt a little preoccupied at lunch. I just stared at my plate while the Robins went on and on about the weekend.

"I think I have two boyfriends now," Iliana said. "Alejandro and Alan, the boy I met at the hospital. Do you think it's bad to talk to two boys on the phone if they haven't officially asked me to be their girlfriend?"

"Apparently not," Patty said. "Derek talks to a bunch of girls at the same time."

"Tell me about it," Shawntae said. "I scratched him off my Boyfriend Wish List as soon as I got home."

"Join the club," Patty said.

"We're all deleting him," Iliana added. "Right, Erica?"

"Sure, yeah. Derek's off my Wish List."

"So what's up with Roberto?" Patty said. "He moped all during social studies. And instead of eating lunch with us, he's hanging out with the Ping-Pong crowd from the other night."

"I guess they're his new friends," Shawntae said. "I should have predicted he'd leave the Robins. But I guess I'm not a psychic after all. I'm just like everybody else. Normal."

"Oh, brother," Patty said. "It's not the end of the world. I'm in that 'everybody else' category, too, but you don't see me down in the dumps."

Iliana said, "Shawntae, you couldn't be normal if you tried. Who else wears pumps every day? Who else can get a bunch of kids on the dance floor? You're a natural-born leader. Isn't she?" She nudged me, but I didn't say a word. "You're going to be the first black woman mayor of San Antonio, remember?"

"I guess," Shawntae said with a bummed-out voice, but then she brightened up. "At least my service learning project went well."

"It was awesome," Iliana admitted. "A whole other class came to listen."

"Thanks to the invitations, the other social studies

teacher decided to join us," Shawntae said. "So I presented in front of two classes!"

"Weren't you nervous?" Patty asked.

"Are you kidding? I was *so* nervous, but I kept it under control."

They talked a bit more and then ate silently for a while. Finally, Patty said, "Check out Roberto. He keeps glancing over. He keeps looking at Erica. He did that during class, too." She turned to me. "You hurt his feelings when you changed seats. He probably thinks you're avoiding him."

I shrugged.

"That's right," Iliana said. "You two were acting weird Saturday night. One minute you were dancing, and the next, you were stomping off the floor."

I still didn't speak.

"Erica!" Iliana said. "Wake up. Tell us what happened. Did you and Roberto get in a fight?"

"Oh, please," Shawntae said. "He's too nice to fight with anyone."

"Then what's wrong with Erica?" Iliana wanted to know.

"She thought she was going to be rich," Shawntae replied, "but her mom didn't win the lottery after all."

"That's not it," I said.

"Well, why else would you be in a bad mood?" Before I could answer, Shawntae went on, "I don't blame you. You probably hate me right now for putting those ideas in your head. I shouldn't have told you about my stupid dream."

"Are you really worried about the lottery?" Iliana asked me.

"No. I never thought we were going to win."

"I knew it!" Iliana said. "So you *did* get in a fight with Roberto. That's why you guys are acting so weird."

"They didn't get in a fight," Patty said, all impatient. "Erica's upset about Derek being a flirt."

"Come on," Shawntae said. "You don't need psychic powers to see that she wanted to win the lottery."

"Or that she had a fight with Roberto," Iliana insisted.

I couldn't believe they were talking about me when I was right in front of them.

"Stop it," I said, but they kept making guesses. I couldn't believe it. My mood ring—my inanimate mood ring!—knew how I felt better than my friends did. "Stop it!" I shouted.

And they did—they completely froze. All three of them looked at me like I was some stranger wearing an Erica mask.

"How can my friends be so clueless about what's going

on in my life?" They didn't dare answer. "Sure, if my life were normal, I'd be upset about boys and lotteries, but I can't think about that right now because my life is *not* normal. My mom's sick, remember? I made a *promesa* to help her, and it isn't working out. I still need a hundred names to reach my goal, but now I have all this homework because I'm about to fail school. Yes, my grades are awful! And I can't help thinking that if I don't keep my promise, my mother will die. Do you hear me? She'll *die!*"

With that, I ran out. They tried to stop me, saying they didn't know and they're sorry, but I kept moving, straight to the counselor's office. She'd told me I could go there whenever I needed to, and I desperately needed to right now.

When I got home, I went to the bedroom to check on Carmen. She was sitting on the bed with a box of paper clips, a stack of envelopes, and a ball of rubber bands, which she was slowly taking apart. "Fourteen, fifteen, sixteen," she counted.

"What are you doing?" I asked.

"Seventeen, eighteen," she went on like a mindless robot.

"Carmen!"

I startled her. She stopped counting and looked up at

me. "Don't interrupt," she scolded. "I lost my place. Now I have to start over."

"Why are you counting those rubber bands?"

"Because I've already counted the paper clips and envelopes."

She was about to start again, but I snatched the rubber bands away.

"This has to stop," I said. "You can't go through life counting things. At first, I thought you were just acting weird, but now I think you've got a real problem. No one counts all the time, not even geniuses."

That's when I noticed two book-shaped rectangles beneath her blouse.

"What's that?" I said, pointing.

She tried to cover up with a pillow.

"Let me see," I insisted.

She shook her head, so I grabbed the pillow. We played tug-of-war for a while, but since I was stronger, she gave up.

"Okay!" she said. "But don't laugh."

She lifted her shirt, and sure enough, she had used athletic wraps to tie two books to her chest.

"What on earth are you doing?" I asked, trying my best not to laugh.

She covered up again. "I was in the library this morning doing more research on breast cancer. Did you know that if your mother has it, you have a greater chance of getting it, too? Some women even have preventive mastectomies, which means they get their breasts removed before they ever have a chance to get sick. But I figure that if I stop developing, I won't have to worry about it. That's why I wanted to come home. I'm going to stop my boobs from growing."

I started laughing. I couldn't help it. I know I promised, but this was too funny. My poor sister thought she was going to die, and all I could do was laugh. I couldn't stop long enough to tell her that she was wasting her time because you can't stop Mother Nature.

"Quit laughing!" she said, but I couldn't. Carmen might be smart and she might be developing, but she was still a little kid, especially when it came to the facts of life.

She threw the box of paper clips at me. It hit the wall and the clips rained down. Then she threw the pillow at me. It hit a figurine on my dresser, making it crash to the floor. I couldn't even get mad.

"Please!" she begged. "Stop laughing!"

I took a deep breath to calm myself. A few chuckles slipped out, but I quickly got them under control. "You're not going to get cancer," I finally managed.

"How can you be so sure?"

She was right. I couldn't make that promise. "Okay, I'm

not sure. If there's one thing I've learned," I said, thinking about Shawntae, "it's that no one can predict the future. But if you start worrying about it now, you're never going to enjoy life. Plus, don't you want boobs? *Every* girl wants to have nice boobs."

I went to my dresser, pulled out one of Mom's bikini tops, and put it against my chest.

"It's way too big for you," Carmen said.

"I know, but someday, I'll be able to wear a bikini like this." I tossed the top to her. "And so will you."

She examined it, and then she removed the books from her chest.

"So why do you count?" I asked.

She shrugged.

"I'm not going to make fun of you. I'm just curious. You're the only person on the planet who counts everything she sees."

She looked at me. I could tell she was trying to decide whether or not to trust me.

"Counting makes me feel better," she said. "I ask myself, how many of this? How many of that? And when I count, I get the answer. I like getting answers, especially when..."

"When what?"

"When I'm confused about things."

"You're *never* confused," I said.

"That's not true. I'm *always* confused."

"About what?"

She gave me a long list, things like friendships and emotions and Mom, mostly Mom. She had the same questions that bothered me, like why was Mom sick and would she get better?

"What do *you* do when you feel like life is out of control?" she asked me.

I glanced at the notebook GumWad had given me. "I started a diary," I said, "and it really helps."

She smiled. Finally, we had something in common.

We picked up the paper clips that had fallen on the floor. It was the first time we had ever cleaned the room together. After a while, Carmen said, "I know we fight a lot, but I'm really glad you're my sister. I owe you, especially for helping me at Derek's party."

I thought about my parent-teacher conference, how I refused to let Carmen help me. But if she owed me one, then maybe tutoring wasn't really helping. Maybe it was a way to pay me back.

I glanced at the mountain of books I'd brought for homework. "Can I show you something?" I asked.

"Sure."

I reached into my backpack and pulled out the math test. She looked it over, and when she got to the word problems and my six pages of reasons why each needed more information, *she* started laughing. My paragraphs really cracked her up. Normally, I'd be offended, but I had to admit that my "divergent thinking" *did* lead me in new, startling, and just plain wrong directions.

When Carmen finally settled down, she said, "Okay, let's start with number one."

4 EXTRA ENVELOPES

Thursday afternoon, I sat on the front porch, waiting for my friends and watching Jimmy scribble on the sidewalk with chalk. The Race for the Cure forms were due, and as soon as Dad came home, I was going to turn them in. But my friends made me promise to wait. They said they had a surprise for me.

I pulled the list of sponsors from my manila envelope and tallied up the names—412. In a way, I felt proud. I had talked to every person I knew and a lot of strangers. So I didn't meet my goal, but hopefully, I'd get credit for trying my best; and in that way, fulfill my *promesa*.

"Gimme car!" Jimmy said, pointing to a toy truck at my feet. I kicked it to him. He rolled it across the curvy line he'd drawn on the sidewalk. The line looped over itself and sometimes trailed off into the grass, but Jimmy kept following it, making zooming sounds as he pushed his truck. And I thought, if I were to draw a line of my life, it wouldn't be straight like the timelines in my history book but tangled like the squiggle Jimmy drew on the sidewalk because you had to change directions sometimes, trail off the normal path—like the way Carmen did eighth-grade math even though she was supposed to be in elementary school, or the way I took care of Mom when she was supposed to take care of me. Maybe there was no such thing as a normal path. Maybe we all traveled through confused squiggles instead.

A sedan pulled into the driveway, and after turning off the engine, Shawntae's mother got out.

"The gang's all here," she announced, and when the other car doors opened, all the Robins, even GumWad, stepped out.

"Hi, everyone," I said. "I didn't know *all* of you were coming."

"Are you ready for the surprise?" Shawntae asked.

"Sure, what is it?"

She laughed. "Not so fast. It's for your mom, too."

I told Jimmy to go get her, so he ran in, calling, "Mommy! Mommy!" A few moments later, Mom and Carmen came outside.

"Close your eyes," Iliana told us.

Mom, Carmen, Jimmy, and I closed our eyes. When the Robins told us to open them, we saw a white banner with bright pink letters that said, "Race for Lisa."

"I love it!" Mom said, clapping her hands like a kid who had just opened a birthday present. She gave Shawntae's mother a hug, and then she hugged each of the Robins.

"Look on the other side," GumWad said as they turned the banner around.

Dozens had signed their names. I didn't recognize every signature, but many were familiar. My teachers, classmates, even guys on my Boyfriend Wish List. I scanned the names, finally finding Iliana, Shawntae, Patty, and Roberto.

"There's more," Patty said. She reached into the car and pulled out four manila envelopes.

"We felt really bad the other day when you got mad at us," Iliana explained. "There we were talking about silly things when the whole time, you've been dealing with some big problems."

"Then we thought about the times you helped us," Shawntae said. "Like when you made those invitations for me."

"And when you helped with my English homework," Patty said.

"And when you found my first dog," GumWad added.

"And when you went to the hospital to help me with the kids," Iliana said.

"But you never asked *us* for help," Shawntae went on. "So when you said you were short one hundred names, we decided to pitch in."

"We didn't think it'd be hard," GumWad said, "if we each got twenty-five people to sign up."

"I got all my relatives to sponsor you," Patty said.

"I set up a fund-raising campaign on my Facebook page," Shawntae said. "Lots of people responded."

"I asked my brothers," Iliana told me. "They think you're cute, like another little sister, and when they heard about your *promesa*, they asked their whole football team to help."

"I went back to the people who had lost their dogs," GumWad said. "They were more than happy to donate the reward money."

I took the envelopes and peeked inside. Each had extra sponsor forms, checks, and real money. With the extra names from the Robins, I knew I had reached my goal.

"Thank you," Carmen and Mom said.

And I said it, too. "Thanks. This means so much to me. I know you helped because you care about me and not for other reasons"—I looked at GumWad—"like feeling sorry for me."

His smile told me that he knew I was apologizing for the night of Derek's party.

"Why don't we take the banner inside," Mom suggested, "so we can sign it, too."

"Good idea," Shawntae's mom said.

We headed toward the house. Everyone went in, but before GumWad and I entered, I grabbed his sleeve to hold him back.

"I'm sorry you wasted all your quarters on me," I said when we were alone.

"They weren't wasted," he answered. "I like helping out. Besides, I really needed to get rid of my gumball machine."

"You got rid of it?"

"Yep."

"What a coincidence," I said. "I just got rid of all my Chia Pets. I didn't throw them away. I just passed them along to children at the hospital."

"Even Scooby?" GumWad wondered. "He was my favorite."

"Sorry. Even Scooby."

"Do you miss them?" he asked.

"I thought I would, but no, I don't miss them at all. Do you miss your gumball machine?"

"Sometimes." He got this faraway look on his face as if

he were remembering special moments with gumballs. I couldn't help laughing a bit.

"Erica! Roberto!" Shawntae called. "You're missing all the fun!"

"Coming!" we called back.

And then GumWad said, "You should call me Roberto from now on too, since I'm not chewing gum anymore."

I held out my hand, so he could shake it. "It's a deal," I said.

He smiled. I had to admit he had cute dimples, cuter since he didn't have an annoying gumball in his mouth. And, like Iliana often said, he could be really sweet sometimes. I could never add GumWad to my Boyfriend Wish List, but maybe, someday, I could add Roberto.

500 NAMES IN PINK

The big day arrived! Dad dropped Carmen, Mom, and me near the Race for the Cure festivities, while he and Jimmy searched for a parking spot. The "Race for Lisa" group planned to meet by the flagpole fifteen minutes before the starting gun went off. We had arrived an hour early, so we had time to look around. Mom wanted to see the sights too, but she quickly got out of breath.

"And to think I wanted to do the whole walk," she said. She lifted a foot to show off her tennis shoes. "Next year," she vowed.

I gave her a hug. "Next year, you and I will *run* the 5K."

"We sure will," she agreed. "But for now, I'm going to sit over there." She pointed toward a row of chairs in front of a stage where an emcee introduced a speaker from the city council. I was glad Mom had come, even though she didn't feel well enough to walk the 5K. She planned to sit near the finish line and cheer for us. "You girls look around, okay?"

"Okay," we said.

Carmen and I walked through the parking lot of the Alamodome, San Antonio's big stadium. The newspaper article I had seen in the valley said that last year, thirty thousand people came.

"I wonder how many people are here today," I said to Carmen.

"I don't know," she answered, "but I don't plan to count them." I smiled, glad that she was getting closer to normal.

Nearly everyone wore the official T-shirt, including Carmen and me. Some people went beyond the shirt by dyeing their hair or wearing pink wigs. One lady had wrapped a pink boa around her neck. She kept sneaking up to people and tickling them with its feathers. Other ladies wore pink bracelets or earrings. And the dogs had pink collars or leashes. One man had dyed his poodle so it looked like a ball of cotton candy on legs. There were so many shades—the pinks you find on roses, lipstick, bubble gum, pencil erasers, and pigs. Even the guys wore pink.

Carmen and I made our way to a tent called the Pink Hat Café. It served strawberry yogurt, apples, bananas, bagels, Gatorade, water, and pink lemonade. Then we peeked through the windows of a giant inflatable castle filled with kids jumping around, and we visited a booth where a woman painted the breast cancer awareness ribbon on our cheeks. At another booth, we got autographs from Spurs and Silver Stars players, and farther down the aisle, we laughed at people singing out of tune with a karaoke machine.

Then, we found the Tribute Tent. When we went inside, Carmen said, "It's just like *el cuarto de milagros*."

I had to agree. I felt as if we had traveled back in time to the day we visited the valley and left our special items at the shrine. Lining each side of the tent were walls. One was called the Wall of Hope, and the other was called the Memory Wall. They had bulletin boards so people could tack up pictures and letters. I saw photos of smiling women, and some of women who were bald from chemotherapy or had arms swollen like my mom's. The letters on the Wall of Hope were mostly prayers, and some were *promesas*. One woman promised to work at a soup kitchen every day for a year. One husband promised to stop watching TV. And a child promised to do his homework "forever and ever." Other letters were thank-you notes or narratives from women who had survived cancer. On the Memory Wall, people who had lost someone wrote letters, many addressed to the women who had died. "We miss you," some said, or "We wish you were here," or "Can you believe that Señora Chavez is dating a younger man?" And, just like in *el cuarto de milagros*, tables were filled with roses, hundreds of pink roses; and teddy bears, candles, balloons, greeting cards, and small statues of saints; and souvenirs like thimbles, refrigerator magnets, baseball caps; and T-shirts from all over the world.

"I thought I'd find you here," Dad said. He was holding Jimmy's hand, trying to keep him from grabbing the items. Jimmy kept saying, "Gimme! Gimme!"

"Do you want to jump in a castle?" Carmen asked him.

"Gimme castle!" he said.

Carmen took his hand. "Let *me* take care of Jimmy for a change." We nodded as she led him out. She'd been taking care of him all week. Maybe Mom and Dad told her to, or maybe she was being nice. After all, she *had* been helping me with math, and little by little, I was starting to understand.

When they were gone, Dad said, "Here's your backpack." He handed it to me. It stored my camera, a bottle of water, and the rest of Mom's bikini tops. I had brought them for good luck. I pulled out the hot pink one, remembering how Mom had left a bikini top at *el cuarto de milagros*. That seemed like years ago. Since then, she'd had surgery and several weeks of radiation therapy. She had a couple of more weeks to go. Then we'd have to wait six months before the doctor ran tests to see if the cancer had disappeared. I knew those were going to be the toughest six months, and that every day, we'd silently ask ourselves, "Is Mom going to be okay?" So here I stood between the Wall of Hope and the Memory Wall, glad that Mom was still with us but also afraid that next year, things might be different.

"Do you really believe in *promesas*?" I asked Dad. "Do you think miracles happen if we keep our promises?"

He put his arm around me and took a deep breath. After a long moment, he said, "I don't know, *mija*. Sometimes, I think *promesas* aren't for the sick person. We do them for ourselves, so we can feel like we're helping in some way. But in the end, it's not in our hands."

That wasn't the answer I wanted to hear. I wanted Dad to be as confident about *promesas* as he was when we visited the valley. I wanted certainty, an answer as straightforward as the answers Carmen got when she counted things.

Dad reached into his pocket, pulled out a slip of paper, and tacked it onto the Wall of Hope.

"What's that?" I asked.

"The receipt from last week's visit to Chuck E. Cheese."

He laughed to himself. "I could hardly hear a word your mother said, and I spent most of the time chasing Jimmy. The pizza was cold, and the soda was warm. It wasn't like our first date at all, but we had fun. As much fun as we had the first time we went to the movies."

Dad didn't know Mom's future, but he knew her present and her past. He was going to celebrate and hope and be grateful, and so was I. So I placed the bikini top on a table and left it in the Tribute Tent.

When we stepped back outside, we saw Jimmy and Carmen. "Look who I found," she said.

The Robins were beside her. Roberto carried the banner, rolled up for now. Patty was kneeling as she put hot pink shoelaces in her tennis shoes. She must have found them at one of the booths. Shawntae had pink tennis shoes instead of pumps, and when she caught me staring at her feet, she shook a charm bracelet in my face. *All* the charms were pumps, each a different color. Iliana was there too, arm in arm with her brothers. They wore their football jerseys with pink bandanas tied over the sleeves.

I could only sigh. They were so cute. Maybe someday they'd see me as more than "another little sister."

"We decided to register so we can run," they said. "See you guys later. We're going to warm up."

I watched them disappear into the crowd. Was it

acceptable to put your friend's older brothers on your Boy-friend Wish List?

"Where's your mom?" Patty asked.

"Near the stage," I said. "Let's go find her."

We headed to the stage and found her talking to a few other women.

"Meet my new friends," she said as she introduced us to fellow cancer patients who planned to cheer for the people walking in their honor. We talked to them for a while. They were going through a hard time too, and it was nice to know that Mom wasn't alone.

"Time to make your way to the starting line," the emcee said.

"We better hurry," I told the Robins. "The race starts in fifteen minutes."

Before I left, Mom grabbed my hand. "I wish I could walk with you, *mija*, but I get so weak."

"I understand," I said.

She pulled me toward her and kissed my cheek. "I'm very proud of you. I'll be thinking about you the whole time you're out there."

"And I'll be thinking of you," I said as I gave her a hug.

At the flagpoles, an army color guard hoisted the Texas and United States flags. Then the soldiers did a short routine, twirling their rifles in unison before marching out.

Roberto and Patty rolled open the banner, each holding an end, and we gathered behind it.

"Let's race for Lisa!" I yelled, and everyone cheered.

All of a sudden, thousands of people packed themselves behind the starting line. The starter stood on a platform and spoke into a microphone, his voice booming through huge speakers.

"Are you ready?!"

The crowd roared with excitement.

"Then get set!" The runners positioned themselves. "Go!" We heard the loud pop of the starting gun and the crowd lurched forward, some running, some walking, but all going in the same direction.

The race was amazing. Music bands were positioned at different points along the route. We heard Scottish bagpipes, a drumming circle, a children's choir, jazz and rock bands, mariachis, and country and western groups. There were dancers too—cloggers, tap dancers, belly dancers, and young men doing something called capoeira, which looked like a combination of martial arts and break dancing. We saw air force recruits marching in full dress uniform, and the Spurs Silver Dancers doing routines with their pom-poms. A whole group of health professionals from the Cancer Therapy and Research Center walked in pink scrubs, followed by groups of firemen and police officers. And others had banners, too. Some were from companies—Saks Fifth Avenue, Teachers Federal Credit Union, Trinity Baptist Church, and my dad's company, USAA—and others from private groups like mine.

At one point, we had to cross a bridge that went over the railroad tracks. I stopped a moment to take a few pictures and found myself in the middle of a huge river flowing with pink, each person like a drop of water. I looked at all the faces passing by, and even though they were strangers, I saw traces of my mother, my sister, and my friends because I felt related to *everyone*. After all, we were like a team, an *army*, fighting for those we loved.

It took us an hour to walk the 5K. When we crossed the finish line, Mom, Dad, and Jimmy cheered.

"Come on," Mom and Dad told us. "We want to show you something."

The Robins and I followed them to a huge sign shaped like the graduated cylinders we used in science class, only instead of milliliters, the sign measured the number of sponsors who had donated to this year's Race for the Cure. It was called "The Top Ten Fund-Raising Teams."

"Erica, look!" Iliana said, all excited as she pointed to

our team, Race for Lisa, which was number eight on the list. I had collected 526 names!

"I told you! I told you!" Shawntae said. She started jumping like a jackpot winner. "I'm a psychic! I'm a psychic!" she kept saying.

"What are you talking about?" Patty said. "Did you dream about this sign last night?"

"No," Shawntae replied. "But don't you get it? Don't you get it?"

We all looked at one another. "Get what?" Roberto finally asked.

"The dream I had about Erica's mother winning the lottery. It wasn't about the lottery at all, at least not *literally*." Shawntae put her hands on my shoulders and faced me. "My dream was telling me that you'd collect five hundred names. The lottery was a symbol. It wasn't about money. It was about sponsors. Don't you see? I am a psychic after all!"

The old me would have pointed out all the details that did not quite match and insisted that Shawntae was over-interpreting things, but the new me looked at my family, my friends, and all the people still crossing the finish line, many smiling even though they wore shirts that said, "In loving memory of," and others, so many others, with shirts that said, "I'm a survivor." And then I looked at my mom and dad. I had always thought they were the strongest people in the world. I thought Dad could toss cars as easily as footballs. I thought everyone did what Mom said, not just me, Carmen, and Jimmy, but the neighbors, the teachers, the president of the United States. I thought my parents had the answers to everything, like the meaning of every word, the solution to every problem, and how to answer the big questions like why is there good and evil or why do some people, good people, get sick. I could never imagine my parents being babies once or toddlers or teenagers, going through everything I was going through. In my mind, they had always been adults, and they would always be there to help me. But then I saw Mom sick and Dad all nervous. Suddenly, they needed me. They weren't weak, exactly, but they weren't as strong as I thought. So *I* had to be strong. Even though I was still a kid, I had to do grown-up things like help around the house and keep everybody calm. But I couldn't do it alone.

I glanced at my ring, expecting it to be pink even though it wasn't a color on the mood ring color chart. Then I looked away from it. I didn't need my mood ring to tell me how I felt. I could see my feelings in the faces around me. When I was sad, they were too, and when I was happy, so were they. I still didn't believe that Shawntae was a psychic and even though I had fulfilled my *promesa*, I couldn't be 100 percent sure that Mom would be cured, but after today, I most definitely believed in the people who loved me and that the real miracles happened when we worked together.

Roberto and Patty lifted the banner. "Race for Lisa!" they cheered. Carmen and I joined in: "Race for Lisa!" Then Iliana and her brothers shouted, and finally my parents. Soon, lots of people, including some we'd never met, were chanting, "Race for Lisa! Race for Lisa!" as we celebrated our five hundred names in pink.

AUTHOR'S NOTE

Dear Readers,

I have known about *promesas* and the story of the pilot who crashed his plane for as long as I can remember. My family has visited the church with the Virgen de San Juan many times, and though I don't make formal *promesas*, I like to leave candles and prayers in honor of whoever is struggling at the time.

Several years ago, my aunt was diagnosed with breast cancer. Luckily, the doctors discovered it in its early stages, and my aunt has been in remission for over a decade. To celebrate her recovery, my cousin invited all her relatives and friends to participate in the Komen Race for the Cure, and I signed up, happy to support my aunt in any way I could.

The first time I participated, I was amazed by the thousands of people who had gathered at the Alamodome, and when I saw them singing, praying, and celebrating their loved ones, I remembered the valley and the *cuarto de milagros*. How I loved reading the letters that people left at the shrine, just as I enjoyed hearing their stories at the Alamodome. This is what inspired me to write Erica's story.

I've seen the power of *promesas* firsthand. When my father learned he needed cardiac bypass surgery, my mother promised to say the rosary every day for two years, and when my uncle learned he had prostate cancer, he promised to visit the shrine in the valley once a month for a year. My aunt didn't make a *promesa*, but her prayers and her gratitude as we gathered to walk in her honor taught me, just as they taught Erica, that the most powerful medicines are hope and the love of family and friends.

Yours,

Diana López

ACKNOWLEDGMENTS

Many thanks to my agent, Stefanie von Borstel; my editor, Connie Hsu; and the whole team at Little, Brown. I am so lucky to have your enthusiasm and expertise on my side. Thanks also to Christine Granados and Carmen Edington, who helped me get those first chapters in tip-top shape, and to my Daedalus friends, whose writing advice continues to guide me even when I am alone with the keyboard. Finally, I couldn't do this without the encouragement of my colleagues and students at UHV and the support of my family and friends, most especially Gene.

overnight. But I started on the process of change long ago. When I came to see you before Christmas I was ready to agree to anything as long as we could be together.'

'Partners?' she said firmly.

'Partners,' he agreed, 'but lovers, too—*and* best of friends.'

Judith flung her arms round his neck and kissed him ardently. 'Oh, Nick, I'm so happy.' She giggled suddenly. 'Only I don't fancy going down to breakfast tomorrow. You know what everyone will be thinking.'

'I can't say I care,' said Nick, his voice muffled as he moved his mouth down her throat. 'But if they imagine I've made passionate love to you all night, it seems a pity to disappoint them.'

'True,' agreed Judith raggedly, her breath catching in her throat at the touch of his hands.

'And,' went on Nick, 'as soon as the weather permits I vote we ask Hugh to drive us back to Friar's Haven, where I intend to lock the door on the world and keep you to myself until well after New Year. If you approve,' he added swiftly.

'Of course I approve—it's a brilliant idea,' said Judith, relishing the prospect. 'I'm very fond of my family, but you and I have a lot of time to make up, Nicholas Campion. I love you so much—I never stopped loving you, ever.'

Nick let out an explosive breath and held her cruelly tight. 'Don't get me wrong, darling—the cuff-links were a very special gift. But just to know you love me is the best Christmas present of all.' He rubbed his cheek against hers. 'Separation from you was like being cast adrift in uncharted seas. I feel I've reached safe harbour at last.'

'What a lovely thing to say,' said Judith unsteadily. 'And just to clear up any possible misunderstanding, you'll always come first with me, babies or no babies,' she assured him, hugging him close.

'I don't know that I can say the same,' said Nick thoughtfully, startling her. 'If we have a daughter like Tab you might have to share my attention a bit.'

'Thanks a lot!' she said indignantly. 'You'll have to share mine, too.'

'True,' said Nick, much struck. 'In which case, it seems only sensible to concentrate on each other exclusively while we still have the chance. Starting now. Does the beautiful, irresistible half of the partnership agree?'

'Wholeheartedly!' said Judith, and with rapture gave herself up to reunion with her husband as the crowning touch to the happiest Christmas Day of her life.

MISTLETOE KISSES

Lynsey Stevens

Chapter One

'THERE they are, the high risers of Brisbane,' Mark said as they rounded a long curve of the freeway. 'Are those two still asleep?'

Jazmin McCann turned and glanced at the couple in the back of the car. 'Sleeping like babies,' she murmured.

'Well, don't wake them,' Mark whispered quickly, 'otherwise they'll take up where they left off in their bid to talk us to death.'

Jazmin suppressed a giggle. Mandy was her best friend, and along with Mandy's current boyfriend, Paul, and his friend, Mark, they had driven straight through from Sydney, a journey of over a thousand kilometres. The four of them were members of the same social club, and it was a matter of continuous amusement within their group that Mandy and Paul were both possessed of the gift of the gab. After spending the past eleven hours with them Jazmin was inclined to side with Mark in his recommendation that they let the other two sleep.

Jazmin gazed with mixed feelings at the skyline growing steadily closer and started when Mark interrupted her thoughts.

'Mandy said you used to live here in Brisbane,' he said softly and she nodded.

'Yes. For a while. Five years ago.' And she'd thought she'd never return. The idea of coming back had never occurred to her, not, in fact, until one short week ago.

That was when she'd called to take her mother on her weekly shopping trip, as she always did, and Brisbane and all that went with it were the furthest things from her mind.

'Can you believe that woman has the nerve to write to me?' her mother began almost before Jazmin had seated herself on the sofa. 'After all this time? And after all she's done. I tell you, Jazmin, when I saw this envelope my heart literally stopped beating for a few moments.' Moira McCann clutched at her ample bosom to emphasise her statement.

Jazmin hastily suppressed a smile at her mother's dramatic pause even though she eyed, with some misgivings and a definite flutter about the region of her heart, the letter her mother held.

'And talking of envelopes, just look at this.' She handed the focus of offence to her daughter. 'Embossed!' she exclaimed with disdain as Jazmin dutifully glanced at the raised red script before passing the letter back to her mother.

'Lorelle and James McCann, Throckley, Newmarket,' Moira repeated in case Jazmin had failed to read the address.

'Well, that's where they live, Mother,' she said drily, and her mother pursed her lips.

'That will be Lorelle's doing. Your grandfather wouldn't be so flagrantly ostentatious.'

'Does it really matter?' Jazmin removed a plump cushion from behind her and settled more comfortably into the sofa. 'They have their lives and we have ours. It's been five years, Mother. Don't you think you should just let it go?'

'And have you?' Moira asked pointedly and Jazmin stiffened.

'Have I what?' She casually picked up a glossy magazine from the polished wooden coffee-table.

'Don't be obtuse, Jazmin. You know very well what I
said. Have *you* let it go?'

'Of course I have.' She flipped the pages of the magazine irritatedly. 'Why would you think I hadn't?'

'I sometimes wonder if you have,' her mother said, an
ominous tone to her voice, and Jazmin dropped the
magazine back onto the tabletop.

'There's really no need to wonder about anything,
Mother. There's no drama. Life simply goes on.'

'Then why don't you ever bring anyone home to meet
us?'

'By anyone I suppose you mean a man?' Jazmin raised
a fine russet brow.

'Well, I don't believe you've had a date, let alone a
boyfriend, since—'

'I have a number of good friends, both male and fe-
male,' Jazmin cut in quickly. 'And I'm quite happy with
my life.'

And she was, she assured herself. She had a good job,
not always as demanding as she might like, but a good
job for all that. She belonged to a social club and played
tennis every week, went on group outings to the theatre
and concerts. Only last week they'd all gone on a car rally
that ended at the beach with a delicious barbecue.

'You work, you go home to that tiny little room,' her
mother interrupted her thoughts.

The fact that three years ago Jazmin had elected to
leave home to live in a small flat, a bedsitter really, was
still a bone of contention between mother and daughter.

'And from Friday I have a whole month's vacation,'
Jazmin stated promptly to divert the direction of her
mother's conversation again.

'And I suppose you're going on a romantic cruise? Or taking a package holiday to one of the Barrier Reef islands, hm?' Moira said sarcastically, and Jazmin sighed in resignation.

'I just might, Mother, for the last couple of weeks.'

Moira McCann gave her daughter a sceptical look.

'But I intend to spend the few days I have off before Christmas doing my Christmas shopping at my leisure, instead of dashing madly about in my lunch break or after work. Now *that* I'm going to enjoy.'

'Have you really booked a holiday?' her mother asked lightly and Jazmin glanced at her doubtfully, highly suspicious of her mother's suddenly appeasing tone.

'No. Not yet,' she replied cautiously. 'But I've collected a few brochures. Why?'

'Oh, no reason.'

'No?' Jazmin queried dubiously into the lengthening silence, and her mother left her position by the picture window and came across the carpeted floor to sit down opposite her daughter.

'Not really.' She fanned herself casually with the offensive letter she still held in her hand. 'It's just this letter from your grandfather. From his wife, actually.' She gave the letter another look of disdain. 'His wife! My God, it's almost obscene.'

'It was Grandfather's choice to marry Lorelle,' Jazmin remarked tiredly and ran her hands through her loose red curls. She'd had this conversation, in its various forms, with her mother on any number of occasions to date. 'And it was Grandfather's business, surely,' she added. 'He was a grown man, certainly old enough to make his own decisions.'

'Old enough to make an old fool of himself, more likely,' Moira exclaimed. 'And Jazmin, you can't deny Lorelle was always so, well, flashy. So obvious.'

Jazmin shrugged. 'She was an attractive woman. She just made the most of herself.'

'Beauty is certainly in the eyes of the beholder. I still think she was low class.'

'Mother!' Jazmin protested to no avail as Moira continued.

'What sort of marriage would they have had? I mean, your grandfather was nearing sixty then and not a well man. Lorelle must be a good twenty years younger than he is. It's really quite distasteful.'

'Mother, enough's enough,' Jazmin stated shortly, 'and I don't particularly want to discuss my grandfather's sex life, if you don't mind.'

'There's no need to be coarse, Jazmin,' her mother remarked one-sidedly, with her regularly portrayed air of wounded sufferance.

'But—'

Moira held up her hand. 'I feel we should change this sordid subject. Besides, I want to talk about the letter.'

'Then let's do that,' Jazmin agreed in barely disguised exasperation, glancing at the gold watch on her slim wrist. 'I thought you wanted to go grocery shopping. I can't see us getting there at this rate.'

'The contents of this letter put everything else out of my mind.'

'Mother!' Jazmin warned again, and her mother sighed loudly.

'They want us to come for Christmas,' she said without preamble, and Jazmin felt her jaw drop.

'Come to Brisbane?' she repeated, sitting forward, her stomach muscles tightening defensively.

'Yes. To Throckley. The three of us.' Moira said with portentous solemnity.

It was preposterous. To even think of going back. To visit the scene of the crime. The thought ricocheted about in Jazmin's head like a bouncing rubber ball and she all but laughed hysterically. The crime? What strictly legal term might cover it?

Robbery? He'd certainly stolen her heart.

Fraud? He'd definitely used false pretences to con her into seeing him as some handsome knight on a white charger, had led her to believe he was free to begin a relationship with her.

Grievous bodily harm? Perhaps. She simply knew she had been emotionally devastated by his perfidy.

Attempted murder? As outwardly insistent as she was that her life had gone on, deep down she knew that part of her, the light at the very centre of her being, had flickered and died five long years ago. And he had killed it.

'Of course, we won't go,' her mother was stating baldly. 'She could scarcely expect us to when she drove us away in the beginning.'

'What?' Jazmin stopped and swallowed. 'Why do they want to see us?' She managed to steady her voice.

Her mother gave another exclamation of disgust and extracted the thin notepaper from the envelope, handing it to her daughter.

Jazmin made herself scan the page, the neatly scripted handwriting.

It seemed that six months earlier her grandfather had suffered a major heart attack and his recovery had been hampered by other smaller attacks. He'd asked his wife to write for him, inviting his daughter-in-law Moira, granddaughter Jazmin and grandson Rick to spend

Christmas with him. He held grave fears for his recovery, and he wanted to make peace with his only surviving family before it was too late.

It would be a pity, Lorelle had written for her husband, that the family should remain estranged over some long-forgotten disagreement, and she was sure no one could recall the reason for it. Lorelle closed with an entreaty to be in touch so that their grandfather could arrange airline tickets for them to fly up to Brisbane to give a very ill man the chance to right any wrongs he may have done.

'They may not remember the reason for the argument but I most certainly do.' Moira frowned. 'Surely he can't expect us to go back as though nothing had happened?'

'Grandfather's prognosis doesn't sound very good,' Jazmin said softly, but her mother continued as though she hadn't spoken.

'From the moment we moved into Throckley after Rick began school up there that woman made us feel like interlopers. Always lording it over me, complaining about everything, mostly your brother's behaviour. Lorelle had no heart. Poor Rick was only a boy and he'd just lost his father. He was distraught.'

Jazmin sighed. Her brother, Rick, had been a terrible child, she'd be the first to admit it. And it was a pity her parents hadn't recognised that fact instead of spoiling the boy. Rick had always thought his good looks could charm him out of trouble, and usually they had. Lorelle was his only failure. This had not endeared her to their mother and it had only further damaged the relationship between Lorelle McCann and her husband's daughter-in-law.

'And as for the way her son treated you, well, how could we stay after that?'

'Mother.' Jazmin began to get up from the sofa, feeling that long dormant, familiar urge to flee.

'Well, it's true,' Moira continued, regardless of the closed, pale face of her daughter. 'Lorelle's son took advantage of you, made a fool of my daughter, and I, for one, won't easily forget that.'

Chapter Two

KAEL Craigen. Jazmin stood in her tiny flat and made herself say his name out loud, and it echoed ominously in the small confines of the room. Kael Craigen. There. She'd said it and the world continued to turn on its axis.

You see, she told herself triumphantly, his name no longer reduces you to a quivering mass.

She'd put it all behind her and she felt no pain. Apart from that knot of ice deep inside her. But if she just kept that buried, undisturbed, she knew she'd be fine.

Jazmin paced the small carpeted area in front of her divan, her arms folded across her chest in unconscious defence, fingers gently rubbing the soft skin of her upper arms. It was a relief in itself to be by herself at last.

Her mother had continued to reiterate the subject of Lorelle McCann and her shortcomings until Jazmin thought she'd scream. But somehow she'd managed to steer her mother around the aisles in the supermarket, wait while her mother went to the bank, return her home and help her stow away her groceries before making her escape to her own flat.

And now she was alone she could give free rein to her thoughts, examine some of the memories that had caused her so much pain five years ago.

However, she had to admit the memories weren't all painful. It was simply that the last agonising one had overridden all the wonderful times that had gone before.

Like the first time she'd met Kael Craigen. The initial uncertainty, and then the incredibly incendiary yet silent message that had passed between them, had continued to flare between them from that moment.

Jazmin grimaced. If she'd known the pain that would follow, the agony of his betrayal, she'd have turned and run from him. Wouldn't she?

She gave a softly bitter laugh. Of course she wouldn't have. She'd been incapable of running anywhere. Apart from towards him. She had simply been another willing and eager moth drawn so easily to his undeniably enticing flame. And her fragile wings had been burned, the damage ensuring she'd been unable to fly. In fact, since then she'd had no desire to even attempt to step off solid ground.

Still, five years had healed her wounds, she told herself, had taught her priceless lessons in life. And if she was now just a trifle cynical, a smidgen cool and reserved, and definitely incapable of taking better than average looks and a charming mien at face value, it was surely more positive than negative.

As she'd told her mother, she enjoyed her job and her casual social life and saw no immediate need for any radical changes to be made. Nevertheless, as convinced as she was that she had put the past behind her, she certainly didn't feel she could go back to Brisbane.

Jazmin frowned slightly. Yet she was sympathetic to her grandfather's plight. What had happened had had nothing to do with him. He was, after all, an old man, a very ill old man, and she knew it wasn't too much for him to expect his family to gather around him. If he should take a turn for the worse? Jazmin bit her lip.

She sincerely wished she could go up to see him. But she had no intention of taking the chance on running across Kael Craigen again. Or his wife and family.

A tiny pain fluttered to life in her chest, and she just as quickly quelled it.

It was all over, she repeated to herself forcefully. Kael Craigen meant nothing to her now. And the cold hard truth of it was that she had never meant anything to him.

For two days the contents of Lorelle's letter had fluttered irritatingly in and out of her mind. That she could cope with, she told herself. But along with it came a disturbing new awareness, a renewed recollection.

To her dismay she found herself looking at men in the street . . . tall, dark-haired men. And remembering.

The feel of Kael's smooth, tanned skin. The strength of his arms as he swung her to him. The taste of his lips. The wild tattoo of his heartbeats beneath her fingers.

And when at their weekly tennis evening during the doubles match she'd completely missed a return simply because she was watching the play of muscles in her male opponent's long legs, she decided it was more than time to take herself sternly to task.

It was hormones, she told herself. Maybe she'd been over-zealous in cutting herself off completely from any physical and emotional interaction with men. Perhaps it was time to start making contact again.

One couldn't judge all men by one man's duplicity. And Jazmin knew she'd been doing just that. Still, leering at every man who crossed her path was something of an over-reaction, she decided.

Then Mandy made it known that she had noticed this change in Jazmin, too.

Jazmin had met Mandy Parker when she began work for a legal firm on her arrival in Sydney. Mandy was also a legal secretary in the same organisation and, after a shy start, they'd become firm friends. It was Mandy who'd insisted Jazmin come along and join the social club.

'It's no use gazing at Mark's attributes in that speculative fashion,' Mandy quipped as they sat down to watch the next match. 'He won't even realise you're doing it.'

'I don't know what you mean,' Jazmin muttered, flushing with embarrassment at being caught out.

'I mean you've frozen him off so often in the past. I know he's as thick as two bricks but even he won't come running back for more rejection.'

Jazmin grinned despite herself. 'You do go on, Mandy. And for your information, should you feel inclined to try matchmaking again, I don't fancy him. Okay?'

'In that you aren't alone.' She glanced across at Mark Dean and shook her head. 'Pity, isn't it? He has got a body that would make a girl's eyes grow wistful.' She sighed loudly. 'Have you noticed how often it happens with the drop-dead gorgeous-looking ones? He's great until he opens his mouth.'

Jazmin tried unsuccessfully not to laugh. 'Sexism aside, aren't you generalising a trifle?'

'Are you kidding? It's an understatement. There's my Paul as the prime example. Robert Redford's jaw, Richard Gere's hair, Tom Cruise's smile and Mel Gibson's behind. But as much conversation as that bench over there. And, let's face it, eventually you have to talk to them. I tell you, it's depressing.'

'Poor Paul. Relegated to the rejection pile like all the others before him.'

'Well, not yet. He's still nice to look at. But I'll admit I'm choosy. Like you, Jazmin.'

Jazmin raised her eyebrows and Mandy continued.

'I'll rephrase that. I'm nearly as choosy as you are. At least I give them the chance to open their mouths and insert their patriarchal feet.'

'It's not that, Mandy. I just don't think I'm ready for a relationship yet,' Jazmin began. Some time ago she'd given Mandy a brief account of her short and painful affair with Kael Craigen.

'Five years is long enough in the wasteland.'

'I know, but—'

'But that guy must have been really something,' Mandy finished quietly.

'I thought he was.'

Mandy sighed again. 'Whoever said life was a pain in the derriere knew what she was talking about.'

They sat quietly for a few minutes and then Jazmin found herself telling her friend about Lorelle's letter.

'My grandfather wants us to go up to Brisbane for Christmas,' she finished, and Mandy turned to her in surprise.

'Are you going to go?'

'No, of course not.' Jazmin shook her head. 'I mean, part of me wants to see my grandfather, but I don't want to see Kael Craigen again.'

'Makes things complicated, doesn't it? Would he be there, I mean, does he still live in Brisbane?'

'I have no idea. Five years ago he was studying. He was staying at Throckley, working sort of part time for my grandfather and finishing his degree.' Jazmin's heart tightened in her breast. They'd not taken all that much time to talk of mundane things. They'd been too much in love, too physically attuned to each other for conversation.

'You could always ring your step-grandmama and ask her,' Mandy suggested, but Jazmin shook her head again.

'No. I don't think I could go back anyway.'

Mandy shrugged. 'I can understand that. No sense in putting yourself through it if you don't have to. It's a shame, though. We could have given you a lift up there. You know Paul and Mark and I are going up to Noosa to Paul's parents for Christmas. You and I could have checked out the festive season in the torrid and tropical north together.'

Jazmin groaned. 'Leave me out of your plans. Please. I see only trouble if they let you loose up in sunny Queensland.'

'No worries, Jazmin. I stopped by good old Santa in the mall the other night. I told him what exceptionally good girls we'd been this year and I asked him especially nicely to slip something tall, dark and handsome into each of our Christmas stockings.'

Jazmin burst out laughing, and she was still smiling at her friend's outrageousness when she let herself into her flat a couple of hours later. She'd barely set down her sports bag when the phone rang.

'Jazmin!' Her mother's voice boomed and she held the receiver a few inches away from her ear.

'Yes, Mother. What's up?'

'I've been trying to reach you all evening,' Moira McCann said reproachfully, and Jazmin sighed.

'It's Tuesday. You know I always play tennis on Tuesdays.'

'Oh, well, I forgot. Honestly, between you and Rick I don't know if I'm coming or going.'

'What's the matter now?'

'Can you come over here?' her mother pleaded, and Jazmin glanced at her wristwatch.

'It's late and I have to go to work early tomorrow. Can't you tell me the problem over the phone?'

'No. Well, yes, I suppose so. I wanted to tell you I've decided we're going to take your grandfather up on his offer. We'll go up to Brisbane to see him.'

'You'll what? But—'

'I've given it some thought, Jazmin, and I think that morally we should go. There's nothing to stop us. Both you and Rick have time off work, and as I was saying to Lorelle . . .'

'When were you speaking to Lorelle?' Jazmin interrupted in amazement. 'A few days ago you were adamant you never wanted to see her again. I got the impression wild horses wouldn't drag you back up there.'

'I called her earlier this evening,' her mother replied evenly. 'I wanted to arrange for the airline tickets.'

'Mother, I'm not going up to Brisbane. And I can't imagine why you are. What changed your mind all of a sudden?'

'Well, the other day I was emotional. You know how I get. It's my age. And I may have over-reacted about, well, about Lorelle. Now that I've had time to reconsider it I can see I was being hasty and maybe a little unforgiving. So I changed my mind.'

'Why?'

'Why what?'

'Why change your mind so suddenly?' Jazmin repeated with a patience she was far from feeling.

'Jazmin, your grandfather may be dying.'

'I know, Mother,' Jazmin said quietly and sighed again. 'What about Rick? How does he feel about going?'

'Rick agrees with me. We discussed it and he thinks we should go to see your grandfather.'

'What's the real reason, Mother? I know there's more to this. I can hear it in your voice.'

'You're imagining things,' her mother said quickly, obviously flustered.

'Let me talk to Rick.'

'He's, well, he's not home,' Moira said evasively, and Jazmin's lips tightened.

'This has something to do with Rick, doesn't it? He must need to leave town for a while. How much does he want this time, Mother?'

'I don't know what you mean, Jazmin.'

'The truth, Mother,' she persisted, and to her consternation her mother began to cry. 'Mother? What is it? Look, I'll come over.'

'No. No. As you said, it is late. And I'm all right. I just—' she gave a muffled sob '—I just don't know what to do. Jazmin, Rick's got himself into a jam, a rather serious one, and he, well, he talked me into using the house as collateral for his loan and—'

'He what?'

'I knew you'd be furious but he assured me it was only for a month or so and that it was a rock-solid investment but things went wrong and now he needs the money right away, quite a lot of money, and I think I may have to sell the house,' her mother finished on another sob.

'How much is quite a lot?' Jazmin asked with more than a little apprehension, trying to force her hand to relax, her knuckles showing white where she was clutching the receiver. When she got hold of her brother—

'Ten thousand dollars.'

Jazmin was speechless. 'Ten thousand?' she repeated huskily. 'Mother, that's—we can't find ten thousand dollars.'

'He has a month to get it and he thought perhaps his grandfather would lend it to him.'

'Rick wants to ask a dying man for money?'

'He'll pay him back as soon as he sells that block of land he has.'

'Which could be any time in the next ten years. The real estate market is at an all-time low and the block of land isn't even in a decent area. For heaven's sake, Mother, Rick had no right to involve you in his hare-brained schemes. How dare he jeopardise your home? And as for approaching Grandfather for the money....' She let the statement hang in the air.

'What else could I do?' her mother's voice shook piti-fully and Jazmin sank into the chair by the phone.

'I don't know, Mother,' she admitted tiredly. 'I guess—' Jazmin sighed '—look, let me go to the bank. I've got some cash put aside and perhaps I can get a loan for the rest.'

'Oh, Jazmin. I hate asking you again—'

'Yes, well, it's better than bothering Grandfather. We'll be flat out at work for the rest of the week so I won't be able to get to the bank until I go on holidays on Monday.'

'Jazmin, I can't ask—I mean, Rick said not to... Oh, dear. You were so angry with him last time he got into a little financial trouble and he said not to tell you.' Moira McCann was crying again.

'Mother, you can't ask Grandfather. In fact, you shouldn't be doing any asking at all. This is Rick's re-sponsibility, and when I catch up with him I'm going to tell him as much.'

'He's really sorry, Jazmin,' said her mother, and Jazmin bit back a scathing reply.

'Rick always is sorry, afterwards,' she said wearily and glanced at her wristwatch. 'Now, you'd best get to bed, Mother, and try not to worry. I'll sort it out next week.'

But Jazmin hadn't had time to begin sorting it out. When she returned home from work two days later, her mother had left a message on her answering machine.

'Rick and I are leaving this morning for Brisbane. I didn't want to ring you at work because I knew you'd be upset. As I told you, Rick didn't want to bother you with any of this and I think it's the best decision. Rick says he may not even need to ask your grandfather as someone has shown interest in his land. Jazmin, you always were your grandfather's favourite, you know. So ring us at Throckley if you change your mind about coming up to Brisbane for Christmas.'

Moira McCann paused. 'And Jazmin, Lorelle said that they're—that Kael's in Canada at the moment. Until the New Year.'

Knowing Kael wasn't in Brisbane had wavered her resolve, but any thought of her brother upsetting their grandfather with demands for money had been the deciding factor. Jazmin knew she simply couldn't allow him to do it. And she knew from past experience that talking to Rick face to face would be the only way to convince him.

So here Jazmin was five days later feeling somewhat numb as Mark drew the car to a halt in front of the high white picket fence that surrounded Throckley, the huge old house that had been in the McCann family for nearly a century and a half.

Mark jumped out of the driver's side door to open the boot, pulling out Jazmin's knapsack and handing it to her with a grin. It was then he saw the house, for the high fence only marked the boundary of the nearly two-acre property.

The house was long and low but perched on top of the hill, giving it a three hundred and sixty degree view of the area.

'Wow! You didn't tell us the family home was quite such a mansion,' he said with admiration and just a little speculation. 'Sure you don't want me to carry this up to the house for you? It looks like quite a climb, but I'll bet the view's worth it.'

'It is. And no, you'd best be on your way if you want to make Noosa before dark.'

Mandy and Paul had joined them by now and both exclaimed over the house.

'It's gorgeous,' Mandy repeated, and Jazmin turned, making herself look at Throckley objectively, to try to see it through impartial eyes.

She had to admit it was impressive. Not only was it historically significant, having been built by her great-great-grandfather in the mid-nineteenth century, but it commanded one of the city's choicest positions. It was named after the small township in Northumberland where her great-great-grandfather was born.

Jazmin only wished she could regard it dispassionately, without the associated pain. For the ache had begun in the region of her heart as they'd turned into the street and started up the hill. Her first sight of the house had threatened to undo her composure, and for a moment she'd had to fight down the urge to tell Mark to turn the car, get right away from Throckley and all its memories.

Physically, the house looked much the same as she remembered, the long single-story building stretching along the ridge top. It was built of local stone, with curved, corrugated-iron-covered verandas running the complete length of the front and back. Two huge chimney stacks reached symmetrically from the roof, and colourful flowering pots hung at intervals along the veranda. Green, beautifully kept lawns stretched down to the fence.

Then she caught a movement off to her left and she shaded her eyes against the sun. Someone was working in the garden around what had used to be and was still referred to as the gatekeeper's cottage. They could just see the high-pitched roof of the small matching stone building behind the shrubs, and the man, for Jazmin thought it was a man, through a break in the low trees.

He had his back to them and was dressed in faded denim jeans and shirt and a wide-brimmed hat for protection against sunburn.

'Who's that?' Mandy asked in a stage whisper, although the man was far too far away to hear them. 'The gardener or the gamekeeper?'

Mark and Paul laughed and Jazmin grimaced.

'Very funny, Mandy,' she said and glanced back at the man. 'Old Joe Roberts used to do the gardening but he's probably retired by now. It must be someone new.'

'He looks okay, anyway,' Mandy speculated, and Paul put his arm around her possessively.

'How can you tell from here?' he asked, plainly disgruntled at Mandy's interest in the other man.

Mark rolled his eyes. 'He's obviously male so that's good enough for Mandy,' he teased his friend.

'Thanks very much for the implication,' Paul said with a frown.

'Oh, stop squabbling, you two.' Mandy pushed them in the direction of the car. 'It's your turn to drive, Paul. Let's get going.'

'Have you got my instructions to take you through the outskirts of the city?' Jazmin asked, suddenly and explicably a little reluctant to see her friends leave, and Mandy flapped the piece of paper at her.

'I've got 'em right here, but Paul assures us he'll know the road when he sees it.'

'And I will. Trust me.' Paul leaned over and gave Jazmin a kiss on the cheek. 'Bye, Jazmin. See you in ten days.'

Not to be outdone, Mark wrapped Jazmin in a bear hug. 'Yes, see you, Jazmin.' His kiss also landed on her cheek as she turned her head slightly and he left her with a sulky frown.

Mandy pulled a face at Jazmin as Mark climbed into the car. 'Bye. And Jazmin, perhaps you should ask for a few pointers on horticulture while you're here.' She raised her eyebrows in the direction of the cottage, and Jazmin could hear her laughing as Paul drove away.

With an involuntary smile Jazmin glanced again at the man by the cottage in time to see him turn back to his gardening. Had he witnessed their farewell? Jazmin shrugged and turned to watch the car disappear around the corner before slinging her knapsack over her shoulder and opening the gate.

She climbed the weathered stone steps and then crossed the wide expanse of lawn with its neat garden beds and low flowering shrubs. Whoever the new gardener was he knew what he was about, she reflected as she reached the wooden steps up to the veranda.

Not giving herself time to change her mind and leave, Jazmin walked up to the ornately carved and painted door and rang the bell.

She turned back to survey the view, and although she was familiar with it, it still took her breath away. And she knew it was even more spectacular at night.

The panorama of the city and suburbs and the long arch of the Gateway Bridge was laid out below her. It was truly a million-dollar view, as her mother was wont to say. She also knew the back of the house looked across to the mountains behind the city.

Unconsciously her eyes fell in search of the new gardener, and she saw he had moved on to another brightly flowering garden bed. Jazmin screwed up her eyes. He had broad shoulders, but then so did a lot of men, and she knew instinctively that he definitely wasn't as old as Joe Roberts.

Just then a child ran around the shrubbery and threw himself onto the man's back, almost knocking him over, but he righted himself and the child slid to sit on the grass beside him. A childish laugh drifted up to her, and Jazmin stiffened, her mouth suddenly dry.

No. The word screamed inside her. No. He was in Canada. Her mother had said so. Jazmin swallowed convulsively, fighting to quell her rush of panic.

The child was androgynously dressed in jeans and a T-shirt, so its sex wasn't obvious from this distance. And it could have been any age. Eight or nine, at least. The question formed in her mind. No. It was too tall. That child would be nearer ten. Wouldn't it?

As Jazmin stood transfixed, the child turned, looked up at the house and must have seen her, for it lifted a hand in a friendly wave before saying something to the man.

Quickly Jazmin spun back to face the door, her heart beating a wild tattoo in her breast. No. It couldn't be. The man was the gardener. It was school holidays and so the child was simply the gardener's son.

In agitation she went to ring the bell again, but before she could it was swung open and her mother stood in the doorway.

'Jazmin!' she exclaimed in surprise. 'Jazmin, you came. Oh, I'm so glad you changed your mind.' Moira McCann enveloped her daughter in an uncharacteristic hug. 'I tried to ring you last night.'

'We were on our way up,' Jazmin explained. 'Some friends were driving north so I got a lift with them.'

'Oh, my dear, your grandfather will be so pleased to see you.' She stopped and lowered her voice. 'His health really has failed considerably in the last five years.'

'Yes. That's why I decided to come up and see him.' Jazmin gave her mother a level look. 'And to make sure Rick didn't do anything to add further risk to Grandfather's health. Has he, Mother?'

'No. No, of course not,' her mother said defensively. 'Rick's hardly been home. Actually, he's looking up some friends in Brisbane.'

'So he can fleece them, I suppose,' Jazmin said bitterly, and her mother pursed her lips.

'I don't know why you're so hard on your brother, Jazmin. He's young and trying to make his way.'

'Rick doesn't want to make his way anywhere, Mother. He wants to be there without having to work for it.' Jazmin ran her hand tiredly through her unruly red curls. 'But we've had this conversation before, haven't we? We could keep having it until the cows come home and it wouldn't change things.' She sighed. 'Can I come in? I'm dying for a cup of tea.'

'Of course.' Her mother hesitated slightly. 'But I feel I should tell you, Jazmin, that—'

Her mother stopped at the sound of footsteps climbing the wooden steps behind Jazmin, and the suddenly stricken look on her mother's face gave Jazmin a split second of warning before she turned, her heartbeat accelerating with more than a little foreboding. For she knew unconsciously who would be there.

Chapter Three

'HELLO, Jazz.' His deep voice rolled over her like cool waves on sun-warmed skin, and she shifted defensively in case he saw her involuntary shiver. 'Welcome back.'

Welcome back? The words echoed inside her and she almost laughed. Or cried. Welcome back. Just like that. So civilised. Well, two could play at that game. Jazmin lifted her chin. 'How are you, Kael?' she asked levelly, proud that her voice betrayed none of the turmoil that reduced her stomach to water.

'I'm fine.' He shrugged. 'And you?'

'Can't complain.' Jazmin could almost laugh at the inanity of their conversation. A true example of social civility covering a seething cauldron of bitterness. At least on her part. Who knew what Kael Craigen was thinking?

'Kael arrived home last night.' Jazmin's mother put in quickly. 'Like you, he made the journey home for Christmas. Isn't it amazing how easy it is to travel these days? Just imagine, he was in Canada one day and Australia the next.'

Jazmin raised her eyebrows slightly at her mother's conciliatory tone as she recalled her mother's set face when she'd declared that Kael Craigen had made a fool out of her daughter and that she'd never forget. If such was the case, Jazmin reflected wryly, then a certain coolness on her mother's part should be the order of the day.

'We've got jet lag,' a young voice piped up at that moment, and Jazmin noticed the child for the first time. He had joined his father on the veranda, and she looked down into eyes almost as brown as Kael's.

And the resemblance didn't end there. The boy had the same thick springy hair that stood up from his head to fall back from a side part, and looking at his strong features Jazmin knew he was going to be every bit as attractive as his father. As his father still was. And the boy must be tall for his age, too, for he looked older than the seven years Jazmin estimated Kael's son would be.

'This is Toby.' Kael put his hand on the boy's shoulder. 'Toby, meet Aunt Moira's daughter Jazmin.'

'Hi!' Solemnly Toby held out his hand and Jazmin silently shook it. She swallowed, the tightness in her throat momentarily preventing her from speaking.

He could have been my son. The thought rose to taunt her, and her blue eyes met Kael's and slid just as quickly away.

'We saw you arrive,' Toby was telling her. 'And Dad said he knew you. Well, he said he'd know those red curls anywhere.'

'Toby!' Kael cautioned evenly, and the boy looked up inquiringly, the grin still on his face. 'Perhaps we should let Jazz go inside and get settled, hm?'

'Yes. Yes.' Moira McCann's fingers played with the strand of beads resting on her ample bosom. 'It's just wonderful that Jazmin could come up here at the last minute, isn't it, Kael?'

'Your grandfather will be pleased to see you,' Kael acknowledged enigmatically.

'How is Grandfather?' Jazmin asked, hoping she sounded as detached as she suspected Kael did.

'Not too bad, considering,' Kael told her. 'My mother has driven him into the city to his doctor's appointment. They should be home in an hour or so.'

'James has always been such a strong man, Jazmin,' Moira took up the story. 'What he's gone through would have been the end of a lesser man. Still, it's taken its toll.' She shook her head. 'But let's not stand out here. I know you'd love a cup of tea, Jazmin, and I'm sure you would, too, wouldn't you, Kael? And perhaps some milk for Toby?'

'Tea would be fine,' Kael said easily.

'Can I have some of your cookies, Aunt Moira?' Toby beamed. 'And I can show Jazz to her room,' he added, picking up on the shortened form of Jazmin's name that only his father used. 'There's a spare room next to mine.'

'Well, I—' Jazmin began, and paused as the air about Kael and her mother thickened with the heaviness of something unspoken.

'That's your old room, Jazmin,' her mother said, obviously uncomfortable. 'You may as well have that one, the bed's already made up.'

'Yes. Because that's—'

'Toby!' Kael interrupted firmly. 'Just help Jazz with her backpack, will you?'

Toby glanced at his father and shrugged. 'Sure, Dad. Here, let me carry that, Jazz.'

Jazmin would have liked to refuse but she sensed that there was more under the surface than she could, or at this stage even wanted to, fathom.

She followed Toby through the solid double doors, the lead light panels on either side of them dancing crazy colourful patterns on the highly polished English parquetry floor of the large vestibule. They took the hallway off to the right and Toby swung open the door to

Jazmin's old bedroom, gallantly standing back for Jazmin to precede him.

'My room's next door and then Dad's is opposite and next to him is Rick's room. Rick's your brother, isn't he?'

Jazmin nodded.

'We met him this morning. Wish I had a brother, or even a sister. I wouldn't mind.' Toby swung Jazmin's backpack onto the bed. 'Everything's ready in here. We had it made up for Cathy.'

Jazmin froze as she went to unzip her backpack. 'Cathy?' She shot a quick glance at the boy.

'My mother.' Toby gazed guilelessly up at her. 'She prefers that I call her Cathy.'

'Oh.'

'She's a doctor,' Toby continued. 'Actually, she's a surgeon. She's in Canada learning some new techniques, really, really gruesome things.' He screwed up his nose. 'So I won't describe them.'

'Thanks. That's very considerate of you,' Jazmin said drily, and Toby chuckled.

'Thought you'd appreciate it.' He sat down on the bed and examined the cloth stickers on her backpack.

'Perhaps I should use another room,' Jazmin began. 'When . . . I mean, will your mother be back?' She couldn't prevent herself from asking the question that burned inside her.

Toby shrugged his shoulders and lifted his hands palms upward. 'Don't know. Maybe she'll make it for New Year. She has to work over Christmas. That's why Dad and I went to Canada. We've already had one Christmas, an early one.' He held up his arm. 'Cathy gave me this watch. Excellent, isn't it?'

Jazmin examined the large wristwatch and nodded. 'Looks like it has everything on it.'

'I can even work out what time it is where Cathy is because it tells you what time it is all over the world. It's—'

'Toby.'

They both looked up to see Kael filling the doorway. And Jazmin felt the now familiar tightness in her chest. She had forgotten just how tall he was.

He folded his arms, muscles bulging beneath his thin denim shirt. 'Not talking Jazz to death, are you, son?'

Toby grinned. 'Who me, Dad?'

Kael smiled and the corners of his dark eyes crinkled, deep indentations bracketing his mouth. And Jazmin couldn't seem to drag her eyes from him. Could it be that he was even more attractive than she remembered? He still exuded that raw masculinity that caused women to stop and take a second look.

'We call Toby the Enemy Number One of Iron Pots,' Kael continued. 'They know their little legs aren't safe around him.'

Jazmin raised her eyebrows in enquiry and Kael's grin widened.

'Haven't you heard that old saying, "He'd talk the leg off an iron pot"?'

'Oh.' Jazmin nodded in recognition. 'I see.' She smiled weakly at the boy, and he grimaced.

'Oh, Dad, come on. Give me a break.' Toby slipped off the bed and put his hands on his hips in mock disgust. 'You'll put Jazz off me before I get the chance to show her what a great kid I am.'

Kael smiled down at him. 'You'll have your work cut out for you there,' he teased. 'Now, go see Aunt Moira in the kitchen. She has some milk and cookies ready for you.'

'Aren't you and Jazz coming, too?'

'Yes. We'll be there in a minute. Off you go.'

Toby left them with a sigh, and Kael turned to face Jazmin, casually sliding his hands into the pockets of his jeans as he leant back against the door jamb.

Her eyes were drawn downwards to his thighs, firm and muscled beneath the taut material, and her mouth went suddenly dry. Taking a firm grip on her control, she made herself look up, and for long moments he held her gaze. He had caught her blatantly ogling him and she cringed with shame, feeling the warmth of colour begin to wash her face.

'You look—' he paused, his voice lowly sensual '— wonderful.'

Jazmin's entire nervous system went crazy. She swallowed shallow breaths. And she was having the devil's own job preventing herself from simply rushing across the short space that separated them to throw herself back into his strong arms, to feel the heady thundering of his heartbeats beneath her questing fingertips.

Her only defence was to turn her back on him, and she began to stow her clothes in the bedside chest of drawers.

'Thank you,' she managed to say with reasonable aplomb, considering the conflicting emotions that warred within her.

'I didn't think you'd come.' Kael's voice played over her again, and she thought she'd explode with wanting him.

Butterflies were holding a disco in the pit of her stomach, and they were all dancing with wild abandon. She shrugged tensely. 'I wasn't going to,' she said and found herself turning involuntarily to face him again. 'I thought you were in Canada.' She heard the edge to her voice, knowing her statement bordered on accusation, and Kael's lips twisted derisively.

'I was in Canada until yesterday. Toby and I went over to see his mother. She's working over there at the moment.'

'I know. Toby told me.' Jazmin sighed tenuously. 'He—' she swallowed again '—Toby looks like you.'

'So everyone says.'

Their eyes met again and Jazmin was the first to look away. Had he seen the pain reflected in them, mirroring the terrible ache in her heart?

Kael ran a hand through his dark hair and an unruly lock fell across his forehead. 'I was hoping you'd come back,' he said. 'Your grandfather missed, still misses, you.'

'I missed him, too,' Jazmin replied thickly.

'Why didn't you come before, when he had his first attack?'

Jazmin's chin rose. 'I didn't know he was ill until my mother showed me Lorelle's letter inviting us for Christmas. Your mother could have informed us earlier.'

'As I understand it, she did.'

'Well, she didn't.' Did he really believe they would have ignored a summons to her grandfather's side when he was so ill? Unless her mother had failed to tell her.

Jazmin cringed guiltily. She had no right to blame her mother. Hadn't she been going to ignore her grandfather's Christmas invitation? 'And anyway,' she lashed out at Kael, 'how can you of all people say I should have come back after—' she gulped a steadying breath '—after all this time?'

'I never wanted you to leave,' he said huskily. 'You must have known that.'

'Oh, I knew that, Kael. I was embarrassingly available, wasn't I? That goes without saying. But it was the rest I was confused about. I mean, what did you intend to do? Start your own harem? Well, that's not my idea of professing everlasting love and devotion.'

'I never—' Kael stopped and bit off an expletive. His eyes narrowed as he looked across at her. 'This isn't the time to go into all that.'

'I have no intention of going into all that, as you so succinctly describe it.'

'Then why did you come back?'

'To see my grandfather.' She made herself smile disdainfully. 'I've had five years to come to my senses, Kael. So I'm sorry if you were under the misapprehension I came back to see you. I didn't. And when I do see my grandfather I'm leaving.'

His dark eyes had narrowed, long-lashed lids shielding his expression. 'You're not staying for Christmas?'

'No.'

'James's greatest wish is to spend this Christmas, which in all probability will be his last, with his family. With you, his favourite granddaughter.'

'His only granddaughter.' Jazmin levelly held his gaze, franticly trying to silently deny the fact that she so desperately wanted to stay. And not just because of her grandfather.

'I have to get back,' she said flatly.

'To what? Or should I say, to whom?'

'To my job.' Jazmin's blue eyes wavered guiltily now, knowing she wasn't being strictly truthful. She was on her annual leave.

'So there's no one special?'

'All my friends are special,' Jazmin retorted and then her throat seized up on her. Was his interest in her love life more than casual? The thought slipped under her

defences and she angrily chided herself for her gulli-
bility.

'Not that guy who bade you such a fond farewell
earlier?'

'Mark? Of course not. He's just a friend,' she dismissed quickly and then wished she'd let the question
hang silently, significantly.

'You know what I'm asking, Jazz. Is there someone
waiting for you in Sydney?' he demanded shortly, determinedly holding her gaze from across the room.

How Jazmin wished she could state the affirmative, tell
him there was, and be done with this cat-and-mouse
game. But she couldn't and her eyes fell from his.

Kael was silent for long moments. 'So there's no reason
you can't stay?'

'I told you, I have to get back,' Jazmin repeated with
less conviction than she would have wished.

'So what would it take?' Kael had silently crossed the
room in a couple of strides to stand far too close to her.
His dark eyes pierced her again.

'To what?' she got out huskily.

'To make you stay,' he replied softly, his deep voice
vibrating through her, creating waves of havoc once
more.

Jazmin thought about the reason she was really here,
to prevent her brother from asking their grandfather for
money. What would Kael say if she told him?

'At the moment, ten thousand dollars,' she heard herself say wryly and she raised her chin defiantly.

'It's yours,' he said with nary a pause.

Jazmin blinked in surprise. 'Don't be ridiculous,' she
said quickly. 'I wasn't serious.'

Kael raised one dark brow. 'Ten thousand was just a
number you picked out of the blue?'

'No. I...I do need ten thousand dollars.' Jazmin swallowed nervously. She couldn't look at him now and she moved over to lean against the chest of drawers, away from him. 'But I didn't mean—I... Well, the ten thousand dollars... You see, I've got myself into a little problem with my finances.'

'To the tune of ten thousand dollars?' he asked, and Jazmin nodded uneasily.

'Well, yes. It was my car. It had to have major repairs and then I got a little behind with my credit card, I mean, my credit cards.'

A frown shadowed his brow. 'Can't you consolidate the debts into a single amount and make one payment on the lot?'

'Well, yes. I wanted to, but it's not that easy. I thought—I mean...' Jazmin straightened. 'Look, Kael. Forget it, please. I was just being facetious.'

'Ten thousand dollars is quite a hefty joke.'

Jazmin shrugged. 'In for a cent, in for a dollar,' she quipped lightly. 'Now, shouldn't we be...'

'You came up here to ask James for the money?' Kael suggested incredulously then. 'Is that it, Jazz?'

'No. Yes.' His statement took Jazmin by surprise and she floundered guiltily. 'I mean, no, of course I didn't.'

'You were going to bite a very sick old man for ten thousand dollars.'

'We were.' Jazmin swallowed. 'I was going to pay him back in a few weeks,' she finished feebly.

'My God, Jazz. How could you? I'll give you the ten thousand. There's no need to ask your grandfather for it.'

Jazmin's eyes rounded in surprise. 'You have ten thousand to give me? Just like that?'

'No, not just like that. It would be a loan, all signed, sealed and delivered.'

'No, I meant—'

'You thought I didn't have two pennies to rub together,' Kael finished cynically.

'Well, you used to... I mean, five years ago you were a student.'

'I also worked for your grandfather. He had faith in me, taught me all he knew. Now I'm a full partner. McCann and Son is now officially McCann and Craigen.'

Jazmin could barely take it in. She knew her father, the son in name only of McCann and Son, had never wanted to be part of his father's real estate and construction business. But for her grandfather to virtually turn the business over to Kael— Still, that was up to her grandfather. 'You've done well,' she said carefully.

'I've worked hard,' he stated levelly. 'Have you?'

'What do you mean by that?'

'I mean, ten thousand dollars is a fairly large amount to be in the red.'

Jazmin's gaze fell again. 'I told you how that happened.'

'And I don't believe you, Jazz. I knew you pretty well five years ago, better than I knew myself, and I have a gut feeling this is all hogwash. You're no more in debt than I am, and putting the bite on your grandfather would be the last thing you'd do. It's not your style. So what's the real story here?'

'Oh, for heaven's sake!' Jazmin bit out, wondering why she'd ever begun this crazy conversation, and refusing to acknowledge to herself that this topic was decidedly safer than the more personal one they'd started to discuss. 'I told you I was joking, that I wasn't serious.'

'And asking for big bucks is a real party pleaser,' he growled sarcastically. 'Everyone's sure to roll around the floor laughing. You should have gone for a million, Jazz. Bigger laughs.'

Jazmin pulled two pairs of jeans from her backpack, her fingers nervously playing with the thick material. 'Just forget it, Kael.'

'And you don't need ten thousand dollars?' he persisted as though she hadn't spoken.

Jazmin made no comment. She lay her jeans on the bed and proceeded to smooth the creases out of them before sliding them onto a hanger.

'I can't see you coming back for money, Jazz,' Kael said, all mockery gone from his voice. 'So if there's ten thousand dollars involved then it has to be your mother or Rick.'

Jazmin refused to meet his eyes as she closed the wardrobe door.

'Tell them to come and see me, Jazz, not James. He has enough on his plate at the moment. I've virtually been in control of the business this past year, anyway.'

'You mean you sign the cheques?' Jazmin retorted bitterly as she spun to face him.

'If you like,' he said with cool arrogance.

'Look, I don't want to discuss this any more, Kael, so I suggest we'd best leave it. Apart from that, my mother will have the tea ready.'

Kael was standing between her and the door, and Jazmin made herself walk toward him, her nerve endings screaming louder with every step she took. At the last minute he stepped slowly aside, silently following her out of the room.

'Remember what I said, Jazz,' he repeated softly before they entered the kitchen. 'Come to me, not James.'

'Oh, there you are, you two.' Moira McCann bustled around pouring tea from the large silver teapot that was a family heirloom. 'We thought you'd got lost, didn't we, Toby?'

'I guess you didn't really need me to show you the way to your room, did you, Jazz?' Toby looked up at Jazmin, wearing a crescent of milk like a moustache. 'Aunt Moira has been telling me that you lived here when you were a little girl.'

'Well, I didn't exactly live here. We visited when I was young, for school holidays, but I was grown up when I stayed here a few years ago.'

Toby nodded. 'Throckley's a great place, isn't it? I love living here. Did you meet me when I was a baby, Jazz?'

The tension in the large old kitchen intensified, and even Toby felt it, for he began to frown.

'No,' Jazmin put in quickly and gave the boy what she hoped was an encouraging smile. 'I guess I left Throckley before you arrived.'

'I think I'll take a rain check on the tea, Moira,' Kael said easily. 'Finished your milk, Toby?'

The boy obligingly swallowed the last mouthful and nodded.

'Good. We've still got a lot to do in the garden. We'll see you both later.' His dark gaze settled for short moments on Jazmin before he turned to the door.

'See you, Jazz.' Toby gave Jazmin a wave as, biscuit in hand, he followed his father. 'Gee, Dad, what a slave-driver. This is child labour.'

A heavy silence fell between mother and daughter until eventually it was broken by Moira.

'Lorelle did tell me they would be in Canada for Christmas,' she said softly. 'I didn't knowingly give you misinformation.'

'I know you wouldn't, Mother.' Jazmin shrugged, fingers wrapped around her thin china teacup. 'It doesn't matter. I won't be here long, anyway. I'll just satisfy myself that Grandfather's all right and talk to Rick, then I'll be going back home.'

She would ring Mandy and catch a bus up to Noosa to join her friends for Christmas. That's what they had originally wanted her to do. At least Mark would be pleased, she reflected derisively.

'You're going back to Sydney? But Jazmin, you have to stay for Christmas. Your grandfather will expect you to. He was very disappointed when we arrived without you.'

'I'll talk to him, explain why I can't stay.' Jazmin stood up, crossed to rest her hands on the kitchen sink, not seeing the beautifully laid out herb garden, the lawns and decorative gardens that spread out towards the view of the distant mountains through the open window. 'Once I talk to Grandfather he'll understand why I'm going back.'

'I don't think he will,' her mother said ominously.

'I can't see why not,' Jazmin replied restlessly and spun around. 'Good grief, Mother. You of all people must see why I can't stay here, face—' Jazmin stopped and her mother reached out to touch her arm.

'If you still feel like that about him then tell him.'

'Tell him what?' Jazmin asked tiredly. 'That I'm ready to make a fool of myself all over again? That doesn't seem to be the most sensible course of action, now, does it, Mother? And that's not taking into consideration the very real moral issue of his wife and child. Home-breaking was not my intention five years ago, and that hasn't changed.'

'I know, Jazmin.' Moira took another sip of her tea. 'But they don't live together.'

Chapter Four

'YOU mean Kael and Cathy are divorced?' Jazmin sat down again as her mother shrugged.

'I don't know about a divorce, but Kael has custody of Toby. I know that because they both live here. Lorelle mentioned in conversation that Cathy has an apartment over near the Royal Brisbane Hospital.'

'She probably has the apartment for when she works late at the hospital,' Jazmin said, trying to decide how she felt about this piece of information.

'Perhaps you should ask Kael?' her mother suggested, and Jazmin raised her eyebrows.

'Oh, yes. Now that's a question one can easily slip into a flagging conversation. Looks like we'll be having a hot Christmas and tell me, are you and Cathy divorced by any chance?'

'There's no need to be caustic, Jazmin,' Moira McCann stated airily, and Jazmin sighed.

'I know, Mother. I'm sorry. I guess I'm just tired.'

'Maybe I should ask Kael. After what he did to you I think I have a right to protect my own daughter.'

'Don't you worry about it,' Jazmin put in hastily, horrified at the thought of her mother subjecting Kael to one of her famous inquisitions. 'It doesn't make any difference anyway. I won't be here that long and I have no intention of becoming involved with Kael Craigen. Or anyone else, for that matter.'

'But Jazmin, you know I hate to see you alone. Everyone needs a soul mate. Even your father, for all his faults, was a good husband and an even better friend. I miss him and I don't want you to deny yourself the chance to build that kind of marriage.'

'I understand, but I'm just not sure I'm ready for that kind of relationship, or that Kael is the man I want to make such a commitment to. And anyway, I would have thought he'd be the last man you'd champion.' On the rare occasions Kael Craigen's name had been mentioned, it had brought only disparaging comments from her mother.

'I'll admit that Kael wouldn't be the man I would have chosen for you, Jazmin,' her mother conceded a trifle disdainfully. 'But I'd have to admit he's good-looking and charming. And I greatly suspect your grandfather will make him his heir.'

'Mother! That's totally mercenary—' Jazmin began.

'That's as may be, but believe me, if one's life is going to be even slightly miserable it's better to be rich. I've been comfortably well off and I've been poor, Jazmin, and I know which I'd rather be.'

'Oh, Mother.' Jazmin gave a half laugh and rubbed a hand over her eyes. 'Look, let's change the subject. I want to talk to you about Rick. That's why I changed my mind and came up here. Do you know what he plans to do about the money?'

Her mother's expression became defensive. 'He's visiting friends at the moment. You know he went to school here, and he's looking up a couple of mates he's kept in touch with.'

'But what about the money?' Jazmin persisted.

'He said he's still hoping to sell his land, even if he has to take a small loss.'

'I just don't want him bothering Grandfather. I'll get the money somehow, as I told you last week. There never was any need to involve anyone else.'

Before her mother could comment, the sound of a car's tyres crunching on the gravel drive behind the house had them both crossing to the window. A silver Mercedes pulled up to the back steps.

'That's Lorelle and your grandfather home. Oh, Jazmin, he'll be so thrilled to see you. You'll be pleased you came, after all.'

With a sigh Jazmin rinsed out her cup and saucer and followed her mother out onto the veranda. As usual her mother had changed the subject from Rick's shortcomings. She wasn't going to put Rick under any parental pressure, which meant, on top of everything, Jazmin must confront her brother herself.

Although she was prepared for some change in her grandfather, her first sight of him shocked her immensely and put all thoughts of Rick out of her mind. To say James McCann had failed considerably in the last five years would be an understatement. His once six-foot frame seemed to have shrunk, and his face was thin and drawn.

Lorelle gave him her arm and he slowly mounted the few steps. When he reached the top his breathing was obviously laboured.

'Grandfather?' Jazmin said softly, stepping forward after giving him a moment to gather himself together.

The old man looked up and his pale face broke into a genuine smile, his faded blue eyes lighting. 'Jazmin! What a wonderful surprise. Your mother said you may not be able to make it. I'm so glad you could. Come give your old grandfather a hug.'

Jazmin grinned and slid her arms around him, her heart contracting as she felt his wasted body. However, his bear hug was surprisingly firm.

She drew back and smiled at him. 'You look—'

James McCann held up his hand. 'The truth, now,' he ordered with mock seriousness. 'Don't sweet talk me.'

Jazmin struck a pose. 'Have you been dieting?' she asked, and her grandfather roared with laughter.

'I hear they're going to make me Weight Watcher of the Year. What do you think, Lorelle?' He turned to his wife, who gave Jazmin a weak smile, her eyes sliding a little defensively away.

'How are you, Jazmin?'

The five years had taken their toll on Kael's mother, too, Jazmin could see. She had aged considerably, as well, and the lines of anxiety were etched beneath her carefully applied make-up.

'Why don't you two go on into the living-room while I put the car away,' she said evenly. 'And perhaps Moira could make you some tea.'

To Jazmin's amazement her mother hurried off without hesitation, saying she'd freshen the teapot. As Jazmin unobtrusively gave her grandfather her arm and walked with him the short distance to the informal lounge, she reflected that perhaps her mother and Lorelle had put their differences behind them.

The soft sofas and chairs formed an intimate circle in the small living-room, which looked out over the back gardens to the hills. James sank thankfully into one chair and Jazmin took the one opposite him.

'I missed you, Jazmin,' he said and she nodded.

'I missed you, too, but—'

'I want to talk to you. While we're on our own,' he said quickly, and Jazmin sat back with a sinking feeling she wasn't going to care for the topic of the conversation.

'Don't tire yourself, Grandfather,' she began, and he waved her protestations aside irascibly.

'Now don't you start pampering me, Jazmin. I know my limitations. And before we start, I know why you left Throckley and why you didn't come back.' James McCann let his white head rest against the chair, and when Jazmin would have interrupted he waved her into silence.

'But first I want to talk about your father and Kael.' He sighed. 'I couldn't think more of Kael if he was my own son. Not that I didn't love your father, but Kael's different. We have more in common than your father and I had. And I don't mean to take anything away from your father by saying that, love.'

'I know,' Jazmin told him. Richard, her father, had had a more artistic temperament and had had no interest in the construction and real estate business that had been his father's life.

'And I love you, too,' her grandfather went on, 'so the whole thing put me in an ambivalent position. Kael on one side and my favourite granddaughter on the other.'

'I didn't mean to upset you,' Jazmin said softly.

'And I can't have things the way I want them just by wanting them that way. Life's taught me that,' he finished regretfully. 'But that doesn't mean I wasn't extremely upset when you and Kael broke up. I'm a romantic old fool. I desperately wanted to see you two together. It was one of the biggest disappointments of my life.'

'Grandfather, I really don't want to talk about that.' Jazmin pushed herself to her feet.

'Sit down. Sit down.' James McCann waved a thin, claw-like hand, and Jazmin sank back into the chair. 'You should be humouring me, you know. I'm a sick old man.'

Jazmin gave a reluctant smile. 'Isn't that hitting a little below the belt?'

Her grandfather shrugged. 'I guess I'll stoop to doing whatever it takes. That's one of the advantages of being in my dotage. You see, I want to tell you, love, just what Kael Craigen has done for me because I didn't get to do that when you left so hurriedly five years ago.'

'Grandfather,' Jazmin appealed.

But the old man belligerently continued as though she hadn't spoken. 'Just let me have my say and we'll be finished with it. When I married Kael's mother he was about twenty years old. He applied for a job I advertised and he told me up front he was studying and wanted the work to pay his way through his university course. Most people would have thought I was taking a chance, that it would be a waste of time. I'd teach him the job and then he'd leave when he was finished his studies. I didn't see it that way. I could see he had potential even then. He worked well from the moment he started and he's more than fulfilled my expectations.

'Later I found out his parents had divorced when he was a youngster and as his father had married again young Kael considered Lorelle, his mother, to be his responsibility. When he brought her along to the office Christmas party, well . . .'

James McCann smiled as his thoughts drifted back, and in that moment Jazmin knew that despite what her mother said, her grandfather cared deeply for his so much younger wife.

'From the moment I met Lorelle,' her grandfather said, smiling, 'my world changed dramatically. She put meaning back into my life. I loved your grandmother, Jazmin, never doubt that, and I've never forgotten her. But I'd been a widower for nearly ten years and I was lonely. I didn't realise just how lonely I'd been until Lorelle walked into my life.'

James McCann sighed tiredly. 'I'm telling you all this, Jazmin, because I want you to know that last year I made Kael a full partner in the business. It was the least I could do. He worked hard and he deserved the partnership. If it hadn't been for him the business would have floundered when I had my heart attack.'

Jazmin sat forward in her chair. 'There's no need to worry about that, Grandfather. I understand completely and it makes no difference to me, to us. I know Dad had no interest in what you were achieving.'

James eyed her steadily and nodded. 'I'm glad. I thought your mother might be a little, well, might think I was being disloyal to Richard's memory. And from what I've seen, young Rick needs to do a lot of growing up before he settles down. But if he wants to become involved in McCann and Craigen the opportunity's there for him.'

Jazmin's eyes fell to her hands. If her grandfather only knew just how irresponsible Rick had been, he may not feel quite so charitable towards his only grandson.

'It's there for you, too, Jazmin, any time you want to be part of it.'

Jazmin looked up, met her grandfather's steady gaze, and wondered just exactly what, or who, he was offering her. But she had no opportunity to ask him to elaborate, for at that moment her mother bustled into the lounge with the tray, and Jazmin rose to take it from her.

It took time and small talk to get the cups filled and distributed, and by the time Lorelle had joined them and they'd finished their tea James was looking visibly tired. Lorelle immediately quashed what was obviously his customary objection and bore him away for a rest.

'I might have a lie down, too,' Jazmin said after she'd helped her mother stow the used crockery in the dishwasher. 'We drove straight through from Sydney and I think the long journey's caught up with me.'

She returned to her room and finished unpacking what was left in her backpack. Removing her joggers, she lay down on the bed, letting her tensed muscles relax.

The canopy-like mosquito net was draped above her, and she drew some comfort from the warm tones of the familiar room. The muted pale lemon flowers on the wallpaper. The off-white ceiling with its elaborately decorated cornices and ceiling rose. The heavy red cedar furniture. And the large brass bed with its porcelain insets featuring the same sprays of lemon flowers. She could have stepped into another world, one of days long gone by, if her imagination had co-operated.

Yet the present held her with a cruel lack of compromise. The burning question crept unyieldingly into her weary mind. Why had she returned? Why had she journeyed back in this season of good cheer to the source of her pain? And she knew she was loath to answer the question truthfully. With a misguided sense of self-preservation she desperately tried to reassure herself.

She'd come back to prevent Rick from upsetting their grandfather with demands for money. And she'd wanted to see her seriously ill grandfather. That was why she'd returned.

And to see Kael Craigen again and to prove to herself that she was over him.

Jazmin squeezed her eyes tightly closed in an effort to shut out his image. But she was fighting a losing battle. His strong, arresting face took shape in her mind's eye—she seemed powerless to prevent it—and the same sharp pain caught her in her chest.

He was just as attractive to her and she was just as attracted to him as she'd ever been, she acknowledged, so the reasons for her return to Brisbane were incidental now. She was here and so was Kael and the spark still flickered strongly within her. And she rather suspected that still smouldering ember burned for Kael, as well.

Something leapt deep within her at the thought and she knew her responses were far from cerebral. They were purely physical and they hadn't caught her quite so urgently for five long years.

Once again she saw Kael standing on the veranda those few short hours ago, and in those first seconds, she conceded, the earth had seemed to shift on its axis. The way it always had when she had come upon him unexpectedly. The sky above had seemed that much bluer, the grass and trees were greener. In fact, it was as though everything had slotted into a sharper focus.

The power of his attraction frightened her now just as it had terrified her the very first time she met him. The first time she met him. Jazmin's thoughts pulled her relentlessly into the past.

When James McCann had married Lorelle Craigen, Jazmin's family hadn't attended the wedding. It had been a quiet, private ceremony, and Moira McCann had commented ominously on its suddenness, much to Jazmin's amusement.

And when Jazmin had occasionally flown up to Brisbane to spend some of her school vacations at Throckley with her grandfather and his new wife, Kael

Craigen had been away on business or visiting his father in north Queensland. So fate had not decreed they meet until five years earlier, just after Jazmin's nineteenth birthday.

Since their father's death, Jazmin's mother had had a worrying time with Rick. His childish pranks had seemed to escalate when he reached high school, until he had been expelled for the second time. It was then that Moira had appealed to her father-in-law, and James McCann had arranged for Rick to be enrolled at a private school in Brisbane. Moira and Rick had left immediately while Jazmin stayed in Sydney to complete the business course she had just started.

She'd joined the family at Throckley six months later, ostensibly for a short holiday before she found a job in Sydney. Her arrival had been much the same as it had been today, except that five years ago she'd flown to Brisbane and taken a taxi out to the house.

She'd hurried up the steps onto the veranda and pressed the doorbell, intent on surprising her mother and brother, but to her dismay, no one had been home. Disappointed, she walked around the back of the house to find Joe Roberts, the gardener, working on the lawns by the garage.

He had informed her that everyone was out, Kael and her grandfather at work, Lorelle visiting friends, and her mother and brother at a school sports meet. Joe had a key for emergencies and he used it to let her into the house.

Jazmin strolled around the many rooms, reacquainting herself with Throckley's beauty, and then, on impulse, she decided to go for a swim. The weather was hot and sultry, so she donned her bikini and collected a fluffy bath sheet from the linen cupboard.

With a smile of anticipation she went down the slate path to the pool which was a focal point in a setting that had been landscaped to form a natural bush habitat. The irregular shaped pool was surrounded by rocks and cascading natural plants and it was kept private from the house by a group of tall gum trees.

The entire area was surrounded by a safety fence, and Jazmin went through the gate and continued down the slate steps to the pool. Sinking beneath the cooling salt water, she allowed herself to float until the tensions and weariness of her trip from Sydney had been soothed away. Then she did a few invigorating laps in an easy crawl.

Eventually she climbed out and began to towel herself dry. As she patted her arms with the bath sheet a tiny shiver of apprehension ran like a rivulet down her spine and she glanced up in consternation. Someone was leaning on the pool gate, someone tall enough to put his arms on the top and rest a square jaw on his hands.

Jazmin swallowed. Who was he? He must be an intruder, and she was here alone. Joe Roberts was nearby but he was partially deaf so there was no way he would heed any call for help she made. But a stranger wouldn't know that. Or know she was alone here.

Trying for an outward calmness she didn't feel inside, Jazmin wrapped the towel around her like a sarong and walked boldly up the steps. The man opened the gate for her and stood back for her to step through.

'May I help you?' she asked levelly with what she hoped was a discouraging aplomb.

The man's lips quirked, and for some reason Jazmin's heartbeats surged into an impossibly faster rhythm. And her anxiety changed timbre, took on a totally different comportment. This man, this intruder or salesman or whatever, was incredibly attractive, she acknowledged, and she swallowed again as she gazed up at him.

'Look, if you're selling anything then I'm afraid I should warn you from the outset that you're wasting your time. I'm not interested.'

The corners of the man's mouth swept upward into a grin, and Jazmin felt as though she'd been struck in the solar plexus. All the breath seemed to have left her lungs and wasn't being replaced.

'Selling anything?' His voice more than matched the rest of him, deep and sensually seductive. 'I'd like to say only myself, but I sense you'd thoroughly wound my fragile ego.' He shoved his hands into the pockets of his pants. 'Actually, I was looking for my mother. I'm Kael Craigen and I'd say you would have to be the elusive Jazmin McCann.'

Chapter Five

'AM I right? Are you Jazmin?' he asked into the lengthening silence, and Jazmin could only nod. 'So, we meet at last,' he added, his voice exuding a low sensuality that seemed to flow between them, to reach out and touch her, spinning a web of wistful longing around her.

Kael Craigen. So this was Lorelle's son, the one her mother had so bitingly referred to as her grandfather's protégé.

He was, Jazmin could only think again, so incredibly attractive. Not in a conventional way. It was more an air of confidence, the way he held himself, as though he had conquered the world and knew he had done so.

His physical attributes only supplemented his bearing. His hair was dark and thick, springing back from his forehead with a careless order that a woman would have laboured to achieve, and at the sides it swept over the tops of his ears, a little longer at the back than fashion dictated.

And his eyes were bright and brown, and fringed by straight dark lashes. Later Jazmin discovered his brown eyes could glow blackly like thick dark chocolate when he was aroused.

His jaw was strong and square and when he smiled, as he was now, two deep creases bracketed his mouth and his white teeth flashed against his tanned skin.

In those initial moments Jazmin had an almost overwhelming urge to flee from him, for he was the most compelling, dangerous man she had ever met. And yet she knew she was incapable of escape, for her fascination overcame her anxious reticence with consummate ease.

From that very first meeting Jazmin's life seemed to sway like a pendulum between ecstasy and disbelief. The ecstasy of being with Kael and the disbelief that someone as handsome, as striking as he was could be even slightly interested in someone as ordinary as she was.

Jazmin couldn't delude herself. She knew she was only of average height, of average build, with a no more than unassumingly pleasant face.

As she saw it, her mop of unruly loose red curls didn't help in the scheme of things at all. Her skin was pale, and she had to take especially particular precautions when she ventured out into the sun as she was very suspectible to sunburn. Her eyes were blue and she had a dusting of freckles across the bridge of her small nose. In other words, she was nothing to write home about.

However, unaware as she was of the clear honesty in those same blue eyes and the strength in the determined jut of her pointed chin, the sum of the above had seemed to appeal to Kael Craigen, and Jazmin was enchanted. And almost from that very first moment she had fallen hopelessly in love.

They spent every spare moment together although it was Kael who kept their relationship on a strictly friendly foundation. When she was alone Jazmin daydreamed about that relationship deepening and she sometimes thought she would die if he didn't kiss her.

She began to wonder if perhaps he didn't care for her as much as she did him, and her heart ached. And then, one evening, they went to the drive-in and the summer weather produced a sudden downpour.

'It's so hot and muggy,' Jazmin cried as they walked up onto the veranda, having left in the middle of the movie. 'It doesn't seem as though the rain has cooled the air down, does it?' She grimaced in the bright glow from the security lights that stayed on for most of the night. 'Yuck, I feel so damp and sticky. Let's go for a swim.'

'It's going to rain again any minute,' Kael remarked as he turned the key in the door and swung it open. A puff of warm air came out of the closed-up house. The rest of the family were out for the evening and not expected home until late.

'It won't matter if it rains,' Jazmin told him. 'We'll already be wet if we're in the pool. Oh,' Jazmin groaned as she lifted her damp hair with her fingers, 'I can almost imagine how cool that water's going to be.'

'Jazz, I don't think this is such a good idea.' Kael leant against the door jamb.

'Aren't you hot, Kael?'

'Yes, I'm hot. And not just from the weather,' he added lowly, and Jazmin flushed.

Perhaps Kael was right. They would be alone in the water. Just as they would be alone in the deserted house, she reminded herself. As they had been alone in the cocoon of the car in the rain at the drive-in, their hot breath and the sparking tension between them fogging up the windows. Maybe they should have gone into the city, found a well-lit, well-patronised disco.

'Okay.' Kael sighed and straightened. 'Let's go swimming. I can't be wetter anyway. The humidity must be one hundred percent.'

'Great.' Jazmin laughed and they both hurried inside to don their swimsuits.

When Jazmin returned, wearing her bikini beneath her cotton beach robe, Kael was waiting for her. Backlit by the lights, his well muscled body seemed to be etched from the surrounding darkness, and Jazmin swallowed as her mouth went dry. She made herself move towards him, the now familiar burning stab of wanting growing in the pit of her stomach.

Without a word she followed him down the steps and along the pathway. He'd switched on the low cosmetic lights so the pool was lit only by the hidden lighting.

'It looks wonderful,' Jazmin said with feeling and tried the temperature of the water with her toe. 'It's barely cool,' she said as she slipped out of her robe, sat down on the side and slipped into the water. 'Come on in, Kael, the water's like smooth velvet.'

Dropping his towel beside her robe, Kael moved around the side, poised there for a moment before diving into the water. He surfaced in the centre of the pool and shook the water from his hair.

'Exhibitionist,' Jazmin teased him and he chuckled.

'I expected it was going to be cooler than it is so I thought I'd get in quickly and not prolong the agony.'

Jazmin swam lazily over to him. 'Now wasn't this a great idea? It feels wonderful. Much better than sitting watching a movie we weren't enjoying.'

Kael laughed. 'Much better.'

They moved over to the shallower end where they could touch the bottom and Jazmin put her hand on his arm, thrusting aside the urge to run her fingers over its smooth wetness.

'You didn't want to stay and watch the movie between showers, did you?' she asked, and he shook his head.

'No. Too violent for me, too. I'm sorry I chose that one. I didn't realise it would be so gory. That type of movie doesn't appeal to me and I'd hate to get so blasé that I'd just sit through it unmoved, as though all that gung-ho stuff was the norm.'

They discussed various movies for a while and then swam a few laps before Jazmin stopped and turned to watch Kael cutting through the water with an economic stroke. The moon was hidden behind the heavy rain clouds, and the subdued lighting barely lit his wet shoulders as his arms left the water, but Jazmin could easily imagine the play of strong muscles in his back.

He had the most perfect body, she conceded. It made her want to reach out and touch him, slide her fingertips over every smooth contour. She ran a hand through her wet hair, feeling a totally different heat begin to wash over her, and she turned away, gripping the edge of the pool with both hands.

She had to stop her train of sybaritic thoughts right there, she told herself. The situation was volatile enough as it was. The small space they'd studiously kept between them all evening was fraught with awareness and fragile at best. If Kael suspected how aroused she was just watching him—

His large hands slid around her waist and his breath cooled the damp skin behind her ear.

'What's this? Chickening out? We've only done a couple of laps.'

'I was—' Jazmin gulped '—just resting for a moment.' Her slight breathlessness, she hoped, would add credence to her words. But her traitorous muscles refused to take direction from her mind. She couldn't seem to push herself away from the edge of the pool. Or away from Kael.

The feel of his hands on her bare skin overrode all of her good intentions. There was a growing buzzing in her ears and her face felt like it was on fire. And the flames were spreading downwards.

Kael didn't seem to be in any hurry to break the contact, and Jazmin swallowed again. She knew she should take the initiative herself. If she made a move she knew he would let her go. But her whole motor system seemed to have short-circuited. There was a breakdown somewhere between her cognisance of the growing tension and her ability to defuse its mushrooming crescendo. She was overcome by a wild desire to dive recklessly into the unknown.

The air around them suddenly stilled and the low rain clouds seemed to droop heavily from the sky. Not that either of them noticed.

Jazmin's entire body was focused on Kael, on the slight pressure of his hands as he turned her towards him. His eyes were dark pools in his face, pinpointed by the sparkle of reflected light as he turned his head to gaze down at her. And she felt his gaze as a physical touch, settling softly on her lips like the brush of the softest silk.

His hold tightened on her waist and then he lowered his head, slowly, taking a second, a decade, until their lips touched, broke away, gently teased again.

Jazmin moaned lowly, a blatantly sensual sound, and her hands clutched at his strong shoulders as her knees seemed to give way beneath her.

'God, Jazz, I knew this would happen,' he breathed rawly against her cheek.

'Don't... Didn't you want to kiss me?' Jazmin asked huskily, and Kael said something unintelligible under his breath.

'Didn't I want to kiss you?' he repeated derisively and gave a humourless laugh. 'I've been wanting to kiss you from the first moment I set eyes on you. Maybe before.'

'Before?' Jazmin's fingers were playing with the wet strands of hair at his nape.

'I like the photograph of you that James has in his study,' he said levelly, and she smiled.

'You do?'

'I do. Very much.' His white teeth flashed in a quick smile and then he just as suddenly sobered. 'And if I don't kiss you again I think I'll go stark raving mad.'

His lips claimed hers again, this time staking a primeval claim, and Jazmin answered his passion with her own. They clung together, bodies fused as one. Kael's hands slid around her, enveloping her, holding her as though he never intended to let her go.

His hands moved, found the slight depression of her spine, fingertips teasing, tantalising each nerve ending. She'd never suspected a man could awaken her body so completely, so intensely, arousing feelings way beyond her wildest dreams.

His hands deftly dealt with the clasp of her bikini top and he drew back to slide the strip of material from her shoulders, exposing her bare breasts to the humid air.

Kael caught his breath, his hands gently cupping the fullness in his palms. 'You're so beautiful,' he said gruffly, his thumbs moving to tease her already aching nipples.

Jazmin moaned as a fission of incredible desire exploded deep inside her, radiating to the very tips of her toes. She felt her head fall back, and Kael took advantage of the movement to rain warm kisses on her firm chin, moving downwards along the exposed line of her throat, nibbling delightfully across her collarbone as his fingers still caressed her swelled breasts. When his lips found one taut peak Jazmin cried out his name, her arms gathering him impossibly closer.

'Oh, Jazz,' he breathed thickly, 'you feel, you taste so good.'

His tongue tip ran riot, teasing her until she thought she'd burst, and when he would have drawn back she clutched him to her again.

'No.' The word broke from her, rasping out through her parched lips. 'No,' she repeated in that same aroused voice she barely recognised as her own. 'Please, Kael. Don't stop.'

'I have to, Jazz,' he said hoarsely. 'Otherwise I won't be able to.'

'I don't want you to,' Jazmin whispered, part of her totally amazed at her audacity.

Their eyes met, held, as immeasurable seconds passed. Kael drew a sharp breath, and as he began to lower his head once more the heavens opened and huge raindrops merged into a deluge.

Kael lifted his head, and Jazmin longed to draw him back. She felt as though she had been set adrift in a murky sea.

'Come on. Let's get out of the rain,' he shouted over the pounding of the raindrops on the surface of the pool. Taking her hand, he pulled her across to the steps and helped her out of the water. They hurried up the path, the rain stinging their bare skin.

When they reached the veranda Kael wiped some of the water from his body with his hands and then disappeared inside, returning with dry towels. Draping one over his shoulder, he wrapped the other one around Jazmin, and she was glad of the warmth. For some reason her teeth were chattering, and she made a big job of drying herself in case Kael saw just how shocked she now was by her response to his kisses.

And her body still tingled, was alert to each nuance of his body. She watched him surreptitiously as he ran the towel economically over his large frame. The rasp of the towel over his skin echoed in her ears, drowning out the steady drumming of the rain on the corrugated iron veranda roof above their heads. And the abrasion of her own towel on her bare breasts only served to remind her of Kael's touch.

'Better get into some dry clothes.' Kael's voice drew Jazmin out of her erotic thoughts, and when she made no move he gently took her hand and led her inside, along the hallway, stopping at the door to her room.

He raised her cool hand to his lips and then, not meeting her gaze, he walked the few paces past her to his own room which was diagonally opposite hers. Was he sorry he'd kissed her?

'Kael?' Her whispered word made him turn and she saw the electrifying answer in his burning dark eyes. The passion she saw reflected there made her tremble anew, and the towel she had draped around her slipped, exposing her breast.

His eyes settled on her, and she felt his tension. With a sob she ran towards him and he met her halfway.

Kael swept her into his arms and carried her into his bedroom. He shoved the door closed with his shoulder and slowly expelled the breath he'd been holding, and it deliciously fanned Jazmin's damp, inflamed skin.

Holding her gaze, he slowly let her slide to the floor, the whispery sound of the slither of their skin echoing in her ears. He lowered his head and kissed her, and Jazmin clung to him. His lips slid downwards to her breasts, taking one taut peak in his mouth. His fingers found the elastic top of her bikini pants and moved them down over her hips. Then he sank to his knees, his lips nibbling a pathway downwards, from the curve under her breasts, across her midriff, her waist, his tongue tip teasing her navel.

'Oh, Jazz,' he moaned. 'I want you so much. I know we shouldn't but—'

'Why shouldn't we?' she asked huskily through dry lips.

'We shouldn't because I'm too old for you,' he said without a shred of conviction. 'And my life's already too—' He stopped, and she heard him whisper her name. Then he was lifting her onto the bed, stretching out the smooth hard length of his naked body beside her.

They clung to each other, kissing deeply, tongues exploring, fingers stroking until Jazmin moaned softly, her body aflame.

'Please, Kael,' she whispered, her voice thick with passion.

'We need—' he gulped a steadying breath '—we need to take precautions.'

The air rushed between them, cooling Jazmin's burning skin, as he rolled away to open the drawer by his bed.

'I've never... I don't know how,' she said, her face flushing.

'Luckily I do,' he said with a quick grin, and he showed her, kissing her again as his fingers renewed their erotic exploration.

Jazmin cried out his name and he lowered his hard body over her and into her, filling her, and they began moving together, matching each other's rhythm, slowly at first, and then faster, until they both cried out and collapsed into each others' arms.

Gradually Jazmin floated deliriously back down to earth, became aware of her surroundings. She knew they were in Kael's room, in his bed, and that the rain still beat a steady tattoo on the roof. And she knew her life would never be quite the same again.

'I love you, Kael,' she breathed against the curve of his neck, and he pulled the sheet up over their still entwined bodies.

'I love you, too, Jazz,' she heard him say thickly as they both drifted over into sleep.

Chapter Six

A TAPPING on the bedroom door had Jazmin springing guiltily upright. She closed her eyes as her head swam and she agitatedly put out a hand to the bed beside her, sinking back thankfully when she felt only the bedclothes.

She had been sleeping, and her dream, her reminiscence, had been so real she had expected to feel Kael's naked body right there beside her. But of course she was alone, and it was five long years later.

And Kael was still married, she admonished herself brutally.

'Jazz.' A young voice broke in on her masochistic preoccupations. 'Jazz, are you awake?'

Jazmin sat up again and swung her feet to the floor. She crossed to open the door. 'Yes. I'm awake.'

Toby grinned up at her with Kael's smile, and something twisted painfully inside her. She wanted to clutch him to her and slam the door at one and the same time.

The boy's smile faded at the expression on her face. 'Are you okay?' he asked uncertainly. 'Aunt Moira said to tell you dinner was ready.'

Jazmin drew herself together and pasted on her best smile. 'I'm fine. I guess I'm still a little sleepy, that's all.'

'Oh.' Toby relaxed, making Jazmin feel even worse. 'Are you going to come for dinner?'

Jazmin nodded. 'Yes, of course. Just let me have a quick wash to wake myself up.'

Grabbing a clean shirt, she went into the *en suite* and splashed cool water onto her flushed face. She pulled off her oversized T-shirt and replaced it with the clean short-sleeved chambray shirt, tucking it into the waistband of her tailored denim shorts. With a grimace at her reflection, she drew a brush through her tousled red curls, forcing them into some semblance of order, before hurriedly slipping her joggers on and joining Toby, who had waited for her in the hallway.

'Guess what, Jazz?' Toby said excitedly as they walked towards the dining-room together. 'Dad and I bought a Christmas tree this arvo, a real live one that we can plant in the garden after Christmas, and tonight we're going to decorate it with lights and everything. Gran found the decorations and stuff and she said we could do it after dinner. Want to help?'

'Oh, well. I don't know that—' Jazmin began.

'Oh, come on, Jazz. It'll be fun,' Toby entreated.

'What will?' his father asked as they walked into the dining-room.

Four pairs of eyes regarded them. James McCann sat at the head of the huge polished wooden table which would comfortably have seated over a dozen people. His wife and stepson were on his right and his daughter-in-law on his left. Toby would be sitting next to his father, Jazmin surmised, which meant she would have the place set beside her mother. Directly opposite Kael.

'I was telling Jazz how much fun it's going to be decorating the tree.' Toby clutched Jazmin's hand. 'You are going to help, aren't you, Jazz?'

'Well, I think we all should,' Jazmin's mother surprised her by stating. 'Between the lot of us we should be able to do a tiptop job.'

Toby laughed delightedly and ran around to slide into his seat. 'You'll see, Jazz. It will be fantastic.'

Jazmin sat down, her eyes meeting Kael's across the table, and she despaired of so much as swallowing a morsel of her meal.

However, she managed to draw herself together enough to make an adequate contribution to the conversation. As her grandfather quizzed her about her job in Sydney she was uncomfortably aware of Kael's absorbed attention.

'Jazmin's underrating herself,' her mother put in proudly. 'She's done so well in such a short time. She's personal secretary to one of the senior partners. In fact, Mr. Dalton speaks very highly of her.'

Jazmin felt like a child praised by an overzealous mother. As her grandfather expressed his delight, Jazmin's gaze met Kael's again. He silently raised his glass of wine to his lips, pausing to acknowledge her before taking a sip.

And she couldn't seem to drag her eyes from the sight of his strong fingers clasping the delicate wine glass. Her mind's eye threw forward stills from her dream and she grew hot remembering the feel of those same fingers caressing her body, setting her aflame.

How she actually made it through that meal she couldn't have told, and it was with great relief that she could push back her chair and help her mother and Lorelle clear the dishes from the table.

They decided to put the tree in the smaller sitting-room, where Jazmin and her grandfather had talked that morning. Kael slid one chair to the side and the tree fitted neatly into the corner.

As they helped Toby add the decorations to the tree Jazmin could almost relax, and she was genuinely sorry

when the tree couldn't hold another coloured bauble.
Toby took such delight in the whole operation the adults
couldn't help but enjoy it, too.

Now, Jazmin sat back on the floor wrapping her arms
around her updrawn legs and gazed at the blinking
coloured lights on the six-foot-tall Christmas tree. Her
mother had just gone to bed, and Lorelle and her grandfather had left them a half hour ago.

'Doesn't it look excellent, Jazz?' Toby asked in awe as
he sat down beside her and ingenuously leant against her
shoulder. Jazmin could see that he was fighting tired-
ness.

'I don't think I've seen a more handsomely decorated
tree,' she acknowledged easily. 'We've done a great job,
and there's no way Santa Claus will miss this one.'

'No way, Jazz.' Toby laughed. 'But I'll remind him
when Gran takes me to see him tomorrow. And I'll be
sure to tell him you'll be here, too, instead of in Sydney.
Unless you've already told him,' he added with a frown.
'Have you?'

Kael had finished storing the empty decoration boxes
in the hall cupboard and he joined them, sitting down
cross-legged beside his son. Jazmin's eyes met his and his
expression tightened. She'd have to tell Toby she was returning home. If she was.

'No. No, I haven't told Santa where I'll be,' she pre-
varicated and Toby wrinkled his nose.

'Bet he'll know where you are anyway. Santa seems to
just know these things. Like he'll know Cathy's in
Canada, too. Don't you reckon, Jazz?'

She swallowed, not looking at his father. 'I'm sure he
will.'

'Do you know it was snowing when we were in
Canada,' Toby continued, 'and Dad and I built a snow-

man.' He grinned at his father. 'Well, we sort of built it. It kind of melted down before we could finish it. But it was fun, wasn't it, Dad?'

Kael smiled and ruffled Toby's dark hair. 'Fun but freezing.'

Toby giggled. 'Especially when snow went down your neck.' He shivered expressively. 'Have you seen snow, Jazz?'

She shook her head. 'It must have been very pretty,' she remarked carefully, desperately trying to keep at bay the mental picture of Toby and his parents playing in the snow. The pain in her chest indicated that she wasn't being all that successful.

'It was like some of the pictures you see on Christmas cards and in books,' Toby told her. 'White on the trees and on the roofs. But it was strange, too. I don't think of snow at Christmas. I think about swimming in the pool because it's so hot and ice-cream and stuff.' He gazed up at Jazmin. 'I guess that must seem weird to people who live in cold countries.'

'I think of fruit salad and ice-cream.' Jazmin smiled. 'But plum pudding and brandy sauce, too.'

Toby chattered on about favourite Christmas food, chocolate crackles and white Christmas, lollies and ice-cold watermelon. He didn't seem to notice that Jazmin and his father added little to the conversation, until suddenly he stopped mid sentence and leant more heavily on Jazmin's shoulder. She glanced down at him to see that his sleepiness had got the better of him and he'd dozed off.

Kael grimaced. 'His batteries have finally run down,' he said softly and pushed himself up from the floor. 'I'll get him to bed.' He slipped his arms under his sleeping son and lifted him away from Jazmin.

And suddenly in the muggy summer heat she felt cool, missed the warmth of Toby's body. 'I should be getting to bed, as well,' she said quickly and went to get up, but Kael stopped and turned.

'No, don't go. Wait for me, Jazz. I want to talk to you.' Jazmin hesitated, her gaze holding his.

'Please. I won't keep you long,' he added and waited until Jazmin reluctantly nodded.

'I want to stay with Jazz and the tree.' Toby stirred in his father's arms and murmured sleepily.

'I know how you feel,' Kael said so softly Jazmin barely heard it but his words sent her blood pounding recklessly through her veins.

She knew what she should do. She should go now, leave, not let him close to her. Especially when they were alone. It was madness and would only expedite a volatile situation. Yet that wanton part of her, the completely sensual section that belonged to Kael and Kael alone, took forceful control and vehemently insisted that she stay. No matter that all logic and astuteness advised otherwise.

God help her, she wanted to hear what he had to say.

Jazmin sank onto the comfortable couch and gazed at the Christmas tree, not seeing its brightly flashing lights, the coloured tinsel and baubles, the tiny gaily wrapped presents and candy canes. Hot tears burned behind her eyes but she refused to allow them to fall. They caught painfully in her throat and she swallowed convulsively.

Their five years' separation might not have been. No wonder she had been so reluctant to journey up here. Her subconscious had known all along what she now recognised. She was still as attuned to him as she'd ever been.

As she'd watched him lift Toby high so the boy could fix the angel onto the top of the tree she'd felt a stabbing pain in her chest. The knot of ice that had enclosed her heart had cracked and begun to thaw. Now she wanted to weep for all Kael had meant to her and for how much it had hurt when she'd discovered the existence of Cathy and baby Toby.

For all that might have been, she told herself angrily. Past tense. And it still was past. She brushed at her flushed cheeks as a teardrop overflowed. Would she never be able to escape the past?

After the night they'd made love, the first of many, they'd been inseparable. When Kael was at work or at classes Jazmin had swum long lonely lengths of the pool or simply sat thinking about him. At that time her whole life had seemed so incredibly simple. She loved Kael and he loved her. Beginning, middle, and end.

How gullibly mistaken she'd been. The excruciating end had come with the escalating antagonism between her mother and Lorelle.

Lorelle had never been taken in by Jazmin's young brother, Rick. His boyish charm had failed to cut any wash with Kael's mother. And whenever Rick was home he seemed to disrupt the household. Jazmin was so used to Rick's behaviour she hadn't noticed Lorelle's growing displeasure. She'd been far too rapt in Kael to notice anything.

So when Lorelle suggested that Moira, Jazmin and Rick move out of the main house and into the gate-keeper's cottage, Moira McCann had taken great umbrage. Lorelle, according to Jazmin's mother, was simply trying to put a wedge between James and his family. She was trying to get rid of them.

Jazmin had just changed into shorts and T-shirt after her morning swim when she'd walked into the kitchen and into the middle of the argument.

'Lorelle? Mother? What's the matter?'

Both women turned to her.

'Lorelle's far too critical of Ricky. The boy's only trying to get attention because he misses his father,' cried her mother.

'Oh, for heaven's sake,' Lorelle exploded. 'Rick's sixteen years old. He's not a baby. You already give him far too much attention, at the expense of your daughter. Perhaps you should be more aware of what's going on with Jazmin.'

Moira's mouth fell open in surprise and she turned to glance at Jazmin, who knew her face had started to redden.

Did Lorelle know about her nighttime visits to Kael's room? She couldn't. They'd been so careful. Jazmin burned with mortification.

'What do you mean by that, Lorelle?' Moira asked furiously, and Lorelle turned away.

She took a deep steadying breath and, in control once more, she turned to face Jazmin's mother. 'Look, I'm sorry. I'm upset. James has been pushing himself so hard at work I'm worried about him, and Kael, well, I worry about him, too.' She glanced at the now white-faced Jazmin. 'And I'm worried about you, too, Jazmin,' she added, her voice a little softer now. 'You and Kael, you spend too much time together and he, well, he has his exams coming up.'

'Are you suggesting—' Moira McCann began but Jazmin put a silencing hand on her mother's arm.

Her eyes were locked on Lorelle's and what she saw reflected there frightened her. There was more to this than Kael's pending examinations.

'What's this really about, Lorelle?' she asked quietly. 'It's not just Kael's exams, is it?'

'I think we'd best leave it. Kael wouldn't like me to discuss, well, anything.' She stopped and her fingers fiddled nervously with the collar of her blouse.

'I love Kael,' Jazmin said levelly. 'And I think he loves me, too.'

Her mother turned to her with an astonished frown. 'In love with him? But you barely know each other.'

'Oh, Jazmin.' Lorelle sat down tiredly and sighed. 'Perhaps it's not my place to interfere.'

'Whatever it is, you might as well finish it now,' Jazmin said with a confidence that was soon to be dashed away.

'Maybe you should talk to Kael,' Lorelle said uncomfortably.

'Talk to him about what?' Moira asked but neither Lorelle nor Jazmin indicated they had so much as heard her question.

The room swelled with a heavy, disconcerting silence until Lorelle sat back, a decision made. 'I'm sorry, Jazmin. Kael's already involved with someone else.'

'No.' Jazmin shook her head. 'That's not true.' Even as she said the words a feeling of apprehension clutched at her. She recalled a number of times Kael had gone uneasily quiet, seemed to drift away from her. 'He would have told me,' she added desperately.

'I'm afraid it is true. He has a child, a little boy. They live not far from here. It's time you knew, Jazmin, before you get any more involved than you already are. I love my son but I care about what happens to you, too, Jazmin. I don't want to see you get hurt.'

Jazmin shook her head again. 'No. I don't believe you,' she said fervently before she turned and left them, hurrying to her room, going inside and locking the door behind her.

Hurt! The word screamed, ricocheting about inside her. It wasn't true. But if it was...

Her mother knocked on the door, called for her to come out but Jazmin told her she wanted to be alone and eventually her mother left her.

She paced the floor of her bedroom, and then sank to sit on the edge of her bed, lost in a cocoon of deep shock that only the sound of Kael's car in the drive could penetrate.

It seemed an eternity before Kael's footsteps came along the hallway, stopped outside her bedroom door. His mother would have had more than time to speak to him, to warn him.

'Jazz. Open up.'

She glanced across the room towards the door and caught her reflection in the cheval mirror. Her skin was chalky white, her face pinched, and her lips almost bloodless. And she didn't think she could make herself move, stand up, cross the room, even if she wanted to. But now that Kael was here part of her didn't want to face him, hear the truth from him.

'Jazz, please. Open the door. Let me explain.'

The words cut through her like a knife and imbedded themselves into her heart. Explain. That one word separated itself from the others. Explanations meant a wrongdoing. Surely it couldn't be true?

In a daze she slowly walked to the door and turned the key in the lock. Kael swung the door open but he made no move to come inside. His eyes met hers and if his words hadn't forewarned her then his expression was an admission of guilt.

'It's true, isn't it? What your mother told me?' she asked flatly, her voice devoid of any expression. She wanted nothing more than to curl up into a ball and shut out the world.

'She had no right to—' Kael stopped and sighed. He ran an unsteady hand through his dark hair. 'God, Jazz. I've been trying to find the words to tell you, to explain, right from the start but—' He shook his head. 'Somehow I couldn't.'

A fissure of pain and anger shot through her, swelled and exploded inside her, and her blue eyes flashed in outrage. 'Trying to find the words!' Jazmin threw at him. 'What was so difficult about it? What's wrong with the plain and simple truth? I have a wife and a child. There's nothing incomprehensible about that. I would have caught your meaning.'

'Jazz, you don't understand,' he began and Jazmin cut him off.

'I'm not that thick, Kael. I'd have understood, believe me. There's nothing ambiguous about it.'

'I meant things are never what they seem. Nothing's ever completely black or white.'

'You mean you haven't got a wife and child?'

'Yes, I have a son but—'

'Then you were never free to make love to me, were you?' Jazmin asked brokenly, and he reached out to clutch the door-frame with his hand, as if to steady himself.

His eyes fell from hers. 'No, Jazz. I wasn't,' he said thickly.

'I don't think there's anything left for us to say, is there? Except goodbye. I'll be leaving as soon as I can get a flight to Sydney.'

'I don't want you to go.'

'And I don't want to stay,' she replied coldly as a myriad feelings turned to ice inside her. 'Now, leave me alone, Kael. I have packing to do.'

'Jazz?'

'I don't want to talk to you or see you ever again.' Deliberately, she closed the door on him and turned the key in the lock. And only then did the tears fall. Silently, they ran in rivulets down her cheeks and soaked her T-shirt.

Jazmin rubbed at the tears now, five years and countless crying nights later. She'd said she never wanted to see Kael again. She'd told herself that for all of those five years.

And now she had seen him. That's why she'd come back to Throckley. Deep down inside her, she'd wanted to see him again. For whatever reasons. And she still did. Even now, knowing he wasn't free, knowing she still loved him as much as she ever had, only added to the pain of remembering.

Jazmin blew her nose and straightened on the couch. She'd simply have to leave. She'd done it before so she could do it again. There was no way she could stay. And she wouldn't knowingly cause any rift between Kael and Toby's mother.

She heard Kael's footfalls on the polished wooden floor and hastily drew herself together, not meeting his eyes as he rejoined her. Silently he sat down beside her on the couch, not touching her but still far too close. Her nerve endings went on alert and she ached again for what might have been.

The heavy silence lengthened until Kael sighed and reached out and took her hand in his.

'Thanks for helping with the tree,' he said. 'Toby was pretty excited about the whole decorations thing.'

'I enjoyed it,' she replied flatly and pulled her hand from his grasp.

'We only had a small tree last year,' Kael continued, not commenting on her movement. 'My mother and James were in New York so we couldn't all be together. That's what Christmas is all about, isn't it? Families being together?'

Jazmin slid a glance at him to find he'd turned slightly sideways and was watching her.

His gaze settled on her lips and they tingled temptingly, almost as though he'd actually touched them. Then his eyes moved downwards to the pale skin where her shirt opened to display a V of creamy flesh.

Jazmin's heartbeats accelerated and she swallowed breathlessly. She put a hand self-consciously to her throat in case he saw revealed there the telltale throb of her racing pulse.

She felt him slide his arm along the back of the couch, his fingers moving in the soft red curls at her nape, and Jazmin was sure she'd never catch another breath.

'Jazz,' he said thickly. 'I want to talk. About what happened five years ago. But, God help me, all I can think about is how good it felt to kiss you, to hold you, and how much I want to do it again.'

His breath was warm and inciting against her cheek, and his lips grazed her flushed skin. And Jazmin couldn't move. She sat there and remembered, too.

He reached out with his free hand and gently took hold of her chin, turning it effortlessly towards him. As her tentative gaze met his a wave of vertigo washed over her and she closed her eyes until the world righted itself.

She knew she should stop him, get up and leave him, but she was drowning in the deep, enticing pools of his eyes as they glowed, hot vivid black coals.

'Jazmin.' Her name tumbled from his lips like the slow flow of water whispering over smooth stones. His mouth hovered over hers for a delayed heartbeat and then he kissed her.

A star burst of desire exploded inside her and she melted into him.

'There hasn't been a day these past five years I haven't thought of you,' he murmured into her mouth as they clung together, submerging into each other.

A small part of Jazmin recognised she was seeping into him, the love she'd kept so neatly parcelled away bursting forth to pour into every inch of him, and she moaned brokenly.

The heavy eroticism of the sound penetrated her senses, pulled her slightly back from the edge, and she pushed weakly against his chest, drawing great gulps of air as their lips parted.

Jazmin's fingers still rested on the solidness of his chest, felt the racing thuds of his heart, and she drew her hands away as if she'd been burned. She squeezed her eyes tightly closed in painful self-disgust, swallowing the aching tightness in her chest.

How could she have allowed this to happen?

'Jazz, don't. Don't push me away. We've both been living for this moment since this afternoon. You can't deny that. We're two halves of one whole.'

Jazmin opened her eyes and shook her head. With no little effort she pushed herself to her feet and for a moment she feared her shaking legs wouldn't bear her weight.

'Jazz.' He was standing now, too, and he reached out for her again, but Jazmin stepped away from him.

'We're physically attracted to each other, Kael. We always have been. I can't deny that,' she added self-derisively, and a wave of disgust washed over her. 'But that doesn't make it right. It's a purely animal instinct—'

Kael crossed to her in one angry stride, his fingers biting into the soft flesh of her arm. 'Don't say that when you don't even believe it,' he commanded.

'Whatever we have, Kael,' she said levelly, 'we have to separate ourselves from it. So please, let me go.'

'You don't mean that,' he said slowly, and Jazmin knew he was speaking the truth.

She drew on her resolve. 'I think I do, Kael. I've been managing to do just that for five years. Not that I didn't think you were vital to my life. In the beginning I did. I thought I'd die without you. But I didn't. I proved to myself that I didn't need you as much as I thought I did. I only needed myself.

'And apart from that, I wouldn't come between you and your wife back then, and I don't intend to now. I can't take my own happiness at the expense of two other people, and neither can you. Especially when one of those people is an innocent seven-year-old boy.'

'Do you think I don't know that?' His voice was icily calm. 'Why the hell do you think I let you go five years ago?'

Jazmin felt her resolve teeter dangerously at the torment in his tense face. 'You didn't let me go, Kael. I went.'

'Without giving me the chance to explain the situation,' he accused, and Jazmin turned on her heel.

'I think we've been through this scene before, and I still don't want to discuss it.' She threw the words over her shoulder as she walked stiffly towards the door.

'Catherine and I were never married,' Kael stated flatly. 'Not five years ago. Not today. And we have no plans to marry in the future.'

Chapter Seven

JAZMIN'S step faltered and she couldn't prevent herself from turning slightly to glance back at him.

'That's the truth, Jazz. I'm not in love with her and, God forgive me, I never was. Cath and I were friends, no more, no less, and Toby was the victim of a mammoth mistake on both our parts. I wouldn't not want Toby now, I love him very much, but—'

Kael shrugged tiredly and looked across the room at her. 'I fell in love with you, Jazz, the first moment I saw you. I still love you, for what it's worth.'

Their eyes were locked together, and outwardly Jazmin's nerves and muscles seemed to be in a state of paralysis. But deep inside, her heart fluttered, began to pound, until it reached a crescendo that reverberated inside her.

Yet still she couldn't take that one small step towards him. Her wary mind continued to caution her with a series of negative scenes from the past and present. She simply stood and looked at him, a mass of pain-filled indecision.

'Oh, Jazmin.' Her mother's voice made her start in surprise. 'I thought you'd gone to bed.' Moira McCann looked past her daughter, and her expression registered a surprise of her own when she saw Kael standing there. 'I was just going to check the light was on for Rick when he comes home.'

Kael seemed to slowly stir himself into action. 'I'll do that for you, Moira,' he said woodenly. 'I was just on my way out.' With that he turned and left the room by the other door.

'Jazmin?' Her mother touched her shoulder. 'You look pale. Are you all right?'

'Yes.' She ran a hand through her hair. 'We, Kael and I, were talking and I was just going to bed.'

Her mother made no comment as they walked along the hall to their rooms, and with a hurried good night Jazmin disappeared into the welcome solace of her bedroom.

When she heard the sound of Kael's car leaving she went into the *en suite* and undressed, then stepped beneath the shower, performing the usual ablutions without any conscious thought. But once she'd slipped into her nightshirt and lay down on her bed all prospect of sleep vanished. Her mind was far too active, tossing around a profusion of scenes and conversations. The disastrous one she'd had with Lorelle. The final devastation of her break with Kael. And now his revelations. Dare she hope?

Her mind shied away from that thought. It was too tantalising, too incredible to even imagine.

But he had said he loved her, she told herself. Yet from all appearances he still had some commitment to Toby's mother. Every possible scenario swirled in her mind until, exhausted, she slipped into a troubled sleep, knowing that Kael had not returned to his room.

EVEN though the weather was hot and sultry, the air heavy with impending rain after weeks of bright sunshine, Jazmin overslept.

She woke thick-headed and physically drained as she struggled to the *en suite* and stood languidly in front of the mirror. Her pale cheeks and strained eyes were reflected back at her, and with a spurt of self-directed anger she made herself splash her face and brush her teeth. Hiding in her room, she told herself, would achieve nothing.

With a mixture of agitated anticipation and a leaden dread, she donned a pair of white cotton shorts and a cool lemon tank top that left her arms and shoulders bare.

She entered the kitchen to find it deserted and all signs of breakfast cleared away. While she waited for her toast she filled a bowl with chilled fresh fruit, diced pawpaw and mango covered with tangy passionfruit and orange juice. She was just rinsing her dishes when an obviously flustered Lorelle joined her.

'Thank heavens you're here, Jazmin,' she stated, and Jazmin tensed with alarm, imagining her grandfather had had another attack.

'Is Grandfather all right?' she asked hurriedly, and Lorelle relaxed a little.

'I'm sorry, I didn't mean to frighten you. He's fine. I'm just annoyed with myself. I promised Toby I'd take him down to the mall to see Santa Claus and I completely forgot James wanted to visit his solicitor this morning. I was coming to find you to ask you if you'd mind taking Toby down to the shops.'

'Well,' Jazmin began uncertainly, wondering what Toby would think of the change of plan.

'Do you need to do any Christmas shopping or anything yourself?' Lorelle added hopefully.

'I do have a few things left to get,' Jazmin acquiesced, 'but I'm not sure—I mean, wouldn't Toby prefer you to go with him?'

'He'd love to have you take him, Jazmin. I'm just his old grandmother. He can go with me any time.' She smiled and then sobered. 'But I'd appreciate knowing just what he asks Santa for. I can't decide between a cricket set and a soccer ball. He seems rapt in both games.' She paused. 'Toby's taken a great shine to you.'

'I like him, too,' Jazmin said honestly.

'He's so much like his father,' Lorelle continued and sighed. 'When I first saw him it was like looking at Kael when he was born, and I, well, I was amazed at how absolutely besotted I was with him.' She gave a wry smile. 'Becoming a grandmother was far more overwhelming than I'd ever imagined it would be. Which, I know, doesn't excuse my behaviour to you five years ago.'

Jazmin's fingers gripped the counter top behind her and she was seeing the scene that she had played out with Lorelle right here in this very kitchen.

'Jazmin, can we take these few minutes to talk, while we're here alone?'

'Where is everyone, anyway?' Jazmin asked, unsure she wanted any more heart-to-heart talks. Her emotions had been stretched to snapping point with Kael last night.

'Well, Kael's at work,' Lorelle told her. 'Toby's with your grandfather, and your mother's gone somewhere with Rick. So we shouldn't be disturbed. Can we sit down? I need to set the record straight about one or two things.'

Jazmin nodded reluctantly and they both took a chair at the old scrubbed wooden table.

Lorelle sighed and shook her head. 'I just don't know where to start.'

'You don't have to say anything, Lorelle,' Jazmin began.

'Yes, I do, Jazmin. Especially to you. Five years ago, well, it was a bad time for us all. We all had our own problems which seemed to preclude us seeing anyone else's. I know it was an especially bad time for you and Kael. I didn't help. But the scene seemed to be set well before you arrived in Brisbane.

'You see, when your mother came up here with Rick, your grandfather wasn't well. He wouldn't see a doctor and he wouldn't let me tell you what a strain he was under. He swore me to secrecy. I love him very much and I was worried sick about him.'

'You mean, he had an attack five years ago?' Jazmin asked, and Lorelle shook her head.

'No, but I'm sure that's part of his problems now. He was just pushing himself far too hard with the project he was working on and he wouldn't let up. Kael and I both talked to him but for some reason he was obsessed with finishing one particularly troublesome job.

'On top of all that I couldn't seem to say the right thing to your mother and I thought it might be better if we had some space between us. That's why I suggested the gatekeeper's cottage. It wasn't meant to mean I wanted to get rid of you but in retrospect I can see it probably seemed that way.'

Lorelle rubbed a hand across her brow. 'I was worried about Kael, as well. He's my son and I love him, too. But he was a grown man and I didn't know how far I should interfere. I could see he'd landed himself in such a mess with Cathy. I knew the situation was weighing him down, and being Kael I knew he wasn't about to shirk his responsibilities.

'And then there was you. Being his mother I also knew how much he loved you.'

Jazmin flushed. 'I loved him, too, Lorelle,' she said simply and brushed a wayward tear from her cheek.

Lorelle handed her a tissue and dabbed at her own eyes. 'Catherine was never his wife, you know,' Lorelle said shakily, and Jazmin's gaze met hers across the short space separating her from the older woman.

'I know that now. But why—'

'Why did I let you think she was?' Lorelle gave a soft, bitter laugh. 'I let you think she was married to Kael because I thought if they broke up I'd lose my grandson. I love Toby so much. If Cathy left I thought I'd lose Toby, too. Can you understand that, Jazmin?'

For brief seconds a burning anger welled inside her but it just as quickly died. If she were honest with herself she would have admitted back then that the signs had been there for her to see if she'd only wanted to see them. Once she'd overheard Lorelle telling Kael he must get his life in order, that it wasn't fair on anyone if he didn't. Jazmin nodded wearily and heard Lorelle expel a relieved breath.

'Kael still loves you,' she said. 'Give him another chance.'

'It might be too late. We're none of us the people we were five years ago. I'm not sure I'm strong enough to face it all again.' But did she have the strength to let him go again? she asked herself.

Lorelle squeezed her hand. 'If you love Kael as much as I think you do then I'm sure you'll do whatever it takes to make it right.'

Toby chose that moment to race into the room. 'Are we going yet, Gran?' he asked excitedly, his face shining. He wore clean shorts and a light T-shirt and some attempt had been made to slick down his dark hair.

'How would you feel if Jazmin took you with her?' his grandmother asked, and Toby grinned.

'That would be great. Would you, Jazz?'

'It looks like you're stuck with me,' she said lightly, and Toby grabbed her hand.

'Are we going now then? We don't want to miss Santa. I've got stacks to tell him.'

Lorelle smiled at Jazmin and passed her a set of car keys. 'Here, take Kael's Jaguar. He went in the four-wheel drive this morning as he has to visit some pretty basic construction sites.'

Toby's enthusiasm had them on the way before Jazmin could so much as demur about driving Kael's expensive and luxurious car, and he kept up an easy conversation with her all the way to the mall.

Of course the shops were gaily decorated for the festive season, and Christmas carols followed them from one end of the shopping centre to the other.

Toby knew just where Santa Claus was ensconced in the central piazza amid a beautifully built tableau of a Christmas theme. The large jolly figure sat on a dais, and parked nearby was his sleigh, drawn by six large kangaroos rather than the traditional reindeer. Koalas and possums in Christmas hats grinned down from the trees, and Jazmin pointed out a cheeky wombat peeking out of a burrow.

She dutifully stood with Toby in a queue of other women and their offspring and surprisingly found herself enjoying it. When it came to his turn Toby bounded up enthusiastically, chatted to Santa Claus and smiled for his photograph.

Jazmin then bore him off to lunch for his favourite hamburger and chips before doing a little shopping of her own.

'What are you getting Dad, Jazz?' Toby asked her, indicating just how his young life centred around his father.

'I don't know,' Jazmin replied. 'Maybe you could suggest something.'

Toby gave the matter some thought. 'Well, Gran's getting him shirts. He needs a couple of new ones,' he told her solemnly. 'I was with Gran when she bought them and helped her choose. So then I got him some new ties to match the shirts.' Toby frowned in concentration. 'He reads a lot.'

Yes, Kael had liked to read. Adventure, espionage, mysteries, if she remembered correctly. 'Then perhaps I could get him a book voucher and he can choose some books for himself.'

Toby nodded and then it was time to collect the photo he'd had taken with Santa Claus. Jazmin suggested they buy a frame for it so he could add the photograph to his father's Christmas gifts. Toby thought that was a great idea, and when they'd made their purchase they headed back to the car.

They sat quietly on the return journey, Toby eating the lollipop he'd been given by Santa Claus.

'Jazz?'

'Mm?' Jazmin turned the car onto Newmarket Road.

'You know when it's your birthday and you make a wish and blow out the candles and you can't tell anyone what you wished for because it won't come true? Well, is it the same with the wish you tell Santa Claus? I mean, will you not get the wish if you tell?'

Jazmin remembered Lorelle asking her to find out what Toby wanted for Christmas and report back to her, and she managed not to smile. 'I don't think the same rules apply for a Santa Claus wish. I could be wrong, but I think it's okay to tell. So, what did you wish for?' she asked, thinking he'd say a truck or a cricket set.

'I said I wanted my dad to be happy all the time and not just when he thinks I'm looking.'

Jazmin was more than a little taken aback. 'I'm sure your father's happy, Toby,' she began feebly, not knowing quite what to say to the boy's revelations.

'Mostly he is. But I really think he needs a proper mother.'

'He has a mother. Lorelle, your grandmother.'

'No. Not that sort of mother. I mean a mother for me. You know, a wife. To hug him and stuff.'

Jazmin was completely speechless.

'When I'm over at Jake's place—' He took his lollipop out of his mouth and turned to Jazmin. 'Oh, Jake's my best friend. He lives down the road and we ride to school together. Well, when I'm at Jake's place his mum and dad hug and kiss all the time.' He shuddered. 'It's pretty gross but they laugh all the time, too. They're really happy. I want Dad to be happy like that, too.'

Chapter Eight

JAZMIN made a big job of turning the car into the steep narrow driveway. 'I don't think there's any need for you to worry about your father, Toby,' she said softly and pulled up in front of the large garage, using the remote control to open the door.

Toby undid his seat-belt as she turned off the engine. 'But I'd like us to be a proper family, Jazz.'

A cold hand encircled Jazmin's heart as they climbed from the car and walked around to the boot to get Jazmin's parcels.

'Maybe when your mother comes back—' Jazmin began, and Toby looked up at her in surprise.

'Cathy? Oh, not with Cathy. I know she's my really mother, and she loves me, but Dad and Cathy don't love each other, you see.' He shrugged without rancour. 'Dad explained it all to me ages ago. How mothers and fathers have to love each other in a special way. That's what I want for my dad.'

'It would certainly be a nice Christmas present,' Jazmin agreed, wanting to hug Toby to her and never let him go.

Instead she walked beside him to the house, and they had barely set the parcels down when a car door slammed outside. Toby ran over to the window and peered out.

'It's Dad's four-wheel drive,' he said excitedly, and Jazmin's heartbeats reacted accordingly. 'But Dad's not driving it,' Toby added, his smile fading with a disappointment that matched Jazmin's.

She headed outside with Toby close behind her.

A burly man in khaki work clothes walked up the steps and took off his battered cap. 'Mrs. Craigen?' he asked uncertainly and Jazmin shook her head.

'Ah, no. I'm a—' she paused '—a friend,' she finished quickly. Old lover would hardly have done, she told herself ironically, and barely suppressed a derisive laugh. 'What can I do for you?'

'Where's my dad?' Toby piped up and the man glanced down at him and smiled.

'Well, young fellow, you'd have to be Toby. Would I be right?'

Toby nodded. 'I look just like my dad.'

'That you do.'

'Is something wrong with Kael?' Jazmin asked, uneasy now, and part of her registered that Toby had slipped a small hand into hers.

'Not exactly.' The man ran a hand through his tousled hair. 'Kael asked me to drop off the four-wheel drive. You see, he had a slight accident. Nothing serious,' he added quickly when Jazmin started.

'Is he all right?' Jazmin got out through suddenly taut vocal cords, and Toby's fingers tightened in hers. 'What happened?'

'He'll be just fine. Took a tumble and cut himself. A stitch or two and he'll be good as new,' the man said lightly.

Surely it couldn't be critical, Jazmin tried to reassure herself, otherwise the man wouldn't be behaving quite so unconcernedly. Or else he was trying to make light of it for Toby's benefit.

'Which hospital did they take him to?' she asked as lightly as she could in case she upset Toby any further. 'We'll go and see him.'

'No point, miss. He'll be here in no time. Pete drove him to the doc's and he's giving me a lift back when he drops the boss off. Want me to put the four-wheel drive in the carport over there for you?'

'Oh. Yes, thank you. Are you sure he's all right?'

'All bar his temper.' The man grinned. 'Been tearing verbal strips off himself since it happened. Come to think of it, never known the boss to be so awkward. It was like he fell over his shadow.' He shook his head as he jumped down the steps and climbed into the truck.

'Will Dad have to go to the hospital?' Toby asked in a thin voice, and Jazmin crouched down beside him.

'I don't think so. The man said he should be home soon.'

Toby slid his arms around her neck, and Jazmin hugged him tightly. 'If he has to go to the hospital do you think Santa will know where he is?'

Before Jazmin could assure him a battered utility bearing the name of McCann and Craigen Constructions on the door drew to a halt at the bottom of the steps and two men climbed out.

Toby released his hold on Jazmin and raced down the steps crying, 'Dad! Dad! What happened?'

Jazmin followed a little more slowly, her knees suddenly too weak to allow her to follow Toby's lead, for she found herself wanting to do just that, to rush into Kael's arms.

Kael lifted Toby up with his undamaged arm and showed his son his clean white bandage. 'A bit of a cut, that's all. I'm fine.'

'We'll get back to it then, Boss.' The first man had joined them.

Kael turned to the two men. 'Okay. Thanks, Dave. Pete. See you tomorrow.'

'Take the day off.' Pete grinned. 'We'll make it sweet with the boss.'

They laughed as they waved and drove away.

'Did you get lots of stitches?' Toby asked wide-eyed, and Kael set him on the ground.

'A couple. It's not too bad.'

'Did it really really hurt?' Toby persisted morbidly and Kael ruffled his hair.

'Not as much as my pride did when I tripped over a plank.' He glanced up at Jazmin. 'I had my mind on other things,' he added enigmatically and she swallowed.

'Toby was worried.'

Kael's dark eyes held hers.

'So was I,' she added huskily.

'Were you?'

Their eyes were holding a far different conversation than their trite words, and Jazmin's heart ached with wanting him. What if his accident had been more serious? she asked herself. And she hadn't had time to tell him how she felt. How much she loved him.

'Would you like a cup of tea or anything?' Jazmin heard herself ask him and she cringed. So prosaic. Tea and sympathy.

'Coffee would be great.' He looked down at his dusty clothes. 'And meanwhile I'll go and get cleaned up.'

'Do you, I mean, will you be able to manage? With your bandage and—' Jazmin's voice gave out on her, and Kael's lips twitched.

'I should be all right. But I might have to call for assistance if I get stuck,' he said and smiled at her, that devastating smile that curled her toes.

And that smile had Jazmin fumbling about the kitchen like someone with five thumbs. She spilled the coffee granules. She almost dropped the mugs she took down from the old-fashioned dresser with the lead light doors. And she found she had great trouble concentrating on Toby's lively chatter. When his mate, Jake, arrived and the boys went out on the front lawn to play soccer, she breathed a steadying sigh of relief.

However, her relief was short-lived, for moments later Kael reappeared, cleanly scrubbed and dressed in a pair of faded cut-off denims and a black sleeveless T-shirt.

He sat down at the table and murmured his thanks as he took the mug of coffee she passed him. A flash of pain crossed his face as he knocked his bandaged arm on the edge of the table.

Jazmin leaned against the counter top on the other side of the table. Her knees had gone distinctly weak from a mixture of sympathy for his pain and the blossoming spread of wanting that his physical presence always had on her.

'Did the doctor give you some painkillers?' she asked as she took a sip of her coffee.

'I had a couple at the surgery.' He gingerly flexed his wrist. 'It's not too bad at the moment. Where's Toby?'

'Out the front playing soccer with Jake.'

Kale took another gulp of coffee and Jazmin sensed he was as ill-at-ease as she was. 'I hope you didn't mind taking Toby with you today,' he said, and she shook her head.

'No. I enjoyed his company. He was no trouble.'

'He's usually a good kid.' He sighed softly. 'To tell you the truth I sometimes wonder how that happened.'

'He has a good father,' Jazmin said simply and her throat tightened as Kael looked across at her, his lips twisting a little derisively.

'I owe him that, Jazz, wouldn't you say?'

Jazmin slid onto a chair opposite him and swallowed nervously. Her skin had grown decidedly warm, and it had nothing to do with the hot summer weather. 'I'd like to hear, I mean, if you still want to tell me—' Her voice died on her and she held her breath, waiting for his reaction.

'I do want to explain, Jazz. I always have.' He sat back in his chair and set down his coffee mug. 'It was the usual. Catherine and I got drunk and we got caught with an unwanted pregnancy,' he stated harshly, and then some of the tension left his taut body.

Sitting forward, he rested his elbow on the tabletop, his chin on the heel of his hand. 'No. That's probably not fair on either of us.

'Catherine and I met at Uni. We clicked as friends, nothing more, we both knew that. We just went around in a group, enjoyed sport, music, talking. I wasn't interested in a relationship, and neither was she. I was working for James and studying part time and she had this burning passion to be a surgeon. It was all she'd ever wanted to be.

'She had no parents and worked as a waitress to make ends meet.' He glanced across at Jazmin. 'I've never met anyone as dedicated as she was. Which was why this became such a bloody mess.

'One night we both ended up back at the house she shared and no one was home. She was depressed because she thought, mistakenly, as it happens, that she'd failed an important exam. I'd just heard that my stepsister...' He paused. 'My father remarried a couple of years after his divorce from my mother, and he had three daughters. Well, that day my twelve-year-old stepsister was knocked from her bicycle riding home from school. She was killed instantly. She was a great kid, and I loved her very much, so I was pretty upset.

'So Catherine and I had a drink together. Then we had another and so on and we ended up in bed.'

Kael stood up and paced the kitchen. 'When Catherine found out she was pregnant we were both devastated. We couldn't believe it had happened. Then we had to decide what to do.'

'You didn't consider getting married?' Jazmin put in through stiff lips.

'Not really. Fortunately we knew marriage would be wrong for both of us.' He took a deep breath. 'Catherine didn't want to have an abortion, and we decided the major consideration was that no matter what we did we'd see that the baby didn't suffer from our mistakes. So she decided she'd put her career on hold until she'd had the child.

'It didn't take long for me to see it was cutting her up and that she regretted her decision. So I offered to support her until she was through medicine. I felt it was the least I could do for my part in the whole fiasco.'

He glanced at Jazmin tiredly. 'I did make two very important mistakes back then, though. I didn't count on a tiny baby wrapping himself around my heart.' His eyes held Jazmin's. 'Or that I'd meet someone who'd make me believe in love at first sight. So,' he added quickly, 'Catherine's now the surgeon she always wanted to be and I'm, well, I'm a single father who's trying to do the best for his son.'

'Who *is* doing the best for his son.' Jazmin said honestly.

'Thanks, Jazz,' he replied softly, and Jazmin pushed herself to her feet and walked around the table to him.

'I'm… I didn't realise…' She swallowed, fighting back her tears, and Kael stood up and took her gently in his arms.

'I love you, Jazz. I always have,' he said simply and his lips claimed hers almost reverently at first.

They clung together, their kisses deepening until they were breathless. Kael sank down onto his chair and pulled her onto his lap.

'You don't know how long I've waited for this moment,' he breathed into her hair, and Jazmin leant back so she could cup his jawline with her hand.

'About as long as I have, I'd say,' she murmured huskily, and he turned slightly so he could kiss the palm of her hand.

'You know, part of me couldn't believe you'd let me go,' Jazmin told him. 'Even when I was waiting at the airport I think deep down I expected you'd come after me.'

'I did come after you. I drove out there like a madman. And then I just stood there helplessly and watched you board the plane. I felt like part of me died that day.'

'Then why—'

'Let you go? How could I have asked you to stay, Jazz? As I saw it I'd made a king-sized mess of my life to date. And not just mine. Catherine's. Toby's. I couldn't add yours to the list. The timing for us was way out back then.

'But I wasn't going to give you up. I decided to try to get my life in order before I came after you to beg you to forgive me. Catherine finished medical school over a year ago. She officially gave me custody of Toby, although she gets to see him whenever she wants to.

'Then James had his attack and my workload doubled. But believe me, Jazz, if you hadn't taken up his offer to come home for Christmas then I'd have come searching for you in the New Year. I couldn't wait any longer.' He closed his eyes eloquently. 'I've been terrified for five long years that you'd find someone else.'

'We've wasted so much precious time, haven't we?' Jazmin said softly.

'That we have. But I think perhaps I needed the time to sort out my mixed-up life.' He sighed regretfully and picked up one red curl to let it spring around his finger.

'I guess as we move through life we all pick up a certain amount of baggage. When we come from other relationships, whatever the relationships may be, we bring the leftovers of those relationships with us. I didn't want to give you my baggage to carry, Jazz. As much as I wanted you, and you'll never know how much I desperately wanted to leave everything behind me and just walk away with you, I couldn't do that. I was filled with a massive guilt. Because of Catherine. Because of Toby. And then because of you.'

'Oh, Kael. I've felt guilty, too. I fell into your arms so easily I thought I deserved to get burned. I mean, I sensed there was something wrong but I wouldn't allow myself to analyse it. I selfishly wanted you too much. I mistakenly thought at any cost.' She grimaced. 'I'm sorry I was so sanctimonious about not letting you explain.'

'I'm not so sure I could have explained it all five years ago. I felt so bad. I thought I'd ruined two lives. First Catherine's and then yours.'

Jazmin laughed softly. 'We've both been such fools.'

'Amen to that,' he agreed and kissed her again. When he raised his head he gazed deeply into her eyes. 'Have I got a second chance to make amends, Jazz? I mean, will you marry me? Will you take on a far from perfect male who comes with a ready-made family but who loves you more than life itself?'

A tear trickled down Jazmin's cheek and he bent to catch it on his tongue.

'I sincerely hope that's an affirmative tear,' he said thickly, and Jazmin nodded and slid her arms around his neck.

'Absolutely affirmative,' she said, and went to slide from his lap at the sound of a car pulling into the driveway.

Kael held her fast. 'I'm not letting you go now, Jazmin McCann, no matter whose mother that will turn out to be.'

In fact, Lorelle and James and Jazmin's mother and brother arrived within a few minutes of each other, and were all genuinely elated by the news. Jazmin's grandfather winked across at her and bade Lorelle fetch the special bottle of champagne he'd bought just for this occasion, firmly declaring he'd known it would all turn out right.

Later Jazmin's mother took her aside to tell her that Rick's land had sold. He'd taken a loss with the price, but he had arranged to pay his debts and they had no need to sell her house. Hopefully, she agreed, Rick had learnt his lesson.

When Kael told Toby the news, he'd thrown himself into Jazmin's arms and squeezed her tightly. 'Can we go down to see Santa Claus tomorrow?' he'd asked delightedly. 'I want to thank him for bringing you up to

Brisbane so Dad could find you. Boy, don't Santa work quickly?'

And much later, after an over-excited Toby had finally agreed to go to bed, Jazmin strolled out onto the front veranda to lean against a post and gaze out at the panorama of the city below her. Watching the blinking lights, the snaking brightness of cars climbing and then descending the arch of the Gateway Bridge, she drew in a deep breath, inhaling the scent of the trees and flowers on the hot summer evening air, and she sighed contentedly.

Could she have asked for a better end to her Christmas journey to be with her family?

She heard a weathered veranda board creak behind her, and Kael slid his arms around her, pulling her against him.

Nuzzling her neck, he murmured appreciatively. 'If I'm dreaming this, don't wake me up.'

Jazmin chuckled and turned in the circle of his arms so that she was facing him. 'Sleep as long as you like, as long as I'm right there beside you.'

'Was that a proposition, Ms. McCann?'

'Of the best kind.'

'My favourite.' He leaned back from her. 'We do need to clean up one last thing though, Jazz.'

'We do?' She slid her fingertips over the smooth bulge of muscle in his arms.

'You're not marrying me for the ten thousand dollars, are you?' he asked with mock seriousness, and Jazmin glanced up at him.

'Do you think that's all I'm worth?'

He laughed softly. 'Very underhanded, Ms. McCann. I think you're priceless, and you know it.'

Jazmin sobered. 'I would never have asked Grandfather for money. You did know that, didn't you, Kael?'

'Of course.' He touched her lips with a quick kiss. 'It was Rick, wasn't it? Does he still need help?'

'No. Thankfully he's sorted it all out.'

'Good. You'll have to tell me that story sometime, but now...' He took something from his pocket and held it above her head. 'This is mistletoe.'

'Mistletoe?' Jazmin chuckled delightedly.

'And of course you know that in some countries it's traditional to steal a kiss underneath a sprig of mistletoe,' he continued solemnly.

'Did you also know that mistletoe doesn't have such a good reputation here in Australia?' Jazmin asked him. 'I've seen it kill gum trees.'

'Where's your romance, Jazz?' he chided. 'That may be so but I have it on good authority that this—' he wriggled the small branch in his fingers '—is a genuine ridgy-didge plastic replica of the real thing. So, we can rest easy knowing the gum trees are safe.'

'I'm suitably impressed.' Jazmin beamed up at him and her teeth flashed in a smile. 'Seems you've thought of everything.'

His lips twitched. 'I try,' he said modestly. 'But where was I? Oh, yes. Mistletoe. Traditionally you stand underneath it and steal a kiss from your true love.'

His eyes met and held hers and all humour left his face. 'The mistletoe might be imitation but I can guarantee the kiss will be the genuine article.'

Jazmin felt her nerve endings prickle to attention. 'I'm pleased to hear that, my own true love,' she said softly and then met his lips with a passion that was very real, and matched his own.

CHRISTMAS CHARADE

Kay Gregory

Chapter One

NINA hated flying. That was why, when the time came to arrange her annual Christmas pilgrimage to Chicago, she booked a compartment on the train.

She also hated being late, so that by the time she boarded Amtrak's silver-grey Empire Builder with its trademark red, white and blue stripes, she had had time to consume three almond-raisin chocolate bars, two brownies and the bag of fudge her roommate had given her in case she felt the need for a light snack.

Releasing a contented sigh after climbing the stairs to the train's upper level, she glanced round her compact cubicle of a bedroom. Yes, it was the same as always. Her own personal hideaway where she could prepare herself in peace and privacy for the stresses of the Petrov family Christmas that lay ahead.

With a speed born of familiarity, she shoved her suitcase under one of the comfortably wide seats that faced each other on either side of the window, and hung her coat in the narrow cupboard beside the door. After that, feeling mildly nauseated now, but deciding there was nothing to be gained from dwelling on the consequences of chocolate, she settled down to watch the remaining passengers bustle along the Seattle platform in search of seats.

Soon the bustling and scurrying tapered off and the train's engines began to throb to life. Any minute now, thought Nina, adjusting the pillow at her back.

A gleam of gold flashed against the window, and she stopped fidgeting to look for its source.

Farther down the platform, a latecomer in a dark grey pin-stripe was striding along the platform as if he owned it. It was the winter sun striking his watch that had caught her eye. He wasn't hurrying. It was as though he expected men and machines to wait for him.

Nina felt herself bristling automatically. If the time ever came when her father, Joseph Petrov III, condescended to board anything slower than a jet plane, she had no doubt he would walk with just the same sort of arrogance. And at the moment she didn't much want to think about her father. She would see him soon enough, and as surely as rabbits bred little rabbits, he would have yet another of his Christmas suitors lined up to court her. He had produced one every Christmas for the past five years—a succession of ambitious young yes-men who were only too anxious to acquire a pipeline to Joseph Petrov's money by marrying the only daughter he was determined to see safely settled down. Preferably with a brood of active children.

Nina had no intention of settling down. And if she ever married, which was by no means certain, her mate would be a man of her own choosing.

Forgetting for a moment that she was in full view of anyone passing by, Nina stuck her tongue out at the imaginary suitor and narrowed her eyes in a squint. At the same moment, the man who had given rise to her gloomy musings drew abreast of her window and stopped.

He took in the tongue and the squint, raised his eyebrows a fraction, and passed on.

Nina shrugged. If he thought she was making faces at him, so much the better. She wasn't interested in men who thought business was what life was all about—and that man had all the earmarks of a hot-shot tycoon.

She traced her finger down a flaw in the glass. He was attractive, though, in an unorthodox sort of way. It was his lips she had noticed at once. Unusual lips. Not wide, but full and alluring, surprisingly sensitive for a man who walked as if he thought he owned the world. He had nice hair, too, glossy brown and wavy. It matched the brown of his eyes. Yet it was a strong face, and that cleft in his chin made him look tough and unyielding. He had the sort of face one would want on one's side in a fight. Funny, though... Nina frowned. It wasn't the sort of face one usually encountered on trains. Men like that were always in a hurry. Like her father.

'Ticket, please.' A brisk and smiling conductor pushed aside the curtain across her doorway, and Nina forgot about the man in the grey pinstripe and reached into her purse for her ticket. A few minutes later a wiry little porter arrived to explain the services of Amtrak. When she told him she had travelled this route many times before, he nodded and moved on to the next room.

Nina realized then that she had been so immersed in her thoughts that she hadn't noticed the train was already on its way. She closed her eyes and prepared to enjoy the peace of her own company until dinner.

That was as long as peace lasted.

When she arrived in the dining-car, the *maître d'* showed her to a seat beside the window. The man sitting across from her was the man in the grey pinstripe. Except that now he wasn't wearing his suit.

He had changed into a soft brown sweater on top of a cream silk shirt. Even so, Nina thought he looked noticeably formal for a train trip. It was probably his power shoulders, she decided. They just weren't made for casual. She herself was dressed in jeans and a loose orange shirt, and compared to him she felt small, frowzy and unbusinesslike. But then she wasn't businesslike. And she *was* small. Involuntarily her lips tipped up.

'That's better,' said the man opposite. 'Your smile is much prettier than your tongue.' He favoured her with a brief, appreciative appraisal.

Oh, lord. A Casanova. With a voice like gravel on velvet. Nina groaned inwardly. 'Thank you,' she said. 'That's a new slant to a well-used line, but I'm afraid I'm not susceptible to flattery. And we both know it isn't true, don't we?'

Just a flicker of annoyance crossed the man's face before his features smoothed out and he replied with easy urbanity, 'What isn't true?'

'That I'm pretty,' Nina snapped, resenting him for making her say it.

'Oh, I don't know.' He tilted his head and studied her with a bold, assessing stare that made her feel like a less-than-impressive heifer up for auction. 'Your hair is a nice light brown, and I like the way you style it—'

'I don't style it,' Nina interrupted. 'It just falls this way.'

A brief smile touched his lips and disappeared. 'Mmm. Straight to your shoulders and then up. I still like it. Your skin isn't bad, either. It goes with that orange tent you're wearing.'

She had known he wouldn't be able to resist getting back at her for that barb about his well-used line. She smiled coolly. 'Thank you again. I'm glad you like it. My shirt, I mean.'

'I don't, particularly. But I do like the shape of your face. Oval and pointed at the bottom. Reminds me of a nice fresh lemon. And your eyes are interesting. I can't make out if they're actually brown or green.'

'Beige,' said Nina through her teeth.

His lips twitched. 'You make yourself sound very dull. But you're not dull, are you, Ms.... Do you have a name?'

'Most people do,' said Nina.

'Very true. Mine's Fenton Hardwick. Fen to my friends.' He extended a hand across the table. A tough, square hand that looked as though it had seen service beyond the boardroom. Was he only masquerading as a tycoon? Reluctantly, Nina gave him her hand, and immediately he wrapped his fingers around it in a grip that sent sparks shooting up her arm. She gasped and pulled away as if her skin had been scorched. Which, to her confusion, was exactly how it felt. She wondered if he had felt it, too. If so, he gave no sign.

Nina hid her hand under the table as their waiter came up, efficiently balancing a tray of salads against the swaying of the train.

When he left again Fenton Hardwick said, 'Well?'

Nina sighed. 'My name's Nina Petrov.' There was no sense being coy about it. And he was unlikely to link her with Joseph. She didn't like being linked with her father. Once people knew she was the daughter of Joseph Petrov III, head of an industrial empire with tentacles that reached around the world, they tended to treat her differently. Though in this case that might not be a bad thing. She wouldn't mind being treated with respect by the smug but seductive Mr. Hardwick.

She lost out on both counts. He knew immediately who she was, and failed to show any sort of reverence.

'Ah,' he said. 'That explains it.'

'Explains what?' asked Nina, knowing she sounded crabby, and not caring.

'The chip on your shoulder, of course. Comes of being your father's daughter.' He took a healthy forkful of salad.

Nina put her own fork down with a clatter. 'I don't have a chip on my shoulder. And even if I had, what would being my father's daughter have to do with it?'

'It shouldn't have anything to do with it. But I've noticed that people who've never had to work for what they have tend to react like the spoiled little rich kids they are when one of the *hoi polloi* dares to ruffle their feathers. You ruffle very nicely, Miss Petrov.'

Nina opened her mouth, prepared to tell this obnoxious and objectionable man just what she thought of his totally erroneous interpretation of her character. But before she could deliver a blistering response, the *maître d'* had escorted another couple to their table—a man and a woman who gave them bright holiday smiles and began to comment on the menu. Nina bit her lip and tried to convince herself that she really didn't care what a nobody like Fenton Hardwick thought of Nina Petrov. Because even though he didn't act like a nobody, she refused to think of him as Somebody.

She ignored the small, nagging voice in her head that suggested she had brought at least some of Fenton's acid on herself. Not that it mattered. For all she knew, he was getting off the train at the next stop.

He wasn't.

When Nina made her way into the Sightseer Lounge later that evening with the intention of watching the movie, she saw that the ubiquitous Mr. Hardwick was there before her. But he wasn't watching either of the two small screens set up at either end of the car. Instead he sat sprawled in a brown leather armchair with his foot hooked over a narrow shelf running beneath the wraparoundwindows. He seemed totally absorbed by the darkness that hid the snow-covered mountains outside.

Nina made a face. All the seats by the closest screen were taken. Which meant she would have to pass by *that man* in order to reach the other end of the car. She hesitated, then squared her shoulders and stepped forward. He wasn't looking her way. And anyway she was damned if she meant to be intimidated by a rude, arrogant pseudo-tycoon who compared her face to a lemon and called her spoiled without the least justification.

He didn't move as she came up behind him. But just when she thought she was safely past, his hand closed over her wrist.

'Don't go away,' he said. 'I want to talk to you.'

Nina pulled out of his grasp, annoyed that his touch had made her jump. 'I don't want to talk to you,' she snapped, starting to move down the aisle.

He patted the empty seat beside him. 'Sit down.'

'I said I *don't* want to talk to you.'

'I heard you. Just the same, I'd like you to sit down.'

'I came to watch the movie.'

'No doubt. But if you'd care to check, you'll find that all the good seats are occupied. This one isn't.' Again he patted the empty chair.

'I can't see the movie from here.'

'I know.' He smiled, a slow, curving smile that made her stomach roll over. 'So you'll just have to settle for me instead.' When Nina stiffened, he carried on blandly, 'And don't look at me as if I'd propositioned you. I don't go in for sex on public seats.'

Nina's mouth fell open, and she was so startled by his effrontery that when the train rocked suddenly, she forgot to maintain her balance and tumbled awkwardly on to his knee.

Fenton smiled again, with cool, suggestive mockery, and she noticed that one of his front teeth protruded slightly as if it had been knocked out of place in a fight. It made him look dangerous—and even more lethally attractive.

'Good girl,' he said, patting her hip now instead of the chair. 'Although it wasn't necessary to fall in with my wishes with *quite* so much enthusiasm.'

'Oh!' Nina struggled to stand up, at which point Fenton put his hands around her waist and without further ado deposited her on the vacant seat beside him. Nina felt its smoothness through her jeans. Quite different from the solid muscularity of his thighs. She swallowed, wishing she had the will to get up and return to her bedroom at once. But, curiously, she hadn't.

There was something very persuasive about Fenton Hardwick.

She sat as far away from him as she could, with her arms pressed into her sides and her hands clasped in her lap as she stared, tight-lipped, into the passing darkness.

'I owe you an apology.' Fenton's low voice rasped across her thoughts, startling her and making her turn towards him.

'What?' she said. Surely his kind of man never apologized.

'I said I owe you an apology. For calling you a spoiled little rich kid.'

'And a lemon,' said Nina without thinking.

He laughed softly. 'No, I won't apologize for that. It fits. Besides, I like lemons. I find their tartness adds a certain pleasing piquancy to most dishes.' His eyes left her in no doubt as to the kind of dish he had in mind.

All right, so the man liked a challenge. Well, she'd figured that. And the best way to make him leave her alone was not to provide it.

'I expect you were right,' she said distantly.

'Right?'

'I probably am a spoiled little rich kid.'

'Probably? Don't you know?'

He had the most irritating eyebrows. Heavy and much darker than his hair, with a habit of arching up in a way that couldn't fail to provoke.

'Not really,' she said, determined not to let him see she was irritated. 'It's true my father is wealthy, of course, and while I was growing up I did have everything money could buy. The best clothes, the best schools, all my friends carefully selected for me. I'm an only child, you see.' She smiled, trying to make a joke of it. 'My father had no one else to keep in order.'

'Hmm. What about your mother?' Fenton appeared to be having trouble with his voice.

'My mother,' said Nina, stroking the hem of her shirt, 'is very beautiful. My father adores her. And she always pretends to do exactly as he says.'

'I see. And you don't?' The idea seemed to amuse him.

'Not always. He wanted me to go to some insipid finishing school in Europe. But I wouldn't. I made a stand and insisted on going to college.'

'Good for you. And did Daddy dutifully cover your expenses?'

Nina hated the mocking lift to his voice. 'He would have done. I wouldn't let him,' she said coldly.

His eyebrows did it again. 'Really? So how did you support yourself? A little flower arranging in your spare time? Or dancing lessons, perhaps?'

'I drove a forklift four evenings a week. In a building supply warehouse.' She didn't look at him, but fixed her gaze firmly on her own reflection in the glass. There were patches of indignant colour on her cheeks.

'Did you now? Well, I'm damned.'

'No doubt,' said Nina.

He made a sound that might have been a laugh. 'You give as good as you get, don't you, Miss Petrov? You must have led your father quite a dance. And my apology stands. I had no business calling you spoiled.'

'Why did you?' She tried to sound as though she didn't care but, oddly, she did.

'I'm not sure. There's something about you that keeps making me want to take you down a peg. Or two. You remind me of a woman I used to know.'

Oh. Was that what this was about? Some woman she resembled who had let him down? Whose assets he'd perhaps had his eye on? Nina felt a sudden stab of disappointment. She'd known enough of that kind in her time. Yet . . . Fen was so much more arrogant, more sure of himself than those executive hopefuls her father was always producing. More disturbingly attractive, too. Now if only . . .

No. There was no point even thinking about that. Nina gave herself a firm mental shake and, for something to say, asked, 'What about you? Were you spoiled?'

In the glass she saw his features suddenly go still. Then he stretched slowly, like a cat getting ready to move in on the kill.

But all he said was, 'No. I wasn't.'

It was all she would get out of him now. She could tell. In her line of work it didn't take long to spot the boundaries of communication. He'd said all he wanted to say, and so had she. There was no reason for her to stay any longer.

Why, then, was she making no effort to move? Was it because he was such a curious mass of contradictions? In some ways like her father, who expected lesser mortals to do his bidding. In other ways like a man who had little sympathy with the trappings of success. She wondered what he did for a living. And what he was doing on the train. But if she asked him, he might think she was interested in a—well, in a more than casual sense. Which, of course, she wasn't.

As a specimen of masculine psychology, though, she had to admit he was fascinating.

Just psychology, Nina? Not physiology? Who do you think you're kidding? muttered an irritating voice in her head.

'I must be going.' She stifled the voice ruthlessly and stood up.

'Must you? Why? Have I scared you off?'

'Of course not. I'm tired, that's all.'

'Hmm.' He tilted his head back and fixed her with a disturbingly speculative eye. The brown had gold flecks in it, she noted. Like the goldstone beads she sometimes wore.

'Sweet dreams then, Miss Petrov. Or may I call you Nina?'

'I can't stop you,' she replied ungraciously.

'No, you can't. And you may call me Fen.'

'I don't want to call you Fen, Mr. Hardwick.'

He shrugged. 'As you wish, Miss Lemon.'

Surprisingly, Nina felt the edges of her mouth curve up. 'Do you *always* have to have the last word?' she asked, but with none of her former acidity.

'Of course. I make a point of it.' He returned her smile lazily, and Nina was horrified to find herself wanting to reach out to run her fingers over those firm and deliciously promising lips—and over that seductive cleft in his chin...

'Good night,' she said, turning away quickly. 'We may not meet again, so enjoy the rest of your journey.'

'Oh, we'll meet again, never doubt it.' His low, amused voice followed her down the aisle as she made her way past the movie—it was something about two dogs and a cat—and hurried back to the security of her bedroom.

Much later—it must have been about three in the morning—she lay on the bunk which the porter had made of the two seats, and listened to the wheels of the train thundering over the tracks. They had already passed through the Cascade Mountains and were now gathering speed through the Columbia River Basin.

Usually Nina found she slept well on trains, lulled by the persistent rocking. But tonight it was different. Tonight she kept thinking of that extraordinarily annoying and objectionable hunk. He seemed to have a remarkable knack for getting under her skin as no man in her past had ever done. Not that there had been many men in her past, apart from her father's Christmas suitors. Who didn't count.

She heaved herself on to her side. There had been other dates, of course, over the years. Casual ones. Yet somehow she had managed to reach the ripe old age of twenty-seven without once having had her heart broken. Something of a record, she supposed. But then having Joseph Petrov for a father had made her a cautious player in the game of hearts, and she had no intention of being used as a rung up the ladder of some ambitious young executive's career.

The train slowed, shuddered to a stop, and she shifted restlessly on her bunk. *Was* Fenton—Fen—just another one of those? An ambitious young executive on the make? Maybe. Although he didn't seem to like her much, and if he was pursuing her with marriage in mind he was going about it in a very odd way.

Nina crumpled the sheet absently in her fingers. It didn't seem likely he was pursuing her at all. There was something determinedly unattached about Fen...

Hmm. She rubbed her ear as an idea, formless as yet, caught vaguely at the back of her mind. She made no attempt to give it shape or substance because she knew enough to recognize trouble when she saw it. And no way would she allow herself to become even briefly involved with that man. If she had to, she would avoid him by remaining in her compartment.

That idea lasted until morning, when the smell of freshly brewed coffee drove her in the direction of breakfast. And she needn't have worried. There was no sign of Fen. Either he had already eaten or he didn't plan to.

When she ventured into the lounge after breakfast and he wasn't there, either, Nina found herself relaxing for the first time since last night. Maybe, after all, he had left the train at Whitefish or Spokane. She shook her hair back and settled down to feast her eyes on the icy splendour of the Rockies as they emerged in majestic white peaks through the clouds. It was a view she had never yet tired of—although today the clouds seemed unusually heavy.

After lunch, and with Idaho and the mountains left behind, the train pulled into Havre, Montana. By that time Nina felt quite safe in alighting with the other passengers to stretch her legs and breathe unconditioned air.

Immediately her interested gaze fell on the gleaming black bulk of an old steam engine—one of the last to run on the Great Northern Line, she learned as she studied the inscription. She was admiring its solid power, its connection with the history of the railroad, when she felt a brisk tap on her shoulder.

'You like engines?' Fen's voice, holding only the faintest trace of amusement.

Nina jumped. 'Yes,' she said, swinging round. 'As it happens, I do. Is there something wrong with that?'

'Not at all.' He brushed the back of his hand across his mouth. 'Don't be so defensive, Miss Lemon.'

'I'm not defensive.' Nina was irritated, and her heart seemed to be beating much too fast. 'And don't call me Miss Lemon.'

'Then you'll have to let me call you Nina, won't you?' He smiled smugly. 'And with a better grace than you've exhibited up to now.'

Nina sighed. 'How far are you travelling, Mr. Hardwick?' she asked pointedly.

'I'm not getting off at the next station, if that's what you're hoping.' When Nina glared at him, he added with a shrug. 'New York. If it matters.'

'It doesn't. Your destination is a matter of total irrelevance to me,' said Nina grandly.

It wasn't though. For some reason the winter sky seemed a little brighter and more challenging now that she knew Fen was still on the train. She decided it must be because his provocative presence added a perverse sort of spice to the long journey.

'Is it?' said Fen. 'Irrelevant. Then why did you ask.'

'I was merely making conversation.'

'I see. Well, come and make it in my bedroom. The train's getting ready to leave.'

'Mr.—Fen! I am *not* visiting your bedroom.'

'All right. We can argue in the lounge if you prefer it.'

'Why should we argue?'

His lips tipped up. 'It's what we do, isn't it?'

In spite of herself, Nina laughed. 'Yes, I suppose it is.'

He nodded. 'So we might as well do it in private.'

'No,' said Nina. 'We mightn't.'

Fen sighed. 'OK, have it your way. Come along to the lounge. I'll buy you a drink.'

Nina didn't particularly want a drink. All the same, a few minutes later she was seated beside Fen in one of the brown armchairs sipping doubtfully on a glass of pink wine.

'Why do you want to talk to me?' she asked, knowing she sounded unnecessarily belligerent.

'It may help to pass the time on this very tedious journey.'

'Why are you making it if it's so tedious?' Nina bristled at once. She didn't like people criticizing her beloved train.

'I hadn't much choice. Unless I was prepared to hurt my sister badly by throwing her well-intentioned gift back into her teeth.'

'You mean this trip was a gift? From your sister?'

What an odd sort of present to give a man like Fen.

'Mmm. She knew I planned to fly to New York on business right after Christmas. So she went out and bought me a train ticket. Then she arranged for me to spend Christmas with our second cousin, Addison, on Long Island.' He examined his hands. 'I have a feeling Addison wasn't altogether delighted. But it's not easy to say no to Christine. I should know.'

Nina glanced at him sharply. There was resignation and wry affection in his voice, but it still surprised her that anyone could make Fen do anything he didn't want to do.

'Why couldn't you spend Christmas with her?' she asked. 'With your own sister?'

'I'd have been excess baggage. She's off to Hawaii on her honeymoon. Which would have left me alone in the house we've shared for the past eight years. Frankly, I was looking forward to it. Christine isn't the most relaxing woman to be around.' He gave an exaggerated sigh. 'But she got it into her head I was working too hard, that I needed a rest. If necessary, an enforced one. Hence this damned train.'

Nina frowned. 'Couldn't you have explained you didn't need the ticket, that you'd rest at home—'

He propped a foot on the shelf below the window and twisted to face her. 'I wouldn't have,' he admitted wryly. 'Chris knows me too well. She also managed to get our doctor on her side. He's an old friend.'

'Even so, you could have—'

'No. I couldn't,' he snapped, obviously losing patience with objections he'd long since considered and rejected. 'Christine was genuinely worried. And I owe her too much to allow her to spend her honeymoon fretting about the little brother she brought up single-handed. At considerable cost to herself. So I accepted the damned ticket and here I am. Bored out of my tree and wishing I could somehow sprout wings.' He grinned suddenly, his ill-humour falling away like a snake's skin. 'That's why I expect you to keep me amused.'

'I haven't so far,' said Nina, wishing she didn't feel a certain sympathy for this energetic powerhouse of a man who had generously placed his own inclinations second to his sister's peace of mind. He might be arrogant and exasperating, but he did have his good points.

'You'd be surprised,' he said, picking up her hand and linking her fingers through his. 'I told you I like a little lemon in my life. You fill the bill nicely.'

Nina didn't know what to say to that, so she said nothing, instead staring out of the window at the snow-covered plains of Montana. Usually she found the sweeping white expanses soothing. But there was nothing soothing about the feel of Fen's hand holding hers. The opposite, in fact. She felt on edge, alive, waiting for something to happen. Something electric and maybe dangerous.

'What about you?' asked Fen, in that rough velvet voice that sent ripples up her spine. 'Why are *you* travelling on this lumbering anachronism?'

'Because I love it. I hate flying.'

'Scared?' It was just a question. She didn't think he was jeering.

'Yes,' she admitted, taking a quick sip of her wine. 'I was in a very bad storm once. We nearly crashed. And I've always had trouble with my ears. So I only fly in emergencies. Which Christmas isn't.'

'No,' he agreed. 'It's an inconvenience, but hardly an emergency.'

She looked at him in surprise. 'Why do you say that? Don't you like Christmas?'

'Sure. It's good for business. It's also a time when people who don't have much of anything are made more aware of what they don't have than usual. You wouldn't know about that.'

'As a matter of fact I would,' said Nina, wondering why it was that just a few minutes of Fen's company was enough to make her want to break blunt instruments over his condescending head. She extricated her fingers and shoved her hand into the pocket of her jeans.

Fen's gaze skimmed over her with ill-concealed scepticism. 'Indeed?' he murmured. 'A time of peace and goodwill, is it? I hadn't realized you were so full of Christmas spirit.'

'I used to be,' said Nina, more irritated by his sarcasm than she wanted him to guess. 'When I was younger. But now—well, I have to admit Christmas has become a bit of a—well, like you said. An inconvenience.'

'Oh? Why's that?' He smiled and leaned back in his chair.

OK, he'd asked for it. 'Because my father always has some tame apology for a man lined up to make sheep's eyes at me, that's why,' she said tartly. 'Some man he wants me to marry.'

'Is that so bad?'

He thought it was funny. She could tell from the way his lip angled up. 'Yes,' she said. 'It is. Because the men are always up-and-coming executives from one of his enterprises. He buys them for me, you see.' She'd meant to speak lightly, but couldn't conceal the frustration and resentment she had never entirely managed to overcome.

Fen didn't pretend he hadn't heard it. 'And that doesn't do a lot for your ego? I suppose it wouldn't. Why does he have to *buy* men for you?'

'He doesn't. I don't want them. But he's desperate to see me married and settled down. Preferably to someone in business. He understands business.'

'So I imagine.' Fen spoke drily and without noticeable sympathy. 'And why is it so urgent for you to marry? Does he think you're likely to run off with the milkman?'

'Not really. He's afraid I'll be corrupted by my job, come in contact with unsuitable people. Or come to some kind of harm. And he thinks that if I'm married I'll stop working and stay safely under the thumb of my husband.'

'Unlikely,' murmured Fen, contemplating the pugnacious angle of her chin. His eyes gleamed suddenly. 'Although it might be worth trying it. Just for the entertainment value.'

'What might?' asked Nina suspiciously.

'Keeping you under that thumb.'

'Forget it,' she snapped.

Fen grinned, satisfied that he'd succeeded in provoking her. 'What are you then?' he asked. 'A policewoman? A private eye? A journalist?'

She shook her head, refusing to look at him.

'Ah.' He clapped a hand to his forehead. 'I've got it. You test parachutes for a living.'

In spite of herself, Nina smiled. 'No,' she said. 'Nothing as exciting as that. I'm a social worker.'

Chapter Two

NINA waited for Fen's eyebrows to rise. But instead they drew into a straight line and he said tersely, 'I should have guessed.'

'Why?' She stiffened at the sudden frost in his voice.

'Miss Cleethorpe.' He bit the name off like a curse. 'I said you reminded me of someone. I suppose it's a kind of aura that goes with the instinct to meddle.'

'Miss Cleethorpe?' Nina repeated, nettled by the implication that she meddled—or was connected to anybody's aura but her own. 'I don't know any Miss Cleethorpe.'

Fen gave a short laugh and pinned his gaze on the endless flat vistas of snow. 'No,' he agreed. 'But if you did, you'd get along famously. She was a lady I used to know well. Thanks to her, I spent my childhood in the perpetual apprehension of being taken away from Christine and put in a home for impoverished delinquents. Not that I got into any more trouble than the rest of the kids in my neighbourhood. Trouble was just a way of life.'

'Oh,' said Nina, as the light began to dawn. 'You mean she was your case worker.'

'I believe that's what she called herself. We had other names for her.'

Nina tried to suppress her irritation. She was aware that criticism and resentment often came with her line of work, but that didn't make Fen's gibes any easier to take.

'Would you like to talk about it?' she asked, as years of training came to her rescue.

'Good grief! You even use the same jargon,' Fen groaned. He strummed his fingers on the arm of his chair and glared at a plane passing beneath a cloud.

Nina said nothing. Experience had taught her that if people wanted to tell her what was eating them, they did so. Unwanted prying would only make Fen more determined to keep his feelings to himself.

It proved the right tactic. After a while he stopped glaring at the scenery long enough to turn his glare on her. Then gradually, as she met his look with disarming mildness, the harsh angles of his face took on a smoother, less hostile aspect and he said, 'No. I wouldn't much like to talk. But I suppose after that undeserved brickbat I owe you an explanation.'

'You don't owe me anything.' Nina gave him a small, cautious smile.

Fen swallowed a long draught of what she supposed was bourbon. 'True. But I can hardly expect you to entertain me unless I pull up my socks and behave like the gentleman I'm not.'

Was that mockery she heard in his voice? Or reluctant penitence?

Nina's smile grew more confident. 'All right,' she said. 'You can start by not calling me a meddler. It's something I try hard not to be. I know what it feels like to be constantly interfered with, which is why I prefer to give help where it's needed and then back off.'

'Is that what you're doing now?'

'What? Backing off?'

'Mmm.'

'I suppose so. If that's what you want.'

He grinned suddenly. 'I'm not at all sure it is. But then just for the record, Miss Cleethorpe wasn't nearly as pretty as you.'

Another come-on? Or was he just trying to mend fences? 'Wasn't she?' said Nina non-committally.

He shook his head. 'No. She wasn't. And I suppose it's even possible she meant well. But backing off wasn't in her character.' He paused, and when she said nothing he switched his gaze back to the snow. 'My mother left us after my father died. She said she had a right to a life of her own now that Christine was old enough to look after me. Not the easiest job in the world, so my dear sister frequently informed me.'

No, thought Nina. It wouldn't be. 'Do you mean your mother didn't come back? Ever?' she asked disbelievingly.

'Nope. To be fair, though, I think my father's death affected her mind. She used to write once in a while at first. Then the letters stopped. I had her checked out a few years back.'

No emotion. Just a bald statement of fact. Nina wondered how long it had taken him to learn to conceal his emotions so effectively—for the bewildered little boy to turn into this tough, hard-headed man.

'Is your mother still alive?' she asked.

'Oh, yes. Alive and living in Texas. In some sort of commune. She seems happy.'

'I see. And so you and Christine were left completely on your own.' The puzzle was beginning to fit together.

He nodded. 'Chris was seventeen when our mother went away. I was seven. And I'm told I kept her on her toes. Hence Miss Cleethorpe.' He shrugged dismissively, as if he felt he'd said more he should have. 'Don't look so stunned. We all survived. Even Cleethorpe. And I've managed to pay Chris back at least some of what I owe her. Thank God she's finally found a man who can give her the life she deserves.'

He spoke without inflection, but Nina wasn't deceived. The abandoned child had turned into a hard, determined man who didn't allow emotion to sway his actions.

But he loved his sister.

Nina had no idea what Fen did for a living, but there was no doubt in her mind that, like her father, and in spite of his brief flashes of humour, he would be ruthless in pursuit of his own goals. This was a man who had learned to take what he wanted from life.

But what *did* he want? For no particular reason, she shivered, and something, some fleeting thought she knew she'd had before, flickered like a shadow across her mind.

'And you?' she asked, carefully now. 'Are you—um—comfortably settled?'

'Shades of Miss Cleethorpe,' Fen muttered. And then, seeing her quick frown, he said, 'If by that you mean, do I have marriage in mind, the answer is no, I do not. I've never found the time to get to know a woman well enough to ask her.'

'Oh,' said Nina, not sure how to interpret the challenging gleam in his eye. 'All work and no play...' She paused. 'You must lead a very dull life.'

Fen shook his head. 'That's what Christine says. She's wrong. I enjoy work. And when I've felt the need for other—shall we say, diversions I've managed to find like-minded ladies.' He put his head on one side and gave her a slow, provocative smile that made her glad she was sitting down when he added softly, 'I promise you it hasn't been dull.'

'I'm not a diversion,' said Nina quickly.

'I was afraid you weren't.' Fen heaved a sigh. 'I can see this is going to turn into a very long and boring journey.'

Oh! Of course. That was *it!* That was what she'd been trying not to remember. Nina stared into the pink liquid in her glass. Fen's dislike of trains, his reluctance to spend Christmas with his cousin...

The idea that she had refused to give credence to in the lonely, creaking hours of the night returned with a sudden insistence. She tried to push it away. But this time it wouldn't let go.

Yes, Fen might be casually on the make and much too autocratic for comfort, but he made her laugh when he wasn't making her want to hit him. And now that she understood something of his background, he didn't seem quite as obnoxious as she'd thought him at first.

It *was* possible. Wasn't it? He was all business, of course. That was as obvious as his pressed grey pinstripe. But from the little he'd said about his work, she didn't think he was a very prominent corporate cog.

He might be glad of free room and board and the chance to get out of spending Christmas with his cousin.

But—did she really have the nerve to suggest it? How was he likely to react? He might refuse and make her feel a fool. That would be—awkward. Worse than awkward. And yet—if she didn't ask him how would she ever know?

She stole a quick glance at his profile. His mouth was still curved in that soft, sensuous smile that set all her nerve ends on red alert. And for the first time, she observed a thin scar running from his hairline to just above his right eye. There were lines beside his mouth, too, that she hadn't noticed before.

What did she really know about this man? Was she just plain crazy? She had to be even to think what she was thinking. So why wouldn't the insanity go away?

Nina swallowed the rest of her wine in a gulp. She might be crazy, but there was one very compelling reason for giving the matter serious reflection.

She would soon be in Chicago with her father. And Fen was a man supremely uninterested in marriage.

She put her glass down abruptly and stood up. 'I have to be going,' she said. 'Um—perhaps I'll see you later?'

Fen stretched his arms above his head and smiled lazily. 'Perhaps. I'm in Room A.'

Nina paused. Was he suggesting what she thought he was? She eyed his sprawled body with suspicion—and when she felt a quick, unwanted frisson of desire, she looked away. 'That's a deluxe bedroom,' she said, because it was the first response that came into her head.

Fen nodded. 'Yes, I'd noticed. Christine had sense enough to know that not even she could persuade me to spend two days cooped up in a box the size of a beer crate. Besides...' He flicked a speck of dust off the fawn trousers stretched so smoothly across his thighs. 'She happens to be marrying the owner of an exceptionally large and successful shopping mall.'

Oh. So that was why he believed Christine's bridegroom would give her what she deserved. In Fen's mind success was probably what counted. Nina felt an odd flare of irritation. Then wondered why it mattered.

Without answering him, she turned to walk down the aisle—and promptly lurched against the back of a seat occupied by an elderly gentleman snoozing over his daily paper.

'Missed,' murmured Fen. 'Better luck next time.'

The elderly gentleman grunted, Nina frowned and Fen gave a low, gravelly chuckle.

Damn him. On second thoughts, maybe her brain-wave hadn't been so brilliant after all.

That evening she enjoyed a congenial dinner with three women heading for a convention. But when it was over, once again Nina found herself alone in her compart-ment contemplating a week spent dodging mistletoe and flabby, groping hands. There was no reason for the hands to be flabby. But they always were. She shuddered, and after a while got up and went into the lounge. No sign of Fen, so she stumbled down the curving stairs leading to the bar. It was filled with smoke. Nina peered through the haze, but no long body sat draped over any of the ob-long tables, and most of the heads that turned her way were bald.

When Fen wasn't in any of the day coaches, either, Nina gave up and made her way back to the sleeping car. She hesitated briefly outside the door of Room A, then had a sudden vision of Fen's sexy smile—and of a predatory hand curling round the back of her neck, drawing her in, then closing the door softly behind her....

The porter, on his way to make up a bed, brushed against her arm. Nina started.

'You OK, miss?' he asked.

She realized then that she had been standing in the corridor with her eyes closed. 'Yes, I'm fine. Thank you.' She gave him a reassuring smile and hurried to her room to collect her sponge bag. Then she headed downstairs to have a shower in the small but efficiently appointed shower room.

When she came up again, demurely buttoned into a yellow brushed-cotton robe and with her hair hanging damply around her face, Fen was standing above her with his arms resting on the rail along the window. He had his back to her and seemed totally unaware of her presence.

Nina paused for a second, admiring the tight stretch of trousers across his rear, and almost at once he swung round. 'I thought I smelled powder and freshly showered woman,' he said softly. He looked her up and down. 'Mmm. Very proper. No breaching those defences, I suppose?'

'I should hope not.' Nina lifted her chin. She hesitated for just a fraction of a second, then said quickly, and before she could change her mind, 'But I do have a proposition to make.'

'Good,' said Fen. 'I thought you'd never ask.' He held out his arms and leered down at her. 'I'm all yours.'

'Not that sort of proposition,' said Nina, suppressing an unexpected and enormously disconcerting urge to take him at his word.

Fen sighed. 'I thought it was too good to be true.' He jerked his head at the door of Room A. 'Never mind. Come in and tell me about it.'

'No, I—'

'You want us to go sit in the lounge car?' His warm brown gaze raked suggestively over her yellow robe.

'I could change.'

'Look,' said Fen, not troubling to hide his exasperation. 'If I had the slightest inclination to rip your clothes off, I could do it right here in the corridor, whether you were wearing that canary-coloured advertisement for chastity or not. So how about you put your lurid imagination on hold and come into my parlour like a good little fly. I have a number of vices, but attacking lemons isn't one of them. And to be honest, I find the suggestion that it might be most offensive.'

He was smiling, but his eyes weren't, and Nina had no doubt that he meant it.

'OK,' she said, taking a deep breath and making up her mind. 'Let's go.'

Fen rolled his eyes at the swaying ceiling and opened the door of Room A. As Nina ducked under his arm she smelled the faint scent of spice. It was a very male smell, ominously seductive. She turned to see him closing the door, and swallowed uncomfortably.

Fen's bunk had not yet been pulled out for the night, and Nina took in at once that his room was more than big enough for two people. It was fitted with a sofa and chair and a pull-out table, and he also had his own bathroom and sink. If her mind hadn't been on another, more pressing matter, she might have regretted her annual refusal to let her father buy her ticket. Joseph would have settled for nothing less than this.

'Have a seat,' said Fen.

She took the chair, then wished she hadn't, because Fen immediately propped a pillow behind his head and swung his legs up on to the sofa. He looked disturbingly alluring stretched out like that—lean, intimate and altogether too available.

'Well?' he said, smiling like a predatory cat. 'What is it you want to propose? I'm open to offers.'

Yes, she had no doubt he was. In more ways than one. And that, of course, was precisely why she was here. It was also why she seemed to be having trouble finding words.

'It's not what you're thinking,' she blurted, nervously checking the top button on her robe. 'You see, what I need—well, want, anyway—is a man.' No, that hadn't come out right. 'Just for Christmas,' she explained, making it worse.

Fen stretched, more catlike than ever, and his gold-stone eyes gleamed at her in the light beaming down from the lamp above his head. 'Interesting. I've never been gift-wrapped before. But I guess I could go for it.'

'No, you don't understand.' Nina put her hands up to her cheeks to hide a blush. 'I meant I need someone to pretend to be a man—'

'Pretend? Now look here, Miss Lemon, I've been accused of many things in my time, but I'll have you know—'

'Stop it,' she said, exasperation overcoming her nervousness. 'Please—just listen.'

'I'm all ears,' he replied, linking his hands behind his head.

He wasn't. He was all sinew and muscle and endless leg, and his lips were... No. Oh, no! Nina pushed herself up straight and took a long, deliberate breath.

Fen ran a careless hand through his hair and closed his eyes.

'Fen,' she said desperately, 'I can't talk to you if you're going to go to sleep.'

He opened his eyes at once, and she wished he hadn't, because they sent her a message so explicit it brought goose bumps to her skin. 'Who says I'm sleeping?' he said.

Nina shook her head. 'You don't understand. The point is—is that I need someone to pretend to be the man in my life.' Oh God! That had come out as if she were asking for a second cup of tea. She tried again. 'Someone who will convince my father to lay off the troops and—and who will go away once the holiday is over. Do you see what I mean?'

'Not really. Wouldn't it be easier, and a lot more honest, just to go along with the troops?' Fen's lazy drawl immediately set her teeth on edge.

'No. No, it wouldn't.' She curled her fingers tightly in her lap. 'Dad picks them for their persistence. The last three followed me to Seattle. *After* they'd spent the entire Christmas week breathing down my neck, dragging me under the mistletoe, and making sheep's eyes at me over the leftover turkey.'

Fen appeared to have something caught in his throat.

'Well,' she asked doubtfully, when she had his attention again. 'Will you do it?'

'What? Make sheep's eyes at you over the turkey?'

Nina gritted her bicuspids. 'No. Be my man of the moment. You—you're rude and impossible. But at least you don't smell of martinis.' When he only gazed at her in what appeared to be total disbelief, she added hurriedly, 'And once the holiday season is over I know you won't ask me to marry you.'

'Mmm. On that you *can* trust me,' agreed Fen. 'I may be rude and impossible, but I've yet to propose to a lemon.'

'So you'll do it?' Nina kept her temper with an effort.

'No. I will not.' He switched off the light above his head, throwing his face into shadowed relief.

He'd turned her down. She'd found the courage to ask him, and he'd turned her down. 'But why not?' she persisted. There was nothing to be gained from giving up now. She had already made herself look ridiculous. 'You don't want to spend Christmas in New York. You said you didn't.'

'I don't much. Nor do I want to spend it in Chicago pretending to be someone I'm not.'

'You don't have to be someone you're not. You can be you. My father won't know you. Will he?'

'I doubt it.'

That was all right then. At least . . .

'Fen—what is it that you actually do?' It probably didn't matter, but just in case she could get him to change his mind, she ought to know that much about him.

'I'm in imported food.' Fen didn't elaborate.

Oh, so he was just a buyer for some fancy food company. That explained the trip to New York. And as food wasn't one of her father's sidelines, there wouldn't be much danger of his knowing more about Fen than he should. Her plan *could* work—if he'd only co-operate.

'Fen,' she said, 'I'm certain there won't be a problem with food—'

'None at all. Because I'm not falling in with your little scheme.'

He spoke pleasantly enough, but he was adamant. She recognized that uncompromising tone. She'd heard it often enough from Joseph. But . . . She held her breath for a moment. What Joseph couldn't demand, he bought.

Nina shut her eyes. She didn't want to *buy* Fen's co-operation. Besides, she wasn't sure he could be bought. But if he could—if he could, she supposed he would be better than the alternative, which would be to spend yet another Christmas dodging moist lips, groping hands and phony protestations of adoration.

Joseph had always told her everyone had his price.

She made up her mind. 'I'll make it worth your while,' she said quickly, before she could change it again. 'How much will it take?'

She heard his indrawn breath, saw the sudden rigidity of his shoulders, and for a moment she thought—hoped?—he would refuse. But after a lengthy silence during which she could almost hear the wheels grinding in his brain, he said in a crisp, businesslike voice that held not the slightest hint of velvet, 'That depends. How much are you offering, Miss Petrov? And precisely what will you expect in return?' There was a glint in his eye that Nina didn't know quite how to take.

She gulped. Why was he responding with such detachment? And he had called her Miss Petrov again, the name he associated with undeserved wealth and privilege. Yet he was apparently ready to strike a bargain. She felt a vague stab of unease.

'I told you,' she said, checking her top button again. 'I—well, I just want you to be my man for a few days.'

'Yes? And exactly what services does the job entail?' He raised his arms above his head and flexed his shoulders against the pillow. 'I've never been paid for my favours before.'

Nina gulped. She couldn't take her eyes off him. And she was almost sure he knew it, and was greatly enjoying her reluctant fascination.

But he sounded about as warm as an iceberg. Did he really think she was the kind of woman who would pay a man to—to... Well, yes. Obviously he did. She swallowed. Maybe this hadn't been such a great idea after all. Surely there was still time to back out....

'How much?' asked Fen, before she could put her thoughts into words. And was that minuscule movement of his lips actually a quickly suppressed smile?

No, it couldn't be. 'I—don't know,' she mumbled, biting the inside of her cheek. 'I didn't mean I expected you to—um—'

'Make love to you? Well, that lowers the price then, doesn't it?'

Oh, God. This was worse than she could possibly have imagined. And now she was so confused that she didn't know *how* to back out.

She moistened her lips. 'How much do you want?'

He named a figure. It wasn't exorbitant. Well within her means. And if Fenton Hardwick thought it was enough, he must be even further down the corporate ladder than she'd imagined. Still, he didn't *seem* to see her relationship to her father as a ticket to his personal advancement. That was something. Better than Joseph's tame suitors.

'Yes,' she agreed. 'Yes, all right. I'll get my cheque book.' She stood up, and beneath her the wheels of the train kept pace with the uneven pounding of her heart.

A few minutes later, with a few quick strokes of her pen, the deed was done.

Fen inspected the cheque she had handed him then gave her a curt nod. 'Seems in order,' he drawled.

'Good.' Nina bit her lip. 'Um—we'll be in Chicago to-morrow night, so do you think we'd better—'

'Practice our Christmas charade?' he suggested, re-moving a hair from her shoulder, studying it, then flick-ing it on to the floor.

'Well—make sure we both tell the same story, at least,' amended Nina, feeling numb.

He nodded. 'Sounds advisable. We'll meet for break-fast, shall we? Good night, Miss Petrov.'

'Good night.' She waited, wondering if he would try to take advantage of their altered relationship. But all he did was reach for the bell to call the porter to make up his bed.

Nina looked back once before she left. Fen was draped across the sofa looking relaxed and sexy. And just be-fore she slid the door shut, she saw him push a hand through his hair. When he lowered it, she caught a glimpse of his eyes. They were lit with a dark, devilish glitter that made her wonder what she had let herself in for.

She shook her head, paused for a moment, then made her way to her compartment feeling much the same as she had felt as a child on the day she learned that Santa Claus was a myth. Which didn't make a whole lot of sense.

You're being a fool, Nina Petrov, she lectured herself as she collapsed on top of her bed. You've got what you asked for. A man to take the heat off over Christmas—a man who won't try to kiss you in corners and who has no intention of remaining in your life.

Except, murmured that tiresome little voice in her head, that being kissed in corners by Fen Hardwick might be an experience that... No. She wasn't even going to allow herself to think it. She had bought Fen, just as her father had bought all the others. And the fact that he could be attractive and amusing when it suited him didn't make him any different from the rest. He was a man. He could be bought. Once he'd done his job he'd be gone. For good. Unexpectedly a lump began to form in her throat. She swallowed, twice, and it went away.

Good. Now, with luck, she would have a peaceful Christmas. And for once when she returned to Seattle there would be no scheming swain in hot pursuit.

Nina settled her head on the pillow and closed her eyes, hoping these bracing reflections would lead to an undisturbed night. But sleep didn't come easily, and by the time she slouched into breakfast the following morning she felt a lot like a soufflé that hadn't happened. Not that soufflés felt anything much, she supposed. She wished *she* didn't. Because there was Fen, already seated at a table, and with his white smile and slightly damp skin, he looked like a gift to womankind from the god of mornings.

'Good grief! The lemon's turned into a lime,' he exclaimed, standing up as soon as he saw her come in. Once she was seated he sat down again and studied her more closely. 'Do you realize your skin has turned green?'

'Thanks,' said Nina sourly. 'I had a bad night, all right?'

'I can see that.' He eyed her shrewdly. 'Having second thoughts?'

'No. Are you? You can return my cheque if you want to.' She held her breath, not sure what she was hoping for but knowing his answer was important.

Fen's eyes glinted with sudden malice. 'Why should I? We struck a bargain. I haven't much use for people who break their promises.'

'In other words you do what you've been paid to do,' Nina said flatly. 'I suppose I ought to respect that.'

'I suppose you ought—since Daddy's money puts you in the fortunate position of being able to buy whatever, and whoever, you want.'

'I thought money was what you wanted,' said Nina dully, resenting enormously the fact that there was some truth to what he said—even though she hadn't accepted help from Joseph for many years. 'And it's not my father's money. It's mine.' She paused while the waiter took her order, then muttered, 'This isn't going to work, is it?'

'Oh, yes, it is,' said Fen. 'You're not getting off that easily, my girl.'

'So you do want the money?'

Fen didn't answer directly. Instead he peeled the foil back from a small square package and began to spread jam on his toast. 'What do you think?' he asked.

'Well—you took it.'

'And you offered it.'

His voice was smooth, unemotional. But he *had* taken the money, so she couldn't have made a mistake. 'Yes,' she said, making a decision. 'I did. So I guess we'll just have to make it work.'

'Oh, it'll work,' said Fen. 'I'll see to it.'

She didn't like the sound of that. The edge was back in his voice, and she had a feeling that although he would keep his side of the bargain, he didn't intend to make it easy.

She was right. The train, which was running a little late, was just pulling into St. Paul, Minnesota, when Fen threw down his napkin and said, 'Come on. We'd better start as we mean to go on. Let the world get a good look at the young lovers—just in case Daddy's spies are on the prowl.'

'They won't be. And I haven't finished my coffee—'

'Then finish it. We'll be in the station in a minute.'

Nina decided the matter wasn't worth arguing about, so she swallowed her coffee and made her way to her compartment to fetch her coat. When Fen met her at the door he took her arm in a proprietorial fashion and marched her briskly out on to the platform.

'Brr. It's cold,' said Nina, making conversation to take her mind off his disturbing proximity.

'Not as balmy as Seattle,' he conceded. 'And I suppose that as the besotted and attentive suitor it's up to me to keep you warm.'

Before Nina could tell him that wasn't necessary, he had looped an arm over her shoulder and tucked her up against his side. Then he began to whisk her along the platform towards the station. 'Better?'

bright, crystalline shores of a nameless Upper Mississippi lake, and at that moment it gave another gentle lurch.

'I didn't. It's called F and C Foods.' Fen's gaze rested on her with unexpected intensity.

'Yes,' said Nina, frowning as she braced herself against the door-frame. 'I've heard of them, I think.'

She had, too. There was a connection somewhere, but her mind just wouldn't quite make it.

'I expect you have,' he said non-committally. His supple body seemed to relax.

'I'm off.' Nina spoke quickly, before the seductive lure of his sudden smile could weave its magic. 'I want to catch some sleep before we hit Chicago.'

'Then I'll see you later,' Fen said softly.

Nina stumbled to her room and closed the door.

There wasn't the remotest likelihood of sleep. She was too tense and restless to close her eyes. But she had needed desperately to get away from Fen. The more time she spent in his company, the more convinced she became that she had bitten off more than she could chew. And what a tasty mouthful he might have been if—if he hadn't been for sale like all the rest.

Nina sighed, and stared out at the white, frozen waters of the lake. Was it possible to become emotionally involved with a man in just two days? She had chosen him as her decoy precisely because it *wasn't* possible. And yet now she found herself unable to think of anything or anybody else. He had filled her mind almost from the moment she'd set eyes on him striding arrogantly down the platform in Seattle. But she wouldn't, *couldn't* allow herself to care for a man who could be bought. Even if he did have the face and form of an Olympian god and could melt her bones with the force of his smile.

It was. Much better. And much too warm. She could feel the lean length of him all along her side. 'Yes.' She cleared her throat nervously. 'Yes. Thank you. I'm fine now. You don't have to hold me.'

'Maybe I like holding you,' he said amiably. Too amiably.

'Oh.' She threw him a doubtful glance as they made their way through the glass doors leading into the crowded station. 'But you can't. It's not part of the bargain.'

'What isn't? Holding or liking?'

Nina didn't answer, mainly because she couldn't think of anything to say. Holding her probably *was* part of the bargain if they were to convince Joseph they were seriously devoted.

Fen had just steered her round a crowd of noisy teenagers surrounding a mountain of packsacks when they almost collided with a harried young mother in pursuit of giggling twin boys. The boys were running determinedly for the exit. 'Roddy,' the distracted mother was shouting. 'Reggie! If you don't come back right this minute, I'll—'

'Allow me,' said Fen. To Nina's immense relief, he released her and strode purposefully after the two offenders. Within seconds he had scooped them up, one squirming little body under each arm. 'Where would you like them?' he asked the mother as she came panting up behind him.

'In a cage,' she groaned. 'But I guess you better put them over there.' She pointed at the nearest row of chairs.

Fen nodded and sat the boys down. 'And no more of your nonsense,' he told them sternly. 'Give your mother one more bit of trouble before she gets you safely on the train and you'll have me to answer to. Understand?'

They nodded mutely, two little black heads with enormous eyes.

The mother grinned. 'Thanks,' she said. 'It's tough travelling without their father. But I bet they'll behave themselves now. Won't you, boys?'

The two nodded again, and Fen grinned at them. 'Good. Just be sure you do.' He turned to look for Nina, who was watching him from near the doors leading out to the street.

'What's the matter?' he asked, going up to her. 'You look as if you've just spotted the Christmas turkey eloping with the Easter ham.'

She laughed. 'No, nothing as surreal as that. I just couldn't quite believe what I was seeing. You like children, don't you?'

'Mmm. Does that surprise you?'

It did somehow. He seemed the sort of man who would be too busy taking care of business to have either the time or the patience for children. Her father had been like that. He had loved her in his way, but as a child she had always suspected he was fondest of her when she was either at school or asleep. His determination to marry her off to the first eligible man who came along was only an extension of that attitude.

'Yes, I guess it does surprise me,' Nina admitted. 'You don't seem the paternal sort somehow.'

'Oh, I don't know,' Fen drawled. 'You have to admit I'm good at keeping brats in order.' The words and his expression were bland. But when he patted her lightly on the cheek, she knew he wasn't referring to the twins.

'You,' she began, 'are the most impossibly patronizing—' She broke off as a disembodied voice blasted over the speaker system announcing that passengers should now reboard the train.

'And are you the maternal type?' asked Fen, ignoring her interrupted outburst. He took her arm and hustled her through the jostling throng on the platform.

'I suppose I must be.' Nina felt uncomfortably warm again and almost certain that Fen knew exactly what he was doing to her blood pressure. Even his hand on her arm was enough to send it soaring. But there was no sense losing her temper. She inhaled deeply and hurried on, 'Most of my work is with disadvantaged kids. Or kids with problems.'

'Like me?' he suggested drily, dropping his hand over her hip.

'No.' Her voice came out high and breathless. '*You* are neither disadvantaged nor a kid.'

'But I'm a problem?'

Yes, he was a problem, all right. And that mocking lift was back in his voice. 'You could be,' she said carefully. No doubt he would enjoy being a problem.

'I aim to please,' Fen murmured. They were outside Room A again, and before Nina could tell him she meant to go to her room to rest, he had opened the door and, putting his hand in the small of her back, had thrust her unceremoniously inside.

'Hey,' she said. 'You can't—'

'Yes, I can. You paid me to do a job. I'm the new man in your life. Remember?'

'Yes, but—'

'And in order to play the role convincingly it's high time we held a practice session.'

'Practice session?' croaked Nina. 'What kind of practice?'

'This kind.' Fen raised his arms and began to unbutton her coat.

Chapter Three

NINA stood frozen beneath Fen's touch. She wanted to tell him to take his hands off her—those hands that were peeling the protective layers from her mind as briskly and efficiently as they were peeling off her coat. Her mind told her she must put a stop to his activities at once. But her mouth wouldn't open. With a strange detachment, she wondered if she was about to lose the gift she had been saving for that special man, here, in this comfortable but confining compartment.

That would be the ultimate irony. She had wanted her father to think Fen *was* that special man.

He finished with the coat and pushed it off her shoulders on to the chair. Nina gazed up at him mutely. There was an unusually bright light in his eyes, all golden and glowing and seductive. And yet gradually, as he unfastened the top button of the yellow plaid shirt she was wearing, she began to get a sense that what he had started almost as a joke, or perhaps to prove a point or to punish, had become something else. Something he had neither expected nor wanted.

Behind the golden seduction, and just before he kissed her, she saw doubt.

Then his fingers slipped under her shirt and around the back of her neck, stroking and teasing, provoking sensations only dimly dreamed before. When at last she could be silent no longer, Nina gave a low murmur of surrender, and Fen's lips closed coolly over hers.

Too coolly. There was something wrong, not as it should be—something controlled and calculating about the way he was easing his tongue into her mouth, pushing his fingers through her hair, cradling the back of her head so she couldn't move. She put her hands on his shoulders, at first in an attempt to inject warmth into an embrace that she sensed was not an embrace at all, but an experiment or—what had Fen called it? A practice.

But after only a few seconds she stopped waiting for the flare of a passion that seemed not to be there. Desire faded, and she pushed him away.

He didn't attempt to hold her, but stepped back at once. In the same moment the train swung round a corner and flung him against the window.

'Are you all right?' asked Nina, as he steadied himself.

A corner of his mouth slanted up. 'In what way?'

'I meant are you hurt.'

'Not noticeably.'

All right, if he wanted to play it that way, who was she to stop him? 'Why did you kiss me?' she asked, picking up her coat and folding it over her knee as she sat down.

Fen sank on to the sofa and immediately the room seemed larger.

He shrugged. 'Sorry. Isn't that what you paid me to do?'

Nina decided not to rise to what she suspected was an attempt to pay her back for having hired him. He might want her money, but she had a distinct feeling he thought less of her for paying it. Not that what he thought of her should matter.

It did, though.

'No,' she said. 'I paid you to spend Christmas with my family and, if necessary, to run interference when my father's latest offering becomes persistent.'

'OK. No kisses unless desperate measures are needed.' He tipped his head back and Nina noticed a thin film of sweat where his neck met the open collar of his clean cream silk shirt. 'So tell me,' he said after a brief silence, 'what do I need to know about you in order to play my part with appropriate conviction? Apart, of course, from the fact that you're used to getting your own way, and that lemon is your flavour of the season.'

'I'm not, and it isn't,' snapped Nina. She eyed him balefully, in a way wanting to forget the whole deal. That kiss had shaken her more than she was willing to admit. Because she couldn't afford to be even remotely attracted to Fen. That was the whole point in hiring him. But if she backed out now he would think he'd made her lose her nerve. Which he almost had.

She waited for her temper to cool then took a deep breath. 'All right,' she said. 'I suppose you should know that I've never had a serious romance, that I work in Seattle because it's a good long way from Chicago—I share an apartment with a friend—and that I love my job. At our house those three subjects are served up every Christmas along with the turkey and Brussels sprouts and plum pudding.'

Fen smiled. This time it was a nice smile, almost as if he actually sympathized. But he spoiled it at once by saying, 'No serious romance? That I can accept, given the general unpalatability of lemons. I can also understand that your father's objections to his daughter's dirtying her hands in a job he considers unladylike might drive you to practise your trade away from home. But why social work, for Pete's sake? What do you know about ordinary people's needs?'

Nina tried not to flinch. She didn't think Fen had actually meant to hurt her. He was just incapable of understanding that one didn't necessarily have to have experienced hunger and deprivation to know that they were bad and to want to do something about them. In a way, she supposed it was just *because* she'd had a privileged childhood that when she grew up she had wanted to give something back. But Fen's childhood had been so different that he couldn't see it. Couldn't see that she had never believed having money in the bank absolved anyone from caring about others.

But there was no point trying to explain, and in the end she said simply, 'I love children. I wanted to help.'

'Hmm.' He stared at her for a few seconds, frowning as if something puzzled him. Then he turned to gaze out of the window.

Nina studied the side of him she could see, the clearly defined bones, the droop of a heavy eyelid and the surprisingly sensitive curve of his mouth. And a sudden urge to reach out to him, to touch him on some level deeper than the merely physical, made her say quietly, 'I'm sorry your mother left you. Sorry that—well, that your life wasn't—isn't easy—'

'What?' He swung to face her, his expression a mixture of exasperation, amusement and disbelief. 'What gives you that idea?'

'You seem—bitter sometimes. And you said you work too hard—perhaps because you've never had much, and mean to have it all some day—'

'I did *not* say I work too hard. My beloved sister did. And I don't know what you mean by "much" but whatever it is, I have plenty.'

Oh, sure. That was why he had accepted what amounted to a bribe. The only thing Fen Hardwick had much of was a misplaced pride and a stubborn refusal to acknowledge reality.

Nina's urge to give comfort evaporated.

'I'm glad to hear it,' she said.

'Mmm.' Fen eyed her sardonically. 'You know, if you look at me like that in front of your father, he'll have me thrown out of the house. And before you know it you'll be married off to the opposition.'

Nina sighed. He was right. Not about her being married off to anyone, but about the need to present an amicable and united front to her father. And if only Fen would co-operate instead of going out of his way to antagonize her, there would be no problem.

She forced herself to smile. 'He'd have trouble throwing you out, I should think. But if we can just manage to behave as though we like each other—'

'Right,' Fen interrupted. 'So start liking.' He patted his knee in invitation.

'I don't mean that way,' said Nina, exasperated. Yet she found herself biting back a smile. She thought for a moment. 'Tell me what I ought to know about *you* to make our story sound convincing.'

'Well,' he drawled, 'you could say you found me in a gutter, picked me up and dusted me off—'

'He might believe that, but he wouldn't like it,' said Nina drily. 'I mean tell me about your job, what it is you actually do. What kind of house you live in. That's the kind of thing Dad's bound to ask. Not your favourite colour or how you like your eggs.'

'Ah.' Fen stretched his arms above his head. 'My job involves buying and distributing food, travel, meetings, some personnel work and—oh, various things that come up. As to my living arrangements, I have recently sold our house and will soon be moving into an apartment. Closer to the office now that Christine doesn't need me any longer.'

'What kind of food?' asked Nina. Getting information out of Fen was like trying to open a tightly sealed jar.

'Oh, caviar, snails and chocolate bees. Some interesting sauces. Pâtés. Cheeses. That sort of thing.'

'Oh,' said Nina. 'Gourmet stuff.'

His eyes narrowed. 'You don't approve?'

She shook her head. 'I'm surprised *you* do.'

'Given my plebeian origins?' he asked, with a familiar edge to his voice.

'No, given your macho-man attitudes,' said Nina.

'I see. As it happens, a lifetime of Christine's economy casseroles gave me a taste for more exotic fare. That's the reason I chose my current line of business.'

Nina recognized a rebuke when she heard one. Once again Fen was calling her attention to the differences in their backgrounds.

'How touching. Rags to riches,' she taunted, because somehow his mild reproof had touched her on the raw.

'Watch it. Your lemon juice is leaking, Miss Petrov. It's my understanding we're supposed to like each other.' If she read the look in his eye correctly, he was about as fond of her as she was of cockroaches.

'Yes,' she agreed, looking him directly in the eye. 'But you don't like me, do you?'

She expected him to shrug and pass it off. Instead he met her look with one equally direct and said, 'I'm damned if I know. There have certainly been moments when I've been tempted to tip you discreetly off the train.'

He stroked his chin, and a pensive smile began to lighten his features. 'There is one thing I'm certain of, though.'

'What's that?'

'That I'd like to take you to bed. Provided, of course, that you make it worth my while.'

'What?' Nina gaped at him, stunned and angry. But just as she was about to tell him in minute and uncomplimentary detail exactly what she thought of men who could be bought, especially for *that*, she saw his smile broaden into a grin. A taunting, attractive, maddeningly complacent grin.

As usual, Fen was baiting her. And she had swallowed the bait whole.

'What would you do if I took you up on that?' she asked, stifling an urgent desire to kick him, hard, on the nice stretch of shin that was well within range of her solid brown travelling shoe.

The grin turned into a villainous leer. 'Why don't you try it and find out,' he suggested, flexing a muscular forearm.

Nina shook her head and stood up. 'You're impossible,' she said, crossly. He'd really had her going there. And it *was* impossible to tell when he was serious and when he was merely leading her on. She still had that odd feeling that although he had allowed her to buy him, he hadn't liked it one bit.

There was something about Fenton Hardwick that didn't add up. She had felt that right from the beginning.

Hardwick... As she made her way over to the door, something, some nebulous memory, stirred and began to tease the back of her brain.

'What company did you say you worked for?' she asked. The train was now winding its way along the

She lifted her chin and fixed her gaze on the pearl-grey sky that hinted strongly of more snow. Then, after a few minutes of watching the passing clouds, she reached for the first of the three books she had brought to read. The books she hadn't even looked at because of Fen.

It was called *Risk Not the Heart*.

'I won't,' said Nina out loud. 'No danger of that.'

But when she went along to the lounge car shortly before lunch and saw Fen's glossy brown head bent over a curly blonde one, it hit her like a blow between the ribs that the danger wasn't as remote as she had thought.

Her first reaction was surprise, followed almost at once by a quick rush of indignation. Then, when she felt her heart beating extra fast and the blood rushing up to her ears, the truth came to her in a crushing revelation. She had not only risked her heart—she was well on her way to losing it altogether.

Nina pressed her lips together and curled her fingers into her palms. This was ridiculous. Fen was only *talking* to the girl. And the fact that he was smiling that white, irresistible smile was none of her business. Nor was it her business that the corners of his eyes were crinkled attractively with amusement.

The girl was very young. Pretty, with a pert little face that was laughing up at Fen with an admiration she wasn't attempting to disguise.

When Nina's throat muscles began to contract, she swallowed hard and made to turn away.

Fen chose that moment to look up, and as soon as he saw her he lifted a finger and beckoned.

Nina hesitated. She didn't want to talk to Fen now, wasn't sure she would be able to hide her quite inexcusable jealousy. Because that's what it was. Jealousy. Of a girl who was flirting with a man she didn't want.

Couldn't possibly want because he was precisely the sort of man she'd been avoiding for years.

Except—except that Fen *wasn't* like her father's eager suitors. On the surface he was. But...

No. No, there couldn't be any buts. Her problem was just a belated attack of lust. She was overdue for one, surely—had never really had one before. At least not like this. And lust she could easily deal with by heading it off at the pass.

There would have to be a slight change of plan.

When Fen beckoned again she stepped forward.

'Hi,' he said. 'Lucy, this is Nina. My fiancée. Nina, this is Lucy. We've been discussing the food in the dining-car. It's remarkably good when you consider the constraints of time and space. Don't you agree?'

Nina didn't care about the food. 'I am not your fiancée,' she said in a cold, clear voice that caused Lucy's eyes to widen in surprise—closely followed by hopeful speculation.

'Fiancée-in-waiting then,' Fen amended, extending an arm along the back of Lucy's chair.

'You needn't bother waiting for anything,' Nina said rudely. 'Fen, I need to talk to you.'

'Talk away.' He leaned back, resting an ankle on his knee.

'Privately.'

Fen arched an eyebrow. 'I'm not sure if I should find that promising or ominous.' He turned to Lucy. 'Will you excuse us? Nina's feeling a little sour today. It happens sometimes with lemons.'

Nina, with great forbearance, managed to resist an immediate impulse to pull his burnished brown hair.

They left Lucy sitting with her mouth agape looking after them as if she thought the two of them had escaped from an institution which featured bars and padded walls.

'Where would you like us to talk?' asked Fen without much warmth. 'In your boudoir?'

'It's too small. We'll have to use yours.'

'We'll also have to make it short,' said Fen, looking at his watch. 'I don't know about you, but I have no intention of missing lunch.'

'I'll be brief,' said Nina grimly.

Fen glanced at her sharply, but said nothing. When they reached his room he held open the door with exaggerated courtesy and waited for her to precede him inside. 'Well?' he said, sliding it closed behind him. 'What is it that couldn't wait till Chicago?'

'You're not going to Chicago,' said Nina.

'Oh?' Fen hooked his thumbs into his belt and leaned against the door. He didn't ask her to sit down. 'Who says I'm not?'

'I do.'

'Do you now? And what makes you think it's up to you?'

'Don't worry, you can keep the money,' she said disdainfully. 'But I've decided I don't need your help. I'll handle Dad's latest candidate on my own.'

'Ah. A woman of independence and courage. And what brought about this gallant change of heart? Was it something I said?'

Just about everything you said, thought Nina despairingly. Not to mention the way you look at me, the way you touch me, and the way my toes curl up just watching you drape your body against that door.

But all she said was, 'No, nothing you said. I just— don't think it will work.'

'I see.' He narrowed his eyes. 'Are you afraid I won't be able to play my part?'

'No.'

'Afraid you won't?'

'No.' The truth was that she was afraid she would be able to play it much too well.

'Then what brought on this sudden attack of independence?'

'I've always been independent. It was just that this year I thought I saw a way to make Christmas bearable. I was wrong.'

'Were you? Am I so unbearable?' His voice was low and suggestive and it made her stomach lurch.

'No, of course you're not.' She steadied herself against the wall. 'I've just decided it will be better if I deal with the problem the way I've always done. On my own.' He wasn't making this easy. She might have known he wouldn't. 'I *told* you you could keep the money,' she said irritably.

Fen bent his head and, removing his thumbs from the belt, thrust his hands deep into the pockets of his fawn trousers. When he looked up, Nina read only indifference in his eyes. 'Thank you,' he said.

'Yes.' She pushed hair that wasn't there out of her eyes. 'I—um—I guess that's it, then . . .' Her voice trailed off. Somehow she had expected him to say more, to raise further objections. Maybe, in the end, to change her mind?

No. She refused to contemplate that. Of course she didn't want to change her mind. She was suffering from an unfortunate case of lust for a totally unsuitable man, and the only way to conquer it was to nip it smartly in the bud and get Fen out of her life before her heart suffered irreversible damage. That had to be the sensible course.

But why be sensible? whispered the devil's advocate living in her head. Sensible is so unadventurous—so dull.

Fen's voice drew her back to reality. 'Mmm,' he was saying. 'I guess it is.'

'What is what?' asked Nina blankly.

'You said that was it. I was merely agreeing.'

Nina shook her head. This whole thing was getting beyond her. Was she really going out of her mind? If she was, it would have to wait until later, because what she had to do now was get past Fen, out of this room and back to the safe haven of her compartment.

But as she stepped towards him, swaying along with the train, he put a hand around her elbow and said, 'Lunch.'

'Lunch?' repeated Nina, as electricity sizzled up her arm.

'Yes. You know, food. I'd like to eat before we hit Milwaukee.'

'Chocolate bees?' she said faintly. Wasn't that the kind of food that appealed to Fen?

'I hope not. I was thinking of a sandwich.'

'You go ahead then. I'm not hungry.'

She was, come to think of it. But she didn't want to sit down to eat with Fen. She wanted to forget about him altogether and concentrate on strategies for surviving another Christmas spent dodging her father's marital machinations.

But Fen's hand was still around her elbow and he was looking at her in a very peculiar way. As if he wasn't quite sure what he wanted to do with her, but was certain he meant to do something.

'Please let me go,' she said, in a voice that was annoyingly breathless.

Fen didn't appear to have heard her. 'Why have you lost your appetite?' he demanded. 'I haven't noticed much wrong with it up until now. Rather the opposite.'

Was he calling her a glutton? Nina glared. 'I certainly haven't lost it because of you,' she replied without pausing to think.

'I didn't suggest you had. But it's an interesting possibility.'

She didn't like the teasing glitter in his eyes any more than she liked the barely controlled quiver in his voice. Frowning, she pulled her arm away. Damn it, what was it about this man that could make her want to kiss him and kick him in the same breath?

'Excuse me,' she said, tilting her nose in the air. 'Please let me pass.'

Very deliberately Fen reached behind him to slide open the door. Even more deliberately he turned sideways so that if Nina wanted to pass him it would be impossible to avoid intimate contact.

As she started to edge forward he smiled.

Chapter Four

IT was the smile that was Nina's undoing.

As she tried to flatten herself into a cross between a pancake and a snake, the lazy curve of Fen's lips made her catch her breath and forget where she was putting her feet. When her brown travelling shoe came in contact with his smartly polished black one, she gasped. Fen put out a hand to steady her, but she was so anxious to escape from him that, to her dismay, her legs became entangled with his. At once erotic imaginings blossomed and began to overwhelm her. Frantic now to get away, she staggered a little and crashed out into the corridor just as a willowy young man wearing miniature skulls in his ears came drifting past the door whistling a popular tune between his teeth.

Automatically Nina's outstretched arms closed around his waist, and for a moment the two of them did a frenzied little dance in time with the motion of the train. Then the young man stumbled and they fell to the floor in an ungainly tangle of flailing arms and legs.

'Nicely timed,' drawled Fen, as Nina extricated an arm and tried to push herself upright.

'Oh! It wasn't—I didn't—' She stopped as it dawned on her that her partner on the floor was making no attempt to get up, but appeared content to stay exactly where he was. 'I'm so sorry,' she said to him firmly. 'My fault entirely. And now I think we'd better find our feet.'

The young man leered. 'I'm not into feet.' He moved his hand a fraction until it rested unobtrusively on her hip. 'I go for the bits further up.' He shifted his hand under her rear.

'How dare—' Nina gasped as he began to move his fingers in slow, suggestive circles. Her gaze flew upward, instinctively seeking Fen's reaction. But Fen was propped against the door-frame with his arms crossed, and he looked amused, unperturbed and totally unmoved by her predicament.

All right, thought Nina. All right. I might have known you wouldn't stir yourself to help. Taking a deep breath, she jerked herself sideways until her body was up against the wall beneath the window and only one of her legs lay trapped beneath the lustful young man's thighs. Immediately he twisted towards her.

At that point Nina heard a resigned sigh issuing from somewhere above her head. An instant later two firm hands closed around her wrists.

The next moment she was dragged upward and into Fen's arms. 'Mine, I'm afraid,' said Fen to the body on the floor. 'Beat it.'

The body took one look at Fen's face, scrambled to its feet and, as advised, beat a hasty retreat down the corridor.

'You could have helped me sooner,' grumbled Nina.

'Why? It's my understanding I was fired from my job as your bodyguard. Besides, you seemed to be enjoying yourself. I certainly was.'

'Oh! You...' Nina gulped, breathed deeply and choked back the furious words. Fen was right. She *had* fired him. She was also entirely capable of looking after herself. In fact she'd been doing it for years. So why in the world, in this particular crisis, had she automatically looked to Fen for help?

She shook her head in confusion and stared at a white button on his shirt. After a while she became conscious that his arm was still around her waist.

Desire stirred deep in her belly and rippled outward. Soon her skin began to feel as if it had taken on a hot, glowing life of its own.

Slowly, very slowly, Nina raised her eyes.

Fen was looking down at her with a small furrow between his brows, as if he wasn't quite sure what she was doing in his arms.

'Yes, I did fire you,' she said woodenly. 'But I wasn't enjoying myself.'

Still the glow wouldn't go away. Which just proved she had been right in the first place when she'd decided that her first priority must be to put a safe and permanent distance between herself and Fen.

The only problem was that in this position, with her body pressed against his so that she could feel every hard, enticing inch of him, it wasn't possible to fool herself that she wanted to be *any* distance from him—certainly not a safe one.

She ran her tongue along her upper lip. 'You—you can let go now,' she finally managed to say. 'He—that creep has gone away.'

'Yes.' Fen nodded and ran an exploratory palm up and down her spine until it came to rest lightly on her rear. 'So he has. And now it's my turn.'

'You don't get a turn,' gasped Nina, as his hand continued its gentle massage.

'Don't I? Want me to stop?'

No. No, she didn't want him to stop. But he must. This was a public corridor. And she couldn't allow him to carry on his activities in private, because if he did there wasn't a doubt in her mind as to what would follow.

But why, oh, why did it have to be *this* man who had stirred to life all those feelings that up until now she had only sensed obscurely as in a dream? This man who had allowed her to buy him.

'Yes,' she groaned. 'Yes. You must stop.'

With a briskness that appalled her, he removed his hand, took her by the shoulders and turned her around.

'OK,' he said, as if it made no difference. 'I'll give you a head start. You go straight to the dining-car and find yourself a table. If you're lucky, by the time I get there, you'll be safely seated with that party from Australia I see coming up from downstairs.'

Nina saw them, too. Two tall young men and their mother, all talking at once. They looked friendly and cheerful and she didn't want to sit with them in the least. She wanted to go back to her own small compartment to cry. Except that she was damned if she was crying about Fenton Hardwick.

'I don't want to eat,' she said stubbornly—and un-truthfully.

'Fine. A little fasting will probably do you good. Off you go, then.'

Dismissed. Just like that. But as Nina lifted her chin and began what she hoped was a dignified stalk back to her compartment, she thought she felt a light tap on her behind. She swung round indignantly to protest, but Fen had already disappeared into his room.

She must have imagined the tap.

Back in her compartment she sank onto the seat and buried her face in her hands.

This was ridiculous. Hopeless and ridiculous. She had known Fen precisely two days. She wasn't in love with

him, didn't want to be in love with him. And once he was
out of her orbit this disturbing uncertainty would pass.
Which meant that all she had to do now was stay in her
compartment until the train pulled into Chicago. Then
Fen would make his connection with the New York train
as planned, and that would be the end of an interlude that
had been—just a minor mistake. Nothing more.

But when, a half hour later, Nina's stomach began to
growl insistently, it occurred to her that there wasn't, and
never had been, anything remotely minor about Fen. Or
about her appetite, for that matter. She was hungry. Very
hungry. But if she went to the dining-car now she was
bound to encounter Fen tucking smugly into a sandwich. And she didn't want to see Fen again. Ever. Nor
did she want to confirm for him what she suspected he
already knew—that she had no more wish to bypass
lunch than he had, and that it was the thought of his
company that had made her take what was, for her, an
unusual decision to pass up food.

In the end she decided pride and her peace of mind
were both more important to her than lunch.

When the train stopped in Milwaukee, she drew the
blind and willed herself to sleep. An hour or two after
that, and a little late due to a fresh snowfall, the Empire
Builder trundled into the terminal in Chicago.

'I MIGHT have known,' muttered Nina, as she spotted the
uniformed man in the peaked cap standing beside a
waiting limousine. 'Doesn't Dad ever give up?'

Of course, as she knew very well, her father never gave
up, and every year they went through the same performance. She would tell Joseph she intended to take a taxi
like everyone else, and he would ignore her and send a
limo. He refused to hire a chauffeur because he insisted

on driving himself, but somehow he never quite found the time to meet his daughter.

Ignoring the wary glances of fellow passengers as she muttered past them, she walked up to the limo driver and laid her two small suitcases at his feet. 'Nina Petrov,' she said. 'I see my father sent you as usual.'

When the driver only blinked and lifted his cap, she shrugged and climbed into the car without waiting for his help. She gave a sigh of relief as she relaxed into the soft leather of the limo's supple seat, for a moment grateful for Joseph's interference. This was a lot easier than looking for a taxi. She closed her eyes and leaned her head back—and was immediately engulfed in a wash of overwhelming desolation. If it had had anything to do with the annual battle with her father that loomed ahead, she could have born it. But she knew it hadn't.

'I hate you, Fen Hardwick,' she groaned.

At that precise moment, the door beside her swung wide, letting in a blast of winter air. 'Do you?' said a man's familiar baritone. 'That wasn't the impression I had.'

Nina's eyes flew open. Fen, once again the ultimate executive in grey, was swinging himself and a briefcase in beside her.

'Get out,' she said, sliding to the far side of the seat. 'At once.'

'Certainly not.' Fen set the briefcase carefully on the seat.

'Driver,' called Nina to the man in front who was busily warming up the engine. 'Don't leave for a moment, please. This gentleman is just getting out.'

'No, I'm not,' said Fen, folding his arms and crossing his legs in a way that told Nina he didn't plan to move. 'Keep going, driver. The Petrov residence, please.'

'Fen.' Nina spoke in a clear, precise voice so there would be no possibility of his mistaking her meaning. 'If you don't leave at once I'm going to call station security.'

'Go ahead,' he said.

'Don't you understand?' She was practically baring her teeth at him. 'I want you out of here. Now.'

'That's too bad, isn't it? Because I have no intention of getting out of my own limousine.' He leaned back, crossed an ankle over his knee and shut his eyes.

Nina gaped at him. 'It can't be your limo,' she protested. 'Dad sent it. He always does.'

'Yes, but when I enquired I discovered your father and I use the same limo service. I called from Milwaukee and cancelled yours. I assure you this *is* my car.'

He still had his eyes closed. Nina contemplated hitting him over the head with his own briefcase and climbing out. But they were already attracting surreptitious attention from passers-by, and this holiday season promised to be difficult enough already without the appearance in the papers of snide little articles about the love life of Joseph Petrov's daughter. The fact that she had no love life to speak of wouldn't cut the slightest bit of ice with any gossip columnist worth his or her salt. And the car was already pulling out from the curb.

'How *dare* you?' Nina was so angry she was almost spitting. 'How dare you cancel my father's car?'

Fen opened an eye and turned his head towards her. 'Easy,' he said drily. 'It was simply a matter of picking up the phone.'

His smile was so coolly complacent that Nina had to look away to prevent herself from punching him on the nose. She didn't believe in violence as a solution to personal problems, but in this case . . .

Damn him. She glared at the passing traffic, thankful that no one could see her face, which no doubt resembled that of a furious porcupine on the warpath.

Fen could think he'd won a victory if he liked. But there was no way he would be allowed through her father's door without an invitation. Which he was *not* going to get. She squared her shoulders. In the meantime, since she didn't seem to have a lot of choice, she would just have to endure his company for the duration of the drive.

She stared at the falling snow which was subtly blurring the hard angles of the skyscrapers, transforming the elevated railway that formed Chicago's central Loop into a magical bridge to the stars. And she tried to ignore the man beside her. He wasn't touching her, but she could feel his presence just as if he was. And although he wore no discernible aftershave, the scent of him seemed to fill the car.

Soon they were driving north along the familiar shoreline of Lake Michigan. And Nina began to feel a new kind of tension—one that for a change had nothing to do with Fen.

In a short while they would be at her family home on the elegant old street where so many of Chicago's rich and famous lived. And the closer they came to that home, the greater her feeling of oppression. She always felt this way at Christmas.

Only this year it was worse.

'Why did you insist on coming?' she asked Fen, breaking a silence that crackled with a tension that came entirely from her side of the car. 'I told you I didn't want your help.' It was dark outside now, and she watched the bare branches of the trees swaying gently in the glow from the streetlights.

She felt rather than saw Fen shrug. 'Maybe I needed an excuse to get off that damned train.'

'Oh.' Unaccountably, Nina's shoulders sagged. 'That doesn't make sense.'

'It makes a lot of sense. Christine will understand perfectly when she hears that I gave up my ticket to New York for the sake of an exceptionally sour but pretty lemon. In fact, she'll be delighted.'

He was laughing at her. She knew he was.

'Especially a lemon who has Joseph Petrov for a father,' she said bitterly, not even caring that he had called her pretty.

'Especially,' he agreed. Nina noted that he no longer sounded amused.

'You'd no right to cancel my car,' she said. 'Not when I'd already told you I wouldn't be needing you.'

'Is that so? But, you see, I tend to make decisions based on my own needs. And as you've just pointed out, you *are* Joseph Petrov's daughter.' He reached across to cup her chin with the fingers of one hand, and when she was forced to face him he added softly, 'Don't tell me you're indifferent to my charms.'

'What charms?' asked Nina, flinching at his touch.

'Want me to show you?' His voice was soft, silky, charged with a seductive kind of menace.

'No.' She shrank back against the door, then remembered she wasn't some timorous maiden from a Victorian novel and sat up straight, looking him squarely in the eye. 'No, I don't want you to show me anything, Fen Hardwick. I just want you to—to...'

'Take my money and run? Not a chance.'

'But—'

She broke off because the limo was turning into the driveway of her father's house.

Nina threw her head back and filled her lungs with air. Home. The Petrov house. No example, this, of Frank Lloyd Wright's influence on the Chicago architectural scene. Joseph's house subdued nature rather than becoming a part of it. Like Joseph himself, it was large, rectangular and solid, made of weathered brick ascending three storeys to the plain pitched roof. Its windows, too, were solid and rectangular, arranged in military rows on either side of a white-pillared door. Only the ancient evergreens rising gracefully from the manicured lawns— and at this season hung with coloured lights—lent an air of grace and permanence to her childhood home.

'Mmm,' murmured Fen. 'Respectable and definitely no-nonsense. I shall look forward to meeting your father.'

'You're not going to meet him,' said Nina. 'This is the end of the road.' She glanced at her watch. 'And now, as I'm already late, I hope you won't mind if I say good night. And goodbye.' She held out her hand, but when Fen didn't take it she dropped it at once and turned to the door which the driver was holding open.

Fen didn't wait for the driver but emerged at once from his side of the car.

'I said you're not coming in,' warned Nina. She turned towards the house, afraid to look at him again in case her resolve to be rid of him weakened.

'Just a moment.' Fen's voice was quiet but commanding. 'You've forgotten something.'

Nina stopped. She didn't want to, but she couldn't help herself. Reluctantly she swivelled around. 'I haven't...' she began. Then she frowned. Fen was holding out a white slip of paper. 'What's that?'

As she continued to frown in perplexity, he took her hand, turned it over and placed the piece of paper on her upturned palm. Then he closed her fingers around it and stepped back.

The whole operation was conducted in silence by the light of the stars and the twin lamps standing sentinel by the door.

Slowly Nina uncurled her fingers. And there, slightly crumpled, lay the cheque she had given Fen to play the part of this year's Christmas suitor.

'What...?' She stared down at it in total bewilderment. 'I don't understand. I said you could keep it. Why are you giving it back?'

A sudden breeze blew the shadow of a tree branch across Fen's face so that all she could see was the very faint gleam from his eyes. It wasn't a gleam she trusted. But when she started to move away he took a sudden step forward and hauled her into his arms.

'This is why,' he said roughly, and covered her lips with his own.

For a moment Nina was too startled to react. She stood totally still, wrapped in the warmth of his embrace, unaware of the coldness of the night, of the limo driver watching in amazement, or of anything except the feel of his firm lips on hers and the soft wool of his cashmere coat against her cheek. But as his kiss deepened, and she felt his tongue begin a more insistent probing, she remembered where she was, and who *he* was, and that some hours ago she had dismissed him from her life.

She started to struggle. 'Don't,' she cried, tearing her mouth away. 'Don't. You have no right. I told you—'

'What you told me was a lot of lemon-flavoured drivel.' He settled her head more securely on his shoulder, tightened an arm around her waist and dropped the other one down across her hips. Now she was plastered so firmly against him that if it hadn't been for the barrier of their coats she would have been able to feel every sinuous muscle in his body. He was moulding her to him as if he truly believed that was where she belonged.

Fen wasn't a man who was easily dismissed.

After a while Nina stopped even thinking of resistance because he was kissing her so thoroughly, with such burning expertise that she no longer knew what resistance was. Or what thought was. She knew only the unbelievable ecstasy of being kissed by the one man in the world who had the power to bring every singing nerve in her body to traitorous life.

She returned his kiss with passion, if not with expertise, and when her soft, delirious moans began to drift out into the night, the limo driver, with a smile and a shake of his head, climbed back into his car and drove away.

Vaguely, Nina was aware of his departure. But only vaguely. And if Fen noticed he gave no sign. Instead he deepened his kiss and moved an arm up to tangle his gloved fingers in her hair.

He was just beginning to slide his free hand with delicious sensuality over her rear when she became conscious that the night was brighter than it had been. Then she remembered that a second ago she had heard a sound that might have been the faint creaking of a door.

Slowly, too slowly, reality returned, as she realized that Fen, without haste or apparent embarrassment, was calmly straightening her coat. When he had finished he took her hand in his and turned her to face the two figures standing frozen in shock at the top of the wide, white steps leading up to the door.

Briefly, time stood still. Then the abrasive bellow of Joseph's voice shattered the tenuous peace of the winter night.

'Nina? Nina! What the *hell* do you think you're doing?' He paused to run a gimlet-sharp gaze over Fen, who
had placed a casually protective arm around Nina's
shoulders. 'And who in the hell is this?' Without waiting
for an answer he stormed on. 'Don't you realize you're
an hour and a half late, miss? If you'd taken a plane like
everyone else, you could have been here two days ago.'

As Joseph growled to a halt, the optimistic notes of
'Joy to the World' rang out pure and sweet from the
throats of a small group of carollers advancing with re-
lentless seasonal cheerfulness down the street.

Both Fen and Joseph looked as though they wished
they could lay their hands on something to throw.

Chapter Five

FEN'S grip tightened around Nina's hand, offering support, and she was surprised to feel a quick glow of gratitude. Gratitude wasn't an emotion she was used to in connection with Fen. But he seemed to understand that she had always hated being late, and that her father's accusation rubbed her where it hurt.

She opened her mouth, meaning to point out that she had never had any intention of arriving two days earlier. But she heard herself saying instead, 'I'm sorry, Dad. The train was held up by the snow.'

'That's what I mean, girl. If you'd taken a plane—'

'I know, but—'

'Leave it to me,' murmured Fen, who didn't seem in the least put out at being caught kissing the daughter of the house in full view of any member of the household who cared to watch.

Nina looked up at him, startled, but before she could ask what he meant, she heard him saying evenly, 'Nina took the train because I asked her to travel with me, sir. I have to be in New York on the twenty-seventh, so I thought we might spend some time together first.'

Joseph's grey eyes seemed about to bulge out of his head. Seeing her domineering father for once at a loss for words, Nina had to struggle hard not to choke.

But Joseph noticed her struggle and scowled. 'What are *you* laughing about?' he demanded, recovering quickly from incipient apoplexy.

'Joy to the earth! The Saviour reigns,' chorussed the carollers.

'Now, Joseph.' Nina's small, blonde mother, Nancy, who up until this point had been quietly hanging back behind her husband, hurried to soothe ruffled family feathers. 'You know Nina always takes the train. She enjoys it.'

'Harrumph. Not the only thing she seems to enjoy.' Joseph turned his scowl on Fen. 'What do you think you're talking about, young man? I won't have my daughter taken advantage of.'

'Of course not, sir,' Fen said gravely. He touched a black-gloved hand to Nina's cheek. '*Was* I taking advantage of you, Nina?'

For a moment she was speechless. Oh, yes, he'd taken advantage of her, all right. He was still doing it, and she felt as if her insides had been turned inside out and hung out to dry in a hurricane. All the same, to the best of her recollection, Fen was the only man she had ever met who wasn't intimidated by Joseph. Since he could obviously look after himself, there was no reason for her not to pay him back.

'Yes,' she said demurely. 'I'm afraid you were.'

In the background Joseph started to rumble, and Nancy made an anxious twittering noise.

'Oh?' said Fen, glancing pointedly at the cheque that, incredibly, was still crushed in Nina's hand. 'Funny. I could have sworn it was the other way around.'

Nina moistened her lips. He wasn't joking now. 'I thought I was doing you a favour. Not taking advantage,' she said quietly.

'Is that so? By allowing me to kiss you?'

'No, I meant—'

'The cheque? Yes, I see. But I'm afraid being bought like some over-priced gigolo isn't my personal idea of a favour.' He spoke pleasantly but with an undertone of very dry ice. 'Of course I realize you've been brought up to think everyone has their price—but it happens not to be true.'

Did he mean it? Nina shook her head in bewilderment. She glanced at the cool slant of his eyebrows, noted the arrogant tilt of his head. He sounded sincere enough. But, damn it, he *had* taken the money.

She felt her normally equable temper coming to the boil.

'If the shoe fits, wear it,' she snapped. 'You weren't hard to acquire. I've picked mushrooms that put up more resistance.'

'Nina!' Joseph's roar thundered down the steps like a concrete drill on full power. 'What the devil is going on? If you owe this fellow money, then pay him and tell him to beat it. If he owes you—I'll take care of him. But your mother and I will not stand out here in the snow while the two of you conduct negotiations in my driveway—'

Only the hard pressure of Fen's fingers on her palm told Nina that her gibe about mushrooms had hit home.

'Mr. Petrov,' he said crisply, interrupting the flow. 'The only thing Nina owes me is an apology. The only thing I owe her is some straight talking. And, like you, I would prefer to see both those debts settled at once.'

Dad's going to explode, thought Nina, watching Joseph's cheeks inflate like pink balloons. She found herself reluctantly admiring Fen's audacity. But when she saw her mother anxiously chewing her lip and twisting her hands at her waist she felt a quick stirring of conscience.

It *was* cold out here in the snow. And of course it was time to bring this absurd Christmas charade to an end. If that could only be achieved by allowing Fen to have his way—again—then so be it.

She turned to look up at her parents. 'This is Fenton Hardwick,' she said formally. 'Fen, my mother and father, Nancy and Joseph Petrov.'

Joseph's eyes narrowed, and suddenly he looked a little less explosive. His keen gaze swept over Fen. 'Hardwick?' he said. 'Hmm. All right, you'd better come in.'

'Thank you,' said Fen. 'I hope it's not an imposition.'

'When has *that* ever bothered you?' muttered Nina.

Fen responded by tapping her lightly on the rear, and Joseph at once replied heartily, 'No, no. No trouble at all. We were expecting young Vickery. He was supposed to be coming for dinner. But the damn fool's got himself engaged. Says he can't make it. Told him I wouldn't have it, but . . .'

Saved by Cupid's arrow, thought Nina, resisting an unwise urge to laugh hysterically. After all the trouble I've taken to protect myself from unwanted advances, this year's suitor isn't going to come up to scratch. I needn't have enlisted Fen's services at all.

'Well, come in, come in,' urged Joseph. 'Not getting any warmer out here.'

Fen raised an eyebrow at Nina and picked up two of the suitcases the limo driver had left in the driveway. 'After you,' he said, inclining his head gravely. 'I believe lemons take precedence over mushrooms.'

Nina gaped at him, too startled to hide her stupefaction. But when she saw a small, malevolent grin part his lips, she turned her back on him so he wouldn't see her own lips curve up in response. Damn him. Did he *have* to

keep making her laugh? As she marched regally up the
steps, it was only the knowledge that he was likely to re-
taliate that prevented her from following her instincts and
turning round to deliver an unladylike punch to his hard
midriff.

'And makes the nations prove the glories of His right-
eousness and wonders of His love,' trilled the carollers as
Fen and Nina reached the top step.

Once they were inside, a formidable figure in black
swooped down to pick up the rest of the cases, and Nina
noticed that Fen relinquished his as if it had never occurred to him that he might not be spending the night.

She swallowed, uncomfortably aware that his sar-
donic brown eyes were surveying her with what could
only be described as complacence—as if he had just
scored a coup and intended very shortly to score another. She turned away with a toss of her head.

The four of them were standing in a big, dark hallway
at one end of which a steep, gold-carpeted staircase led
to a three-sided gallery above. The only visible con-
cession to Christmas was a green vase filled with holly
which stood on an antique table beneath a still life featuring dead game birds and something that looked like
hundred-year-old cheese.

Nina stared glumly at the holly and wondered what
she'd let herself in for. When she felt a hesitant hand on
her shoulder, she jumped. Then she smelled the sweet,
cloying scent of lavender and spun round to fling her
arms around her mother's swan-like neck.

'There, there, dear,' said Nancy vaguely, patting Nina's
back as if she were a baby needing to be burped. 'Your
father and I are so happy to have you home, dear. And
we're delighted you've brought your young man...'

'He's not my young man,' wailed Nina, crumbling in the face of her mother's gentleness. 'He's a—a...'

'Decoy?' suggested Fen from behind her. 'Smoke-screen? Fraud?'

'Skunk,' said Nina through her teeth.

'Now, now, Nina,' muttered Joseph. 'No need to be rude to young Hardwick. Next thing you know, you'll be asking me to have him thrown out.' He chuckled as if he'd made an excellent joke.

Nina closed her eyes as a vision of fisticuffs in the front hallway flashed improbably into her mind—with Fen thoroughly enjoying himself in the centre of a pugilistic throng of family retainers. No, she didn't want him thrown out. She wanted him to leave of his own volition.

But as she watched her father lead him into the main drawing room with a friendly hand on the shoulder, she saw the likelihood of that happening grow dimmer with every passing moment.

'Come along, dear. You'll want to put your things away,' said Nancy. 'You father will take care of your Mr. Hardwick.'

Her mother sounded so pleased and happy that Nina couldn't bring herself to repeat that Fen wasn't, and never had been, 'her' Mr. Hardwick.

When she went downstairs twenty minutes later, she discovered Joseph and Fen enjoying a drink together in front of a roaring fire. Beside them stood an enormous Christmas tree with a revolving gold angel on the top.

'Ah,' said Joseph. 'There you are, Nina. Your mother's arranged a fire in the small sitting-room. More private in there if you and Hardwick—'

'We don't need to be private, Dad,' said Nina firmly. 'I don't have a lot to say to Mr. Hardwick—'

Fen's nostrils flared briefly. 'We'll see about that,' he said, putting down his glass and standing up.

'That's the spirit,' said Joseph. 'Don't put up with any of her nonsense, lad. She'll lead you a dance if you do.'

'Yes, I've noticed that,' said Fen, with a non-committal smile. 'Come on, Nina.' He took her arm firmly and led her out into the hall.

Nina didn't even think about resisting. She couldn't. Because this was far, far worse than she'd imagined.

If she read the signs correctly—and she was almost certain she did—Joseph had taken in Fen's well-cut suit and air of assurance and come to the erroneous conclusion he was marriage material. A worthy replacement for young Vickery. And there was only one thing to be done about it. She must convince Fen once and for all that she wasn't interested. After that, surely he would leave.

'Where to?' asked Fen.

Nina gestured at a door across the hall, and Fen propelled her ahead of him into a firelit sitting-room fitted with heavy, overstuffed furniture that loomed massively in the glowing orange light.

'So you don't have much to say to me,' he said, clicking the door shut and leaning against it as if he expected her to stage a panic-stricken break-out.

'No. Not much.' She started to edge away from him. He looked terribly grim, and she didn't trust the dark glitter of his eyes in the firelight.

'I see,' said Fen. 'Then perhaps a different kind of communication will work better.'

No, thought Nina, as he moved purposefully towards her. No. Not again.

It was her last coherent thought before Fen's arms were wrapped around her back and she lost the will to do anything but respond to the virile body entwined so intimately with hers.

The touch of Fen's lips was as drugging and overwhelming as it had been when he had kissed her in the driveway. But now that they were no longer wrapped in heavy winter coats, there was an immediacy to their contact that set the blood singing in her ears. She could feel every lean inch of him against her softness—and when his hand closed over the silk shirt covering her breasts, this time no roaring father appeared to shatter the seductive closeness of the moment.

'Fen,' murmured Nina, shifting her hips against him as his teasing fingers began to drive her wild. 'Fen...' Her hunger was explicit. And yet she didn't know what it was exactly that she wanted—what she waited so eagerly to receive...

Then, when she was certain she wouldn't be able to bear the waiting and the incompleteness a moment longer, Fen let her go.

'There,' he said. 'That should loosen your tongue.'

It didn't at first. Nina discovered that although she could open her mouth, no sound would come out. But when the room stopped spinning, and she finally regained the power of speech, words were tumbling from her lips like water streaming over a dam.

'Yes,' she said. 'It's loosened it all right. Fen Hardwick, you are without a doubt the rudest, most indefensibly self-satisfied man I have ever known. *And* the most arrogant and bossy—'

'That,' interrupted Fen, 'is not what I'd call an apology.' He settled his shoulders more firmly against the door.

'It wasn't meant to be. Why should I apologize? I bought you, didn't I?'

'No, as a matter of fact you didn't.'

'Oh? And I suppose you expect me to believe that you came home with me just to give me back my money.'

'Why else?'

'For the sake of a bigger pay-off, of course,' She hated the break in her voice and attempted to steady it. 'Once you discovered I was a sucker for your kisses, you figured I'd be ripe for the plucking. You're not married, my father is Joseph Petrov III. And he seems to have fallen for your line. That's why you came after me, isn't it?'

A log cracked in the fireplace, and Nina took in for the first time that they were glowering at each other in semi-darkness.

It didn't matter.

Fen reached behind him, flicked a switch and flooded the room with revealing light. Nina screwed up her eyes against the glare.

'Would you like to say that again?' he asked quietly.

'No,' said Nina, warily studying the harsh lines etched into his face. 'I wouldn't. I've said all that needs to be said. Let me pass, please.'

'Why? So you can run to your most estimable father and spill the beans? He won't believe you, you know.'

'He might,' said Nina, feeling drained and cold in spite of the warmth of the fire. 'You won't be the first fortune-hunter he's sent packing.'

'Thank you.' Fen gave her a small, sarcastic bow. 'I've never been called a fortune-hunter before.'

'Then I've enlarged the scope of your experience,' said Nina with deceptive sweetness. 'Now, are you going to let me pass, or do I have to scream?'

He shrugged. 'Want something to scream about? It'll make it much more convincing.'

'What I want,' said Nina, ignoring the bright challenge in his eyes, 'is for you to move.'

'Sure?'

'Of course I'm sure.'

Fen's mouth flattened, but he stepped back and swung open the door. As Nina scurried past him she heard him murmur, 'Get rid of the blinkers, Nina, and face the truth.'

She stopped dead. 'What's that supposed to mean?'

'It means that instead of walking tall, and accepting that there are plenty of men who might just want you for yourself—for your compassion and your independence and your strength—you've chosen to wear your mistrust like a badge of honour and assume the worst of every man who comes along. And one of these days you'll find no one comes any more. Your father understands that. Even if you don't.'

Nina lifted her chin a little higher and didn't answer. The last thing she wanted to hear at this moment was that, inexplicably, her father and Fen had become allies. That her wonderful scheme had so hopelessly backfired.

She didn't look back to see if Fen was watching, but hurried up to her room at the head of the stairs. *Had* her scheme backfired? Had her father really been taken in by Fen?

'It doesn't make *sense,*' she groaned out loud. 'Dad's no fool. He *must* see that Fen isn't one of his executive hot shots. He must, because if he doesn't... Oh, my God!' She sank down on her blue quilted bedspread and put both hands up to her face.

Was it possible that *Joseph* had planted Fen on the train? Was young Vickery nothing more than a—a red herring? Had her father, all along, been playing a game with her? Could he be that devious?

Could Fen be? Her lips tightened and she bunched her hands into fists and pounded them into the pillow. Oh, she wouldn't put it past either of those two. Not for a moment. And *that* would explain why Fen had been so determined to hand her money back.

To her horror, Nina felt tears pricking at her eyes. They were partly tears of rage, but mixed with the rage was a terrible feeling of desolation and betrayal. Because if Fen was really Joseph's man, that meant he was just another ambitious suitor on the make. And in spite of all her efforts to pretend otherwise, in her heart she had never wanted that to be true.

A clock chimed loudly in the hall, and Nina jumped and glanced at her watch.

Dinner time. It was always served promptly in Joseph's house, and if she didn't move fast she'd be late. As for Fen . . . No, she didn't want to think about Fen.

She showered hastily—no time for a leisurely bath—and pulled on a soft, cream wool dress with long sleeves. Then she attached the ruby pendant and earrings she didn't often have a chance to wear and hurried downstairs to the drawing room.

Fen, Joseph and Nancy were finishing pre-dinner drinks. 'Just in time,' said Joseph, not offering a drink to his daughter. 'Shall we go in?' He took Nancy's arm and the four of them moved sedately down the hall to the dining-room.

Fen made no attempt to take Nina's arm. 'You're looking very glamorous,' he remarked as they sat down. 'Not for my benefit, I assume?'

'You assume right,' snapped Nina.

Fen's eyes gleamed, and she knew that once again she'd fallen into a trap.

Dinner was a scrupulously polite affair that sizzled with tension beneath the civilized veneer of discussion about the journey and the weather. Nina noticed that her father kept throwing speculative glances at Fen, and that Nancy kept giving him nervous smiles. Were they wondering if Fen had succeeded where others had failed? Were they trying to decide if he would do for their daughter? Or had Joseph decided that long ago?

For his part, Fen appeared oblivious to the unspoken currents circling all around him, and joined in the conversation with an easy charm that made Nina want to hit him.

She spoke very little herself, and as soon as dinner was over, Joseph announced that he and his wife were planning an early night. 'Leave you young people to yourselves,' he said, beaming as if he were Santa Claus handing out presents.

'Dad, you never go to bed before ten,' protested Nina.

'Your mother is—um—tired,' said Joseph, looking shifty. 'Hardwick, I suggest you use the small sitting-room again. We've kept the fire going.'

Before Nina could offer further objections, Joseph had taken Nancy by the hand and towed her out into the hall.

'All right. Your move,' said Nina once they were alone. She couldn't quite keep the bitterness from her voice.

Fen was leaning against the wall with his hands plunged deep into the pockets of his elegant grey trousers. His mouth looked as though it had been drawn by a ruler. But after a few seconds he jerked his head peremptorily at the hallway, and Nina decided there was nothing to be gained by refusing to talk.

As soon as they were back in the small room with the fire, she edged away from him and sank into a red brocade chair by the hearth. Then after a while she heard his footsteps on the carpet and sensed that he had come up behind her.

'What do you want from me, Fen?' she asked tiredly. When he didn't answer she tilted her head back. He was bending over her, and she could feel his warm breath on her cheek.

'I'm not sure I want anything,' he said. Nina stiffened, and almost absently he dropped a hand over the soft swell of her breast, as he added thoughtfully, 'Although I did, at one point, think I might want you in my bed. Possibly on a permanent basis.'

'Permanent? I'm flattered,' said Nina, automatically tensing beneath his touch. 'Particularly as you've only known me for a few days. But I do, of course, see the obvious benefits of being married to Joseph Petrov's daughter.'

The hand stroking her breast clenched convulsively and was immediately withdrawn. 'Yes,' Fen agreed, so coldly that she flinched. 'So you've already said. And I'm afraid I haven't the patience to wait for you to discover your mistake.'

Nina twisted around, trying to see his face, but he had stepped back into the shadows. 'What mistake? Did my father set this up?' she asked wearily. 'Did he arrange for you to be on the train?'

Fen was so long answering that for a while Nina thought he'd left the room. Then his voice seemed to come to her from a distance. 'No, Nina, he didn't. We've never met before. And to save you the trouble of asking, he also knows I'm not remotely interested in your money.'

There was a bleakness in the way he spoke, a cold withdrawal, that stirred an answering coldness in her heart. And suddenly she *knew*. With chilling clarity. Fen was telling her the truth. Had probably been telling it all along. She wasn't sure why she knew now, when she hadn't believed him before. It had come as a kind of revelation.

She reached for him blindly, then realized he was still speaking.

'There's something else you should know before I leave.'

'What's that?' Nina whispered. Fen was leaving? When there was so much still left unsaid? She wanted to tell him... She shook her head, trying to remember what it was she had to say.

'You should understand,' Fen was explaining, 'that when I accepted your commission on the train, it was as the joke you didn't see it was. And partly, I admit, to pay you back. It's not flattering to be mistaken for Rent-a-Stud of the Week. I thought you could do with the lesson.'

Very slowly Nina lifted her head and turned to face him. He was standing with his hand on the doorknob. His mouth was curved in a smile, but his eyes were as blank as one-way glass.

'I *don't* understand,' she said at last, tracing her finger round a red brocade leaf.

'No. I see that.' Fen shut his eyes. 'Perhaps I expected too much.'

'What *did* you expect?' Nina was too lost and confused to think straight any more.

His mouth turned down. 'That you would realize I'd never have kept your money—even if I'd needed it. Which, as it happens, I don't.' He paused, then seemed to make up his mind. 'Remember F and C Foods?'

Nina nodded. 'Yes. You work for them.' She frowned. Wasn't there something else? Something she'd tried to remember? Something about—oh, yes, now she had it.

The company had donated an extraordinarily generous supply of foodstuffs for the agency's Christmas hampers for needy families. She had supplied some of the names of the recipients herself. And the food hadn't been useless things like caviar and chocolate-covered bugs. She remembered all the staff had been delighted at how practical and yet imaginative F and C's selections had been.

F and C... F, the president, had made the delivery himself, according to a starry-eyed receptionist who had waxed poetic about muscled shoulders heaving boxes, and a delectable masculine backside displayed to great advantage as the boxes were shifted into place. The receptionist had also gushed breathlessly about glossy brown hair and eyes like an evening in autumn...

Oh, God! F! Fenton. F and C. Fenton and Christine? Could it be...

She raised her eyes to Fen's coldly blank face.

And had her answer.

'You *are* F and C Foods. Aren't you?' she groaned with despairing certainty. 'You don't just work for them.'

'No,' said Fen. 'I don't. At least not in the way you mean—and not that there's anything wrong with honest work.'

'Of course there isn't. Because you're the president. It's your company. Your very *successful* company. You *didn't* need my money. *That's* why you gave it back. Not because you wanted to marry Joseph Petrov's daughter.'

'Go to the top of the class.'

Fen stared down at her impassively, and when he didn't seem inclined to continue, she demanded with a kind of desperation, 'Why didn't you tell me before? I can understand why you couldn't resist taking me up on my offer. It must have seemed a joke to you at first. And like you said, a way of teaching me how foolish it is to make superficial judgements. But later—'

'Later you were too busy playing Lady Nose-in-the-Air dismissing the upstart servant. I saw no reason to waste my time on explanations you obviously weren't willing to listen to. Besides…' he smoothed a hand over his jaw. 'It seemed a shame to waste such a virtuoso performance.'

Nina ignored the taunt. 'But you still cancelled my father's limousine,' she said, twisting the pendant at her neck.

'Mmm. I had this misguided idea that in spite of your background and general perversity, maybe I'd at last found a woman I might make time for. Once she'd got over the idea I was for sale.' He shrugged. 'Apparently I was wrong.'

Nina hadn't thought brown eyes could look so passionless, or that Fen's seductive body could seem so unapproachable.

Had her suspicions and accusations gone too far? Fen, with his quirky sense of humour and his contempt for the rich and the spoiled, had been playing a game with her all along. Oh, he hadn't intended to be cruel, that wasn't his way. But how could he possibly have understood what it was like to grow up in Joseph Petrov's shadow, to have spent most of your young adulthood fighting tooth and nail for every inch of independence you gained? And how could he have understood about the suitors?

Fen, after all, was a man.

A man who was already halfway through the door and about to walk out of her life.

She stood up, but the door was already closing in her face.

Nina stared at it, heard it snap shut—felt her heart slump down to her red shoes. And that was when she knew for sure that she didn't want Fen out of her life. It was too soon to be sure, of course. Yet she was.

Fen was the one.

And if she didn't move fast she would lose him.

The thought prodded her into action, and she skidded across the thick Turkish carpet as if a hundred crazed camels were in pursuit.

But by the time she gained the hallway, Fen had disappeared.

She glanced around, searching for a clue to his whereabouts—and heard her father's unmistakable voice saying loudly, 'Nonsense, my boy. All Nina needs is a firm hand—'

Another, quieter voice interrupted, and the rest of Joseph's speech was cut off.

Nina gazed, mesmerized, at the closed door of the drawing-room. Fen must have told Joseph he didn't mean to marry his daughter. And Joseph was trying to persuade him otherwise, telling Fen how to handle her. As for Fen's hands, firm or otherwise . . .

His voice, brisk and businesslike, interrupted her wayward imaginings. 'I agree, sir. Nina could certainly do with—'

'A good boot in the right place,' said her father. 'I have faith in you, Hardwick. You can manage her.'

'It's a tempting thought,' Nina heard Fen admit. 'Although that wasn't exactly what I had in mind. And as I'm not given to violence, I'm afraid . . .'

She didn't hear any more, because a lump, hard and painful, was beginning to form in her throat. Dammit, how *could* those two arrogant men—and particularly Fen—stand there discussing her as if she were a horse? A horse that he was obviously unwilling to train. It was evident from the dry politeness of his voice. And if he thought . . .

All at once the lump in her throat burst. And a rage that was part agonizing grief because she knew she'd lost him, and part resentment that both Fen and her father seemed to think she was a commodity to be *managed*, rose up to propel her through the drawing-room door. She'd show Fen. He might not want her, but by the time she was through with him, one way or another, she would have him grovelling in the dust at her feet.

She didn't pause to reflect that grovelling and Fen didn't go together. Nor was dust permitted to settle in Joseph's house.

In the end it didn't matter, because when she came to a stop on the threshold, she saw at once that Fen was already at her feet—although not in supplication or surrender. He was searching for something among the array of colourful packages piled beneath the huge Christmas tree.

Briefly, very briefly, Nina was reminded of the receptionist's comment about a delectable male backside bending over boxes. After that, all she could think of was her overpowering need to let Fen know exactly what she thought of him. Not that she knew what she thought of him any longer. She just knew his dismissive comments hurt. Unbearably.

'Skunk,' she said, very clearly and precisely. 'Fenton Hardwick, did anyone ever tell you you're a skunk?'

Fen, looking hard and formidable in his grey executive suit, rose smoothly and deliberately to his feet.

Nina swallowed and squeezed her eyes shut. He wasn't a skunk. He was a strong, beautiful man. And all she wanted to do was throw her arms around him.

'Here it is, Mrs. Petrov.' Fen ignored Nina and handed a topaz brooch to Nancy with a smile. 'The clasp must have come loose while you were decorating.'

'Oh, thank you so much. My eyes aren't what they used to be, you see.'

Nina glanced sideways to where Joseph was standing beside a solid Victorian table with a lot of carved scroll-work around the edge. His gaze flicked keenly from Fen to his daughter.

'Ah, there you are, my dear,' he said blandly. 'Your mother and I were just off to bed.'

'You've already used that one,' said Nina.

'Have I? Well, well.' He smiled innocently. 'Good night, my dear. Good night, Hardwick. I'm glad you made things clear to our little girl. Come along, Nancy.'

'Wait a moment.' Nina swallowed. 'What—what was that you said? About making things clear?'

Joseph cleared his throat. 'Humph. Young Hardwick here. Knew who he was the moment you introduced him. Heard about his career. Started as a stock-boy, worked his way up to the top, then bought the company. I admire that kind of ambition.' He scratched his head and tried to look artless. 'Could see you'd no idea, though.'

'Dad! Then why didn't you *tell* me?'

Joseph cleared his throat again. 'Didn't think you'd like it. Haven't liked it when I've approved of other young fellows.'

'But they were different. They—' Nina stopped abruptly, because Joseph's smug smile was practically splitting his face.

'That's what I thought,' he said, nodding. 'Different.' Then, seeing Nina's furious expression, he said, 'Nancy. Let's go.'

'Now, Joseph.' Nancy threw an anxious glance at her daughter. 'I don't think Nina wants—'

'Yes, she does,' said Joseph. 'Take my word for it.'

'Well...'

But Joseph already had his wife by the hand, and as she was no match for his determination to remove her from the scene, a minute later Nina was once again alone in a firelit room with Fen. Only this time the fireplace was bigger and made of stone, and Fen was gripping the back of a wing chair looking as if he was about to deliver a stern lecture on manners, deportment and the respect due to presidents of companies that imported fine food.

Nina put her hands behind her back. The indignation she had felt on hearing Fen discuss her with her father was still there. But it wasn't *entirely* Fen's fault—and somehow it didn't seem to matter much any more. Only one thing mattered. Perhaps, in her heart, she had known that all along.

'*You* forgot something this time,' she said quietly. If she didn't get to the point at once she would lose her nerve. And Fen might actually get round to that lecture.

'Did I?' he asked. 'I doubt it. Your mother said she'd see my suitcase was brought down. All I have left to do is call a taxi.'

Nina shook her head. 'No, that's not what I meant. There's something else.'

Fen glanced at his watch. 'Then you'd better tell me. I've a flight to catch.' His goldstone eyes were about as promising as a cobra's.

Nina took a deep breath and lifted her chin to give herself courage. 'You forgot the apology you said I owed you.'

Only a brief twitch of his eyebrows betrayed that he was taken by surprise. 'So I did,' he agreed. 'I suppose it seemed a little meaningless in the circumstances.'

'No,' said Nina. 'It isn't meaningless. It matters to me. I should have known when you gave back my—my bribe—that I'd misunderstood everything from the start.'

Fen didn't respond, just looked through her as though he didn't really see her. Nina had to struggle not to drop her eyes. 'I'm sorry,' she said, meaning it, but suspecting she sounded surly and defensive. 'You were quite right when you told me I've become so blinkered and mistrustful that I can't tell the pearls from the swine—'

'That's not quite the way I put it,' murmured Fen. His eyes came back into focus and he brushed a hand across his mouth.

'Well, no,' agreed Nina. Had she really seen the ghost of a smile on his lips? 'I wouldn't exactly call you a pearl—'

'You called me a skunk, as I remember.'

'Yes, but never a swine. Fen, I didn't *know*. There's never been anyone—I mean, every man I've ever met who's known about my father has had his eye on a prize that isn't me. I didn't understand…that is…' She gulped hard, trying to dislodge the lump that had come back into her throat. 'I suppose I should have seen that you weren't like all the others. I *did* see that you enjoyed teasing and provoking me and I—well, in a way I liked it—' She broke off because Fen wasn't responding and she couldn't think of any more to say.

She couldn't blame him for not understanding. Even when he had handed her money back she had refused to see what had always been right under her nose—that although Fen had a wicked sense of humour, he was a man of integrity and compassion and pride. No wonder he'd been insulted by her bribe.

She gave a small sigh and allowed her eyes to drop. On the other side of the room, a fresh log flared in the grate, and for a moment there was an acrid smell of smoke.

Fen didn't move, and without looking up Nina murmured, 'I'll call a taxi for you,' before she turned away.

She had almost reached the door when she felt Fen's peremptory hand close on her shoulder.

'And where do you think you're going?' he asked.

'I told you—'

'Yes, and you're not doing anything of the sort.'

'But I—' She gasped as he turned her around and placed a hand on the small of her back. 'I...' She looked into his eyes, all narrowed and golden, and couldn't remember what she'd meant to say.

The muscles in her stomach began to clench, and when the room swam out of focus, automatically her body swayed towards him. Fen placed two steadying hands on her shoulders.

'Hold it,' he said, his voice coming to her softly from a distance. 'No fainting. Your father would have my scalp.'

'I never faint,' said Nina. She opened her eyes extra wide and made herself meet his gently sceptical gaze. 'And you never part with your scalp. Do you?'

'No,' he admitted. 'But I doubt that would stop your redoubtable father from giving me a run for my money. I like him, Nina.'

He stepped back and looked her over so thoroughly that after a while she felt obliged to inform him that she wasn't one of his exotic foods being considered as an addition to his stock. 'I've no intention of being added to your inventory,' she told him, a little breathlessly.

Fen ran his thumb across her lips. 'You needn't worry. Lemons are too commonplace for my shelves.'

'Oh.' Nina knew she ought to come up with a suitably deflating rejoinder. But she couldn't think of one. His teasing remark had cut too close to the bone.

'On the other hand,' said Fen, 'as I think I told you before, I do like a little tartness in my life. It keeps me from getting bored.'

His hand was on her back again, and suddenly he moved it lower, making her gasp. Lord, she couldn't stand this much longer. She knew Fen teased out of habit, but it wasn't his teasing her body craved now. And on top of that she longed for reassurance, for some sign that he cared enough to find out if she was really a woman he might—what had he said? A woman he might finally find time for.

'I'm not here to spice up your jaded palate,' she told him, wishing he would stop whatever it was he was doing with his fingers. It was so distracting she couldn't keep her mind on the subject at hand. Which was—which was what? Dear heaven, she couldn't even think straight.

With a groan of frustration she attempted to pull out of his arms.

But Fen wouldn't let her. Instead his hand spread out across her lower back and he drew her so firmly against him that she couldn't fail to be aware of his arousal. His other hand was curved round her neck, and once again she felt as if the floor had dissolved underneath her so that Fen was her only anchor to a world that no longer had any meaning beyond his touch.

Her heart sounded loud in her ears. She could feel the blood pounding in her veins, and his invading lips were warm and wonderful and gentle—the lips of the man she wanted to spend her life with.

No. No, wait. That couldn't be true.

Now Fen was dropping feather-light kisses on her neck and along her jaw. But Nina discovered she had somehow come back to earth.

The smoky smell was stronger now. She would have to see to that fire.

'Fen,' she whispered. 'Fen, please, we can't—'

'We can,' said Fen, touching a pulse at the base of her throat. 'Maybe not here, in your parents' house. But very soon— '

'No. I don't want...' Nina swallowed, unable to finish.

'What don't you want?' He smiled, an achingly sensuous smile that tugged at her heart.

'I don't want to be just another of your handy bodies—'

Fen gave a snort of disbelief. 'Not much danger of that,' he said drily. 'So far you've been exceedingly unhandy.'

Nina tried to smile to show it didn't matter, but when the corners of her mouth began to quiver, she gave up.

At once Fen wrapped both arms around her and drew her head against his chest. 'Hey,' he said, absently stroking her hair. 'There's no need to cry, little lemon.'

'I'm not crying.' Nina sniffed loudly into his elegant grey jacket. 'And I'm not a lemon.'

'And no sniffing. Nina, look at me.' He put a finger under her chin and tilted it upwards.

Nina sniffed again, but only because he smelled so nice.

'Nina—lemon, I'm sorry, too,' he said softly.

Nina blinked. Surely the light in his eyes was unusually bright. And his mouth—his mouth was all tender and wry.

'What are you sorry for?' she asked blankly.

'For not understanding. I couldn't see—was too blinded by my own prejudices to see—that your whole experience has been so different from mine that you were bound to be mistrustful of me at first—bound to think I was just another man on the make.' He held her away, smoothed her hair from her face and shook his head. 'Especially when I was fool enough to accept payment for services not rendered. I didn't think about your feelings much, I'm afraid. Didn't think you had any to speak of.' He gave her a rueful, self-deprecating grin.

'Thanks,' said Nina. Was she going crazy, or was this really Fen apologizing and looking at her as if she were an ice-cream he longed to melt slowly and deliciously on his tongue? She tried a smile and was vaguely surprised to find that this time it stayed on her face. 'If you had known—would it have stopped you?'

'I don't know.' His answering smile was guarded now, hinting at regret. 'Probably not. At the time I thought you could do with a good shaking up. But I found myself being shaken up instead.'

Did he mean it? Or was he only teasing again? 'What changed your mind about me?' she asked, still suspicious.

'You did,' he said promptly. 'You called me a skunk—twice—which as a term of endearment leaves something to be desired. But then you apologized so bravely and looked so sad that it came to me you must feel strongly about skunks.' He slid a finger slowly and deliberately down her spine. 'Even, perhaps, to the point of learning to trust one.'

'I do trust you,' said Nina, burying her face in his neck. She wrinkled her nose appreciatively. 'Mmm. And I had no business calling you a skunk.'

Fen twisted a lock of her hair around his hand and drew her head back. 'No, you hadn't,' he agreed. 'And I think it's time you lemons started showing a little more respect towards us skunks. You can start by kissing one.'

Nina shook her head. 'Won't do any good,' she said sweetly. 'Only frogs are supposed to turn into princes.'

'Kiss me anyway,' ordered Fen, with a gleam in his eye that promised delightful trouble if she didn't do as she was told.

Nina kissed him. And it turned out he was right, because the moment her lips touched his, she knew he would always be prince enough for her.

WHEN Nina hurried into the drawing-room early on Christmas morning, she found Fen waiting for her. He was standing beneath the tree looking sexy and strokable in a soft brown sweater. As soon as he saw her he held out his arms.

'Are you my Christmas present?' she asked, walking into them.

His answer was a deep and passionate kiss. It ended abruptly when the door behind them was suddenly flung open.

For a few seconds there was total silence. Then Joseph's voice rang out, smugly triumphant. 'Aha. We've done it, Nancy. And about time, too. We've finally found a man for Nina.'

Nina decided not to spoil her father's Christmas by pointing out that she'd found Fen all by herself.

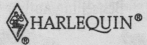

HARLEQUIN®

Don't miss these Harlequin favorites by some of our most distinguished authors!
And now you can receive a discount by ordering two or more titles!

HT#25483	BABYCAKES by Glenda Sanders	$2.99	☐
HT#25559	JUST ANOTHER PRETTY FACE by Candace Schuler	$2.99	☐
HP#11608	SUMMER STORMS by Emma Goldrick	$2.99	☐
HP#11632	THE SHINING OF LOVE by Emma Darcy	$2.99	☐
HR#03265	HERO ON THE LOOSE by Rebecca Winters	$2.89	☐
HR#03268	THE BAD PENNY by Susan Fox	$2.99	☐
HS#70532	TOUCH THE DAWN by Karen Young	$3.39	☐
HS#70576	ANGELS IN THE LIGHT by Margot Dalton	$3.50	☐
HI#22249	MUSIC OF THE MIST by Laura Pender	$2.99	☐
HI#22267	CUTTING EDGE by Caroline Burnes	$2.99	☐
HAR#16489	DADDY'S LITTLE DIVIDEND by Elda Minger	$3.50	☐
HAR#16525	CINDERMAN by Anne Stuart	$3.50	☐
HH#28801	PROVIDENCE by Miranda Jarrett	$3.99	☐
HH#28775	A WARRIOR'S QUEST by Margaret Moore	$3.99	☐

(limited quantities available on certain titles)

TOTAL AMOUNT	$
DEDUCT: 10% DISCOUNT FOR 2+ BOOKS	$
POSTAGE & HANDLING	$
($1.00 for one book, 50¢ for each additional)	
APPLICABLE TAXES*	$_____
TOTAL PAYABLE	$_____

(check or money order—please do not send cash)

To order, complete this form and send it, along with a check or money order for the total above, payable to Harlequin Books, to: **In the U.S.:** 3010 Walden Avenue, P.O. Box 9047, Buffalo, NY 14269-9047; **In Canada:** P.O. Box 613, Fort Erie, Ontario, L2A 5X3.

Name: _____

Address: _____ City: _____

State/Prov.: _____ Zip/Postal Code: _____

*New York residents remit applicable sales taxes.
Canadian residents remit applicable GST and provincial taxes.

HBACK-OD

On the most romantic day of the year, capture the
thrill of falling in love all over again—with

Harlequin's

Valentine
Bachelors

They're three sexy and *very single* men who run
very special personal ads to find the women of
their fantasies by Valentine's Day. These exciting,
passion-filled stories are written by bestselling
Harlequin authors.

Your Heart's Desire by Elise Title
Mr. Romance by Pamela Bauer
Sleepless in St. Louis by Tiffany White

Be sure not to miss Harlequin's Valentine Bachelors,
available in February wherever
Harlequin books are sold.

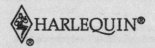

VB

Harlequin® Historical

LOOK TO THE PAST FOR FUTURE FUN AND EXCITEMENT!

The past the Harlequin Historical way, that is. 1994 is going to be a banner year for us, so here's a preview of what to expect:

* The continuation of our bigger book program, with titles such as *Across Time* by Nina Beaumont, *Defy the Eagle* by Lynn Bartlett and *Unicorn Bride* by Claire Delacroix.

* A 1994 March Madness promotion featuring four titles by promising new authors Gayle Wilson, Cheryl St. John, Madris Dupree and Emily French.

* Brand-new in-line series: DESTINY'S WOMEN by Merline Lovelace and HIGHLANDER by Ruth Langan; and new chapters in old favorites, such as the SPARHAWK saga by Miranda Jarrett and the WARRIOR series by Margaret Moore.

* *Promised Brides,* an exciting brand-new anthology with stories by Mary Jo Putney, Kristin James and Julie Tetel.

* Our perennial favorite, the Christmas anthology, this year featuring Patricia Gardner Evans, Kathleen Eagle, Elaine Barbieri and Margaret Moore.

Watch for these programs and titles wherever Harlequin Historicals are sold.

**HARLEQUIN HISTORICALS...
A TOUCH OF MAGIC!**